CHAPTER 1
SUPERMAN

Theo isn't quite sure why he keeps watching Max.

He's nothing special, nothing out of the ordinary. That is, if you disregard the black clothes, the piercings, the Dr. Martens and the black eyeliner, all of which goes perfectly with that dark, messy hair and those intense, blue eyes. No, he's nothing special. Really.

Compared to Theo, though, he is. At least, Theo thinks so. Because Theo really *is* nothing special, with his plain jeans and light brown hair, boring shirts and complete lack of piercings. Compared to Max, compared to anyone, he just feels so incredibly dull. And it doesn't help that he's nerdy to the point of embarrassing, and can't show it off because his friends would never stop mocking him for it; as someone who belongs to a group that's at least reasonably popular, he can't really afford to deviate too much from the norm.

And if nothing else, Max is really smart. Like, genius-level smart, at least from what Theo can tell, from the classes they have together, and from what he's heard.

He doesn't like Max. He hates him. He and his friends hate him, and they hate the goth crowd that Max hangs out with.

Theo hates those black clothes that suit him so perfectly. He hates that messy, black hair that looks just long enough to pull fingers through and grab onto, and he hates that black eyeliner and that stupid piercing, that dark silver ring that circles Max's bottom lip, right in the center. He hates those dark blue eyes and that surprisingly cocky smirk that makes him look like an angel who's been kicked out of heaven.

Yeah, he hates Max. He really does. And he's crushing on him so hard that it's not even funny.

There's nothing special about today. It's just a day like any other, with boring classes and obnoxious students, all there to make the high school experience as genuine as possible, it seems, and it's on this completely ordinary day, that Theo makes his way outside after lunch, rounding the corner of the nearest building.

There's no real reason for it, it's just a short cut to his next class, and no one ever goes through here, which is kind of nice; it's behind one of the school buildings, right at the edge, surrounded by bushes and trees. It's also out of eyeshot from the rest of the schoolyard, and it's generally abandoned, which is why Theo actually stops dead in surprise, when he actually sees someone there. And when he realizes who it is, it makes it even worse.

As Theo rounds the corner, Max barely looks up. Instead, he just glances at Theo, eyeing him up and down quickly, before looking straight ahead again. He's leaning against the brick wall, one hand in the pocket of his black jeans, the other holding a cigarette between his fingers. He pulls on it, and Theo fidgets a bit.

Oh, shit.

4

SWEATERS & CIGARETTES

Mika Fox

But no, he can do this. It's no big deal. No big deal, at all.

He slowly starts making his way past Max, but doesn't even make it there, before a cloud of smoke hits him practically in the face, and he stops dead. He blinks away the stinging smoke, before turning to Max, who just looks at him, a small smile shaping his lips.

"Sorry," he says, not meaning it in the slightest, and Theo turns to him. He tries to suppress the way that unusually low and rough voice of Max's makes him shiver, and he absently grits his teeth a little.

Theo is standing only a couple of feet away from Max, almost next to him, and those blue eyes are locked on his green ones, as Max raises his cigarette to his mouth. Theo deliberately looks away, but just as he moves to leave again, Max actually blows out smoke at him *again*, practically in his face, despite the distance between them. And Theo suddenly feels annoyed, nervousness temporarily forgotten.

"The hell you think you are, man?" Theo says, but Max just smirks at him, looking oddly mischievous. Along with his dark, messy hair and black-lined, fierce eyes, it makes him look weirdly intimidating.

Max lowers his chin a bit, intensifying his dark blue gaze.

"I'm Batman," he says, in a voice that somehow sounds even deeper and more gravelly than normal, and Theo involuntarily shivers. *Damn.*

He doesn't show it, though. Instead, he just scoffs and looks away, intending to leave. And Max quirks a tiny smile and looks away, as well.

"Then again," he murmurs, to Theo's surprise, but mostly to himself. "Superman would kick his ass."

Theo frowns then and turns back to Max, who takes a long, slow drag on his cigarette. And Theo swallows hard. It's unfair how hot Max looks when he does that. It's just *unfair*, on so many levels.

"Whose?" Theo says, involuntarily starting up a conversation, going against every instinct saying that he should leave, because this guy is a douche, crush or no crush. And Theo doesn't even want to admit said crush, to begin with. "Batman's?"

Max cocks his head, now slowly blowing out smoke through just slightly parted lips.

"You gotta be kidding me," Theo murmurs, and now it's Max's turn to frown.

"What?" he says, and Theo feels uncharacteristically bold.

"Superman has powers, sure," he says. "But without them, Batman would kick *his* ass."

Max raises a pierced eyebrow, turning to look at Theo.

"Oh, really?" he says. "How do you figure?"

"It's just facts," Theo says, sounding cockier than he's used to. And Max straightens a bit then, his brow furrowing into a frown again.

"Superman can fly," he says, as though this is obvious and anyone contradicting it is an idiot. "And he can shoot lasers with his eyes."

Theo shrugs.

"So?" he says. "Batman doesn't need all that. And he still kicks ass."

Max seems to deliberate for a moment, still frowning.

"So, you're telling me," he says, actually getting out of his slouch, his back no longer leaning against the wall, hand now out of his pocket, "that some brooding billionaire is better than Superman?"

"Superman is an alien," Theo says, mirroring Max's frown. "Unfair advantage."

"Unfair—" Max actually cuts himself off, glancing away and taking a breath, as though to calm himself down. Then he looks back at Theo. "He's all alone, basically a god. And he uses his powers for good, when he could just as easily take over the world."

"Batman's all alone," Theo retorts, actually starting to get a bit worked up. "And he could just as easily sit back and ignore everything that's going on in Gotham, but he doesn't. He could just spend his money, have fun, and *not* dedicate his life to fighting crime."

"Superman isn't even appreciated for it," Max says. He's as worked up as Theo now, defending his superhero. Neither of them seems to think about how unreasonably pissed off they're both getting over this, especially considering that they've never even spoken before. "People just bitch about him wrecking stuff."

"Batman gets crap all the time," Theo exclaims, throwing up his hands. He and Max are facing each other now, rather than standing almost next to each other. "They call him a menace."

"You can't seriously tell me that Batman is better," Max says, frowning incredulously, but Theo just cocks his head.

"At least he's got a decent disguise," he says. "I mean, Clark Kent? Really? He doesn't even wear a mask, that's just retarded."

"Oh, and Bruce Wayne is such a genius?" Now Max throws his hands up, cigarette still lit, still secured between his fingers.

"As a matter of fact, yes." Theo feels unusually secure now, mouthing off with this guy like this. They've never even spoken before, and he's still on some level somewhat embarrassed about just how hard he's crushing on Max, but he's too wrapped up in their argument to think about it. Instead, he feels oddly riled up. But in a very good way.

Max takes a deep breath and steps closer to Theo, before raising his hand and pointing at him, cigarette held between his index- and middle finger.

"You don't know what you're talking about," he says, lowering his voice slightly.

"I think you're confusing me with you," Theo retorts, lowering his voice to the same level. He can see Max's jaw working, those blue eyes fixed on his.

"If you call Superman retarded again," he says, raising his eyebrows, "I swear to god."

"Well, he is retarded," Theo says, cocking his head. "At least his so-called secret identity is."

"Shut up."

"Make me."

The next second passes in a blur. All Theo is aware of is Max flicking his cigarette away on the asphalt, before stepping closer and gripping Theo's sweater with his hand, pulling him to him. And then, suddenly, he's kissing him. Just like that.

Theo widens his eyes in shock, but to his own surprise, he doesn't react or push Max away. Sure, he's got a massive crush on this guy, but still. They're at school, in the middle of the day, and anyone could see them. And if nothing else, Theo has tried to convince himself that he hates Max, mostly because he has figured that Max hates him.

But as he feels those lips against his own, that stupid piercing hard against them, the metal warmed from Max's mouth, he can't really think at all.

Max seems honestly surprised when Theo kisses him back, tensing up a bit, but then moves his hand from its grip on Theo's sweater and up to his face, cupping it. Theo, meanwhile, closes his eyes and half-hesitantly puts his hands on Max's waist. He's wearing only a black, long-sleeved t-shirt, and Theo can feel the outline of his stomach and muscles and hip bones through the thin, warm fabric. Max groans slightly then, and pushes his tongue into Theo's mouth; his tongue is pierced, too, Theo notices with some surprise.

Max claims his mouth, pushing his body against Theo's with such surprising force that it makes Theo actually stagger a bit, and Theo lets out a soft moan of surprised pleasure. Max tastes like cigarettes, but it doesn't matter. In fact, Theo realizes he finds it kind of hot.

Theo isn't entirely sure how long they keep at it, but when Max slowly pulls away, he feels oddly dizzy and disoriented. Max's hand has moved back a bit from his face, his fingers now digging into Theo's short, light brown hair, the other hand casually slipped into the back pocket of his jeans. And Theo finds himself breathing heavily, while Max lets out a slow, deep breath.

"Shit," he says, his voice barely even a whisper. Theo opens his eyes. Their lips are just an inch away from touching, and he can see that Max's eyes are closed. "Fuck."

Theo swallows hard.

"What?" he says, his voice low and surprisingly hoarse, and Max swallows, too.

"That was awesome," he says, still barely whispering, and Theo feels a shiver run down his spine. Max opens his eyes then, and Theo finds himself staring into that dark, brilliant blue, framed by pitch black, just slightly smoky, eyeliner.

"I was just gonna make you shut up," Max says. "Just for a second. But *damn*."

Theo feels a bit self-conscious then, mixed with the weirdest sense of pride.

"Right," he says, in lack of anything else, and he watches Max's eyes wander across his face, his eyes, his mouth. And Max licks his lips.

"What was your name again?" he says.

"Theo," Theo replies, and Max nods slowly.

"Theo," he repeats. "I'm Max."

"I know." Theo grits his teeth slightly at the stupid reply, but Max doesn't seem to notice or care. "Hi."

Max quirks a smile and looks back up into Theo's eyes.

"Hey," he says. That mischievous smirk is back, but unlike before, Theo finds it incredibly hot, as well as intimidating.

Max straightens a bit, putting some more distance between the two of them, and Theo hesitantly pulls his hands away from Max's waist, as Max's hands leave his body. Then Max eyes him up and down, and Theo clears his throat a bit.

"Right," he says unnecessarily. "Well, I've got class, so…"

Max looks back up at him and nods.

"Yeah," he says. "Yeah, me too."

He seems to hesitate for a bit.

"We should do this again, sometime," he says, and Theo's throat constricts, from some kind of mix between nervousness and surreal excitement.

9

"Yeah," he agrees. "Sometime."

Max nods slowly, and Theo forces himself to look away from those intense, blue eyes.

Only a few seconds of silence pass, though, before it's broken again.

"How about right now?" Max says, and Theo looks up at him. He doesn't even hesitate.

"Sounds good to me," he says, moving closer and grabbing Max's shirt, this time, pulling him to him with surprising roughness. He glimpses that cheeky, mischievous smirk, before he kisses him, and Max's tongue and mouth and hands make him forget all about Batman and Superman and about whoever would win in a fight.

CHAPTER 2
SMOKE

Max is everywhere.

It was fine before, when he still didn't really seem to know that Theo existed, when he never even shot him a glance, as they passed each other in the halls. It was fine when Theo would walk with his friends, and he would glance over at Max, hanging with his friends, the two of them never interacting. It was fine.

Now, however, Max sees him. Now, he definitely knows that Theo exists, and he no longer ignores him as they pass each other in the halls. He'll catch Theo's eye, just for a moment, and smirk in that trademark way of his, looking gorgeous and slightly intimidating, all at once. And Theo will feel a slight jolt and look away, but then glance over his shoulder when Max has passed him by. And almost every time, he wonders what Max is thinking, what's going through his mind.

He wonders if he's thinking about that kiss, like Theo is.

Kiss probably isn't the right word, though. It happened over and over again after that first one, the two of them eventually ending up nearly pressed against the brick wall of the school building, hands practically all over each other (well, Max's hands, at least, seeing as how Theo isn't exactly used to that kind of thing). It was amazing and hot and spontaneous and completely unexpected, and they only stopped when they heard someone coming, pulling apart and quickly stepping away from each other. They didn't say anything, only exchanged a look, before going their separate ways; it was more about getting caught skipping class than getting caught kissing, the latter something that Theo has the distinct feeling that at least Max wouldn't have the slightest problem with.

Theo, for one, has never done something like that before, which just makes it all the more surreal, and all the more amazing, as well as slightly terrifying.

But either way, that was how it ended. And that was three days ago.

Theo still can't quite wrap his head around it. He still can't quite believe that he and Max actually made out behind the school, and the only thing keeping him convinced that it actually happened is the way Max looks at him now. The way he catches his eye now and then, and the way he gives him just the slightest, teasing smirk, like they share a secret no one else knows about. Which, as far as Theo knows, is the case. God knows, he hasn't told a soul.

Theo has lost count of how many times in the last three days Max has looked at him like that. He has lost count of how many times he has shyly looked away from that dark blue gaze, how many times he has had to pretend that he has paid complete attention to what his friends are saying, even though his thoughts are completely and utterly wrapped up in Max. Wrapped up in the way he ruffles his black hair with his fingers sometimes, and the way he rolls his tongue piercing between his teeth when he's thinking. Theo has seen him do it in class, every now and then, and he suddenly finds it oddly endearing. He's not sure why.

Today, though, during lunch, Theo doesn't look away from Max. Not this time. Because this time, there's something else about that look, something more than just simple, albeit teasing, acknowledgement.

As Theo steps out of the classroom and stuffs his bag into his locker, he spots Max through the crowd milling through the hall, everyone hurrying to the cafeteria. He's standing at the end of the hallway, by the school's entrance, completely still, head slightly tilted, hands in his pockets. Theo stops dead, and they just look at each other, until Max smirks at him and backs away a bit. And he keeps his eyes on Theo, before turning around and exiting the building.

No one else seems to have noticed their exchange, but Theo glances around anyway, deliberating. And then, he closes his locker and makes his way down the crowded hallway and out through the big, double doors. His friends are already at lunch; they won't miss him.

The schoolyard is practically empty, apart from a few students here and there, hanging out on the grass. It's already autumn, so the air is crisp and just a bit too chilly to be out in for too long, sitting on the ground. But they seem to insist on it, and Theo shoves his hands in his pockets as he passes them by. Max is out of sight, but he has a pretty good idea of where he has gone.

As usual, there's no one around here, and Theo is barely surprised when he rounds the corner of that particular school building to find the area deserted. Deserted, except for Max, that is, who's standing there, hands in his pockets, waiting for him.

Max gives him a wicked smile.

"Hi," he says. It's odd how every word out of his mouth sounds as though it's made of pure corruption and charismatic persuasion, drawing you in and making you want to do bad things. At least, that's how it makes Theo feel.

"Hey," he says, taking a step forward, so that the two of them are only a few feet apart. He eyes Max up and down quickly, he

13

can't help it; despite the sheer simplicity of that long-sleeved, black t-shirt, those black skinny jeans and black Dr. Martens, it suits him better than anything Theo could ever think of. He can't help but wonder what he looks like, in comparison. Probably boring and utterly ordinary, in his long-sleeved, brown Henley shirt, washed-out jeans and Converse sneakers.

"So," Max says, pulling a cigarette out from behind his ear. Theo didn't even notice it until now. "How you been?"

He asks the question with a joking glint in his eyes, and Theo doesn't answer. He has wanted to talk to Max again ever since last time, wanted to be alone with him. He just never really thought of what he would say, if he got the chance.

Max quirks a small smile at Theo's silence, putting the cigarette in his mouth. It stays loosely secured between his lips, as he gets a lighter from his pocket and flicks it on, cupping his hand around the small flame, pulling on the cigarette to get it lit. Within seconds, thin tendrils of smoke start drifting through the air, and he pockets the lighter again.

He blows out some smoke.

"Do I make you uncomfortable?" he asks after a few moments, and Theo glances away for a split second, before looking back.

"I'm here, aren't I?" he says, and Max chuckles.

"That's not what I asked," he says, moving the cigarette up to his mouth again.

"Then, what?"

Max seems to hesitate, breathing out another stream of smoke.

"You seem uncomfortable," he finally says. "These past few days."

Theo swallows. So Max has actually noticed. He has actually paid attention to Theo, and not just looked at him like that to tease him.

"I wouldn't say uncomfortable," Theo says.

"Then, what would you call it?"

Theo hesitates.

"I guess I'm just not sure how to act," he admits. He doesn't sound as shy and nervous as he suddenly feels. Instead, he sounds rather sure and steady, which he's grateful for. "I don't usually hook up with guys behind the school."

He even adds that last part with some dry humor, but Max still confuses him by looking just the tiniest bit surprised.

"You don't?" he says, and Theo frowns a bit.

"No," he says, shaking his head slightly. "I don't. Why?"

Max just shrugs, that surprise on his face gone. Maybe Theo just imagined it.

He pulls on the cigarette again, before glancing at it, and then glancing at Theo. And then he holds out the cigarette to him, and Theo glances up at Max's face. Max cocks his eyebrows, somehow half-encouraging and half-amused, and Theo glances back at the cigarette. It's kind of embarrassing to admit, but he has never actually smoked before. You'd think he would have, given other things he has tried, but no. He has just never really had occasion, or wanted to.

He takes the cigarette from Max's fingers, a bit hesitantly, and slowly moves it up to his mouth. He puts his lips around it and inhales, figuring it's just as simple as breathing in. It's not. The smoke travels down his throat and into his lungs, and the burning sensation of it makes him cough, just a little at first, surprised. But he soon leans forward, coughing louder and more violently, his body convulsing and instinctively forcing the poison out of his lungs. He feels his eyes tear up, and he can hear Max chuckle.

"I'm guessing you haven't done this before," he says, a smile in his voice, as his hand moves to gently snatch up the cigarette from Theo's fingers. Theo takes a deep, rasping breath as the coughing subsides, and slowly looks up. Max's blue eyes are on him, that trademark smirk on his face.

There's something different about it, though, Theo thinks. That smirk looks just a bit softer than usual, more like an actual smile.

Theo opens his mouth to reply, but decides against it; his throat feels raw, at the moment. Instead, he just cocks his head awkwardly, glancing away as he straightens up again. If anything is more embarrassing than not having even tried something so common, and something that Max seems to spend half his time doing, it's this, his reaction to trying it for the first time, himself. He feels very embarrassed, and so pathetically inexperienced, somehow.

"It's okay," Max says, to his surprise, and Theo glances back at him. He doesn't sound teasing or mocking or sarcastic. Instead, he sounds completely neutral, and he looks at Theo. "How about we try something else?"

Theo frowns a bit, confused, as Max lifts the cigarette up to his mouth and pulls on it. It's a slow, deep inhale, and Theo just stares as Max lowers the cigarette again, those blue eyes fixed on his. Then, Max moves closer to him, until they're only inches apart, and Theo tenses up a bit. He doesn't move as Max's hand moves up to his face, his thumb gently sliding along Theo's bottom lip, eye-contact unbroken, and automatically, Theo parts his lips, just the slightest bit. And Max opens his mouth a little, exhaling slowly, and as Theo feels the warm smoke against his lips, he inhales, just as slowly, even though Max hasn't even told him to.

This time, the smoke burns less, as Theo slowly pulls it down into his lungs. It still tickles his throat a bit, but he keeps himself from coughing, and he keeps his green eyes locked on Max's, as he breathes in his exhale, Max's hand still by his face.

And for some insane, stupid reason, Theo suddenly feels so turned-on right now, that he doesn't quite know what to do.

Max's exhale ends after a few seconds, and Theo breathes out slowly, traces of the smoke swirling out of his mouth, dissipating into the air. Max's lips are very close to his now, so close he can practically feel the warmth of them, the metal piercing just the slightest bit cooler than the skin.

He barely has time to take another breath, before those lips are pressing against his.

Theo closes his eyes as Max's hand moves to pull fingers through his hair, reciprocates the kiss as his own hands

16

automatically find their way to Max's hips, tilts his head a bit and lets Max slide his pierced tongue into his mouth.

They haven't kissed again since the other day, when they spent the better part of half-an-hour just making out against the wall, haven't even spoken since then. But right now, it's like no time has passed at all.

Theo feels his whole body tense up as Max moves closer, pressing against him. It's somehow softer, though, this time, not as urgent. But Theo is still painfully aware of how it seems to make his skin burn, how the feeling of Max's muscles moving beneath his clothes makes Theo want to slip his hands underneath that black shirt and touch his skin.

But he doesn't. He doesn't dare to.

Theo's head is spinning, though, just like last time. Although, it takes a few moments before he realizes, as the spinning intensifies, that it's not just Max causing it, but rather a pretty intense rush of nicotine. Not that he minds the two together; one seems to intensify the other, and he's not sure which is which, at this point.

Max is still holding the cigarette in his other hand, but simply drops it limply to the ground, before slowly moving his hand to Theo's waist, his other hand still twisted into that light brown hair.

Neither of them utters a sound, a moan, nothing. The kiss is slow and quiet and hot, a sharp contrast to the eager urgency of their last one, and Theo feels a burning sensation somewhere deep in his stomach, spreading through his body and carrying through every single vein, making it hard to breathe.

When Max slowly, finally, pulls away, Theo doesn't open his eyes at first. It's only when he feels that Max is still incredibly close that he does open them, and he sees Max's eyebrows slightly furrowed in a frown. Max is looking at Theo's mouth, and he swallows hard, as though thinking about something. Then he looks up into Theo's eyes. His own are intense and blue and framed by that black eyeliner that Theo used to try and convince himself he hated.

17

"I should go," Max says, but taking another second or so before actually moving away, and Theo tries not to think about how cold the absence of him feels. That burning inside is slowly fading, the further away from him Max moves.

"But, um…" Max glances away for a moment, looking uncharacteristically subdued, somehow. He seems to hesitate a little bit. And then he looks back at Theo. "Give me your phone."

Theo actually raises his eyebrows in surprise, but when Max holds out his hand, palm up, he doesn't question it. Instead, he reaches into his pocket and gets his cell phone, putting it in Max's hand, and Max starts fiddling with it, navigating through the menus and apps, eyes fixed on the screen. And after a minute or so, he hands the phone back to Theo, who takes it, confused. Max puts his hands in his pockets and backs away a bit.

"You'd better use that," he says, nodding at the phone, suddenly back to exuding confidence, like he always does, and Theo glances at the phone in his hand. The screen is black, turned off, and he looks back up at Max. And Max smirks in that mischievous, angelic way of his.

"I'll be waiting," he says, before turning around and walking away. And Theo keeps his gaze on him as he leaves, keeps his eyes on that black-clad, lean frame, until Max rounds the corner of the building and is out of sight. And then Theo looks back at the phone. He turns on the screen, and it takes a few seconds to process what he's seeing.

Max, it says. And below the name is a number, entered into Theo's contact list. Theo swallows hard, suddenly feeling oddly insecure and nervous. Max gave him his number. Just like that.

Theo exhales slowly, still tasting some cigarette smoke, and he closes his eyes for a moment, head still spinning. He puts his phone back in his pocket.

"You'd better use that. I'll be waiting."

He opens his eyes, and he swallows hard, before making his way back to the school.

CHAPTER 3
PHONE CALL

Theo has spent a long time staring at his phone, now. A ridiculously long time.

Max gave him his number. And he specifically said that Theo "better use it". So why is Theo hesitating, sitting on the edge of his bed, cell phone is his hand? Max told him to use his number, so he should. Right?

He doesn't even know what Max wants, though. He clearly doesn't seem to take Theo too seriously, yanking him around like that, with his blue eyes and angelic smirk, making Theo feel like he'll do basically whatever he asks. Theo thinks about earlier today, about that kiss, and he can't really see straight.

Damn. Just... *damn.*

As he sat down with his friends at lunch, after that, he could have sworn it was written all over his face. No one seemed to notice, though. His friend Hannah frowned and asked why he smelled like cigarette smoke, but he just shrugged, and she dropped it, and they all went back to talking amongst themselves. And Theo sat there, poking at his food, trying not to think about it. He didn't see Max for the rest of the day, and now he's sitting here, trying to pluck up the courage to text him.

Theo takes a deep breath. And then he opens up a new text message. He's really not the kind of guy to do this; he's shy and awkward and nerdy, even though he doesn't necessarily look the part. God knows, he used to, all ugly sweaters and no eye contact. But then he started hanging out with Hannah, and Michael, and their friends, and gradually, this changed. At least, on the outside. Despite Theo's occasional, successful bouts of sarcasm and dry humor, he's still pretty insecure, and despite the fact that he doesn't really look like a complete, stereotypical nerd anymore, he still really feels like one.

He still feels awkward and self-conscious, and so, when someone like Max gives him this kind of attention, he's just at a complete loss as to what to do. Especially when he's got the biggest crush on Max, as it is. And he can't ask anyone for advice; his friends wouldn't be very helpful, given how much they all seem to hate and look down on Max and his crowd.

So Theo is on his own, and he swallows hard as he starts typing.

I'm using it, he writes, in lack of anything else, referring to Max's comment earlier today. *Happy?*

He hesitates for a moment, before taking another deep breath, and pressing *send.*

It takes about a minute, before his phone beeps in response, and he opens up Max's reply.

Very. That's all it says, and Theo just stares at it. Then he frowns, annoyed. How the hell is he supposed to answer that? Could Max be more of a douchebag? Isn't it enough that he's making Theo text first, couldn't he at least help him along a little bit?

Theo groans and puts the phone down on his bed, suddenly more uncomfortable than a moment ago. He really doesn't know how to answer that. This is stupid.

It's when the phone suddenly rings after another minute or so, that Theo actually starts and looks at it, wide-eyed. Max. Max is actually *calling* him.

Shit. Theo swallows hard and nervously picks up the ringing phone. He stares at it for another second or so, chewing his bottom lip, before he answers it.

"Hello?" he says, trying to sound casual, not entirely sure he's succeeding.

"Hello, Theo." Max's voice sounds rough and low, and Theo has the distinct feeling he's smiling. Or smirking, probably. "Good to hear from you."

How does this guy manage to make pretty much anything sound suggestive, seriously? Not to mention the fact that hearing him say Theo's name like that makes Theo tense up and tingle in all the right places.

"Well," Theo says, looking at the floor, glad Max can't see him. "You did ask me to."

Max chuckles, and it makes Theo shiver, for some reason.

"That, I did," he says, and he sighs into the phone. "You wanna hang out?"

Theo tenses up. Well, that came out of nowhere.

"What?" he musters, his voice embarrassingly high, and Max chuckles again, as though amused.

"Hang out," he explains. "As in, being in the same place, together."

Theo swallows hard.

"Why?" he says, and grits his teeth immediately. Damn it. He didn't mean to say that.

Max doesn't seem to be bothered, though. Instead, he still sounds like he's smirking, amused and entertained at Theo's reactions.

"Because I think you're cute," he says simply. "And I like to think we have fun together."

21

He sounds completely sure, confident, and it makes Theo squirm, for some reason.

"And I'm curious to see what else that tongue of yours can do."

Theo blushes then, hard, and that warm burning suddenly comes out of nowhere, shooting through his body. He involuntarily makes an uncomfortable, slightly strangled sound, and Max laughs.

"Too much?" he says, and Theo clears his throat.

"A bit," he says, sounding tense and awkward. "Yeah."

"Sorry," Max says, not sounding sorry, at all. "My bad."

Silence lingers for a second or so, before Max speaks again.

"Tell you what, though," he says, in that gravelly voice. "You come over, and I promise I'll behave."

Theo's heart starts beating a bit faster, and he squeezes his eyes shut. He exhales slowly. It's ridiculous, but just hearing Max talk like that actually makes him feel uncomfortably turned-on, and he fidgets slightly, sitting on his bed. He clears his throat again.

"Right now?" he musters, and Max makes a thinking sound.

"That would be ideal," he says. "Seeing as how I haven't been able to stop thinking about you, all day."

Jesus Christ. Theo bites down on his lower lip and looks up at the ceiling. He has never heard anyone talk to him like this before, and the fact that it's Max makes it so much worse. And the way he says it, as though it's the easiest thing in the world, as though he just *knows* that Theo won't be able to resist, is doing very bad things to Theo's self-control and better judgment.

"Okay," Theo says, to his own surprise, and he can practically sense Max smiling.

"Great," he says, an almost predatory edge to his voice. "I'll text you the address."

Theo nods, even though Max can't see him.

"Yeah," he says. He can't really seem to find any words, right now.

"See you soon, then," Max says. "Bye, Theo."

Theo doesn't have time to reply, before he hears Max hang up on the other end, and he lets out a slow, shaky breath, as he lowers the phone from his ear. It takes only a few seconds, before he receives a text from Max, with his address, followed by a short message of *don't be late*.

Theo swallows hard. This is not how he thought this was gonna go.

Theo manages to actually get to Max's house, before he starts to fully realize what the hell he's doing.

His parents didn't question it when he said he was just going "out", and after checking the address Max sent him and noticing that it's not that far from his house, he decided to walk. It took him only fifteen minutes or so, and now he's here, hands in his pockets, staring at the front door. The sun has just started setting, he notices absently—it'll be dark in a little while.

Theo takes a deep breath and raises his finger to the doorbell, but before he even manages to press it, the door opens. And he's met by Max, who eyes him up and down, leaning against the doorframe, while Theo awkwardly lowers his hand again. Max smiles wickedly.

"Come on in," he says, stepping aside, and Theo actually averts his eyes as he steps over the threshold and into the house. Somehow, he feels like a prey stepping into a predator's lair. He's not sure which surprises him most; that it feels that way, or that he really doesn't mind.

The front door closes behind him, and he looks around absently, until Max makes his way past him.

"Parents are out," he says, making his way into what Theo assumes is the living room. "Got the place to ourselves."

Theo swallows hard then, not lost on the tiniest, suggestive hint in Max's voice. He still reanimates, though, and soon enough, he sheds his jackets and shoes, and follows Max into the house.

"Sit," Max says as Theo enters the living room, and Theo does, without objection. There's a couch, in front of a big-screen

23

TV, and he sits down, feeling rather awkward and out of place. Max doesn't seem to notice or care, though. Either that, or he's just amused by it, like with everything else Theo says or does, apparently.

"Can I get you anything?" Max says, pierced eyebrow slightly raised, and Theo just looks at him, before shaking his head the tiniest bit. He's not sure why, but somehow he just assumes that everything Max says is laced in sarcasm, and he doesn't want to answer, really.

Max cocks his head and makes his way over to Theo and sits down beside him. Neither of them speaks for a few moments.

"Relax," Max suddenly says, and Theo turns to him. He's sitting with his elbows against his knees, leaning forward slightly, so he supposes he doesn't look very relaxed, and he gets what Max is saying. He doesn't straighten, though. Because he isn't relaxed, and sitting next to Max like this is oddly terrifying.

Max quirks a smile.

"You're a bit weird, you know that?" he says, and Theo frowns at him.

"You're calling *me* weird?" he says, and Max smiles a bit wider, cocking his head.

"Touché," he says. "But at least I'm obvious about it. You…"

He eyes Theo up and down, the smallest frown on his face, as though he genuinely can't make sense of him.

"I can't figure you out."

Theo swallows uncertainly. He has never heard that one before. Most of the time, people don't really bother trying to figure him out.

"Well," he says, a bit uncomfortably, half-shrugging. "I'm nothing special."

"I don't know about that," Max murmurs, still looking at him. Then he leans in a little bit, and Theo almost flinches. Max pauses for a moment, looking into his eyes.

"I'm gonna kiss you now," he says simply. "Okay?"

Theo doesn't say anything, suddenly frozen in place. But after a second or so, he manages to nod, and Max doesn't need telling twice.

A moment later, he's pressing his lips against Theo's, and Theo closes his eyes. He slowly straightens in his seat, as Max moves one hand to his shoulder and gently pushes him back against the backrest of the couch. And then, to Theo's utter surprise, Max moves up and straddles him, sitting down on his lap with one knee on either side, leaning against Theo so that his back presses against the couch. And Theo's head is spinning again, taken completely off-guard.

"I've wanted to do this for days," Max murmurs against his lips, hands sliding down along Theo's neck, his shoulders. "You've been on my mind the whole time."

Theo actually finds himself wincing a bit then, and Max notices. He stops kissing him and pulls back a bit, and Theo feels oddly embarrassed.

Max just looks at him for several seconds, head slightly tilted.

"You don't believe me?" he finally says, but Theo doesn't answer him. Honestly, he does find it a bit hard to believe, what Max is saying. No one sees him that way, and no one ever has. It just doesn't make sense. And hearing it from Max is enough to make him uncomfortable.

Max keeps his eyes on him, before he sighs quietly, leaning in again. He plants a soft kiss on Theo's lips.

"Would it help if I told you," he says, his voice just above a rough whisper, "that I got off while thinking about you, the other day?"

Theo tenses up, his whole body suddenly rigid. He turns away, and Max kisses his jaw, slowly. Theo swallows hard.

"You can't just say stuff like that," he manages to say, and Max pulls back just a little bit.

"Why not?" he says. "It's true."

Theo slowly looks back at him, looks into those blue, black-lined eyes. They're completely sincere, unwavering, dangerously hungry, and Theo reluctantly admits to himself that it's turning him on.

"I think you're hot, Theo." Max leans in closer, his lips just barely brushing against Theo's, his words a warm whisper against his skin. "And I can't stop thinking about you."

Theo starts breathing heavily, as he feels Max slowly start grinding against him, feels his own hands move down to those hips.

"That kiss, the first time around… It was amazing," Max continues, his voice still low, still rough, whispering against Theo's mouth. "And I kept waiting for you to make a move after that, but you never did. So I had to improvise."

Theo doesn't look away this time. Instead, he closes his eyes, suddenly aching for those lips, aching to feel Max move against him, bodies pressed together. He swallows hard.

"I know you want me," Max whispers, still teasing at a kiss, his mouth tantalizingly close to Theo's. Theo tightens his grip on his hips. "And honestly, I'm getting hard just looking at you."

Theo involuntarily groans. How can Max talk like that? Theo has never heard *anyone* talk like that, not to him, and hearing it from Max's mouth, so close to his own, those hips grinding against him as Max straddles his lap, is close to unbearable. He doesn't know what to do, doesn't know how to react.

He can hear Max's breathing getting heavier, can feel it, and he tries to focus. Why is Max doing this? Why won't he just get this over with, do something, *anything*, instead of teasing Theo like this?

Then Theo realizes it; Max wants *him* to make the move. So Theo does.

Max's lips are a fraction of an inch away, and as soon as Theo steals them with his own, he knows he's done for.

Max's entire body presses against him, grinding slowly, hands moving down along his chest and digging into his hair, Theo's tongue pushing into his mouth and brushing against that metal ring in his bottom lip. Max emits a small moan, as Theo's hands wander up along his back and down over his ass, pulling him closer. He's breathing heavily, quickly, while Theo is trying to remember how to breathe at all.

Theo's skin is on fire. He can feel Max's hands skimming along his body, smoothing over his chest, the kiss deepening as Theo slips one hand underneath that black, thin shirt, *finally* getting to feel Max's skin against his fingers. And he can feel Max tense up, groaning against his mouth, tugging at Theo's bottom lip gently with his teeth. It's a complete overload of sensation, like Theo has never felt before, and he's so wrapped up in it that he barely even notices the hard-on underneath his jeans. And as he feels Max grind against him, he can tell that Max wasn't lying before; he's hard, too.

It's only when Max's hands move down to the fly of his jeans that Theo reacts, and he actually flinches, making Max pull away again. He looks surprised and a little bit confused. And Theo feels so annoying, all of a sudden, for interrupting this thing, over and over. Max must think he's ridiculous.

"What?" Max asks breathlessly, and Theo swallows, glancing away. Max seems to consider this for a moment, before lowering his chin a bit, eyes on Theo.

"You have done this before, right?" he says, and Theo shifts uncomfortably, but doesn't reply. And Max takes a deep breath, as he gets it.

"So," he says, a bit hesitantly. "You haven't…?"

Theo looks up at him, and Max cocks his head a bit, asking a silent question, and Theo grits his teeth.

"Not exactly," he finally admits, his voice gruff, as he looks away from Max again. He can see Max nodding, out of the corner of his eye.

"Right," he says, and Theo suddenly feels very embarrassed, rather than turned-on and impatient. He hadn't thought about this, about this question actually coming up. He hadn't thought about the fact that although he has done *this* before, making out and such, he hasn't gone further. He has never gone further than this, not with anyone.

"Huh." Theo frowns at the small sound coming out of Max's mouth, and he looks at him.

"What?" he says, a bit defensively, and Max shakes his head.

"Nothing," he says. He looks a bit pensive. "Just surprised, that's all."

"Yeah, well," Theo grumbles, looking away again, embarrassed. "Whatever."

Neither of them says anything for a few seconds, and Theo suddenly feels the urge to just run, to leave this room and this house and never come back. Because Max has *clearly* done this before, and he must think Theo is completely ridiculous, and Theo tries not to think about it.

After a little while, Max sighs.

"It's fine, you know," he says. "We don't have to do this right now, if you don't want."

Theo looks at him. He could have sworn that Max almost sounded sincere, just now.

"I mean," Max continues, way more nonchalantly, as though noticing the almost suspicious look on Theo's face. "If it's too much, or whatever…"

He glances away then, looking oddly subdued. Theo is reminded of earlier that day, when Max gave him his number; he had that same look then, a sharp contrast to the cocky, predatory one he usually wears.

"Yeah," Theo says quietly, and waits for Max to say something.

Then, suddenly, Max exhales and turns back to Theo. He leans in and kisses him on the mouth, but not like he did before. It's softer, this time, slow and surprisingly chaste, with no tongue and no impatience. When he pulls away, Theo just stares in surprise.

"Wanna watch *The Dark Knight*?" Max says, and Theo blinks.

"What?" he says, and Max raises his eyebrows slightly.

"Well, I don't want you to leave," he says, as though it's the most obvious thing in the world, and Theo just keeps staring at him. He's honestly surprised. He was half-expecting Max to not be the least bit interested in *actually* hanging out, and the fact that Max is, makes him feel oddly warm inside.

"I thought you didn't like Batman," Theo says, and Max smirks.

"I never said that," he says. "I just find him inferior to Superman."

He cocks his head, as well as his eyebrows.

"And I watch it mostly for the Joker's sake, anyway."

He smiles at Theo then, an actual smile. It's the first time Theo has seen his expression look so soft, somehow. It looks unfamiliar, but he likes it.

"Fair enough," he says, and Max nods, before glancing away and wiping that smile off his face, as though he can feel how unfamiliar it looks.

"Great," he says, getting off Theo's lap and standing up. Theo just sits there for a few seconds, watching as Max gets the movie started. He feels oddly soft and relaxed, a complete one-eighty from how he felt just minutes ago, and he exhales slowly.

Max eventually sits back down beside him, and Theo looks at his profile, as Max leans back against the couch. Then Max turns to him.

"What?" he says, but Theo just shakes his head, turning to look at the TV, where the movie is starting.

He does his best not to smile.

CHAPTER 4

ROOF

Theo has never really been good at studying, at least not when it comes to certain subjects. He has always been eager to learn, though, always done the work and tried his best. But his attention span doesn't always seem to cooperate, so some subjects, like math, are a bit trickier, and he often ends up in the library, pouring over his books.

Today is no exception.

The library is virtually empty; Theo supposes that most people don't use their free periods to study. But on the bright side, it gives him the peace and quiet he needs to focus, or at least try to, and he actually manages to get some work done.

His friends, Hannah, Michael and Ben, were here too, a little while ago, but Theo's not quite sure where they went. They're not as ambitious as Theo is, and get bored with the studying pretty fast. Except for Michael, but everything seems to come so easily to him. And he's on the basketball team, too, which means that academic grades aren't really quite as valuable to him as they are to Theo.

Theo's been sitting in the corner of the library, by a small table, for about an hour, now. There's a small, sturdy, wall-like parting right next to the table, a few feet high. It stands parallel to the longer side of the table, and Theo is sitting at the far end, which puts the wall to his left. He appreciates it; it kind of shields him from the rest of the large room, and gives him some peace and quiet.

At least, until someone suddenly shows up beside him.

Theo almost jumps in his seat, and turns to look at the newcomer. And at once, he spots Max, who lightly hops up and perches on the parting wall, swinging his legs over the edge and planting his feet on the seat of a chair in front of the wall, by the table. Theo suddenly feels startled, surprised, and oddly nervous, all at the same time.

"Jesus, Max," he mutters, glancing down at the table. "Don't do that."

Max ignores the reprimand.

"Hey, baby," he says, and Theo looks up at him again. Max is wearing that smirk, the one that makes him look like a rebellious angel, and Theo fidgets a bit. *Baby.* Max hasn't called him that before. *No one* has *ever* called him that before.

Theo automatically glances around them, and Max notices.

"Relax," he says, sounding bored. "Your stick-up-the-ass friends aren't here."

Theo looks at him.

"You shouldn't talk about them like that," he says, but Max isn't fazed.

"Really?" he says, eyebrows raised. "You mean, as opposed to how they talk about me and *my* friends?"

He gives Theo a pointed look, and Theo looks down at the table. He can't argue with that.

Max sighs quietly.

"What are you doing?" he asks, and Theo keeps his eyes on his notes, as he replies.

"Studying," he says. "Or trying to, at least."

Max nods. Theo can see it out of the corner of his eye.

What is Max doing here, anyway? They had fun the other night, sure; Theo hasn't had that much of a good time in ages, with anyone. But still.

When he came over to Max's place, they really did just hang out—at least, after the whole make-out session on the couch, which left Theo feeling very turned-on and awkward, all at the same time.

They watched *The Dark Knight*, commenting on it now and then, Max occasionally pointing out how Superman would have handled this and that situation way better. But he mostly did that to tease Theo, and Theo didn't mind.

Although, a few times during the movie, they did catch each other's eye, and then Max would lean in and kiss Theo on the mouth. He didn't take it further than that, though, not after that first time, when it had gotten really intense, when Theo had basically told him that he was a virgin. Instead, he kept it rather soft and slow, and only got into it more, if Theo wanted to. And after the first few times, Theo even plucked up the courage to kiss Max, taking the initiative, to Max's obvious and pleased surprise.

Theo left only when it was getting really late, that night, after the movie was over, and Max's parents would be back home soon. He didn't want to, he remembers. He wanted to stay there, wanted to stay on that couch, Max's warm body right next to him, and watch that stupid movie over and over again.

Max kissed him goodnight, though, before he left. It was a really good kiss, soft and warm and greedy, all at once, and Theo smiled almost all the way back home.

But still. He has no illusions about what Max wants from him, or about what kind of relationship, if any, they have. He's not stupid, or naïve; despite his own crush on this guy, he doubts that Max feels the same. He clearly isn't into that kind of thing, from what Theo can tell, and he's still kind of shocked that Max actually wanted to hang out with him the other night, and didn't just send him home as soon as it became clear that he wasn't getting any.

So why is Max here?

Several seconds of silence follow, and the whole time, Theo is painfully aware of Max sitting there, looking at him. He's a bit higher up than Theo, sitting on that little wall, but Theo can practically sense him watching him. And then, Max suddenly makes a small thinking noise, and Theo frowns. He looks up at him.

"What?" he says, and he can see Max considering whether or not he should answer. He's got the smallest frown on his face, eyes on Theo's notes. And then he seems to decide to say what he's thinking.

"That one goes there," he says, pointing at the notes, and Theo looks back at them. And then it dawns on him.

"Right, I forgot," he says, just a little bit bitterly. "You're a genius."

He hears a small chuckle from Max, more like a scoff, and when Theo looks up at him, he looks oddly self-conscious, beneath that confident expression.

"Is there anything you can't do?" Theo asks, with a hint of sarcasm, the kind he barely ever manages to pull off. Max smirks, that self-consciousness gone.

"You'd be surprised," he says. Then he looks back at the notes on the table in front of Theo, and sighs. "However, algebra is not one of those things."

He looks at Theo, and extends his hand, a question written on his face; *May I?* Theo doesn't answer him, just hands him his notes, full of equations and formulas, and Max takes the notepad from him, placing it in his lap.

It somehow looks odd, Theo thinks, as he watches Max. He's sitting on that small dividing wall, black Dr. Martens planted on the chair's seat in front of and below him, a notepad full of formulas and mathematical scribbles in his lap. He looks at it with complete focus for a few seconds, brow slightly furrowed, rolling his tongue piercing between his teeth—for some reason, Theo loves that quirk of his. He has no idea why.

Finally, Max lets out a deep breath and actually hops off the dividing wall, feet landing with a soft thud on the floor.

"Alright," he says, pulling up a chair and sitting down. He squeezes in beside Theo, even though there's barely any room at the end of the table, where he sits. He moves so close that their shoulders brush together, and Theo just stares at him, while Max keeps his eyes on the notes, not bothered at all. "Here's how it works."

He's clearly referring to Theo's algebra, and Theo glances down at the notepad, confused.

"You're helping me with my homework?" he blurts, and Max glances up at him. Theo could have sworn that there was the slightest hint of nervousness in those blue eyes, just now. But if there was, it's gone now, as Max frowns a bit.

"Don't make a big deal out of it," he grumbles, rather unlike his usual, confident self. "It's not like I've got anything better to do."

They look at each other for another moment or so, before Max turns back to the notes.

"Right," he says, clearing his throat. "You gotta—"

He doesn't get to finish his sentence. Theo, on some kind of impulse, puts his hand by Max's face and angles it, so that he can kiss him on the mouth, and it shuts him right up.

The kiss only lasts for a few moments, but Max reciprocates it, and when Theo pulls away, those black-lined eyes are just a little bit widened. And Theo just looks right into them, until he realizes that maybe this was a bad idea. Maybe he went too far. And for a split second, he panics. But then, Max blinks, and he swallows hard, before turning back to the notes.

It's a few minutes later, when Max has explained to Theo how to solve his current problem, that Theo gives it a try. And as he leans forward slightly and tries to focus, he feels the lightest brush of Max's lips against his neck, in a soft, chaste kiss. And he smiles.

♦

"Are your parents *ever* home?" Theo asks, and Max glances over at him. They're at Max's house, in his room, this time, and they're all alone.

"Not often," Max replies. "My mom works nights a lot, and my dad goes out of town on business. So actually, I guess they're home, just not when I'm home."

Theo nods.

"But hey," Max says, smiling suggestively. "More privacy."

Theo can't help but quirk a small smile, but still glances away. He still feels really shy around Max a lot, especially when he talks like that.

"What about your folks?" Max says, making his way over to the bed, where Theo is sitting.

He came over here after school, and for the past twenty minutes or so, he's been awkwardly sitting in the same spot, cross-legged, on Max's bed. Somehow, he didn't expect to see Max's room; last time he was here, they didn't even leave the living room, and this feels much more... *personal*, somehow. Although, he doubts that Max sees it that way.

He's not sure what he expected Max's room to look like, but it seems to fit him perfectly. The walls, one of them slanted, are plastered with posters, ranging from bands like Korn, Marilyn Manson and Seether, to movie posters with prints from *A Clockwork Orange, Underworld* and *Queen of the Damned,* and Theo just sits there, taking it in. He likes this room, he decides. It's messy and cluttered, but Max's personality seems to be written all over it. Even the music playing in the background sounds like him; it's not really Theo's style, but he doesn't mind.

And the room smells like him. Theo tries not to think about that.

Max sits down in front of Theo, who's sitting practically in the middle of the bed, which is placed practically in the middle of the room, its headboard against the wall below the room's only window. He crosses his legs, mirroring Theo, and Theo looks back at him and meets his eye.

"They're pretty ordinary," he says, in response to Max's question. "My dad's a mechanic, and my mom's a grade school teacher. And if they're not home, there's always my little brother."

Max frowns the slightest bit, as though in a question, and Theo explains.

"His name's Riley," he says, and he knows that the affection for his brother is clear in his voice. It seems that he will never grow out of that. "He's fourteen. Kind of a genius. You two would get along, I think."

He adds that last part a bit jokingly, and Max actually smiles. And again, Theo is struck by how Max's expressions have slowly started going from smirks to smiles, softer and more genuine. Or maybe he's just imagining it. Max seems to notice, though, and when he does, he quickly tries to stop smiling like that, as though it feels uncomfortable and unfamiliar on his face.

"I'll have to meet him, sometime," he says, glancing away for a moment, before looking back at Theo. "So, I'm guessing there's not much privacy at your house?"

Theo cocks his head.

"Not really."

Max nods slowly, and then, for several seconds, he just stares. He just stares at Theo, an unreadable expression in those dark blue eyes, and Theo can't help but stare back, shifting slightly in his seat. And then, suddenly, Max blinks, as though coming out of some deep thought, and he clears his throat.

"Sorry," he says, in that typical tone of *I'm not really sorry at all* that he seems to use a lot. "I know I shouldn't."

Theo frowns.

"Shouldn't what?" he asks, honestly confused, and Max exhales slowly, a small smirk on his face. He licks his lips.

"I'm exercising a lot of restraint, here," he says. "I just want to kiss you, and I know I shouldn't."

Theo swallows nervously.

"Well, you can," he says with some hesitation, but Max shakes his head a bit.

"No, you don't understand," he says, an oddly hungry, slightly amused look on his face. "I want to kiss you, but I also want to pin you down and rip your clothes off. And I think that crosses the boundaries we've set up."

He adds that last part with narrowed eyes, which gives it some kind of joking sarcasm, but there's some seriousness underneath, and Theo tenses up. The prospect of Max pinning him down and ripping his clothes off is simultaneously terrifying and extremely arousing, and for a moment, he just sits there, unsure how to react. It doesn't help that they're sitting on a bed, on *Max's* bed, and Theo swallows hard. Max sighs.

"See," he says. "Now I've freaked you out again."

Theo shakes his head jerkily.

"No," he says, sounding so much less composed than a moment ago. "No, I just…"

He looks down, and exhales.

"Okay, maybe a little bit, yeah."

Max sighs again.

"I'm sorry," he says, and this time, it almost sounds like he means it. "I'm just not used to…"

He seems to hesitate, deliberating, and Theo looks up at him again.

"I'm not used to showing restraint," Max says, with an expression that says he's fully aware of how stupid that sounds. "But you've asked me to, so I will."

His eyes scan Theo's face, gaze wandering down along his mouth and his throat, down over his body.

"Even though looking at you does things to me."

He murmurs the words, his voice low, and Theo shivers slightly at its gravelly tone. Seriously, how can Max talk like this?

It makes Theo feel so immensely uncomfortable and turned-on, all at the same time.

And on some level, he appreciates Max trying, when he really doesn't have to. He doesn't have to show restraint; he could just pick someone else, instead of Theo, and skip that part altogether.

"Well, if it helps," Theo hears himself say, and Max looks up at him. "It's mutual."

He swallows hard, can't believe the words coming out of his mouth.

"Looking at you does things to me, too."

The words hang in the air. Theo has never talked like this before, has never said anything like that to another person, in his life. It's just so straight-forward, and inappropriate on so many levels.

Max doesn't seem to think so, though. Or maybe he does, and that's why hearing it from Theo's mouth makes him tense up a bit, blue eyes suddenly completely fixed on Theo's green ones. He looks at him like he wants to eat him alive, and suddenly, Theo feels like that's what he wants, more than anything in the world. But he doesn't say anything.

Instead, he wonders what, exactly, his own expression looks like, since it makes Max react this way.

He wonders what it is that makes Max suddenly lean forward and kiss him, any thought of restraint seemingly gone from his mind.

It doesn't start off slow, or soft. It doesn't escalate, transforming from a relatively innocent kiss into something more heated. No, instead, Max's mouth rams into Theo's, pushing them both back down onto the bed, Theo's hands gripping onto Max's shirt, as Max's fingers dig into his hair. His other hand is against Theo's shoulder, firmly pressing him down into the sheets. Theo groans in surprise, but closes his eyes and grabs a fistful of black, thin fabric in one hand, the other trailing up underneath Max's shirt, touching his skin. He feels Max tense up above him.

There's no restraint, whatsoever.

Theo isn't used to this, though. He's not used to someone just *attacking* him like this, body pressing down against his, grinding against him. But even though it's unfamiliar and just a little bit scary, feeling Max's weight on top of him, black hair brushing against his forehead as Max leans into him, it's thrilling. He likes this. He likes the way Max groans against his mouth, as Theo moves both his hands up underneath his long-sleeved t-shirt, feeling his skin.

Max moves a bit then, getting up on his knees. He grabs the back of his shirt, blue eyes on Theo, and pulls it over his head, messing up his hair in the process. Just the sight of it makes Theo tense up in the best way, but as Max throws the shirt aside, he feels his eyes widen. He lets his gaze wander across Max's naked torso, momentarily mesmerized.

Tattoos. *Tattoos.*

Of course Max has tattoos, Theo think to himself. *'Cause it's not like he's hot enough, as it is.*

There are several inked images along the skin of his upper arms, some of them still incomplete, by the looks of it. Theo is too distracted to pay attention to what they depict, exactly, but he can't help but stare at them, as his eyes trail over Max's bare chest, to his other arm, taking it all in.

Theo finds himself moving his hands up to touch the inked skin on those arms, and Max lets him, at least for a moment. Then he swoops back down and claims Theo's mouth, and Theo closes his eyes again, pulling him closer.

Hands are everywhere, that pierced tongue sliding along Theo's bottom lip, before pushing into his mouth, Max's skin smooth underneath Theo's hands, blood rushing downward, that sudden hardness straining against the fabric of his jeans. Theo's shirt comes off, expertly discarded by Max's eager hands, and Theo is vaguely aware of it landing somewhere on the floor. He's breathing heavily now, wrapped up in a hot, intoxicated haze, and he can feel his heart pounding frantically.

Max moves to grab Theo's hands in his own, pressing them down against the mattress, on either side of Theo's head, before wrapping his fingers around his wrists. It sends a surge of excited fear through Theo's body, and he lets out a breathless moan as Max moves his mouth down along his throat and his collarbone, kissing his chest. The kisses are slow and hungry, and Theo closes his eyes, overwhelmed, as the sensation builds and makes him squirm. He's close. He can feel it.

And that's when he opens his eyes, suddenly panicked.

"Wait," he manages to get out, desperate for Max to stop what he's doing right now, because he simply can't take it, embarrassing and ridiculous, as that is.

Max's reaction surprises him, though. The sound that comes out of his mouth is one of almost whiny impatience, almost as though he's in pain, and Theo freezes and just stays completely still, as Max stops kissing him and instead rests his forehead against Theo's bare chest.

"Um," Theo says hesitantly after a second, not moving, and Max groans loudly against his skin.

"I swear, you'll be the death of me," he murmurs, and Theo swallows hard.

"Sorry," he says, in lack of anything else, but Max looks up then and meets his gaze. His blue eyes are shining, practically glowing with impatient arousal. Just the sight of it makes Theo's entire body tense up.

"No," Max says. "No, I'm just… overreacting."

He sighs heavily. Theo doesn't need to tell him more explicitly that he wants them to stop, he gets it. Although, Theo isn't quite sure *why* he wants it to stop; it's not like he's not enjoying it.

"It's fine." Max closes his eyes for a moment, as though trying to calm down. "You might actually be killing me, though."

He says it lightly, and Theo relaxes a bit, but he still feels a bit self-conscious at Max's words. Not to mention that reaction.

Max lets out another sigh and opens his eyes. They're calmer now, not as intense, but it's still painfully obvious that he's holding back. He leans in slightly, scans Theo's face with those eyes, before planting a soft kiss on his mouth. It's soft, but it's also hungry, and he pulls away after only a second.

"Alright," he says, moving his mouth lightly down along Theo's throat, until he reaches his collarbone, where he presses his lips against the bare skin. It's enough to make Theo shiver, and Max moves his hands away from Theo's wrists, slowly, as though he really doesn't want to.

"Put your shirt back on," Max says, getting up, so that he's sitting on top of Theo, rather than almost lying down against him. "My self-discipline can only amount to so much."

Theo just looks at him, and Max quirks an eyebrow, before taking in the sight of Theo, spread out underneath him, and lets out a sad sigh. Then he gets off of him and swings his legs over the bed's edge, reaching for his black shirt that landed on the floor earlier. And Theo glances over at him, only to almost start in surprise.

"Holy crap," he murmurs involuntarily, and Max glances over his shoulder at him.

"What?" he says, but Theo doesn't answer him. Instead, he just reaches out and touches Max's back, mesmerized.

He knows Max has tattoos, now; he has seen them, and he has felt them, even though it may take a while for him to get used to it. But he didn't know about *these*. He hasn't seen the wings that mark the skin on Max's back, sprouting from between his shoulder blades and trailing down, all the way to the small of his back. They're made from black ink, not shaded, only outlines, but they're still beautiful, and Theo just stares at them.

Max feels his fingertips touch his skin, and he starts, before visibly relaxing.

"Oh," he says, absently turning his shirt the right way, seeing as how it landed inside-out on the floor. "They're not done yet."

Theo glances up at Max's profile.

"They're beautiful," he says, despite himself, and he could have sworn Max froze for just a split second, just now.

"Thanks," he says. "Just need to spend another ten hours or so under a needle to get them filled-in, but... All in due time."

He pulls the shirt over his head, obscuring the tattoos, both the wings and the ones on his arms, and Theo feels slightly disappointed.

"How do you have so many?" he asks. Max really does seem very young to have so many tattoos, already.

Max exhales.

"Well," he says, "I'm eighteen. Even if my parents weren't okay with it, I'm technically an adult. As in, I can get as many as I like. And I started pretty early."

He picks up Theo's Henley from the floor and hands it to him.

"And as for money," he continues, "I've worked part-time since I was thirteen. And a friend of mine's the tattoo artist, so he gives me a discount. Although, seeing as how society doesn't exactly approve, and especially not in high school, I have to cover them up, most of the time. Which sucks. Most people think the piercings are bad enough."

Theo doesn't answer him, slowly sitting up and putting on his sweater.

"My parents would freak," he says. "They're not exactly into that kind of thing."

Max looks at him, from the edge of the bed.

"It's your body," he says simply, shrugging. "And you're legal."

He frowns then, almost suspiciously.

"I'm assuming," he adds, and Theo looks at him.

"I turned eighteen last month," he confirms, and Max nods.

"Then, there's my point," he says. "You're an adult. And it's your body, your skin. Who the fuck cares, right?"

Theo just looks at him, wishing it were that simple.

"Yeah, I guess," he says. And for another few seconds, neither of them says anything.

"Fuck, I need a smoke," Max finally murmurs to himself, and Theo watches as he clambers over the bed and opens the window above the bed's headboard. Then, he simply climbs out, and

Theo realizes, after a moment of shock, that there's a roof right outside. Max turns around, crouching.

"You mind?" he asks Theo, gesturing to his bedside table. Theo looks over, and sees a pack of cigarettes and a lighter, lying there. He reaches for them and hands them to Max.

"Thanks." He pulls away and out of sight, and Theo hesitates for a moment, before climbing out the window, himself.

The roof lines up almost perfectly with Max's bedroom window, and it overlooks the house's backyard. Max is sitting with his back against the outside wall, knees pulled up in front of him, and Theo slowly sits down beside him, with some hesitation. He mirrors Max, who just glances at him, before lighting a cigarette. Neither of them speaks for a few moments, as he pulls on it, sending tendrils of smoke through the chilly air.

It's after a little while that Max actually hands the cigarette to Theo, who eyes it warily. Max says nothing, not a word of encouragement or judgment. But Theo takes the cigarette anyway, to his own surprise, and moves it to his mouth. He's prepared this time, and takes a careful inhale that doesn't go down into his lungs, before blowing the smoke out again. Max chuckles, but in an oddly fond way.

"Look at you," he says, taking back the cigarette as Theo hands it to him. "I feel like I'm corrupting you."

He takes a slow drag on the cigarette.

"What would your friends say?" he adds, and Theo glances at him.

"What would *your* friends say?" he retorts. "You, hanging out with me?"

Max chuckles, eyes directed straight ahead. Theo likes him from this angle, likes watching his profile.

"I honestly don't think they care much," he says. "And even if they did, I wouldn't care."

Theo feels absently surprised at the warm feeling that gives him inside.

"Maybe Beth, though," Max says, and Theo frowns.

"Who?" he says, involuntarily jealous.

43

"Friend of mine," Max explains, tapping the cigarette against his knee, ashes falling. "She's into me."

Theo hesitates.

"You sound very sure," he says, and Max cocks his head, eyebrows raised pointedly.

"She's made it very clear," he says, glancing at Theo suggestively. Theo swallows hard, unsure why he's asking this.

"And?" he says, and Max exhales, looking straight ahead again.

"And," he replies, "I've told her I don't swing that way. I mean, I've tried it, once or twice. But it's not really my thing."

He sighs heavily.

"I like dick," he says, without flinching. "Simple as that."

He turns to Theo, taking a pull on his cigarette.

"What about you?" he asks, and Theo glances at him. He shakes his head.

"No," he says. "No, I..."

Max raises an eyebrow.

"You, what?" he asks pointedly, knowing full well that Theo is simply too uncomfortable to answer. He's just being an asshole. "You like it, too?"

Theo sighs uncomfortably and looks away, his silence confirmation enough. But Max is unrelenting.

"You can say it, you know," he says, a smirk on his face. "Dick."

Theo shifts in his seat, refusing to look at Max.

"Just say it." Max shrugs, clearly amused at Theo's uncomfortable reaction. "Or would you prefer cock?"

"Stop it," Theo mutters, and Max lets out a chuckle.

"Why?" He takes another slow pull on his cigarette. "You have one. I have one. And they obviously like each other. So what's the big deal?"

He looks over at Theo, who can feel his face heating up. He can't *believe* Max is so comfortable talking like this.

44

"Are you blushing, Davis?" Max says, using Theo's last name, and Theo deliberately doesn't look at him, annoyed and embarrassed about the increasing heat creeping up his neck.

"Shut up," he mutters unnecessarily, and Max chuckles, a little bit more benevolently, this time.

"It's fine, I don't mind," he says, tapping away some ash from his cigarette. "Actually, I kinda like it, getting you all flustered."

He looks at Theo, eyes him up and down.

"Makes me feel kinda special."

Theo slowly turns to him, then. Max's dark blue eyes become fixed on his green ones, and they narrow slightly.

"I like making you blush," he says, his voice a bit lower and a bit more gravelly than a moment ago, the tiniest smile on his lips. "And I like that I get you hard."

Theo actually gulps, but keeps his eyes on Max, to his own surprise. Maybe he's getting used to Max's way of talking, albeit very, *very* slowly, and it's just enough to keep him from looking away. Max seems to like that, too, at least judging from the way his expression shifts just the tiniest bit. For a split second, he looks almost impressed. Then he smiles crookedly, eyes skimming over Theo's face.

"Such a pity," he says, his voice just a murmur, as though he didn't intend to say it out loud.

"What is?" Theo says, his voice slightly lowered, and Max glances at the cigarette in his hand. The brief look on his face confirms that he in fact didn't mean to say those words out loud, but that he figures it's too late now.

"The whole virgin deal," he says, still eyeing his cigarette, his voice still low. And Theo's pulse quickens a bit.

"Why?" he gets out, not sure why he's even asking. And Max focuses completely on the cigarette now, moving it up to his mouth with a small smile.

"Because you are one, and that's restricting," he says, fiddling the cigarette between his fingers, not looking at Theo. "And 'cause if I could, I'd fuck you senseless."

And just like that, Theo feels the weirdest mix of panic and excitement bubble up inside, making him feel restless and paralyzed, all at once. He swallows hard, heart thumping in his chest. He has no idea how to react to that. But somehow, he still finds some words.

"Why do you talk like that?" he suddenly says, sounding oddly breathless, and Max turns to him, frowning slightly. He pulls on the cigarette.

"What do you mean?" he says, looking honestly confused as he blows out some smoke. Theo scoffs nervously.

"You say stuff like that," he says, "so easily."

"I'm just being honest," Max says with a small shrug, and Theo shakes his head.

"No." He turns away slightly, unable to look Max in the eyes right now. "No, that's not it."

"You have a problem with me telling you how I see you?" Max asks, sounding oddly defensive.

"At the moment," Theo admits, "yeah. A bit. It's crass."

"Crass?" Max actually laughs then.

"Yeah." Theo doesn't relent, turning back to him. "There's a fine line between being honest, and just being an asshole."

Max just looks at him for a few seconds, confused and slightly annoyed surprise on his face.

"Well, I'm sorry," he says sarcastically. "Were you under the impression that I *didn't* want to fuck you?"

Theo doesn't answer him. Instead, he just keeps his eyes focused on those dark blue, black-lined ones, for several, silent moments.

"No," he finally says. It's true; he hasn't for one second been under the impression that Max *doesn't* see him that way. It has been quite the opposite actually, and it has been a bit confusing to him, seeing as how Max seems to just simply want to hang out with him, regardless.

He figures, like he has from the very start, that Max only wants him for sex, if anything at all. And somehow, he's been fine with that, even if he does have a crush on him. He never

46

expected it to go beyond that, for the two of them to actually hang out. He honestly did think that Max would just toss him aside, as soon as he realized that Theo was an inexperienced virgin who wasn't about to put out.

So far, though, he has been proven wrong. And it's very confusing, to say the least.

Eventually, Max sighs, looking straight ahead.

"I'm not gonna lie," he says. "I think you're hot, and if I could, I really *would* fuck you senseless."

He flicks some ashes off his cigarette.

"Hell, just this morning, I thought about you in the shower."

Theo involuntarily groans, mostly from discomfort, but also from something else. He hates to admit it, but despite how awkward it makes him feel, he likes hearing Max say things like that. On some level he has never been quite aware of before, he likes knowing that Max thinks about him that way, that he thought about him in the shower this morning. It makes him squirm, but just as much from an awkward hard-on as from discomfort, and he *likes* it.

Damn.

"But, like previously mentioned," Max says, looking back at him, "you've asked me to behave. So I will."

Theo actually quirks a small smile at that, which Max seems to notice, because he mirrors it, giving him an unusually soft expression. It's gone after only a second, but it's enough, and for the moment, Theo is content.

CHAPTER 5
WINGS

Everything is happening so fast. With Max, things have moved so
quickly, that Theo hasn't even stopped to think about what
anyone around him might say or think. At least, not very
consciously.

He knows how his friends feel about Max and his crowd,
though, and that's something he has been thinking about. But so
far, he hasn't been with his friends any of the times he has
bumped into Max at school, and therefore hasn't had to face it.

Until today, that is.

Theo is waiting for Michael to get his stuff out of his locker,
talking to Hannah and Ben, when Max walks by, in the hallway.
It's pretty crowded, between classes, but he still catches Theo's
eye, and looks at him deliberately. Theo tries not to look back,

but he can't help it; those intense eyes, framed by black, are impossible to ignore.

Hannah seems to notice Theo's distraction, and frowns, following his gaze. Then she catches sight of Max, who, while passing them by, actually turns around while keeping his focus on Theo, eyeing him up and down with a smirk on his face, as he backs away a few steps, through the crowd. Then he gives Theo a sly smile, full of wicked, sinful promises, before turning back around and walking away, disappearing among all the students.

Theo just stares for a moment, tensed up, heart racing. He's resisting the urge to hurry after him.

"What was that?" The sound of Hannah's voice breaks his trance, and he looks at her, blinking.

"What?" he says dumbly, and Hannah raises her eyebrows pointedly.

"Why was he looking at you like that?" she asks.

"Who?" Theo says. "Max?"

The moment he says the name, he knows he's screwed. Hannah immediately reacts and folds her arms, after absently pulling a strand of blonde hair out of her soft, pretty face, away from those brown eyes.

"*Max*?" she says, a bit snidely. "What are you, buddies, now?"

Theo doesn't answer right away. He honestly doesn't know what he and Max are, and even if he did, he's not entirely sure that he would answer Hannah truthfully.

"He's bad news, Theo," she says, before he can reply. "You know that."

"Who is?" Ben interjects, and Hannah turns to him.

"That goth kid," she says. "Him and his friends."

"Oh, yeah," Ben says, nodding, hazel eyes tired and his expression oddly stoned-looking, even though Theo knows that he never uses any drugs of any kind. And that tangled mess of brown hair doesn't exactly help. "That guy."

He looks between Hannah and Theo.

"What about him?"

"Nothing," Theo says, uncomfortable at the attention. He also finds himself surprisingly annoyed and defensive about Max, not appreciating his friends talking about him that way. Although, he's pretty sure Max wouldn't even care. "It's nothing."

Hannah shoots Theo a glare, but Ben doesn't seem to notice. Either that, or he doesn't care, and he drops the subject, which would actually be completely typical for him.

"Whatever," he says tiredly, shaking his head, ruffling through his hair with his hand. "We gotta go, come on."

Michael closes his locker, and Ben and Hannah follow behind him as he leaves.

"You coming?" Michael says, and Theo fidgets a bit on the spot.

"You know what," he says, "I forgot something in my locker. I'll catch up."

Michael shrugs. He's tall, conventionally handsome, with his short, dark hair and dark eyes, and he tends to look oddly regal, somehow, with his calm, confident posture. He's clearly the leader of the little group, and as the three of them leave, Hannah glances at Theo almost suspiciously, over her shoulder.

Theo really hopes she won't make a big deal out of this; it's the last thing he needs, and he just needs to settle down for a few seconds.

"Don't listen to them," a voice suddenly says behind him, and Theo whips around. "She's just being stupid."

Theo frowns at the newcomer. It's a girl, with long, red hair and a kind, pretty face, with high cheekbones and big eyes, at the moment accentuated by black-framed glasses. She's clutching a notepad to her chest, almost obscuring the print on her red t-shirt; it's the symbol of the Flash, a yellow bolt of lightning.

"I know," Theo says, a bit confused, and the girl just stares for a while, before reanimating.

"Oh, sorry," she says, laughing nervously. "I'm not eavesdropping, or stalking, or anything. I just overheard your conversation."

She chews her bottom lip for a moment.

"I'm Cassie," she says, and Theo just looks at her for a moment.

"Theo," he says, and Cassie smiles.

"Hi," she says, with an awkward little wave. Then she seems to catch herself, and she looks at the floor.

"What do you mean, by the way?" Theo asks, and Cassie looks up.

"Well," she says, "Max. What she said about him. I mean, I don't really know the guy, but I've talked to him a few times, and he's really not that bad. He's a bit of an asshole, sure, but he's not mean, or anything."

Theo can't help but quirk the smallest smile at Cassie's description of Max. It's pretty on the nose, after all, and he realizes that just thinking about him makes him feel all warm inside.

Cassie reanimates after a moment, and straightens slightly.

"Right," she says. "Well, now that I've made a first, stalker-impression on you, I should go."

She smiles.

"It was nice meeting you," she says, and Theo smiles back.

"You too," he says, and Cassie starts making her way past him. "And thanks."

She glances back at him and nods, before walking away, and Theo takes a deep breath, before adjusting the bag over his shoulder and making his way to class.

♦

"Are you ever gonna stop doing that?" Max asks, his voice low and rough. Theo glances up at his face.

"Sorry," he says self-consciously, pulling his hand away from Max's skin, where he's been tracing his tattoos. But Max snatches up his hand again, to Theo's surprise.

"I didn't say I mind," he grumbles, and Theo hesitantly resumes what he was doing, relaxing.

The two of them are lying on Max's bed, sprawled across the sheets, Max on his back and Theo lying right next to him.

This has started to become something of a routine now, Theo coming over here after school, the two of them hanging out. Sure, most of the time, hanging out consists of kissing and touching and making out on various surfaces, but lately, it has become more than that. Lately, they've actually started talking more, getting to know each other, sharing their likes and dislikes.

For instance, Theo now knows that Max loves coffee and thinks that *Bronson* is a thoroughly underrated movie, and Max now knows that Theo has a crush on a doctor in that stupid hospital show on TV, and that he can be bribed pretty easily with pie. And Theo knows that Max is ticklish just above the waist, that he has been smoking since he was fifteen, and that he feels that Nietzsche "kind of had a point, although he was mostly a dick".

It feels like they know each other now, more properly, and as they're lying there, on Max's bed, Theo just can't stop staring at him, can't stop touching him. They had a pretty intense make-out session a little while ago (which Theo, as per usual, cut short, due to his own overwhelming nervousness), and now they're just lying there, next to each other. They didn't get dressed, this time; they're both shirtless, which Theo really appreciates. It means that he can look at Max properly, take in the sight of him and his tattoos, tracing the inked skin with his fingers.

"So, you don't mind?" he says, in reply to Max's previous comment, and Max grunts.

"Not really," he says, sounding oddly awkward. "It's... it's kinda nice, actually."

Theo glances up at his face. Max is lying with his left arm under his head, against the pillows, the other draped over his stomach, and Theo has rolled over onto his side, to be able to touch Max more easily.

"I like them," Theo admits, looking back at the tattoos. They're on Max's upper arms and parts of his shoulders, some almost reaching down to his elbows, and a few of them flow together so perfectly that it's hard to tell where one ends and another begins.

"Thanks," Max says. "They'll probably be full sleeves by the time I'm done. Just give me a few years."

Max sighs contentedly then, and looks at Theo.

"Maybe we should get you inked up," he suggests with a mischievous smirk and cocking of his eyebrows, and Theo scoffs, smiling.

"I don't think so," he says, trailing his fingers along a tattoo depicting an intricate image containing poker cards, covering most of Max's right upper arm. "Even if my parents were okay with it."

"Again," Max points out, "it's *your* skin, not theirs."

"Still, though." Theo keeps his eyes on Max's body, rather than his face, and neither of them says anything for a few moments.

"You wanna see it?" Max suddenly asks, sounding just the tiniest bit hesitant, and Theo frowns.

"See what?" he says, and Max sighs quietly.

"How it's done," he explains. "The whole tattoo-thing."

Theo looks up at him, looks into those dark blue eyes.

"What do you mean?" he says, and Max cocks his head.

"I'm having the wings finished," he says. "In a couple of days. You could come along. If you want."

Theo doesn't answer him right away, surprised.

"You want me to come with you?" he finally says, disbelieving, and Max glances away for a split second.

"If you feel like spending hours just sitting there, while I get tortured, then yeah," he says dryly, looking at Theo. "I guess I could use the company."

Theo swallows, a bit nervously. That's an odd request. But he immediately feels like saying yes, realizing at the same time that he just really wants to spend time with Max, even if it does mean just sitting there for several hours.

"Yeah," he says, nodding. "Sure."

Max quirks a smile, that trademark cockiness never really leaving his face, and he plants a quick kiss on Theo's mouth.

"Cool."

♦

That Saturday, Max and Theo make their way to the tattoo parlor, for Max's appointment (which has already been booked about two months in advance). It's getting colder outside, now, the air crisp with a late autumn chill, and Theo is glad for his warm jacket. He also weirdly enjoys seeing Max in that black coat of his, which reaches almost to his knees. It's not a leather coat, not like what most of Max's friends wear. Instead, it's more of a trenchcoat, which Theo, personally, thinks looks much better.

The bell above the door jingles slightly as they step inside the tattoo studio, and Theo looks around. It's a rather small place, with tattoo designs and artwork plastered all over the walls, and with a counter that divides the rest of the room from a smaller area, which houses a tattoo chair. There's no one else there, except for a man, sitting on a bar stool by the counter. He's sketching something, but Theo can't tell what, from this distance.

The man looks rather short and stout, middle-aged, with short, dark hair and scraggly brown stubble bordering on a beard. He looks up as Max and Theo enter the parlor, and his face breaks into a smile when he spots Max.

"There he is," he says. "My favorite customer."

His voice is gravelly and low, with a certain burned whiskey rasp to it, and the British, slightly slurred accent is hard to miss.

"Kiss-ass," Max says, making his way over to the man, who just laughs.

"I'm the one with the needle, boy," he says warningly, but with a great deal of affection hidden underneath the blatant menace. "Don't test me."

Max quirks a smile at him, shrugging off his coat and hanging it over a chair. Then, the man's eyes wander to Theo, who's still standing awkwardly by the door.

"And who's this, then?" the man asks, and Max looks over at Theo.

"That's Theo," he says simply. "He's keeping me company today."

The tattoo-artist glances at Max knowingly, before looking back at Theo.

"Really?" he says, getting up from his stool and beckoning Theo closer. Theo hesitantly obeys, and the man looks at him.

"Always nice to meet a friend of Max's," he says, holding out his hand. "Gavin."

Theo glances at the outstretched hand, before shaking it. He doesn't say anything. Honestly, he's intimidated by this man, but then again, who can blame him? Even disregarding the tattoos that seem to cover pretty much every inch of his arms and neck underneath that shirt, and the general roughness of him, there's a certain sharp intelligence about him that Theo can't quite put his finger on. He's sure it's nothing bad, though; even Max used to intimidate him like that. He's just not used to this kind of people.

Gavin keeps his eyes on Theo for another moment, as though observing him, before stepping away.

"Right, then," he says, turning to Max. "Have a seat."

Max locks his arms behind his back for a bit, stretching, rolling his neck and loosening up his joints and muscles, and Theo just looks at him, confused. Then he remembers Max telling him that this will take several hours, and he realizes that it's probably so he won't get too stiff, sitting there for so long.

Gavin starts making preparations, and Theo tentatively sits down on a nearby stool, while Max takes his shirt off. And as Max does, Theo feels himself involuntarily tense up at the sight of it, shifting slightly in his seat. He's pretty sure that his jeans are doing a decent job of hiding the fact that he's suddenly getting hard, but it still makes him fidget a bit.

It's a complete surprise, honestly; he can't remember reacting so strongly and so suddenly to anyone but Max, before, and it's started happening more and more lately, even in public, like this. That can't be good.

55

He knows that it doesn't show, but when Max looks over at him, that teasing smirk on his face says that he *knows*. And of course he does. He knows exactly what kind of effect he has on Theo, and he likes it. He has made that abundantly clear.

Max turns to the chair, but rather than sitting in it, he straddles it and leans his chest against the backrest, leaving his bare back completely exposed, and Theo watches as Gavin preps the already tattooed skin with disinfectant.

"Ready?" he says, and Max grunts in confirmation.

"Just get it over with," he says, and Gavin chuckles, before getting started.

It's rather fascinating to watch, Theo realizes. The wings on Max's back are already in place, and all that's left to do is shade them, so that they look more like they have actual feathers.

Theo watches as the loudly buzzing needle traces the skin, Gavin wiping away a mixture of blood and black ink every now and then, with paper clutched in a white-gloved hand. It looks rather morbid, not to mention painful, but Max's expression barely shifts, and when he catches Theo looking at him, he frowns.

"What?" he asks, and Theo glances at his back.

"Doesn't it hurt?" he says, and Max cocks his eyebrows.

"It does," he admits casually. "A lot. But it only lasts for so long, right?"

Gavin glances up at him, a small, approving smile on his face.

"The pain's worth it," Max continues, and Theo has to admit he has a point. It's only temporary, after all, while the artwork stays on forever.

It's after an hour or so that the bell above the door jingles, and they all look up, only to see a woman enter. She looks to be in her late thirties, clean-cut and with a kind face, her auburn hair pulled back into a loose bun.

"There you are," she says, sounding exasperated, and Gavin stills his hand to look at her. "Is your phone off, or something? I've been trying to reach you."

Gavin seems to consider that for a moment, glancing away, an expression on his face that looks oddly soft and innocent, for a man like him.

The woman by the door sighs.

"You left it at home again, didn't you?" she says, and Gavin looks back at her. The suddenly half-guilty look on his face and slight shrug of his shoulder confirms it. And the woman rolls her eyes.

"Never mind," she says, and then notices Theo and Max. Her blue-gray eyes fall on the latter.

"Hello, Max," she says, and Max half-raises his hand in greeting.

"Amanda," he says simply, and the woman—Amanda—turns her gaze back to Gavin.

"We have reservations for tonight," she says, sounding a bit edgy. "Did you forget?"

Gavin just looks at her, slight confusion on his face.

"That's tomorrow, love," he says, an odd softness to his raspy voice.

Amanda frowns then, deliberating. Then she seems to remember, and she glances away, pursing her lips.

"Right," she says, clearly reluctant to admit it. "My mistake."

She looks back at Gavin, who now has a small, affectionate smile on his face.

"I'll see you at home, then," she says, pushing open the door, her tone just a bit snappy. "And don't forget to pick up groceries on the way."

"Yes, dear," Gavin says, and with that, the bell above the door jingles again, as Amanda leaves.

Theo hears a quiet chuckle from Max, and looks over at him.

"What?" Gavin says, and Max sighs.

"You are so whipped," he says.

"Oi," Gavin replies. "That's my wife you're talking about."

"See, that alone is just adorable."

Gavin glares at the teenager, who just smirks to himself, before settling down again and letting the artist resume his work.

The whole thing does take several hours, occasionally interrupted by breaks for coffee, snacks and cigarettes. Theo had no idea how taxing something like this can be, but although his part in it consists of just sitting there, watching, the three of them talking every now and then, he doesn't mind. He actually likes it. He likes spending more time with Max that doesn't involve making out (not that he minds that at all, but still).

Gavin is apparently a friend of the family; Max's father knows Amanda from college, and met Gavin through her. Over the years, Gavin has been like an uncle to Max, and it was through him he discovered his love of tattoos. He's also the reason Max gets a discount, hence him having so many tattoos at such a young age. At least, that's part of the reason; Max seems to be devoid of the usual fear of branding something very permanent into your skin, despite being only a teenager.

Hours later, on the walk home from the tattoo parlor, Theo can tell that Max is uncomfortable and in pain, at least from the way he fidgets as the fabric of his clothes brushes against his sore back. There's a layer of plastic taped over the fresh tattoo, not to be removed for several hours, but still.

"How's it feel?" Theo asks, hands in his pockets. It's already dark outside, and it's a bit chilly. Max shrugs, flinching slightly as he does.

"A bit raw," he says. "But pretty good."

Theo nods, and Max looks at him. He doesn't say anything for a few moments, worrying at his pierced bottom lip. Those black-lined eyes look just a bit less composed than usual.

"Thanks for coming with me," he eventually says. "I mean, you didn't have to. But the company was nice."

Theo feels slightly surprised at the sudden softness in Max's rough voice, but doesn't mention it. Instead, he just smiles nervously.

"Yeah, well," he says. "I would have held your hand, but you'd probably just punch me in the face."

He meant it as a joke, and he can tell that Max knows that, so he's not surprised at the small smirk he gets in return.

He is surprised, however, when Max suddenly stops walking, making Theo stop as well. Max then glances down and slips his hand into Theo's jacket pocket, taking his hand and pulling it out into the chilly night air. Theo looks down and just stares, as Max slowly laces their fingers together, before he reanimates and looks up.

"Okay," Theo says unnecessarily, and Max looks up at him, turning so that they're standing in front of each other, face-to-face. He's pretty much the same height as Theo, but still, the way he's looking up at him is something Theo hasn't seen him do before.

"Dammit, Davis," he says with a sigh, shaking his head. "I actually kinda like you."

Theo swallows again, nervously this time.

"Okay," he repeats, his voice low and weak. His heart is pounding, though, pounding against his ribcage so hard it's almost uncomfortable.

"I mean," he adds, catching himself, fumbling. "I— I kinda like you, too."

He feels a blush creep up his neck, reaching his face, but he's hoping that Max can't tell in the dim light of the streetlamp they're standing under.

But he does notice, of course he does. And he smiles.

"You're blushing," Max says, with just a hint of smugness, and Theo actually turns his head the other way, exhaling slowly. He doesn't need this right now. It's enough that his pulse seems to be going haywire and that he's so acutely aware of Max's warm hand in his—he doesn't need to have it pointed out.

Max chuckles then, and Theo glances at the ground instead.

"Hey," Max says, putting his hand by his face, making Theo look up at him again. Max lets his dark blue gaze wander across his slightly freckle-dusted face for a few moments, taking it in. "I like making you blush, remember?"

He catches Theo's eye for a moment, before looking at his mouth. And Theo doesn't move a muscle when he leans in slightly and kisses him, so softly it's actually surprising. Surprising, because there's no urgency, this time, no greed or impatience.

Instead, it's just... sweet. It's a kind of kiss that Max hasn't really given him before.

So Theo relaxes into it, savors it and kisses him back, and just for a little while, the night air doesn't feel quite as cold.

CHAPTER 6

TOUCH

It's not unusual for Theo's parents to be gone in the morning, when he gets ready for school; they're not always gone early, but sometimes they are, and this is one of those mornings.

Theo doesn't mind. It does, however, mean that he's responsible for breakfast, and making sure his brother has some before leaving for school.

"You don't have to do that, you know," Riley says, sitting down at the kitchen table.

Theo is perfectly aware of the fact that Riley is fourteen years old and completely capable of making his own breakfast, and that he really doesn't need Theo's help. But he likes doing it; he has always done it, when their parents are gone. It's a habit he's having a hard time breaking.

"I'm making some for myself, anyway," Theo replies. It's the truth, but it's also an excuse he has used to cook for Riley, ever since they were kids.

He's standing by the kitchen stove, frying up some eggs and bacon, and Riley sits at the table, watching his back.

"Fine," Riley says, skimming through a book. Theo isn't surprised; Riley is really smart, especially for his age, and he always seems to have a book or something in front of him.

The brothers don't talk for a little while, the morning silence occasionally broken by the popping and sizzling of the frying pan, until Riley closes his book and slides it into his bag.

"Hey," he says. "I saw that goth kid yesterday."

Theo tries not to flinch. He's almost entirely sure that Riley is talking about Max, and just the thought of Max makes his heart skip a beat. And it makes him smile, too, as he's reminded of the other night, when they walked home together from the tattoo parlor. When Max held his hand and kissed him like that.

Theo is so wrapped up in his own thoughts, that he's barely even surprised at Riley's mere mention of the guy, and he slowly comes back to his senses.

"So?" Theo musters, trying to sound casual. No one really knows that he and Max even know each other, and he has gotten used to pretty much lying about it.

"Well, you're friends, right?" Riley says, plainly.

The question is simple, innocent, but it still makes Theo stiffen. After a moment, though, he reanimates and continues to stir the bacon.

"What are you talking about?" he asks, hoping that he sounds convincing.

"You and that guy," Riley explains. "Max, or whatever. You're friends, aren't you?"

Theo hesitates. He's racking his brain to figure out when, where and how, exactly, Riley might have come to that conclusion. Not even his friends seem to know that he and Max hang out.

And if nothing else, he can't help but react at the word *friends*. Are he and Max friends? Even disregarding the whole physical part of their relationship, which actually came first, Theo has started to feel like they're a whole lot more than just friends, at this point, even the benefits-kind. But he doesn't know. He doesn't know what Max thinks.

"Dammit, Davis. I actually kinda like you."

The words still echo in his mind. He can't really shake them, and he can't shake the feeling of that kiss Max gave him, just moments later. Because friends don't do that, right? Maybe making out, hooking up, sure... But holding hands? Hanging out like they've been doing lately, saying stuff like that, and kissing like they actually care about each other?

As far as Theo knows, friends don't do that. But again, who knows what Max thinks.

Theo flips the bacon in the frying pan, clearing his throat slightly.

"Yeah, maybe," he finally says, unsure what to reply. "What makes you say that?"

"Nothing," Riley says, and Theo knows he's shrugging, even with his back turned. "You just seem to like him, that's all."

Theo nearly drops the spatula, but saves it in the last second.

"You okay?" Riley sounds concerned, but knowing, in that annoying, precocious way of his.

"Yeah," Theo says, turning off the stove and taking out a pair of plates. "Yeah, I'm fine."

He divides the eggs and the bacon between the two plates (with a couple of extra slices for his brother, out of habit), and gets out two forks, before setting the food down on the table. Riley looks up at him as he sits down opposite him.

"It's okay, you know," he suddenly says, but Theo doesn't look at him. Instead, he starts spearing some bacon on his fork.

"What is?" he asks, a bit too casually.

"That you like him." Riley sounds calm and completely certain, and Theo slowly glances up at him. His hair is darker than Theo's, and a little bit longer, his eyes hazel, rather than green. Looks-wise, he takes after their father more than their mother, but although Riley still has some childlike features, being in his early teens, he does bear some resemblance to his big brother, and Theo guesses that the two of them will look more alike when he's older. "I can tell."

Theo doesn't confirm nor deny, suddenly very uncomfortable. But Riley notices how he wants to know *how* Riley can tell, even if he's not saying anything.

"You've been smiling a lot, lately," he says. "And you haven't been home as much, you've been going out more."

Riley digs into his bacon, looking down.

"And it started when you met him."

Theo swallows hard. He hasn't even spoken to Max in front of other people, at school. How the hell does Riley know?

"How—" he starts, but Riley cuts him off.

"You're my big brother, Theo," he says simply. "I've seen the way you look at him, at school. And I've seen the way he looks at you."

He puts some bacon in his mouth and looks at his brother.

"I don't know if anyone else can tell," he says, with his mouth full. "But I can. And you like him."

Theo doesn't say anything for several seconds. Somehow, he's worried that Riley will react the way his friends would, the way most people would, at him liking a guy like Max. But he doesn't. Instead, Riley just half-smiles at him, like the happiest, most supportive little brother in the world, who seems so much older than fourteen. And Theo exhales slowly.

"Don't tell mom and dad, okay?" he says, his voice slightly subdued, and Riley nods. Theo doesn't have to explain why, because Riley is smart, and he knows exactly why. He knows how most people would react to Theo and Max being together, especially their parents, considering how Max isn't exactly conventional, and he knows that Theo really doesn't need that.

Theo appreciates it. But he doesn't tell Riley the other reason for his hesitation, that he simply doesn't really know what, exactly, he and Max are. Because they're not just friends, not at this point, not even the benefits-kind.

But he's too scared to think that they just might be something more.

♦

It has been two days since Theo last saw Max. He hasn't seen him since the tattoo session, and it's Tuesday by the time he actually runs into him again.

They've kept in touch, though, since then. They've texted a lot, more than Theo has probably ever texted anyone, just talking about random crap that serves no other purpose than to make him smile. He can't help but think that he must have made Max smile, too, with all those stupid texts they've been sending back and forth.

It's at school that Theo sees him.

Theo is standing by his locker, none of his friends in sight. There are students milling about in the hallway, but Michael, Hannah and Ben have already gone to class, and Theo is just getting some last minute stuff.

He tugs at his t-shirt uncomfortably; it's a black one with the Batman logo on the front (in dark grey, rather than yellow, though), with a dark green hoodie over it. He feels oddly restless, like he can't focus properly, like he's in withdrawal, or something.

Theo is tense and restless, but when he suddenly feels the slightest hint of a familiar scent right behind him, he relaxes his shoulders a little.

"Hey, babe."

Theo can't help but smile stupidly; he knows that scent, and he knows that voice. He'd know it anywhere.

"Hey," he says, as he turns around. He doesn't even flinch at the use of the word *babe*, this time.

Max is standing rather close to him, he notices. He's close enough for Theo to really look at and take in the features of that gorgeous face, but not close enough for it to look weird to anyone else, and when he catches Theo's eye, his entire expression actually seems to light up a little bit. It's an odd sight; Theo isn't used to seeing Max like that, all dark and brooding as he generally is.

Not that he minds. His heart is kind of doing a backflip, right now, anyway.

It's after the first few moments of just general joy at seeing Max, though, that Theo realizes something else. This is the first time Max has approached him like this, in plain sight of everyone else, here at school. It's the first time, because, as far as Theo is concerned, sneaking around and making out behind the school, talking in a corner of the library, and occasionally looking at each other in the halls, doesn't really count.

And Max actually seems to agree. At least, judging from the way he seems just the tiniest bit hesitant about it, in a way that most other people probably wouldn't even notice. He looks just the slightest bit uncomfortable, and Theo is pretty sure he can tell simply because he has spent so very much time looking at Max's face, by now.

"Batman?" Max eventually says, even going so far as tugging lightly at the hem of Theo's shirt. "Really?"

Theo can't help but smile a little bit, as he glances down.

"What, you mind?" he retorts, with just enough blatant confidence for Max to raise his eyebrows a bit, impressed.

"Well, now you're just being provocative," he says, but when Theo's small smile widens a little bit, there's an obvious softness in those dark blue eyes, as though making Theo smile actually makes him happy.

Theo sighs.

"I gotta go," he says, after a few seconds of silent, mutual staring. This is just terrible timing, really. He doesn't want to go, but he has class, and Max knows that.

Max nods and takes a step back.

"Yeah," he says. Theo may be imagining it, but Max looks just the slightest bit disappointed. "Sure."

Theo just looks at him, though, doesn't say anything.

Max glances away for a split second, and Theo just looks at that face, lets his gaze wander from those cheekbones to those eyes, to that metal stud in the left eyebrow. He looks at that black, messy hair and the eyeliner to match, down to the dark metal ring in Max's bottom lip, the touch and feel of which he has become all too familiar with. And suddenly, he's hit with an almost overwhelming urge to kiss him, right then and there, to feel Max's lips against his own. Not because he wants to fool around or anything, but just because he wants to kiss him. Because he *misses* it.

Theo doesn't kiss him, though. They're at school, and despite Max coming up to him like this, in plain sight, Theo still has no idea how Max actually defines their relationship, and he's afraid of doing anything too obvious or out of line. So instead, he hesitates for a moment, before straightening, and Max steps aside so that Theo can walk past him.

Theo only makes it a few feet, though, before he stops and turns around.

"Hey, Max," he says, actually loudly enough for anyone else paying attention to hear him, and Max stops and turns around, as well. Theo hesitates, before asking. "See you later?"

There's some uncertainty and hesitation in his voice, and Max just looks at him for a moment, clearly surprised but almost succeeding in hiding it. Then, he puts his hands in his pockets, in an unusually soft posture, and he actually smiles.

"Yeah," he says, and Theo smiles back. He nods, suddenly feeling a bit awkward, but in a pretty good way, and neither of them says anything else, before turning back around and going their separate ways.

♦

Theo is never going to get tired of kissing Max. He has decided that. He's never going to get tired of the way Max pulls his fingers through his hair, as he tugs gently at his bottom lip with his teeth.

He's never going to get tired of the way Max touches him, mapping out his body with his hands.

They're in Max's bed, making out, and although Theo doesn't mind, he can't help but absently think of how he would like to be able to do this at his house. Not because he doesn't want to be in Max's room (the privacy that comes with his parents pretty much constantly being gone is nice, after all), but because he, weirdly enough, simply wants to take Max home. He wants to take him home, and show him *his* room and *his* house. He wants him to meet Riley, and even his parents. Although, at least the latter part feels like a bit of a pipe dream.

But he can't help it. He just really likes Max. Somehow, he wants him to be part of his life, properly.

He would never admit that, though. Who knows what Max might do if he did? Given how he seems to view their relationship (and any other kind of relationship he has ever had), Theo seriously doubts that Max is into the whole meeting-the-family-thing.

But Theo tries not to think about it. Instead, he focuses on how *this* feels, right now. The way Max's body presses down against his, as he straddles him, that pierced tongue in his mouth, that black hair against his fingers.

"Fuck, how are you doing this?" Max's voice is low and rough, as he murmurs against Theo's lips.

"Doing what?" Theo asks, not opening his eyes or moving his lips away from Max's more than a fraction of an inch.

"This," Max says. "Making me act like this."

He moves his lips down to kiss Theo's jaw, slowly, before nipping the skin below his ear gently and smoothing it over with his tongue. And Theo actually moans. He has gotten more comfortable with that, now; he's not quite as self-conscious as he was in the beginning.

"I'm not doing anything," he murmurs, Max moving back up to his mouth.

"You're doing *something*," Max insists. "You make me wanna do all kinds of things to you."

Theo tenses up a bit. He may have gotten used to Max's way of talking like that, but it still makes him simultaneously uncomfortable and turned-on.

"I can think of a few things right now, actually." Max's tone is teasing and hungry, as he smoothes one hand down over Theo's bare chest.

That Batman shirt was disposed of pretty much as soon as Theo arrived here, earlier, although Max is still wearing a black tank top that shows off his tattoos. The wings on his back are hidden; they're not healed yet, and he doesn't really want to show them off until they are, as he puts it. Not to mention the fact that his skin is still sore, and not exactly up for being touched too much.

"Like what?" Theo can't help asking, half-afraid of the answer. He hasn't forgotten Max telling him how he would like to *fuck him senseless*, and he can't help but feel nervous at the mere thought of it.

"Well," Max murmurs against his mouth. "One thing in particular, right now."

Theo shifts uncomfortably, then.

"Max," he says, slightly subdued, knowing that Max knows how he feels about that. "Not yet, okay?"

Max chuckles, for once without any of the teasing malice he tends to use.

"Don't worry," he says. "I wasn't talking about *that*."

Theo frowns, confused.

"Then, what?" he asks, and Max pulls away far enough to look into his green eyes. He half-smiles, almost mischievously.

"Something else," he says pointedly, as though waiting for Theo to catch on. There's a kind of impatient hunger in his eyes, as though he's really reining himself in, at the moment. But Theo still doesn't get it. He opens his mouth to answer, but ends up just shaking his head a bit, still frowning. And Max gets the tiniest hint of amused fondness in his expression, for just a second.

"I'm saying I'd like to go down on you, Theo," he suddenly says, simply, calmly, with a completely straight face.

But Theo, of course, isn't quite as calm.

"What?" he sputters, in that never-failing, eloquent way of his. But Max doesn't seem to mind. Instead, he quirks a small smile, again, bordering on mischievous.

"I want to go down on you," he repeats, voice low and husky, moving closer and brushing his lips against Theo's. "As in, I want to blow you."

Theo swallows hard. He can't deny the fact that he's getting really hard just hearing Max say that, his heart suddenly pounding.

He also notices how Max's way of putting it sounds just a bit too *soft* to be him, but Theo suspects that he's consciously avoiding any more direct and explicit terms, at the moment. He doesn't want to make Theo too uncomfortable, and using words more explicit than *blow*, at least right now, would definitely send Theo over the edge.

Max's words are enough, though, enough to make Theo feel a quiet rush of excitement move through his body. But like always, just the thought of something like that makes him so nervous it's not even funny.

"Um," he mumbles, and Max kisses him, that metal ring hard against his lips.

"You don't want me to?" he asks, practically purring now, and Theo closes his eyes, breathing heavily. He can feel Max's breath against his mouth, the heat of those hands as they smooth over his skin. "It's okay if you don't."

He kisses Theo again, slower this time, before slowly sliding his tongue along his bottom lip, making Theo's entire body shiver. There is a distinct shift in mood right now, much hotter and much more impatient and greedy, than just moments ago.

"But I really want to," Max whispers, now grinding slowly against Theo, nails dragging lightly down along his sides. "I've wanted to for quite some time."

Theo makes a strangled noise in the back of his throat, squeezing his eyes shut. He feels his grip tighten on Max's hips, as they move against him in a slow, agonizing rhythm.

"But it's up to you," Max almost surprises Theo by saying, voice still low. "We can do whatever you want."

He lets out a slow, deep breath, trailing his lips down along Theo's throat, tensing up as he maps out Theo's bare skin with his hands.

"Tell me what you want, Theo," he whispers, suddenly sounding completely wrecked, kissing his neck and smoothing over the kisses with his tongue, any trace of restraint gone. "I'll give it to you."

And just like that, it's as if Theo's insecurities suddenly just vanish. At least for a split second, because that's when he replies, with just one word.

"Okay."

It's more of a breath, but it's enough for Max to stiffen for just a moment. Then he reanimates, moving back up to Theo's mouth.

"Okay, what?" he says, voice still low and husky, but a bit unsure.

Theo opens his eyes, and looks straight into those deep, dark blue ones.

"Okay," he repeats, and Max just looks at him for a moment.

"You want me to?" he asks, his tone just the slightest bit hesitant, as though he doesn't want to risk getting anything wrong. And Theo just looks at him, before nodding jerkily. His insecurities are gone, at least for now.

At least, until Max gets some kind of predatory look in his eyes and kisses him deeply, hungrily, before moving down along his throat, down to his chest.

It's about then that Theo starts to realize what's happening, and his heart starts pounding. It's about then that he realizes what Max is about to do, and he looks down as he feels those sure fingers tug at his jeans gently, pulling them down a little bit. He swallows nervously.

Max's mouth is planting searing kisses all over his bare skin, over his stomach and just above the waistline of his underwear, moving further down, while his hand slowly smoothes over the hard bulge in Theo's boxers. And Theo's throat hitches, one hand instinctively gripping the sheets, as his whole body tenses up at that touch. He shouldn't be so nervous, he really shouldn't. He doesn't even have to *do* anything, except just lie there.

But he *is* nervous, because he has never done this before. No one has been so close to him before, not like Max, and no one has seen this much of him before and kissed so much of his skin and made him shiver like this. No one has touched him like this before, and the way Max exhales as he ghosts his lips over the stretched fabric of Theo's underwear is so deliciously new and amazing, and just the thought of Max actually *wanting* this, wanting *Theo*, is enough to make Theo's head spin.

Max is clearly impatient, but he still moves slowly, carefully, as though giving Theo a chance to stop him. But Theo doesn't, to his own surprise. Instead, he just takes a deep breath, as Max slips his fingers underneath the hem of his boxers and pulls them down. And Theo tenses up, heart pounding, waiting, before it suddenly just happens.

Theo gasps.

It's hot and wet and smooth, unlike any sensation Theo has ever felt before, and after the initial shock, he realizes that he can actually *feel* that stupid tongue piercing against him. He can feel it, and he can feel that metal ring in Max's bottom lip, Max's mouth moving together with the slick swirls of his tongue. It's enough to make Theo arch off the bed a bit with his hips, only to have Max pin him down firmly with his hands, causing Theo to quickly start scrabbling pointlessly at the sheets with his fingers. He squeezes his eyes shut, letting out a deep, strangled moan.

He doesn't know what's happening, he can't think straight. Everything is suddenly just a haze of pleasure and confusion, mixed together in the most exquisite way.

Theo knows what blowjobs are supposed to be like. He has heard it from a bunch of guys, and they all say it's the most amazing thing. He has always figured they're exaggerating, though; it can't be *that* good, right?

But, as he lies there, suddenly squirming and panting and moaning, reduced to nothing but a hot mess under the intense and eager persuasion of Max's mouth, he realizes that they're really not exaggerating at all. Because this really is the most amazing thing. Just the feeling in itself is mind-blowing, and knowing that it's Max... Well, that just takes it to a whole other level, entirely.

It's when Theo bites out a particularly load moan that Max moves one hand up and grabs Theo's wrist, and Theo can't help but look down as Max deliberately moves Theo's hand to the back of his head. Theo automatically threads his fingers through that black, messy hair, and as he does, Max moans deeply, causing a vibration that makes Theo tense up all over, making him grip Max's hair tightly. Max actually looks up at him then, the equivalent of a mischievous smirk in those eyes, and Theo swallows hard. The eye-contact only lasts for a moment, though; those dark blue, black-lined eyes looking at him like that, while Max is doing what he's doing, is so much more than Theo can handle right now, and he looks up at the ceiling, instead.

Max doesn't seem to mind. Instead, he keeps going, more intensely now, and Theo finds himself pressing gently against the back of his head with his hand, wordlessly urging for more.

He's getting close, so close. They haven't even been at it for very long, but god help him, he's really not going to last, and he knows he should feel embarrassed, but this just feels so good that he can barely think.

"Max." Theo says the name breathlessly, without thinking, and he can practically feel Max tense up against him. Theo's eyes are closed now, his mouth half-open, as he finds himself getting closer and closer to the edge. He doesn't know what to say, but he wants to say something, and Max's name is pretty much all he can think of. "Oh god, Max."

He says his name like a prayer, desperately and earnestly, and as though it affects Max in some way he's not aware of, that grip on Theo's hips tightens, one hand working over what Max's mouth can't take, that pierced tongue swirling around in the most perfect way. And in a matter of seconds, Theo just comes completely undone, his breath quickening to the point where he's nearly hyperventilating.

It's the most amazing feeling. Before he knows it, Theo suddenly goes rigid, fingers digging into that black hair, mouth opening in a stuttering groan, as he feels that blissful, white hot release, making him tense up and stay completely still for just a second or so. Then, his entire body seems to relax, and he softens against the sheets, his suddenly shaking fingers absently loosening their grip on Max's hair.

Damn.

He barely even notices Max lifting his head and pulling Theo's boxers back up, even zipping up the fly of his jeans. Instead, Theo just lies there, eyes half-closed, staring at the ceiling, while Max moves up and lies down beside him, on his back. Theo just keeps breathing, slowly, simply overwhelmed.

Max clearly notices, because he chuckles.

"You okay?" he says, his voice sounding just a bit hoarser than before. He sounds a bit out of breath, too.

Theo doesn't move, every muscle in his body suddenly turned to jelly.

"Yeah," he breathes, swallowing dryly. He sounds completely finished. "That was amazing."

He didn't mean to say that out loud, not really, but he can't help it. He feels high, or at least like he's coming down from being high, and *amazing* doesn't even quite cut it.

Max chuckles again, sounding a bit surprised, this time.

"Thank you," he says, and Theo quirks a small, exhausted smile. No matter what, Max somehow always manages to sound confident and downright cocky.

Neither of them speaks for a few seconds, and soon, Theo actually closes his eyes. He only opens them again when he feels Max shift slightly beside him, and is surprised to find him turning over on his side, so that he faces Theo properly. Then, slowly, hesitantly even, Max drapes his arm over Theo's bare chest, so that his hand ends up by Theo's neck, and Theo swallows hard.

They haven't really done this before. Or at least, Max hasn't. Theo hasn't been able to help himself, really, often cuddling up next to Max as they lie together in his bed.

Max has never cuddled back, though, always keeping a safe distance, despite never objecting to Theo's closeness.

He's definitely not objecting now. This time, Max is the one moving closer. And Theo's heart starts beating faster, for an entirely different reason than a few minutes ago.

He doesn't say anything, though. He just lies still on his back, turning his head to face Max, whose gaze is currently wandering over Theo's chest and collarbones. Those slender fingers start to lightly stroke the bare skin just below Theo's hairline, and Theo feels a pleasant shiver run across his skin. He wonders if Max notices.

Max looks up at him then, eyes dark blue and locked on his green ones, and for several seconds, they just stare at each other. Until Max sighs quietly.

"Shit," he murmurs, looking away again. "I wasn't expecting this."

Max looks back at Theo's chest, fingers still softly stroking the back of Theo's neck. Theo isn't even sure he's aware of doing it, but he's not about to stop him. It feels good.

"What?" Theo asks softly, honestly confused. But Max doesn't answer right away. Instead, he just keeps staring at Theo's chest absently, now rolling his tongue piercing between his teeth, like Theo has seen him do so many times, by now. It means that he's thinking, and Theo would very much like to know exactly what he's thinking about.

He doesn't say anything, though, doesn't press the matter. Instead, he waits, patiently. And finally, Max replies, gaze unmoving.

"I wasn't expecting that I'd actually fall for you."

And just like that, Theo's throat seems to constrict, a weird sensation settling in his stomach; warm and cold, calm and chaotic, all at the same time. He doesn't know what to say, how to react. And for what seems like several seconds, he just stays in shock, waiting for something to prove that he just heard Max wrong.

But no such proof comes, and eventually, Max slowly turns his gaze back to him. Those intense, blue eyes are so much softer than usual, unsure, even, and Theo can barely believe what he's seeing. Max never looks unsure, *ever*, and he always has some witty comeback, some dry comment, to ease any kind of tension.

But not this time. This time, he just looks at Theo, softly.

"I really like you, Theo," he says, that smoky voice unusually soft, as well. "A lot."

But Theo still doesn't say anything. Instead, he just keeps his green, slightly widened eyes on Max's blue ones, unmoving. And after a few seconds, even Max, who always seems so impervious to any kind of social awkwardness and tension, gets uncomfortable.

"Look, I—" he starts, but he doesn't get to finish. Theo stops him by planting a hard, deliberate kiss on his mouth, not even caring where Max's mouth has just been, and Max really doesn't seem to mind. He just kisses him back, relaxing against Theo's body, and when they finally pull apart, he quirks a typical Max-smile.

"It's mutual, then, I take it?" he says, and Theo exhales slowly. He can't help but smile back, and gives Max another quick kiss. Max chuckles against his lips.

"So, what?" he murmurs. "Am I like, your boyfriend now, or something?"

Theo feels a ridiculously strong rush at the word *boyfriend*, and at the way Max seems to struggle between saying it softly and saying it dryly, since it's a word that doesn't usually come out of his mouth in any serious sense.

"Do you wanna be?" Theo says, heart pounding. Max cocks his head.

"Well, I've never been anyone's boyfriend, before," he admits. "Not really."

He kisses the corner of Theo's mouth softly, hand still stroking the back of his neck, pulling through his hair slightly.

"I wouldn't mind being yours."

Theo is suddenly elated. Suddenly, he can't think of anything that would make him happier to hear, and for the first time since he has met Max—yearning, long-distance crush aside—he allows himself to really feel it. He finally allows himself to really feel those butterflies in his stomach, the way his heart pounds against his ribs, and the way just a look from Max makes him feel high.

He lets himself feel it, and he moves closer to Max, so close that they're practically breathing in each other's breaths, shifting so that he's lying on his side, properly face-to-face with Max. He moves his hand to Max's waist, smoothing over the fabric of his black tank top, while Max gently pulls his fingers through Theo's hair, moving as close as he can possibly get, a small, content sigh escaping his lips.

Theo kisses him softly, closing his eyes as he leans their foreheads together.

"Okay."

CHAPTER 7
REBEL

Theo is pretty sure that there's a neon sign above his head; a giant, red arrow pointing down at him, letting everyone know that he's so happy right now that he can barely function.

Riley sees said arrow. He sees it the moment Theo comes down the stairs the next morning, not even twelve hours after the milestone Theo and Max just passed in their relationship.

Relationship. Because they actually have one, now. Max is suddenly his boyfriend, and Theo can't really seem to wrap his head around it.

His parents are home, though, so Riley doesn't say anything. Instead, he just gives Theo a quizzical look, before somehow realizing what's up, and his face cracks into a smile. Their dad, Eric, is too focused on his newspaper to notice, and their mother, Amy, is on the other side of the kitchen, back turned. But Theo still barely dares to respond to Riley's smile, only hints at one, as he makes his way to the fridge. And that seems to be enough for Riley, who turns back to his schoolbook. It's baffling, really, how mature he can be for such a young kid.

"Good morning," their mom says, giving Theo a peck on the cheek. "I was just about to check if you were awake, yet."

Theo just smiles, a bit awkwardly. To be honest, he barely slept at all last night, too stirred up by the butterflies in his stomach to get any real rest.

"I'm good," he says, grabbing a piece of toast. "In a bit of a hurry, though."

Amy nods, tucking a strand of long, blond hair behind her ear.

"That's what happens when you sleep in," she says, a bit chidingly, giving him a pointed look with those eyes that almost match his own. Eric looks up over the edge of his newspaper.

"Don't forget your brother," he says, and Theo frowns, turning to him.

"Dad," Riley says, exasperated. "I'm not a kid, I can walk to school by myself."

"You're going to the same place," Eric retorts, looking back at his newspaper. "Might as well."

"Wait, what?" Theo says, confused, chewing a bite of toast. Riley turns to him.

"Ellie's sick," he says, referring to their neighbor, and Riley's childhood friend. "And dad doesn't think I'll survive the walk to school by myself."

Theo raises his eyebrows slightly at the obvious sass, and glances at their father. Ellie and Riley have walked to school together since forever, pretty much, sure, but making Riley walk with Theo instead is a bit of an overreaction.

"It's not out of your way, right?" Eric says, only the top of his dark-haired head visible, really, as well as his hazel eyes, as he glances at Theo. Theo then glances at Riley, before shaking his head.

"No," he says. "It's fine."

79

He looks back at his little brother, and can't help but smile teasingly.

"So she's home sick, huh?" he says pointedly. "I bet she'd be really grateful if you bring her the homework she's missing."

Riley just makes a face, but the way he starts blushing furiously makes Theo's smile widen.

"Shut up, Theo," he mutters, turning back to his book, and Theo just chuckles, as he chews down the last of his toast.

It's about fifteen minutes later that the two brothers leave the house, and as soon as they have rounded the corner of their block, Riley looks up at Theo pointedly.

"You did something, didn't you?" he says. It's almost more of a statement, than a question.

Theo widens his eyes slightly, taken completely by surprise.

"Whoa," he says, glancing around. "What?"

"You know what I mean."

Riley gives him a pointed glare, and Theo exhales.

"Fine," he admits. "Yes. Why?"

Riley shrugs, half-smiling.

"No reason," he says. "I'm just pretty sure other people will be able to tell, this time."

Theo frowns.

"What's that supposed to mean?" he asks, knowing full well about the metaphorical neon sign above his head. He's just really hoping it's not as obvious as it feels.

Riley gives him another pointed look, which he figures is reply enough.

"So," he says, instead, after a while. "Are you two together now?"

Theo actually blushes, knowing that he's referring to Max.

"Maybe," he mutters, unable to completely hide the small smile that creeps into his expression. "Yeah."

Riley smiles, then. His expression is a mix of brotherly teasing and genuine happiness, and Theo is eternally grateful that him and his brother so close, despite being four years apart in age.

"Good," Riley says. "That's good."

He looks straight ahead, as they keep walking.

"You know what this means, right?" Riley says, and Theo looks at him.

"What?" he asks, and Riley sighs quietly.

"Mom and dad are gonna find out," he says. His voice is neutral, just a little bit sad. "You should be the one to tell them."

Theo sighs. For the first time since last night, he feels his stomach drop. He knows what their parents are going to think, what they're going to say. They wouldn't like Max, at all. Especially his dad probably wouldn't even give him a chance. He would just take one look at him and decide that he's some deadbeat who's out to corrupt his son, and not want Theo anywhere near him.

"Let's not get ahead of ourselves," Theo says, slightly subdued. "Don't think we're quite there, yet."

Riley nods slowly, understanding. Then he half-smiles.

"Well, I should meet him, at least," he says, looking up at Theo. "I think I should know what kind of guy my brother's boyfriend is."

Theo blushes again, looking down at the ground. He still can't quite comprehend that Max is his *boyfriend*. He has never even had a boyfriend, never had any relationship like it, at all, and now he's with Max. *Max*. The gorgeous, amazing, really smart guy he has fallen for so completely, and who now, for some reason, has fallen for Theo and actually wants to be with him. It's just surreal, really.

When they reach the school, Theo and Riley go their separate ways, and Theo can't help but look around a bit as he makes his way to the main building's entrance. On one hand, he's anxious about just how obvious the arrow above his head is (Riley practically said that everyone would be able to see it this time, after all), and on the other, he can't help but scan the area for Max. It's almost as though he *needs* to see him, just to make sure that last night actually happened.

Theo doesn't see him, though, not for a few hours, at least. It's not until right before the last class before lunch, that he sees him.

It's odd, Theo realizes, that even though he and Max have spent so much time together lately (and *done* so much, he remembers, blushing to himself), and even though they're actually a *couple* now, apparently, they're still practically strangers at school. After weeks of basically ignoring each other in front of other people, it has become a habit, so much so that Theo doesn't really know what to do when he spots Max, several feet away.

Max is over near the end of the hallway, in a little crook by a window, where he's perched on the windowsill. One black boot is firmly placed against the surface of it, knee pulled up, the other leg dangling over the edge. He's leaning with his back against the window frame, the entire left side of his body pressed against the glass of the big window, and he's got a closed notepad in his lap.

He's not alone; a few of his friends are standing or sitting nearby. From a distance, Theo recognizes Jay, a skinny guy who somehow looks even skinnier with all that black and those heavy, silver-buckled boots, and Rachel, a girl whose blond hair has been knotted into long, pale dreadlocks, in stark contrast to her black makeup. There's also Beth, who looks a little more common in comparison, with dark brown, curly hair, and a wicked smile that's only accentuated by her blood red lipstick.

She's smiling at Max. She's short enough to be at about eye-level with him, as she stands up and he sits on the windowsill, and her obvious and blatant flirting makes Theo's stomach twist into knots. He shouldn't care, though; Max said that he has made it very clear to Beth that he's not interested. But still. Theo can't help but feel extremely uncomfortable and inadequate, not to mention jealous, all at the same time, as he watches her watch Max.

He's on his way out of a classroom when he sees Max, over there, and he stops as Michael does, when they reach his locker. Hannah is with them, too, and she waits patiently while Michael rummages through his locker, Theo at his side.

Theo tries not to look at Max. He really tries, especially while Max is with his friends. Theo hasn't even spoken to them, after all (not that Max has ever spoken to Theo's friends), and he's pretty sure that they wouldn't much approve of him, anyway. And he has no idea what difference it would make if he looked. He's still not entirely convinced that last night wasn't just a dream.

But he can't help it. Michael and Hannah are busy talking to each other, and Theo lets his eyes wander over to Max, where he sits, several feet away. He's just so beautiful. He's so beautiful it's stupid, frankly, and Theo kind of hates what it does to him. Max is so out of his league, and for a moment, he feels something like panic.

Of course last night never happened, he thinks. That would be too amazing and too surreal and just too *good*.

But then, Max sees him. It's just a glance, at first, but then those intense, blue eyes focus on Theo, as though seeing him for the first time, and Max's entire face seems to light up. Theo can see it, even from so far away, and he feels his heart do a double take, as Max simply, unbelievably, smiles.

Theo takes a deep breath, trying to still the way his entire body seems to tense up in anticipation. And the way Max is smiling at him, so softly, yet with such unabashed affection and something that looks an awful lot like hunger (because it's Max, and he seems unable to *not* look at Theo that way)... He's convinced. Last night *did* happen, and it wasn't just a dream. And Theo hesitantly, just barely, smiles back.

"What do you think, Theo?"

Hannah's voice comes from somewhere far away, and Theo barely notices. He doesn't answer her, whatever it is she and Michael are apparently talking about. He can't. He's just too distracted by the way Max is looking at him from several feet away, and all of a sudden, he feels as though he's physically forcing himself not to move, lest he run over there and attack that stupid, beautiful face with his mouth.

"Theo." Hannah's voice is a bit harsh now, as though she can clearly tell that he's distracted. "What's the matter with you?"

"Uh-huh," Theo musters, eyes still on Max. Then Hannah notices, and turns to look. Her entire face twists into a confused, annoyed frown, as she realizes just who he's looking at.

"Really?" she exclaims, and Theo glances at her briefly, before looking back at Max. "Theo, we've talked about this! What are you doing?"

Theo looks at her properly, then, suddenly anxious. Michael has closed his locker, and his eyes are on him, as well, slightly disapproving and suspicious. Theo swallows hard. He's pretty sure anyone can tell that he's immensely uncomfortable and kind of scared, right now. He doesn't know what to say. These are his friends, sure, but he just knows that they'll hate him forever for hooking up with someone like Max, and he hasn't exactly told them, yet.

"I—" he starts, but doesn't really know what to say. Out of the corner of his eye, he can see Max tensing up slightly, straightening in his seat, as though paying more attention. Almost as though he's *concerned*. "I just—"

"You just what?" Hannah says, frowning angrily. "He's not worth it, Theo!"

She gestures vaguely in the general direction of Max and his friends, glancing over there with thinly veiled disdain.

"I mean, look at him."

Theo's face flushes. Not from embarrassment, but from anger, and he suddenly feels a strong urge to defend Max, to tell Hannah to simply shut up, that she doesn't know Max and has no idea what he's like.

Not to mention the fact that Max is beautiful in every single way, and that she clearly has no idea what she's talking about.

But Theo has never been good with confrontation. And he has never been good at speaking his mind, especially not when it comes to his friends.

So he grits his teeth, trying to think of something to say, anything.

He's only vaguely aware of Max making his way over to them, out of the corner of his eye, and it's not until he's suddenly right there, that Theo actually reacts.

Max simply walks up to them, puts himself between Theo and Hannah, Michael standing right next to them. He then glances at Hannah briefly and hands her his notepad, practically pushing it against her chest, making her simply catch it in her hands, in surprise. Meanwhile, Theo just stares, eyes slightly widened in confused surprise, as Max turns to him. But then, those dark blue eyes focus on his, and the smallest, mischievous smile shapes those lips, before Max simply puts his hand by Theo's face, and kisses him.

Theo barely has time to react. He knows that he should be surprised and uncomfortable, somehow, but he isn't. Instead, he just feels a rush of warmth and shivers, as his mouth recognizes Max's, and he closes his eyes, reciprocating the kiss.

Max pushes against him slightly, just enough to softly press Theo's back against the locker behind him, and Theo puts his hands by Max's waist, pulling him closer, Max's free hand slipping into his back pocket. That tongue slides into his mouth, metal stud hard and warm, and Theo forgets how to breathe for just a few seconds.

Because that's how long it lasts, just a few seconds, before Theo opens his eyes as Max pulls away. He feels dazed and light-headed, and he watches those blue, black-lined eyes as they refocus on him; they're filled with amused excitement, and Max smirks as he removes his hands from Theo's body. Then he turns to Hannah, who's clutching the notebook against her chest, eyes wide and mouth half-open. Max glances at her, pierced eyebrow raised, before grabbing his notebook and pulling it out of her grip.

"Thanks," he says, giving her a smile that's like poisoned honey. Then he turns to Theo, expression softened. He gives him a quick, chaste kiss. "Later, babe."

Theo doesn't answer him, simply nods weakly, and Max gives him one last, amused smirk, before turning around and simply walking away.

Nobody moves for several seconds, but finally, Hannah speaks.

"What the hell was that?" she says, sounding angry, rather than confused. Theo doesn't answer her, still staring after Max, who is just disappearing from view.

"Theo," Hannah insists, sounding appalled. "Listen to me. I don't know what he's done to you, but this is not okay. He's gross—"

"Shut up, Hannah." Theo says it with a low voice, sounding bored, more than anything. He's too annoyed and too happy to care about how he's saying anything like that to her for the first time ever, and he doesn't even turn to see her expression. "Just shut up."

It turns out that speaking up like that might not have been the best idea. At least, it didn't have quite the effect Theo expected.

Hannah basically just huffed indignantly, shocked at Theo's comment, and she pretty much stormed off, Michael in tow. Theo was surprised, to say the least, both at what he said, and at her reaction to it, but he didn't think about it, at the time. Instead, he was just *happy*. Happy about what Max had done, and happy about how it was simply out there, now. The whole thing had pretty much saved him from a painfully awkward and judgmental conversation with his friends, and he was just too blissfully high from that kiss that he couldn't think about the consequences.

Said consequences came later.

For the first time in the past year or so, Theo is sitting alone at lunch. He hasn't always been friends with Michael and Hannah and the rest; it was something that just sort of happened. Theo and Michael were paired up during class once, and Michael sort of took him under his wing, after that. And because Michael is fairly popular, Theo's social life significantly improved, because of it. Hell, before that, he barely talked to anyone, really.

But now, Theo is learning the hard way that the small social status he actually had is crumbling pretty fast, and all because of what he did earlier, just a couple of hours ago.

At lunch, he entered the cafeteria and searched the room for his friends, as usual, but when he spotted them, Hannah gave him such a venomous glare that he felt physically repelled, and Michael didn't exactly reprimand her for it. So Theo quietly made his way over to an empty table across the room, where he sat down with his lunch.

He's been sitting there for about ten minutes, eating, thinking about the whole thing. He doesn't really mind sitting alone; honestly, he's used to it. He was always alone before he became friends with Michael and Hannah. But still. It feels unusually cold, now that he knows what the warmth of company feels like.

"Hi, Theo."

Theo looks up at the sound of someone speaking, right next to him, and he relaxes a bit when he sees who it is.

"Hey," he says. "Cassie, right?"

Cassie nods, a tentative smile on her face.

"That's me." She glances around a bit, as though hesitant. Then she turns back to him. "You look like you could use some company."

Theo sighs quietly, glancing around at the empty table. Then he nods, a small, tired smile on his face, as he looks up at her.

"Yeah," he says. "I'd like that."

Cassie smiles properly, this time, and she sits down opposite him, with her lunch.

"I know I've said this before," Cassie says after a little while, "but don't mind them. They're idiots."

Theo frowns slightly.

"How do you know—"

"I heard what happened," Cassie interrupts him simply, with a sympathetic look. "Actually, I'm pretty sure everyone's heard."

Theo just stares at her, blinks, trying to determine what she means.

"You and Max," Cassie explains, as though a little bit amused at Theo's confusion. "The whole *public display of affection.*"

She says it tentatively, as though not sure how to put it, and Theo actually blushes a bit, looking down at his food. He hadn't thought about that. It didn't occur to him for a second that the hallway wasn't exactly empty when Max did that, and that other people, besides his friends, were bound to have seen it. If he's surprised at anything at all, it's that Cassie—or everyone, as she says—already knows about it, just hours after it happening. Then again, he shouldn't be surprised. This isn't exactly a huge school.

"For the record," Cassie says, "I think it's really cool."

Theo looks up at her, hesitantly.

"Really?" he asks, and Cassie shrugs.

"Yeah," she says. "I mean, it's nice that you two have found each other. Unexpected, and a bit weird, but nice."

She pauses.

"I mean," she adds, unsure. "It is you two, right?"

Theo nods.

"Yeah," he says. "I mean, I think so. We kind of decided that, recently. It just sort of happened."

Cassie nods, looking oddly pleased.

"So, you've been seeing each other for a while?" she asks.

"Yeah." Theo nods, poking at his food with a fork, looking down. "You could say that."

"And you're finally out with it?" Cassie continues. "Okay with the whole public-thing?"

Theo frowns at his food, then looks up at her.

"Yeah," he says, a bit confused at her question. "Why?"

Cassie half-smiles.

"Because he's coming over here."

Theo nearly jumps and looks over his shoulder, just in time to see Max come up behind him. He stops dead, and Theo has to lean his head back and look straight up to see his face. Then Max smiles wickedly and leans down, smoothing his hands down over Theo's chest and tilting his head slightly to kiss him on the mouth, and in the midst of the pure, pleased surprise Theo feels at the action, he also feels uncomfortable.

"What are you doing?" he asks when Max pulls away from his mouth about an inch or so.

Max raises his eyebrows, his expression bored and amused, all at the same time, not to mention currently upside-down.

"Saying hello," he practically purrs, and Theo shifts slightly in his seat.

"Yeah, well, there's people everywhere," he mutters, and Max cocks one pierced eyebrow.

"You mean, they might see us and draw all kinds of conclusions, based on the physical proximity of our greeting?" He leans in and kisses Theo on the mouth again, before adding in a murmur: "I think we're pretty fucked in that department, don't you?"

Theo has to admit that he has a point, and he doesn't object when Max gives him one last, quick kiss, before pulling away and sitting down on the chair beside him, instead.

Theo just looks at him, follows him with his gaze, and Max does the same, their eyes not leaving the other's for a moment, really. And as he sits down, Max smoothly takes Theo's hand and laces their fingers together, holding their hands underneath the table. It takes several seconds of silent staring, before Max suddenly turns to Cassie.

"I've seen you before," he says, and Cassie nearly flinches. It's obvious from her expression that she's intimidated by Max, both by the way he looks, and by the way he practically exudes confidence.

"Uh, yeah," she stutters, and Theo remembers her mentioning that she has talked to Max, once or twice. Max frowns, thinking, eyes narrowed. Then he tilts his head.

"Cassie," he says, and her hazel eyes widen, clearly surprised.

"Yes," she confirms, and Max nods.

"Thought so," he says. "Good to see you."

He smirks, but in a way that looks more amused than mean, and Cassie half-smiles back, clearly a bit more relaxed.

"Thanks for keeping him company," Max says, cocking his head toward Theo, eyes still on Cassie. "Seeing as how his so-called friends are assholes."

Theo opens his mouth to object, but then realizes that he doesn't really want to. They *are* assholes. Friends don't just up and abandon you for being with a certain person, after all.

But he says something anyway, as though automatically defending them, even though he knows it's not right.

"It's fine," he says, looking down at his food, and he can practically feel Max bristling.

"You do realize," Max says, and Theo looks up at him again; those blue eyes are slightly narrowed. "That they have *literally* distanced themselves from you?"

He pauses, eyes on Theo.

"Like, *physically*," he says, making a pushing motion with his hand. "They have actually, deliberately, made you move away from where they are, and are currently ignoring you. Just because you're with me."

He cocks his head.

"So I'm sorry, but I really don't see the point in giving an ounce of a shit about calling them something like that."

Theo is shocked at the sheer gratitude and affection he suddenly feels for Max, at the way he so fiercely comes to his defense, just like before. He's struck by just how determinedly Max just came up to him earlier, in the hallway, and kissed him, in front of Theo's friends and in front of everybody, claiming him for his own for them all to see.

And Theo swallows hard, oddly overwhelmed, and he squeezes Max's hand gently under the table. Max squeezes back.

CHAPTER 8

WARMTH

You would think that Theo would have paid attention to pretty much every part of Max by now, but no.

He hasn't before noticed or paid attention to the tiny, barely noticeable scar he has on his chin, or the way cricks his neck a bit, every time he straightens up.

Or his habit of quirking a tiny smile to himself, whenever he manages to solve something—Theo noticed that the last time they actually studied together. It doesn't happen often, and when it comes to math, for instance, Max is definitely on a whole other level.

But it does happen, and when it does, Theo always finds it hard to focus on his homework, when Max is so much more interesting to watch. Because when he works, when he's thinking, it's just fascinating, somehow, how he gets so into it and looks so pleased when he gets it right.

Tonight, though, Theo is paying attention to something else about Max.

They're sitting on the couch in Max's living room (his parents are out, as usual), watching *Buffy the Vampire Slayer* reruns, and although Theo loves this show, he's having a hard time paying proper attention to it, right now. Instead, he glances as Max's profile, on his left, as they sit next to each other, watches him watch the screen. Theo's gaze skims over his face and his neck, until it lands on his ear; both Max's ears are pierced, but his right one has a black earring that fits the stretched earlobe perfectly, and Theo is paying attention to that, this time. He has no idea why. Maybe it's just that it's part of *Max*, and that makes it interesting.

The piercing isn't that big, not big enough to really look twice at if you just glance at it. It kind of looks like a black button, the earlobe only stretched out a little.

Theo shifts a little bit closer to Max's side. He touches Max's ear, then, and Max raises an eyebrow at him.

"What are you doing?" he asks, but Theo isn't fazed.

"Did this hurt?" he says, and Max glances at Theo's hand, realizing that he's talking about his piercing.

"Not really," he says. "You sort of just work your way up to the size you want, little bit at a time."

Theo nods, fiddling with the black, round piercing for a moment, before trailing his fingers softly up along the shell of Max's ear. He can practically feel Max shiver at his touch, and it makes him smile; he still can't get over the fact that he affects Max that way.

"Stop that," Max murmurs after a little while, and Theo glances at his face. Max is looking straight ahead, absently fiddling with his lip piercing, using his tongue and teeth, while he watches the TV, and Theo pauses for a moment. But then he starts again, slowly moving his fingers along Max's ear and up to the metal stud pierced at the top of it, to the dark metal ring even further up. And Max shivers again, noticeably, eyelids fluttering just the slightest bit.

"Theo," he says warningly, but Theo can't help but smile slightly, as he watches Max's face, his reactions.

"Yes?" he says, and he can tell that Max is slightly surprised at his bold tone.

"Don't do that," Max says, the tiniest smile quirking at the corner of his mouth, eyes still fixed on the TV.

"Why not?" Theo moves his fingers back, slowly pulling them through that black, messy hair. And Max actually closes his eyes for the briefest moment. He sighs.

"Because it does weird things to me," he says, that raspy voice low, and Theo licks his lips. He suddenly feels oddly brave.

Max nearly flinches when Theo leans in and plants a kiss against his neck, but in a way that's more surprised, than anything. Theo can tell, because a moment later, Max is relaxing against the couch, inhaling slowly. And Theo takes that as encouragement, kissing him again, slowly moving his lips along his throat, up to the curve of his jaw, and Max lets out a deep, slow breath.

Theo doesn't say anything, and neither does Max. Instead, Theo just keeps kissing, slowly, softly, fingers pulling through Max's hair, while his other hand slowly smoothes over his chest. And Max lets out the smallest, barely audible, moan. Theo is shocked at how good it feels to hear it.

It spurs him on, though, and Theo finds himself moving. He's not sure who's more surprised, him or Max, but before he knows it, he's suddenly sitting on Max's lap, straddling him, and Max just looks up at him, wide-eyed.

"Well, look at you," he murmurs, and Theo is pretty sure he would be smirking, if he weren't so shocked.

Theo doesn't answer him, instead just looks at him for another moment, before leaning down. He doesn't kiss him, though, not right away. He simply hints at it, that metal ring brushing against his bottom lip, and he can both hear and feel Max breathing heavily, hands sliding up to Theo's hips, tentatively, greedily. Theo slips his tongue out, touches Max's lips lightly, making him tense up underneath him. And Max swallows hard.

"What are you doing?" he breathes, but Theo doesn't answer him, just slowly tightens his grip on Max's hair, his other hand smoothing up along his neck. He doesn't answer, because he doesn't know what to say. He doesn't know what he's doing. He has never done anything like this before.

Theo wants to kiss him, he really does. But he also loves this, loves being just on the brink, Max moving just the slightest bit underneath him. So Theo starts moving, too, just a little bit. Just enough to grind slightly against Max, who immediately tightens his grip on Theo's hips, exhaling slowly, heavily.

The TV is still on, but Theo barely hears it. Instead, all he hears is Max's breathing, the way he moans quietly, as he gently pushes Theo's hips down against him with his hands, moving their bodies together. And Theo closes his eyes, leans their foreheads together, trying to breathe slowly, but to no avail.

Theo didn't mean for this to happen. He only meant to tease a little bit, maybe kiss Max, innocently enough. But it's like he can't keep his hands off of him, and he's vaguely aware of how shy and uncomfortable he was about all of this just a few weeks ago. He never would have done something like this. He barely let Max do it, and now, he's the one straddling him, grinding against him with gradually more pressure and more determination, fingers digging into his hair, feeling those steady hands on his hips.

Theo is surprised, but at the same time not at all, when he feels the fabric of his jeans suddenly straining over his unexpected hard-on; it was bound to happen, he supposes. He's a bit more surprised, however, to feel that Max is having the same reaction, and that Max is the one pressing their bodies together, seemingly doing everything in his power not to kiss Theo, right now, keeping his eyes closed and taking heavy, shuddering breaths. He sounds like he wants to say something, but he doesn't, his body arching against Theo's, as Theo presses down against him, harder.

It's only a matter of seconds, really, before it becomes too much. Theo still isn't used to this, and he's still not good at the whole endurance-thing, and he can feel it building, already. And they haven't even done anything, haven't even taken a single layer of clothing off. They're not even *kissing*, for god's sake. But it's still happening, still building, and for a second, he starts slowing down; it would simply be too ridiculous and too embarrassing for him to come, right now.

But then, Max kisses him, out of nowhere, and it's like pouring gasoline on a fire.

Theo hears himself moaning against Max's lips, surprised and pleased, all at once, and he tightens his grip on Max's hair, when he feels Max slip one hand underneath his jeans and grab his ass. *Shit.* This isn't working, he's not going to last.

But just when Theo is about to actually pull away—to avoid any embarrassment that he knows will come if they keep going—Max stops him. He places one hand firmly at the back of Theo's head, the other still on his ass, pressing their bodies together, kissing him deeply, claiming his mouth with his tongue, and Theo moans in surprise at the sheer intensity of it.

Damn it. Shit.

Max lets out a deep, pleased groan, and that's it. That's all it takes for Theo to tense up and squeeze his eyes shut, body shuddering with the untimely orgasm he has tried to contain for the past couple of minutes. And although it feels so amazing he might just pass out, it's almost immediately overshadowed by an intense sense of embarrassment.

Shit. He can't believe that just happened. He feels like such a *virgin* that it's not even funny.

Max doesn't seem to notice, though. He doesn't seem to notice, because only a second or so later, he completely stops moving, muscles tensing up, pressing Theo and his mouth so close against him that it almost hurts. The piercing is hard against

Theo's lips, and he notices a low, choked moan coming from Max, before, a second later, Max relaxes again underneath him.

And it takes another second, before Theo realizes what just happened, green eyes widening slightly. He pulls away a bit.

"Did you just—" he says, unable to string together a coherent question. But the way Max is breathing heavily, blue eyes dazed as he looks up at him, is answer enough.

"I mean," Theo says, almost stuttering, disbelieving. "Did I just make you—"

"Come?" Max says, cocking his eyebrows, looking oddly exhausted, practically panting. "I think that's the word you're looking for."

Theo just stares at him, mouth falling open, as he tries to wrap his head around it.

"Really?" he says, dumbly, and Max does some tired cross between an eye-roll and a smirk.

"Yes, really," he says. His hands are still on Theo, one in his hair and the other on his ass. He frowns. "And honestly, I'm as surprised as you are."

He swallows dryly.

"I mean, don't get me wrong," he says, cocking his head. "It was amazing. But *damn.*"

He leans his head back against the backrest of the couch, exhaling loudly, and Theo moves his hands down to smooth them over Max's chest. He can feel Max's heart beating frantically, under his palm. And then it sinks in, and he can't help but smile.

He did this. He made Max come. And he didn't even take his clothes off, barely even touched him. And suddenly, he feels oddly pleased, and oddly proud.

"I didn't mean to," Theo says, and Max looks up at him. He licks his lips.

"Well, fuck," he says, narrowing his eyes. "That just makes it worse."

He pulls Theo's face down to kiss him, slowly and deeply, before pulling away again.

96

"If you weren't even trying," he says, "how am I gonna survive, when you actually do try?"

Theo feels himself blushing, ridiculously enough, and Max smiles as he sees it.

"God, I love it when you blush," he murmurs, moving one hand up to smooth over Theo's cheekbone with his thumb. And for a few seconds, they just stare at one another, valiantly ignoring the sticky discomfort they've caused in each other's underwear, Theo absently deciding that it's not important, right this second.

"You wanna come over, sometime?" he suddenly asks instead, surprising himself, and Max gives him the smallest frown, which makes Theo clarify. "To my house. Just hang out, or whatever..."

He trails off, suddenly feeling very silly, under the intense gaze of those dark blue, black-lined eyes, and simply considering the whole situation they're currently in. It's all rather ridiculous, really.

But then, Max smiles.

"I'd like that," he says, and Theo noticeably relaxes. He lets out a breath, smiling back.

"Okay."

♦

It's not like Theo has suddenly decided to drop this bomb on his parents—no way. It's more a matter of wanting Max to see his home, *his* room, seeing as how he has never actually been there, before.

And they have been together for over a week, now, after seeing each other for the past month or so. It seems only appropriate, like it's about time. At least, that's how Theo sees it, after spending so many hours at Max's house.

It has taken a few days to find the opportune moment, though; Theo's parents are rarely away from home any longer periods of time, but tonight, there's an exception. Both his mother and father are away together, at some dinner party with friends, at the edge of town, and seeing as how both Riley and Theo are old enough to look after themselves, their parents are staying with their friends for the night, rather than driving home. And this means privacy, which isn't something Theo is about to turn down.

"Do mom and dad know about this?" Riley asks, sitting at the kitchen table, doing his homework, while Theo absently finishes up the dishes (it's his turn, as he and Riley do them every other day).

Theo sighs, pulling the plug in the sink, after putting away the last, cleaned plate.

"No," he says, watching the foamy water swirl down into the pipes. He hears Riley sigh softly, and he looks over at his little brother. His expression is sad and slightly disapproving, and Theo is reminded, like he always is, about how precocious Riley can be.

"Don't give me that," Theo says, wiping down the counter with a dishrag. "You know how they get."

Riley murmurs in agreement.

"I know," he admits. "But you really should tell them. If not, they're gonna find out from someone else, and then they'll be really pissed."

Theo looks over at him, and Riley starts, eyes wide.

"Not from me!" he clarifies, a bit frantically. "You know that." Theo knows it's true; Riley would never sell him out like that. Riley relaxes in his seat.

"I'm just sayin'," he says, and Theo cocks his head, before putting away the dishrag.

"I will tell them," he says, looking at Riley. "But I figured, you could meet him first."

Riley smiles a bit then, and Theo smiles back. Regardless of what his parents would say about him dating someone like Max, he's very happy that at least Riley is on his side.

The doorbell rings, and Theo practically jumps, instantly nervous. He shouldn't be, though; Max coming to his house shouldn't be such a huge deal, especially not now. Max is his boyfriend, after all.

Boyfriend. Theo's heart skips a beat, as he makes his way to the front door.

Riley stays seated at the kitchen table, but Theo knows he can hear anything that happens out in the hall, so he tries to play it cool when he opens the door. That plan fails completely, though, because as soon as he sees Max, it's like he physically has to stop himself from letting out a pathetic sound of pure joy and stunned affection.

"Looks like I got it right," Max says, as Theo opens the door, glancing up at the house. "Awesome."

He turns back to Theo, who just stands there for a few seconds, hand on the door handle. Max is wearing his black trenchcoat, hands in the pockets, and he raises his eyebrows, with a small smile.

"You gonna let me in, Davis?" he says smoothly. "Freezing my ass off, here."

Theo reanimates, then, pausing for a confused moment.

"Uh," he says eloquently. "Yeah."

He steps back, allowing Max to step over the threshold and into the warmth of the hall, and Theo closes the door behind him. He swallows dryly, confused as to why this makes him so nervous.

Theo barely has a chance to lock the door and turn back around, though, before Max's hands are on either side of his face, pulling his mouth to his own, and Theo widens his eyes in surprise for a moment. But the moment fades away very quickly, and he's relaxing against Max's body, absently moving his hands to rest on his hips. Max's coat and shoes are already off, and his hands are chilly against Theo's warm skin. Even his lips are cool, the piercing even more so, but Theo doesn't mind; it just makes him want to warm Max up, and fast.

Max pulls away after a moment, keeping the kiss rather soft and chaste, and Theo just exhales, softening his posture a bit. Why was he nervous, again?

"You okay?" Max asks, quirking a small smile, and Theo nods.

"Yeah," he says softly, before remembering where they are. He lightly takes Max's hand. "Come on."

Max doesn't seem the least bit anxious about being in a new place, merely looks around with slight interest, as they eventually make their way to the kitchen, Theo leading the way. There, they find Riley, still sitting at the kitchen table, and he looks up as they enter the room, straightening slightly in his chair.

"Riley," Theo says, lingering with Max by the doorway. "This is Max. Max, my little brother, Riley."

Max nods at Riley.

"Hey," he says, and Riley looks at him for a second, before speaking.

"Hi," he says, but that's it. Theo then waits patiently for another couple of seconds, as Riley eyes Max up and down, very quickly, with a look of detached, neutral interest. It doesn't faze Max, who is used to it, although the complete lack of judgment or distaste on Riley's face is something Theo is pretty sure he's less used to.

Riley frowns a bit, as his gaze lands on Max's face.

"I like your piercings," he says, and Theo actually raises his eyebrows slightly in surprise. He glances at Max, who keeps his eyes on Riley.

"Thanks," he says, and Riley nods.

"Got any more?" he asks, and Max hesitates for a moment, before simply opening his mouth and rolling out his tongue. Riley looks slightly surprised, at the sight of the tongue piercing.

"Cool," he says weakly, as though he really means it, and Max cocks his eyebrows, closing his mouth. Riley seems to deliberate for a second, before he turns to Theo.

"So, can you feel that?" he asks. "When you make out?"

Theo starts blushing furiously, hoping that it's not as obvious as it feels.

"Riley!" he says, in lack of anything else, but his little brother just shrugs.

"What?" he says. "Just curious. Can you?"

100

Theo opens and closes his mouth, instantly very uncomfortable. And then, Max makes it worse by turning to him, an over-nonchalant look on his face.

"Yeah, Theo," he says, eyebrows slightly raised. "*Can* you?"

Theo glares at him, but Max just smiles mischievously, until Theo sighs in frustration.

"Yes, I can," he mutters, glancing at Riley. "Happy?"

Riley smiles in a way that seems reserved for teasing his big brother.

"Yeah," he says, and Theo shoves his hands into his pockets, pulling his shoulders up a bit in discomfort. Max chuckles.

"Don't be like that," he says, with a tone of fondness that Theo isn't quite used to hearing, yet. "You know you like it."

Theo shoots him another glare, but the sincere, albeit slightly teasing, smile on Max's face makes him relax a bit, and he exhales.

Riley clears his throat a little bit, and Theo looks over at him. He's wearing that precocious look on his face, eyebrows slightly raised.

"You guys go ahead," he says. "I've got homework, anyway."

Theo feels a bit embarrassed at his words, but grateful, and he gives his brother a small nod, before turning toward the staircase. Max follows right behind him, but gives Riley a small salute, before climbing the stairs to Theo's room.

It's only when Theo opens the door to his room that it hits him; he has never had a guy in his room, before. Well, he *has*, but not like *this*. He has never had anyone in his room before, that he feels this way about. This is a first, and he tries not to fidget too much, as Max enters and looks around.

"Hm," Max hums absently, blue eyes scanning the walls. Theo becomes almost uncomfortably aware of the rather extreme geekiness of the place, with posters ranging from *Star Wars* and *Batman*, to *Gattaca* and *The Fifth Element,* and he hopes Max won't pay too much attention to the miniature Mjölnir he got for his birthday a couple of years ago; it's a tiny replica of the hammer belonging to Marvel's Thor, serving as a kind of paperweight, on his desk. Maybe he should have hidden that.

"You really went for it, didn't you?" Max says, and Theo fidgets uncomfortably. Then Max looks at him, though, quirking a small smile. "I like it."

Theo lets out a barely noticeable breath of relief.

"Thanks," he says, with a tiny hint of sarcasm, and Max's smile widens a bit.

It's weird, Theo thinks, how he barely ever sees Max smirk at him, anymore. He still does it, sure, but more often than not, he just smiles. Just smiles, properly. Like he's happy.

"The nerd-thing is actually pretty hot," Max admits, making his way over to Theo, who's standing pretty much in the middle of the room. "It's all kinds of interesting."

Theo scoffs, smiling. He nods.

"That's good," he says, hands in his pockets, and Max nods too, as though agreeing with himself.

Theo looks at Max properly, then, just takes in his features, his body, the way his black hair looks like it has been messed up from chilly wind. And then he sees it, and he widens his eyes just the slightest bit.

Suspenders. Max is wearing suspenders, black ones, thin and inconspicuous, over a black, long-sleeved t-shirt, and attached to his black skinny jeans. Theo swallows, surprised at how much he likes the way it looks on him, honestly shocked at how hot he finds it.

Theo doesn't say anything, at first, just looks at Max, before slipping his finger underneath one of the black, elastic straps.

"You're wearing suspenders," he says dumbly, murmuring, eyes on Max's chest.

"I *am* wearing suspenders," Max confirms. "What about it?"

"You've never worn that before."

"Actually, I have," Max points out, cocking his head slightly, thinking. "You've just never seen it."

Theo doesn't immediately answer him. Instead, he just keeps staring, fiddles with the strap lightly between his fingers.

"It's hot," he says, to his own surprise, and he can practically sense Max raising his eyebrows.

"Did you just say it's *hot*?" he asks, as though honestly surprised, but at the same time wearing a teasing smirk.

Theo blushes slightly.

"Yeah," he says. "So?"

Max half-shrugs, and Theo looks up at him.

"No reason," Max says, smirking. "It's just that you've never said that before."

Theo doesn't reply right away, simply frowns.

"What?" he finally says.

"You've never said that before," Max repeats, as though amused at Theo's confusion. "You've never called me hot, before. Or my clothes. Or anything, for that matter."

He doesn't say it bitterly, more like it's an interesting observation, but it still takes Theo by surprise.

"I have," he says defensively, but Max just shakes his head.

"Nope." He sounds completely certain. "Not once."

Theo racks his brain, before realizing that *damn it*, Max is right. Of all the billion times he has thought about just how hot Max is, it never occurred to him that he wasn't actually saying it out loud. He has never actually *told* Max that. And he suddenly feels weirdly embarrassed, especially seeing as how Max has told him exactly what he thinks about Theo's appearance, on more than one occasion.

Theo looks down awkwardly, smoothing along the suspender strap between his thumb and forefinger, absently.

"Well, I guess I figured it was obvious," he mutters. "Self-explanatory."

Max chuckles.

"It's fine," he says. "I don't need you to say it, or anything."

Theo swallows hard.

"I do think you're hot," he says, eyes still on his fingers, fiddling with that strap. "Like, *really* hot."

He adds some proper emphasis on *really*, simply because it still baffles him how someone like him ended up with someone as hot as Max, and he continues, his gaze now trailing up along Max's chest.

"Everything about you is gorgeous," he mutters, as though not confident enough to say it outright, despite how true it is. "Everything."

He finally, hesitantly, looks up at Max's face again, meeting those dark blue eyes with his green ones. Max looks oddly surprised, frozen. Theo is pretty sure there's even the smallest hint of fear, there.

"You're beautiful."

Theo has only seen Max look even remotely nervous or uncomfortable once or twice, maybe three times. It's rare enough, that he can barely believe it when it happens. Like right now.

Max doesn't say anything for several seconds, just stares at Theo, blue, black-lined eyes slightly widened, as though honestly shocked. Then, finally, he clears his throat a bit and puts on a typical Max-expression of charming nonchalance.

"I guess that sounds pretty good," he says lightly, "now that I think about it."

Theo understands that he's trying to ease the tension, or at least, whatever tension Max seems to be feeling, at the moment. But he can't help himself.

"It's true," he says instead, with a completely serious, straight face. And Max is visibly affected, as though surprised for a second time. This time, though, he looks almost confused, and just stares at Theo for another moment, before actually glancing down at the floor.

"Fuck," he mutters, his voice so low that Theo can barely hear him. "You really mean that, don't you?"

Theo is surprised at his reaction, even a bit confused.

"Yes," he says, surprised by the steadiness in his own voice. "I really mean that."

Max looks up at him again. *There it is again*, Theo thinks. *That fear*. It dissipates slightly after a moment, but it's still present enough for Max's attempt at an ordinary, casual half-smile to look just a bit awkward and still kind of scared.

"What?" Theo asks, frowning slightly, and Max glances away.

"It's just, uh..." he says, as though looking for the right words. "No one's ever called me that, before."

He sighs, deliberating what to say.

"At least not—" He cuts himself off, chews his bottom lip for a second, thinking, frowning.

"At least not, what?" Theo says, waiting. Then Max sighs again, turning back to him.

"At least not without getting laid," he says. There's a bitter, almost sad edge to his voice that Theo wonders if he meant to let slip. "No one's ever said stuff like that to me before, without wanting something. This is... unfamiliar."

Max doesn't look sad as he says it, not really. He looks more as though it's a fact he doesn't like, but that it's simply there, and he can't do anything about it. And it breaks Theo's heart.

"What?" he says dumbly, simply shocked to hear this. But Max just shrugs.

"It's weird hearing it like that," he admits, gaze flicking away for a second, in uncharacteristic, unsure distraction. "I mean, there's nothing in it for you, and you say it anyway. It's weird, that's all."

Theo doesn't know what to say. He can't believe that Max hasn't been told this before, by anyone, like this. It seems impossible.

But then he realizes what Max is like. If there's one thing he's comfortable with and secure about, it's sex. He has no problem saying pretty much anything about it, no matter how inappropriate or explicit, and he seems to have no problem with the action itself (Theo is pretty sure he has tried pretty much everything, too, honestly).

But then, in contrast, Theo remembers the first time Max actually made a move and *cuddled*. The hesitant way in which he touched Theo, as though he hadn't done it before, and the way he used to complain about Theo touching him so much, one second, and then practically grab his hands and keep them there, the next.

Theo realizes that slowly, very slowly, Max has started touching him more. Not sexually, not even very much, but just in little ways. Brushing his fingers against his, occasionally pushing his hair back with his hand, very lightly brushing his lips against his skin if they're close together for longer than three seconds. Theo remembers how surprised he often looks when Theo does these things to him, for no apparent reason.

Max may know sex, Theo realizes. He may know all about that and how to act and what to do and how to simply say what he wants, and then ask for it (or give it). But he doesn't know touching. He doesn't know caressing and simply being close, just for the sake of it, or showing affection simply because you want to.

So feeling that Theo's compliments are weird, it makes sense. It makes sense, because desire and affection aren't necessarily the same thing. Sex and intimacy are not necessarily the same thing. And Max has only ever really had one and not the other.

Theo is almost shocked at how intensely he's suddenly aware of this, and he just looks at Max, dumbstruck. Then he just goes on instinct, and cups Max's face in his hands, softly, without even really thinking about it.

"You are beautiful," Theo says. He's vaguely aware of how weird that probably sounds, and how he has never said that to another person, but he can't help it. It's true; Max is the most beautiful person in the world. "All of you. Inside and out."

Max just stares at him, as though torn between suspicion and surprise. And there, somewhere in the background, is something that looks oddly like terrified joy. It's enough to make Theo keep going, and he plants a soft kiss on Max's lips.

"I don't want anything from you," he says. "There's 'nothing in it for me'. I just want you to know that. Because it's true."

He smoothes his thumb over Max's cheekbone, on some kind of impulse, and he can feel Max react, almost as though he's tensing up and relaxing, simultaneously.

"You're the most gorgeous person I know."

Max just stares at him. Someone could just as well have slapped him in the face, with that expression he's wearing, and for a moment, Theo is genuinely worried that Max is actually going to pull away, and run. But he doesn't. Instead, he just stands there, for several, long seconds, until he finally exhales slowly and swallows, dark blue eyes refocusing.

"Um," he says, and Theo resists the urge to smile. Max is speechless. For the first time since Theo met him, Max is actually *speechless*, and it's ridiculous how that makes Theo feel. It makes him feel all warm and happy, in some inexplicable way.

He can tell that Max is uncomfortable, though, that maybe Theo just went a little bit too far. They don't generally talk like that, after all, especially not Max, and Theo feels just a little bit self-conscious, in the midst of it.

So he lowers his hands from Max's face, and Max visibly relaxes, as Theo takes a small step back.

"Sorry," he mutters, hoping that Max knows he's referring to the way his words made Max feel, rather than the words, themselves. "I just... Wanted to let you know."

Max doesn't answer him, just keeps staring, eyes still slightly widened, and Theo stares back, before looking down. Yeah, he definitely went too far.

Theo feels the odd discomfort settle in, and he fidgets slightly, unsure of what to do. But then, he's shocked to find Max moving closer, and he looks up.

Theo isn't sure Max has ever really hugged him before, not like this. Sure, they've kissed and made out, even cuddled a bit, and a lot more than that, but never *hugged*. It's enough to make him just stand there for a split second, surprised at the way Max just puts his arms around him and moves in really close. The split second is over immediately, though, and Theo reciprocates the hug, pulling Max as close to his body as he possibly can.

Max's face is by Theo's shoulder, nuzzling against his neck, and Theo frowns slightly at the way he can feel Max gripping onto his shirt, arms tightening around him. It's desperate, somehow, almost as though he's clinging to him, and Theo automatically hugs him tighter.

Neither of them says anything, and although quite a few seconds pass as they still hold on to each other, Theo doesn't have any intention of pulling away. Because Max needs this, just like Theo does. He can tell.

Max wants this, and Theo isn't about to deny him anything.

CHAPTER 9
STEPS

Having Max over turns out to be a much less nervous experience than Theo at first expected.

After spending an hour or so in Theo's room, the two of them decide to go back downstairs, since there's not much to do up there, anyway (besides making out, which Theo honestly finds himself a bit uncomfortable doing, with his little brother downstairs).

They find Riley still sitting at the kitchen table, still studying, and he looks slightly surprised to see them.

"You still working?" Theo asks, equal parts confused and disbelieving, and Riley gives him a look that Theo imagines will one day evolve into a full-blown bitchface.

"It's due tomorrow," he says, and Theo cocks his head, making his way over to the fridge.

"You want anything?" he asks, directing the question to both Riley and Max, and they actually glance at each other for a moment.

"A Coke," Riley says, turning back to Theo. "If we have any."

"Sure thing," Theo says, extracting a can from the fridge, before looking over at Max, who deliberates for a second. Then he gives a small smile.

"Coke's fine," he says, and pulls out a chair at the table, while Theo gets another can.

Riley glances as Max apprehensively, as he just sat down almost right beside him, Riley sitting at the end of the table. But Max doesn't seem to care. Instead, he leans over the table's corner the slightest bit, looking at Riley's homework.

"You stuck?" he asks, and Riley frowns a little.

"Yeah," he says. "How'd you know?"

Max doesn't answer him. Instead, he just keeps his eyes on Riley's book and his notes, chewing the inside of his cheek, thinking. Then he picks up a pencil from Riley's pen case and doodles on his notes, and Riley just stares, apparently completely taken aback by Max's disregard for boundaries. He looks up at Theo, who sits down at the table, opposite Max, a questioning look on Riley's face. But Theo just half-shrugs, and after a few seconds, Max puts the pencil back down and pulls back, lacing his fingers together and resting his hands against the table. Riley looks down at his notes, and raises his eyebrows.

"Hey," he says, surprised. "I hadn't thought of that."

"You were doing it backwards," Max says, unfolding his hands to open his can of soda. "Common mistake."

Riley looks up at Max, who takes a sip of coke, then looks at Theo.

"Oh," Theo says. "He's a bit of a genius."

Max looks at him fondly, putting his can down and moving one hand up to rub the back of his neck.

"It wasn't exactly genius-level," he says, quirking a small, tired smile. "But thanks."

Theo responds with a small smile of his own, and for a few seconds, they just look at each other from across the table, Riley sitting between them. His eyes dart back and forth between the two of them, until he makes a small, almost disgusted sound.

"Gross," he mutters, looking down at his homework, and Theo snaps out of his trance, instead turning his attention to his soda can. He's suddenly blushing slightly.

"Well, sorry, dude," Max says smoothly. "But unless you can think of some better way I can spend my time, I'm just gonna keep staring at your big brother."

Theo blushes harder, then, and he looks up at Riley, who is suddenly glaring at Max in a surprisingly familial way. And Max just smirks, in that almost mischievous way of his, and Theo waits for Riley's reaction.

"Like what?" Riley finally says, almost suspiciously, and Max raises his eyebrows in mock innocence.

"You mean besides undressing him with my eyes?" he says, and Theo's mouth actually falls open a bit, and he looks back down at the table, blushing furiously. Max makes a small thinking-noise. "I couldn't help but notice, you've got a PS3 in there."

He jabs his thumb over his shoulder, toward the living room, and Theo is almost surprised at Max's observational skills; there's a direct line of sight between part of the hallway and the TV in the living room, but still. He must have seen it, on the way in. And sure enough, they do have a Playstation 3, in there.

Riley seems as uncomfortable as Theo at Max's blatant comment about undressing Theo with his eyes, but more in a grossed-out, little brother kind of way, and he scrunches up his nose.

"Ew," he says, and Theo looks up at Max, cocking his head, looking slightly embarrassed, as though to say that Riley has a point. But Max just laughs.

"What?" he says, folding his arms. "He's fourteen, he's not a little kid."

Theo glances at Riley, and is surprised to find that he looks weirdly glad about that comment, and Theo suddenly feels his embarrassment being slightly replaced by gratitude, towards Max.

"I'm not," Riley says, a bit defensively, but clearly agreeing, as he looks down at his notes.

"Exactly," Max says, simply, and he turns to Theo. "So, tell me. Got any violent, bloody games we can waste some time with?"

Theo just looks at him for a moment, while Riley can't see, and relaxes when he sees Max's smirk soften into a sincere smile. A smile he seems to have reserved for Theo, one that Theo still hasn't gotten used to. And Theo smiles back.

"If Riley's finished with his homework, sure."

Riley finishes his homework in a matter of minutes, with a little help from Max, and soon enough, they're all in the living room, spread out on the big couch.

They end up playing *Mortal Kombat*, and they all get pretty into it. Theo, especially, gets surprisingly competitive, which means that when he loses, Riley laughs and rubs it in his face, while Max takes it upon himself to smirk smugly and kiss him on the cheek. And Theo, being a bit sore about losing, pulls away, until Max subdues him and plants kisses all over his face, making Riley retreat to the corner of the couch, looking simultaneously amused and grossed out, trying to get as far away from the two of them as possible.

They have a lot of fun, but since it's a school night, Max eventually has to leave, and Theo walks him to the door, while Riley stays put in the living room, playing some other game.

Theo patiently waits while Max gets dressed for the cold walk back home, hands in his pockets, and eventually, Max is done. He looks at Theo, exhaling tiredly. Then he smiles, hooking onto a belt loop on Theo's pants with his finger, and pulls him closer.

"I had a good time," he says, and Theo automatically puts his hands by Max's waist.

"Me, too," he says, and Max studies his face for a moment, seemingly lost in thought.

112

"You were right, you know," he says, looking back up at Theo's eyes. "About your brother. I do like him."

Theo scoffs, smiling.

"I think he likes you, too," he admits, and Max cocks his head as if to say *well, who wouldn't?*

They just stare at each other for a few more seconds, and Theo feels an almost overwhelming urge to ask Max to stay. But he can't, and he knows that. And he can tell from the look on Max's face, that he probably wants to stay, just as badly.

Neither of them says it, though, and Max leans in and kisses Theo on the mouth, softly and slowly. But just as he's about to pull away again, Theo stops him by putting one hand by his face, keeping him close, and Max relaxes against him, moving a bit closer. Theo is half-annoyed and half-grateful that there are several layers of clothing between them, right now, and he savors the kiss, eyes closed, until they finally have to separate.

Max looks at him, blue eyes soft.

"See you tomorrow?" he says, his voice low, and Theo nods, hand still by Max's face.

"Yeah," he says, and Max nods in return. Then he looks over at the living room, and Theo's hand slowly falls from his face.

"See you around, Riley," Max calls, and Riley looks over his shoulder.

"Yeah," he says, before turning back to his game.

It takes five more kisses and *see yous* and *byes*, before Max finally leaves, and when he does, Theo closes the door behind him, exhaling slowly. He's not sure if he has felt this before, this light, fluttering feeling in his chest. He likes it.

When Theo enters the living room, Riley glances at him, a big grin on his face.

"What?" Theo says, sitting down on the couch, next to him.

"Nothing," Riley says innocently, and Theo narrows his eyes at him. He punches his little brother lightly in the arm, and Riley relents.

"You really like him," he states, and Theo leans back in the couch, eyes on the TV.

113

"I guess," he says, slumping against the backrest.

"Good." Riley sounds amused, but sincere, and Theo glances at him. "I like him, too."

Theo feels weirdly glad about that.

"I mean, not like you do," Riley adds. "Obviously."

"That's nice to hear," Theo says sarcastically, and Riley smiles, eyes on the game.

"You're in love with him," he says, sounding so completely sure and sincere, and Theo looks at him again.

"What?" he says, and Riley half-shrugs, still smiling.

"You're in love with him." He doesn't even flinch, as he says it, and Theo is taken too much by surprise to give any kind of retort. So he just sits there for a moment, before he looks back at the TV, a soft warmth settling in his stomach, as he fights a smile.

"Shut up," he mutters. But his heart isn't really in it.

♦

"Still not talking, huh?"

Theo looks up at the sound of Cassie's voice, and realizes that she has caught him looking over at Michael and Hannah. They're on the other side of the hallway, pretty much ignoring him, and Theo sighs quietly.

"Yup," he says, turning back to his locker.

"Dude, that sucks," Cassie sympathizes, and Theo gives her a small, appreciative smile.

"Yeah."

Cassie sighs heavily, leaning against the closed locker, next to Theo's.

"How are things with Max?" she asks, and Theo looks at her. She wiggles her eyebrows suggestively, and Theo scoffs, smiling as he looks away.

"It's, uh," he says. "It's good."

Cassie nods, looking pleased.

"Glad to hear it," she says. She's clutching a notepad to her chest, as usual, and Theo absently wonders if it's because she's

114

somehow an insecure person, or if the notepad is just really important to her.

"By the way," she says after another moment. "They're showing *Thor* next week, at the movie theater, with the sequel coming up."

She shrugs.

"You wanna go?"

Theo looks up at her, honestly surprised, for a moment, and he wonders why. Then it hits him; his friends have never asked him something like that. Sure, he, Michael and Ben went to see *The Avengers*, when it came out, but that was different. Actually paying to go see a movie that has already been out for a few years, at a movie theater, is something that they wouldn't do. It's a different level of fandom, and Theo has kind of gotten used to having to downplay his nerdiness. The fact that Cassie doesn't make that necessary is really refreshing.

So Theo smiles at her, nodding.

"Yeah," he says. "Sounds like fun."

Cassie smiles.

"Awesome," she says, straightening from her slump. "I'll text you the details."

Theo is confused for a split second, but then remembers that they exchanged numbers, the other day.

"I gotta go," Cassie says, moving away from the locker. "Class."

Then she looks over Theo's shoulder, though, and raises her eyebrows a bit.

"And also," she says, her voice low and conspiring, "hottie boyfriend, six o'clock."

Theo actually starts, and looks over his shoulder. Max is over there, talking to his friends, and Theo feels his entire body suddenly tingle, somehow.

It's the sound of Cassie laughing softly that makes him look back at her.

"God, you're not even trying to hide it, are you?" she says fondly, and Theo blushes a bit. "You should go over there."

Theo looks over his shoulder again. Max is in the middle of a conversation with Jay and Beth, and he really doesn't want to interrupt.

"He looks busy," Theo says lamely, turning back to Cassie, who simply raises her eyebrows at him.

"For serious?" she says. "He's your boyfriend. Go over there."

"Well, I don't—"

"Hey, Max!" Cassie calls out casually, and Max looks up. When he spots her, he quirks a small, friendly smile of recognition, and Cassie gives him a small wave. Then Max spots Theo, and his entire expression changes.

Cassie makes her way past Theo, dropping her voice to almost a whisper.

"See, not busy," she says.

"Cassie—" Theo says, almost warningly, but she ignores him.

"Good luck," she trills, sweeping past him, and Theo glances after her as she leaves, before looking back at Max.

Both Jay and Beth seem a bit surprised at Max's sudden distraction, but Jay doesn't seem to mind. Instead, he turns to Rachel and starts talking to her, while Beth looks almost comically offended at Max's abrupt ending of their conversation.

Max's eyes are fixed on Theo, and Theo closes his locker. He wants to go over there, simply because he just wants to be *near* Max, but he doesn't really move. He's embarrassed to admit it, but he's kind of intimidated by Max's friends. Okay, *very*, just like he was intimidated by Max before he actually got to know him, and he's not really into the idea of just throwing himself into their group.

But Max seems to know this (of course he knows, that dick), and instead of going over to Theo, he tilts his head, raising his eyebrows slightly, as though daring Theo to come to him. And Theo glances around for a moment, gripping the shoulder strap of his bag a bit tighter, before taking a breath.

This shouldn't even be an issue.

So Theo goes against his instinct of simply avoiding Max's friends, and makes his way over there, one hand in his pocket and the other still firmly gripping his bag. And Max smirks as he comes closer, fond amusement clear in those eyes.

"Hey," he says, when Theo reaches him, and Theo tries not to glance at Max's friends, who all look up at him. Max doesn't seem to care, and so, Theo decides not to, as well.

"Hey," he replies, and Max gently grabs his wrist, making Theo take his hand out of his jeans pocket, so that the two of them can lace their fingers together.

Theo has never spoken to any of Max's friends, but he recognizes them, and when he actually looks over at them, their expressions are hard to read. There's Rachel, with her white-blond, long dreadlocks, a stark contrast to the black eyeliner, red lipstick and black clothes, and she looks so bored it's almost funny. Theo doesn't feel any welcoming vibes from her, but when she glances at Max, as though asking something, Max looks at her pointedly, and she softens a bit.

"Come on," she says, tugging at Beth's black sleeve, before turning around to walk away.

Jay lingers for a second, and meets Theo's eye. He's skinny, looking oddly fragile in the layers of black and buckles, especially with the black eyeliner and black hair, along with silver-buckled, black boots that somehow look to heavy for him. When he catches Theo's eye, though, he quirks a small, friendly smile.

"Later," he says, and Theo is too surprised to reply. Instead, he just stares as Jay turns around to follow after Rachel.

Beth stays put for another second, though, but Theo doesn't think about it, turning back to Max.

"I—" he starts, but shockingly, Beth cuts him off.

"Excuse me," she says, frowning at him, and Theo looks at her. "We're talking. How about you mind your own business?"

Theo is so stunned, and frankly so insecure at her sudden, venomous attitude, that he doesn't know what to say. He's just shocked at how much blatant rudeness can come out of such a small person with such a pretty face. Then again, it's not like it's the first time he has been proven wrong, when it comes to someone's appearance.

Max spares him the trouble of answering, though, and only a second or so passes, before he turns to Beth.

"How about you go fuck yourself?" he says lightly, without flinching, looking straight at her. "God knows, someone has to."

Beth snaps her mouth shut, and the look she gives Max is downright deadly. But Max doesn't seem to care, instead just raises his eyebrows pointedly, and after a few seconds, Beth actually turns around and strides away, catching up with Rachel and Jay.

Max exhales tiredly, and Theo watches Beth leave for a minute.

"She doesn't like me, does she?" he asks softly, and Max cocks his head, as though confirming it.

"Well," he says. "To be fair, she doesn't really like anyone."

He looks back at Theo, and gives him a soft smile. So soft, that Theo still isn't used to it, and it makes a warm feeling settle somewhere in his stomach.

"So, hey, listen." Max says after a moment, glancing down at Theo's chest. He tugs slightly at the lapels of his jacket, as though pulling them back into place, like they were messed up, to begin with. "You got any plans this weekend?"

Theo doesn't answer for a moment; he's too distracted by the way Max suddenly, adorably and uncharacteristically, avoids eye-contact.

"No," he says. "Why?"

Max glances up at him, before looking back at his chest, as though the front pockets of his dark green jacket are extremely fascinating.

"Well, I was thinking," he says, almost muttering. "You wanna stay over?"

Theo raises his eyebrows the slightest bit, slightly surprised. And then, of course, after the split second it takes for that question to sink in, he feels his heart beat a bit faster.

"Stay over?" he asks dumbly. "You mean, like..."

Max looks up at him, eyebrows slightly raised, as though amused at Theo's confusion.

118

"Spending the night," he clarifies. "My parents are away for the weekend, something about a business conference. My dad's the one going, but mom's coming, too. Like a little vacation, or at least that's what they called it."

Theo has a hard time imagining Max saying that string of words in any way that doesn't sound sarcastic; *like a little vacation*. And sure enough, Max's voice is practically dripping with sarcasm, as he says it. Theo is a bit more unprepared for the oddly bitter tone that laces the rest of his statement, though, but he doesn't mention it.

"Yeah," he says, nodding. He clears his throat uncertainly. "I mean, if you want."

Max smirks, the slightest hint of amused affection in his eyes.

"If I didn't want you to," he says, "I wouldn't have asked."

Theo gives him a small smile, glances down at the floor for a moment. Then he nods, tightening his grip slightly on the shoulder strap of his bag.

"Then, yes," he says, looking back up at Max. "I'd like that."

Max blinks, as though just the tiniest bit surprised, but in a very good way. And he smiles, as though a bit relieved.

"Okay," he says, nodding. He tugs absently, one more time, on Theo's jacket, before leaning in and kissing him softly, chastely. "It's a date."

CHAPTER 10
PIZZA

Right. Okay.

Theo distractedly looks around his room, wondering what, exactly, one is supposed to bring when spending the night at their boyfriend's house for the first time. Toothbrush? Change of underwear? Somehow, it feels weird to plan it out, like the whole thing should somehow be spontaneous and completely relaxed and natural.

Yeah, right.

He ends up taking the shoulder bag he uses for school; he and Max both figured that they might as well try and get some studying done, too. Although, Theo isn't entirely sure they're actually going to do that. But it's a good excuse to bring his bag, where he can casually place a toothbrush and a change of underwear. You know, just in case. No big deal.

Theo doesn't usually pay too much attention to what he wears; he mostly just goes with what's comfortable. Although, Michael and Hannah did give him a small makeover when he first started hanging out with them, trading in all his ugly sweaters for slightly more fashionable ones, Hannah teaching him the basics of how to match stuff, and Michael dragging him along to the gym every now and then.

Theo remembers feeling a bit awkward about all of it, mostly because he didn't understand what difference it would make. But he has come to realize, since then, that it was all probably a good idea. He knows how to dress properly, now (despite the occasional, geeky t-shirts), and he's in pretty good shape, thanks to the mild workout habit Michael practically forced him into. If he's completely honest with himself, he *does* look way better, physically, than he did only a year ago. Even though he is still pretty much the same awkward, shy nerd on the inside, and the most interesting his outfit ever gets is washed-out jeans and a dark green Henley.

Right, Theo thinks, absently double-checking his bag. Toothbrush, schoolbooks—

Condoms?

Theo's head snaps up so fast he feels like he might get whiplash, and he just stares at the opposite wall, eyes wide. He lets that thought sink in for a moment, before he starts blushing furiously, swallowing hard.

No. No, he did not just think that.

Yes, you did, a tiny voice says. *You did just think that.*

Theo actually covers his face with his hands, groaning slightly. It's not like the thought hasn't occurred to him before, but it was still distant, then, in the future. Now, it's suddenly here, *tonight*, and he can't avoid thinking about it.

What if that's what happens tonight? What if Max is actually *expecting* that? They've been together for a little while, after all, after seeing each other for much longer, and it's not like they haven't done stuff like that before. And Theo must admit that he really does *want* something to happen.

121

But tonight? He *is* a virgin, after all, and Max most definitely isn't. What if Theo doesn't get it right? What if he somehow messes it up?

What if he's just not ready for it? Sex is a pretty big deal, after all. At least to him, seeing as how he hasn't actually done it, before. And he's kind of embarrassed to admit that for a guy, he really is a bit of a romantic. He can't imagine having sex with just anyone, especially not the first time around.

But Max isn't just anyone. He really isn't.

Theo sighs heavily, removing his hands from his face and feeling his skin cool off as the nervous blushing fades. He chews his lip, thinking.

No, he's not bringing condoms. And even if he were planning to, he doesn't even have any. Which is somehow embarrassing enough, as it is.

Theo checks his cell phone as he leaves his room; it's just past six p.m., so Max is expecting him any minute, now.

He barely makes it down the stairs and into the hall, before his dad talks to him.

"Hey," he says, sitting at the kitchen table. He's just home from work, reading some magazine about cars, while Riley sits across from him doing homework. Amy is standing by the stove, frying something. Theo doesn't know what it is, but it smells good, and he feels his stomach rumble a bit.

"Yeah?" he answers his father, putting on his shoes, and Eric looks up.

"You doing the dishes tonight?" he asks, and Theo deliberates for a second.

"Uh," he says absently, without thinking. "No, I won't be home, tonight."

It's not until his father looks at him quizzically that he realizes that that might have been a bad answer, even though he was going to let them know, anyway. He's just not ready for the question that follows.

"Really?" Eric says. "Where are you going?"

Theo keeps his eyes on his bag, tries to not seem too flustered. His father has the same dark brown hair and hazel eyes as Riley, but he also has the same way of coming off as though he knows more than he's letting on. He generally lets it go, though, as opposed to his youngest son, and Theo vaguely wonders sometimes, how much like him Riley will be when he grows up. Hopefully, he won't be as gruff.

"Just, uh..." Theo eloquently musters, snapping his bag shut. "Going out."

He can practically feel his dad narrowing his eyes slightly, and he can feel Riley sitting at the kitchen table, eyes darting back and forth between them.

"With who?" Eric says, and Theo fidgets a bit.

"Just a guy," he says, uncertainly. He's not quite ready for this conversation, just yet.

Eric picks up on it, but Amy is the one who chimes in.

"A guy?" she says, with typical, motherly interest, as she turns around. "What guy?"

"A guy," Theo mutters, shrugging. Of course, Max is so much more than just *a guy*, but he's not about to go into that now.

"Who is he?" Amy says, and Theo can hear the suggestive smile in her voice. He sighs.

"Just a guy I'm seeing, okay?" He can feel himself starting to blush. "It's not important."

"This *guy* is seeing my son," Amy retorts fondly. "I think it's pretty important."

Riley fidgets a bit in his seat, Theo can see it out of the corner of his eye.

"I've met him," Riley finally says, a bit uncertainly. "He's cool."

"What?" Theo tenses up a bit, as he hears his mother's tone. She sounds mostly surprised, but also the tiniest bit confused. "You've met him?"

"Yeah." Riley shrugs, downplaying the whole thing.

"Well, who is it?"

Riley doesn't answer her.

123

"Theo," Amy says, turning to her oldest son. "Who is it?"

"Can we not do this, right now?" Theo says, reaching for his jacket. He *really* doesn't want to deal with this, at the moment.

"Why?" Amy sounds genuinely confused, even concerned. Eric says nothing, just watches from the kitchen table.

"I just—" Theo sighs, putting on his jacket. He turns to his mother. "I just don't want to do this, right now. Okay?"

Amy presses her lips together, frowning slightly, as though trying to decide whether or not this discussion is worth having, right this moment. It makes her kind, soft face scrunch up in a rather sweet way, and she absently pulls a blond strand of her long hair out of her eyes. They're green, like Theo's.

Theo waits, and then, after seconds of painful, drawn-out waiting, Theo relaxes his shoulders a bit, as his mother finally replies.

"Alright," his mother says, a bit warningly. She points at him with the spatula. "But we *are* talking about this."

This seems to be good enough for Eric, who returns his attention to his motor magazine, and Amy sighs, leaning against the counter.

"Just," she says, hesitating, "be good, okay?"

Theo fidgets uncomfortably, glancing away.

"Yeah, mom," he mutters, awkward about his mother saying something like that; so many things are implied in that statement, after all.

"Okay." His mother nods, smiles a little, and turns back to her cooking. And Theo glances at Riley, who looks back, and shrugs slightly. Theo takes a breath and hopes his gratitude is conveyed through his expression, before he picks up his bag and slings it over his shoulder.

"Alright, well," he says dumbly, "I'm out. See ya."

Riley gives him a slight wave, Eric doesn't really look up, and Amy calls a *bye* over her shoulder, and before long, Theo is out the door. He takes a deep breath of chilly air, as the door closes behind him, and he swallows hard.

That was a close one. His parents aren't exactly overprotective, and despite the fact that Theo hasn't really had a boyfriend before, he *is* eighteen years old, and they know well enough to leave him alone and not pester him about it.

But it's not the boyfriend-thing that's the problem. The problem is that Max isn't exactly the kind of guy they would want their son to have as a boyfriend.

It's not a long walk to Max's place, but Theo knows that, already. He remembers the first time he walked there, several weeks ago, nervous and just a little bit confused, as well as really excited. He's surprised to find that he feels the exact same way, right now, but in a completely different manner and for completely different reasons.

He has never spent the night at a guy's place like that before. He has never spent the night with someone he desperately wants to touch and kiss and hold, and is simultaneously terrified of going near. It's a very odd feeling, one he honestly wonders if it will ever go away. As it is, it's kind of nerve-wracking.

When he finally reaches Max's house, Theo takes a deep breath, before ringing the doorbell. He's not sure why he's nervous, this time. He has been here so many times before, now, that it has become something of a routine, and it really shouldn't be such a big deal.

It doesn't take more than a few seconds, before the door opens, and Max meets his eye, a smile instantly lighting up his face. And the smile is contagious, making Theo smile back, a soft, pleasant warmth spreading from his chest; it even makes him forget about the cold, for a moment.

"Hi," Max says, stepping aside so that Theo can come in, and Theo absently scuffs off some dirt from his shoes, against the doormat.

The door closes behind him, and he looks up, only to find Max standing there, looking at him, hands in his pockets. There's a tiny smile on his face, and Theo suddenly feels the urge to kiss it. So he does, relishing the fact that he can, in fact, kiss Max whenever the hell he wants, as he leans in and presses his lips against that warm, soft mouth, a somehow pleasant contrast against the metal piercing.

Max kisses him back, becomes plaint against him, and lets out a slow, soft breath that sounds so content that it makes Theo feel oddly happy inside.

"Finally," Max murmurs as they pull apart, and Theo frowns.

"What?" he asks, and Max smiles pointedly.

"You're finally here," he says, but Theo keeps his frown.

"It's not like I haven't been here, before," he says, a bit uncertainly, and Max smiles a bit wider.

"True," he says. "But this time, you don't have to leave."

He cocks his eyebrows a bit.

"At least not for a while."

Theo smiles, since Max definitely has a point.

He hadn't expected it to be so different, just knowing that he won't have to leave until tomorrow, but it is. It makes Theo feel oddly relaxed, now that he's actually here, as though there's no pressure, no deadline.

"We've got two options," Max says a little while later, standing in the kitchen. "Pizza, or pizza."

Theo scrunches up his face in thought, before sighing dramatically.

"I think I'll go with pizza," he says, and Max nods, looking impressed.

"Good choice," he says, and about twenty minutes later, after calling in the order, the pizza arrives at the door. Max pays the delivery guy, shuts the door behind him, and turns to Theo.

"At the table or in the living room?" he says, and Theo opens his mouth to answer, but Max cuts him off.

"Or," he says, holding up his finger, "we could sit *on* the table. *Sixteen Candles* style."

He cocks his eyebrows with a sly smile, and Theo can't help but smile back.

"Let's not get too carried away," he says lightly, as he takes the pizza box from his boyfriend. "At the table is fine."

"Well, you're no fun," Max mutters, as he leans in and plants a kiss on Theo's cheek. But Theo doesn't mind; he's still smiling stupidly when they sit down to eat.

Theo has never before, in his life, enjoyed eating pizza this much. He has never been so completely content, as he is right now, just sitting there, across from Max, at the kitchen table, an open cardboard box of pizza between them. And the pizza isn't even that special; there's a bit too much cheese, for Theo's taste, and the crust could be a bit less crispy. But it doesn't matter. Because the pizza is the least important thing at this table, right now.

"So, I was sixteen when I got my first tattoo," Max says, picking up a slice from the box. "Got it for free, a birthday present from Gavin."

"Which one?" Theo asks, taking a bite of pizza. Max gestures to his right upper arm.

"This one," he says, and although his inked skin is covered by black fabric, at the moment, Theo is pretty sure which one he's referring to, even before he says it. "It was only supposed to be some playing cards, at first, but we ended up adding to it. Haven't really been able to stop, since."

Theo nods slowly. He really likes that tattoo, the one depicting a royal flush, intricately flowing together with the other images on Max's arm.

"What about the piercings?" he asks, and Max narrows his eyes for a moment, thinking.

"This was the first one," he says, pointing to his stretched earlobe. "I think. The rest followed pretty quickly, it's hard to keep track."

He quirks a small smile.

"This one is the newest, though," he says, sticking out his tongue. "And I think it's my favorite."

"Mine, too." Theo catches himself right after he says it, in a low voice, and freezes. Max pauses for a moment, before his smile slowly widens.

"I bet it is," he says, voice slightly lower, slightly suggestive, and Theo actually blushes, looking down at the pizza slice in his hand. He can't believe he just said that. Although, it's true; he really does like that piercing, for several different reasons.

They keep talking, about nothing and everything, even after the pizza has gone cold and they've both eaten as much as they want. It's later on that they move into the living room to watch a movie, and as Theo sits down on the couch, Max hands him a cold beer.

"Thanks," Theo says, opening the bottle. He doesn't usually drink beer. Not because he doesn't like it, but because he just never really drinks, and his parents wouldn't even let him near the stuff before he turned eighteen. He got it from Michael, instead, and from Hannah and Ben.

He gladly accepts it from Max, though, who sits down beside him as the movie starts. This time, they're watching *Man of Steel*, mostly to even out the fact that they've watched a Batman movie, but so far none with Superman.

"It's not as awesome as it could be," Max admits. "With Chris Nolan and Zack Snyder, you'd expect some more greatness, but... It's fine. The fight-scenes are pretty cool."

Theo nods. He actually hasn't seen it, yet, but he understands the reference about the moviemakers, nonetheless. And as he does, he can't help but smile a bit; it's nice to hear someone else geek out about movies like that, someone who gets it and doesn't roll their eyes at him, when he does it.

He looks over at Max, who's slumped in the couch, right next to him, and Theo absently thinks of his first time here. They were sitting on the couch then, too, only slightly further apart (until Max climbed onto his lap, that is). And he was so nervous, and so tense, and when Max kissed him, it had been the most amazing thing.

"I'm gonna kiss you now. Okay?" he remembers him saying.

Max actually warned him, actually gave him a heads up. Theo chuckles at the memory, and Max turns to him, frowning.

"What?" he says, and Theo just smiles.

128

"Nothing," he says. "Just thinking about the first time I was here."

Max seems to consider that for a moment, before his mouth shapes into a smirk.

"Yeah, that was a good night," he says. Then he chuckles, and looks at Theo with amusement. "You were adorable."

Theo groans. He had almost forgotten about the whole embarrassing, virgin-admission he made, that night.

"I'll bet," he says sarcastically, looking at the TV and taking a sip of beer. But then Max takes his hand and laces their fingers together, and Theo looks back at him.

"You were," Max says fondly, still looking a bit amused. Then his expression softens. "I actually felt kinda bad, after that."

Theo frowns.

"Why?" he asks, and Max cocks his head.

"I don't know," he says. "Jumping you, like that. I had no idea it was a new thing, for you."

Theo just looks at him, honestly a bit confused, but vaguely remembering how Max looked just the tiniest bit surprised, back then, when it turned out that Theo was, in fact, a virgin.

"Why not?"

Max seems to hesitate.

"Well," he says. "I guess I just assumed you had done it before. Lots of times. I mean, I figured that someone that hot couldn't possibly be untouched, as it were."

He says that last part with some joking sarcasm, but mostly to take the edge off, Theo can tell.

"Well, I was," Theo mutters, unsure how to feel about Max thinking that about him, back then. It still makes him a little nervous. "Still kind of am, I guess. Though, maybe not quite as much."

He cocks his head with a small smile, and Max grins.

"You almost make it sound like that's a bad thing," he says lightly, and Theo bites his lip, smiling as he looks away.

"It's not," he says. "I just..."

He sighs, wondering if he should admit what he's thinking about, right now. If he should admit to how he felt about Max, back then, too.

Max squeezes his hand.

"What?" he asks, and Theo looks back at him, hesitantly.

"I kinda have a confession to make," he says, and Max frowns. He looks relaxed, intrigued, and honestly suspicious, all at the same time.

"Okay?" he says, seemingly unconsciously turning the statement into a question, and Theo takes a deep breath.

"First time we met," he says. "Behind the school? I kinda had a crush on you, then."

Max doesn't answer him, at first, and Theo feels his heart beat a bit faster, anxiously.

"I'd had a crush on you for a while, actually," he continues. "And then that happened, and... Well, it was all a bit surreal."

Max still doesn't say anything, but Theo decides to keep his mouth shut, until he does. And finally, after several seconds, Max speaks.

"You had a crush on me?" he says, almost uncertainly. And Theo swallows nervously, nodding.

"Yeah," he says. "A pretty big one."

Max just looks at him, mouth slightly open.

"Well, damn," he murmurs, and Theo nods, too nervous to really notice how Max looks oddly pleased and smug at this new information, blue eyes promising that this will probably come up again, some other time.

"Yeah," Theo says unnecessarily. "But I was pretty convinced you didn't even know I existed, and that even if you did, it wouldn't exactly be reciprocated."

Max cocks his head the slightest bit.

"I did know you existed," he admits. "Just... I thought you'd be this insufferable asshole."

"Why would you think that?" Theo says, frowning, slightly offended.

"Because your friends were insufferable assholes," Max says pointedly, eyebrows raised, and Theo has to admit he has a point.

"Fair enough," he says, and Max just looks at him for a few seconds.

"I didn't know you," he says. "And honestly, I didn't *want* to know you, due to the impression I had of you. That's not to say I wouldn't have banged you, if I'd gotten the chance."

He adds it jokingly, with a small, suggestive smile, and Theo glances away shyly. No, he's still not used to Max seeing him that way, not really.

"I just didn't think you'd be that interesting," Max continues. "Or interested, for that matter, not in someone like me."

Theo meets his eye again.

"But then I had the chance," Max says, grinning wolfishly. "And I kissed you. Mostly, just to mess with you."

Theo scoffs, smiling, and doesn't move an inch, as Max slowly moves in closer.

"And then," Max murmurs, lips coming closer to Theo's, "you kissed me back. And then, you kissed me again."

He squeezes Theo's hand gently, while his other hand moves up to softly trace the outline of his jaw, and Theo feels himself shiver.

"And I just couldn't stop thinking about you, after that." Max's voice is lowered to almost a murmur, and Theo watches his mouth, as it moves closer to his. Max plants the softest kiss on his lips.

"And I thought we'd just have some fun," he says, voice still low, and he plants another soft kiss at the corner of Theo's mouth. "That it wouldn't be a big deal."

He exhales slowly, cupping Theo's face.

"But then," he almost whispers, "you were just the sweetest guy. And I couldn't do that to you."

Theo isn't sure what to say. He's not used to hearing Max say things like that, and although the sudden honesty is unfamiliar, it makes him feel oddly warm inside.

Max chuckles against Theo's lips.

131

"And then I fell for you," he says. "So fucking hard."

Theo can't help but smile, then. He likes this, having Max so close. He can smell him, feel him, the touch of those fingers against his face the sweetest feeling in the world.

"You almost say that like it's a bad thing," Theo says, his voice as low as Max's, and Max chuckles, as his own words are turned back at him.

"I thought it was," he admits. "Until I found out that you felt the same way."

Theo sighs softly, squeezing his boyfriend's hand, and Max pulls back, just far enough to look into those green eyes.

"It is a good thing," he says. "You're a good thing."

He leans in then, slowly, and kisses Theo on the mouth. The kiss is slow and gentle, affectionate and sincere, enough to make Theo close his eyes. And Max pulls away the slightest bit, pulling his fingers softly through Theo's hair.

"The best thing."

CHAPTER 11
SKIN

It's not like Max's bed is small. It's normal-sized, Theo supposes, maybe a bit big for one person, comfortably so. But as he looks at it, it suddenly looks tiny, like there will be no way whatsoever for the two of them to lie anywhere but practically on top of each other.

He swallows hard. No big deal.

It turns out that bringing a toothbrush was a good idea, and Theo puts it in the cup by the bathroom sink, after using it. It's in the middle of the night, by now, and he's all done by the time Max takes his turn, planting a quick kiss on Theo's mouth, as he slips into the bathroom and locks the door behind him.

Theo has been in Max's room before, a bunch of times, and he knows this house pretty well, by now. But, like so many other things this evening, it suddenly feels new and scary. Even the bed, where they've spent a frankly ridiculous amount of time together, seems to glare at him from across the room. So Theo tries not to think about it. Instead, he strips down to boxers and a t-shirt, and sits down on the bed, in lack of anything else, before realizing where he sat down. So much for not thinking about it.

Max is still in the bathroom, so Theo just sits there for a minute, a bit awkwardly, unsure of what to do. He ends up looking around, studying the posters and trinkets that litter the room, eyes landing on Max's bedside table. It's small and dark brown, with a drawer, and beside the lit lamp standing on it, is an array of things. There's a box of cigarettes, a lighter, some bracelets that Theo has seen Max wear, as well a small pile of books, ranging from advanced algebra to a *Hellblazer* graphic novel. Theo picks up the *Hellblazer* one and flips through it, but is distracted by something else; there's a folded piece of paper there, previously hidden underneath the graphic novel, and Theo frowns.

He glances over his shoulder, before picking it up.

It doesn't seem very important, at first, and as Theo unfolds it, he's confused to find that it's a paper that has been torn in half, and even more so when he realizes that it's the lower half of a math test. At the bottom is a score, which is the highest one, and Theo raises his eyebrows slightly, surprised and at the same time not; he knows how smart Max is. It's the writing at the bottom, though, that catches his eye.

Good job! Love you / Mom.

Theo just stares at it. There's no way of telling how old or new this paper is, but either way, he's so stunned by it, that he doesn't react for several seconds. Why would Max keep something like that, hidden under a book, on his nightstand? It just seems really weird, especially for him. And somehow, on some, subconscious level, it makes Theo feel oddly sad.

Theo doesn't have more time to think about it, though; he hears the bathroom door across the hall open, and he hastily puts the note back where he found it, placing the *Hellblazer* book on top of it. He's not sure why, but he feels like he's snooping, and he's got a feeling that Max wouldn't want him, or anyone, to find what he just found.

He turns slightly where he sits, so that he sits more on the bed than on the edge of it, and he watches as Max shuffles into the room. He's rubbing his eyes, and Theo looks at him, as he sighs heavily and moves his hand from his face and up to card through his black hair.

Theo actually straightens a bit, then. Something is different. He only has to think about it for a split second, though, before realizing how something is different, and as he does, he tilts his head a bit.

Max isn't wearing makeup. For the first time, Theo is seeing him without that black eyeliner, and although it's a little unfamiliar, he really doesn't mind. It somehow simply softens Max's face, and Theo just looks at him for a little while.

He's gotten used to seeing those dark blue eyes framed by black, but despite this being unfamiliar, he finds that Max looks just as good without eyeliner, as he does with it. Not that Theo doesn't love the way that black usually makes the intense, dark blue of his eyes pop, because he most definitely does. This is simply a different kind of hot than he's used to, and he doesn't mind.

Max notices Theo looking at him, and he stops dead, narrowing his eyes.

"What?" he says, and Theo shakes his head.

"Nothing," he says. "I just... I haven't seen you like this, before."

It seems to take Max a second, before realizing that Theo is referring to his lack of makeup, and he tilts his head a little bit.

"And?" he says, and Theo pauses, before cocking his head and putting on a *meh*-expression. And Max actually pulls back, eyebrows raised in surprise.

"Are you sassing me, Davis?" he says incredulously, and Theo quirks a small smile.

"Maybe," he says. "How am I doing?"

Max just looks at him for a moment, chewing at his bottom lip, before he smiles and actually glances away, suddenly looking uncharacteristically shy.

"Could use some work," he says, but his trademark cockiness is laced with something like affection, and Theo's smile widens, as Max looks back at him. He sighs.

"We all have our secrets," Max says dramatically, making his way over to the bed. "I must admit, I feel kind of exposed, right now."

He raises his eyebrows pointedly, and Theo doesn't argue. Seeing as how that black makeup is such a fundamental part of Max's look, despite it being so small, he can imagine that it feels a bit weird to let someone see him without it. Even if it is Theo.

"I like it," Theo says, looking up at Max, as he places himself by the other side of the bed, still standing. "It's different. But I like it."

Max just looks at him for a moment, before scoffing, with a small smile.

"I'm glad," he says, grabbing the back of his long-sleeved, black t-shirt and pulling it over his head, exposing his bare skin. Theo can't help but practically gulp, as he sees it, but Max doesn't notice, as he turns around and makes his way over to the dresser and pulls out a drawer.

When he turns around, though, Theo really reacts. His eyes actually widen, as they catch sight of Max's back.

The wings. He had almost forgotten about those.

Max has deliberately kept the huge tattoos hidden for the past couple of weeks, as they've been healing, and although Theo has been itching to see them, ever since they left that tattoo parlor, he has almost forgotten about it, at this point. Now, though, he can't help but simply stare, as those wings move so perfectly with the motions of Max's body, over his muscles, that they look practically real. They're beautiful, finished and shaded to perfection.

Theo is vaguely aware of how he gets up from the bed and makes his way across the room, and it's only when he's standing right behind Max that he realizes how brave he suddenly feels.

Max doesn't seem to have noticed, actually folding up his shirt and putting it in a drawer of his dresser. Theo watches him for a moment, and then can't help but reach out and touch his bare back.

Max nearly jumps, but immediately relaxes, as Theo slowly moves his fingertips down along the contours of those dark feathers; the skin is smooth and soft, completely healed, and he can feel Max shiver slightly, under his touch. He swallows, moving in a bit closer.

His hands are hesitant, gentle, as they place themselves against Max's shoulder blades, where the wings look like they're sprouting from his skin, touch slow and attentive, as it smoothes down over his back. He can feel Max tense up slightly, as he slowly exhales, and Theo keeps his eyes focused on those beautiful, detailed wings. His hands slide down along Max's sides, and before he knows it, he's actually leaning down slightly and kissing the base of Max's neck, softly and tentatively.

Theo actually feels the shivers, this time, feels the way Max's muscles tense up and the way the hairs rise along his skin. And it somehow spurs him on, moving his lips up along the back of Max's neck, to the side, kissing him just below the hairline, hands trailing down his waist and down to his hips. He moves in closer, presses his chest against the inked skin of Max's back, and he suddenly wishes he wasn't wearing a t-shirt; he wants to feel that skin against his own.

Max exhales heavily, slowly, tilting his head back the slightest bit, and Theo closes his eyes as Max places one hand over his, on his hip. Max laces their fingers together, gently squeezing, and when Theo uses his tongue to smooth over the kisses he places against the side of Max's neck, he hears him moan quietly, the sound vibrating slightly through his back.

It's enough to make Theo swallow hard and squeeze his eyes shut for a moment, tightening his grip on Max's hips ever so slightly. *Damn it.* He's already getting hard.

Either Max notices this, or he doesn't, but either way, he suddenly moves Theo's hands from his hips and turns around in his arms, so that they face each other. And he lets his dark blue gaze trail over Theo's face, his mouth, before leaning in and kissing him.

It's a surprisingly soft kiss, surprisingly slow, and Theo feels his breath quicken, as Max's hand slips in underneath his t-shirt. He doesn't stop him from pulling the shirt over his head, and he doesn't stop him, when he gently steers him backwards, toward the bed. Instead, Theo keeps his lips pressed against Max's, while fumbling slightly with the fly of those black skinny jeans, and Max moans quietly against his mouth.

Getting Max's pants off is surprisingly easy, and before Theo knows it, the two of them are underneath the covers, tangled together, fingers pulling through hair and smoothing over bare skin, and Theo absently realizes that he has never done this before. He has *never* done this before, has never been practically naked with someone like this, bodies moving together, grinding and touching, as he and Max lie on their sides, as close together as they can possibly get.

Theo has never done this before, and his heart is pounding. He has never kissed someone like this before, has never pulled someone closer like this. He has never moved his hand downward like this, before, like he moves his hand down over Max's bare, hard stomach, and lets his fingers ghost over the stretched fabric of his boxers.

He's not sure which turns him on more; the way Max inhales sharply at the touch, or the way he's actually hard, because of Theo.

Theo's not entirely sure what he's doing. Sure, he knows what feels good, since he knows himself and what he likes, but this is another person. This is *Max*, and he tries his best to make him moan and tense up under his touch, as he grips onto Theo's hair

138

tighter, Theo's hand rubbing and stroking slowly, as they kiss. He does his best, and he seems to be doing well.

He doesn't get to keep going for long, though, before Max rather suddenly pulls back, and Theo opens his eyes, confused, automatically pulling his hand away from Max's crotch.

"What's wrong?" he asks softly, mostly out of uncertainty, and Max looks at Theo's chest, avoiding his eyes.

"You don't—" he starts, then sighs and seemingly revises. "You don't *have to*, you know."

Theo frowns.

"What?" he says, and Max looks up at him.

"We don't have to do anything," he says softly. "I mean, that's not why I asked you to stay over."

It takes several seconds for Theo to get what Max is saying, and when he does, he blinks in surprise. He hadn't even thought about that. He just wants to be close to Max, and it hasn't really occurred to him in the past few minutes that Max might misinterpret that as him feeling obligated, somehow.

He's vaguely reminded of his rather intense nervousness before, though, earlier tonight, about this very issue. But he's not nervous now, not in the same way, at least.

"I know," he says, shuffling a tiny bit closer to his boyfriend and looking right into those gorgeous, blue eyes, hoping to convey his own honesty.

Max's expression is one Theo hasn't really seen before. Since they started hanging out, ever since that first kiss behind the school, Max has been pretty obvious about what he wants, physically. And ever since he found out about Theo's inexperience in the matter, he has taken it slow, after all, reining himself in, for Theo's sake.

But he has always wanted more, and he has always shown it, and Theo has always been pretty okay with that.

This is different, though. This is Max looking at him like he's almost worried, like he really doesn't want Theo to feel like he's being pushed, and Theo somehow doesn't know how to deal with that.

139

"I just want to be close to you," he ends up saying, his voice low, and more honest than he expected. "I like that."

As he says it, he moves in even closer, his hand trailing up along Max's side, over his ribs, where the skin is still untouched, unmarked by ink. And Max takes a slow, deep breath, his dark blue eyes fixed on Theo's green ones. He moves his hand up to Theo's face, his thumb smoothing along his bottom lip.

"I like that, too," he says, almost whispering. He looks relaxed now, put to ease by Theo's words, and Theo does nothing to stop him, when he moves in and kisses him.

The kiss is slow and hungry, but the heat is still there, the urgency. And Theo instinctively moves as close to Max as he can, again, pressing their bodies together, hand smoothing over his bare, soft skin, kissing him as though he's the most important thing in the world. And he supposes that right now, he kind of is.

Theo is about to go back to what he was doing before, when Max pushes him gently, making Theo lie down on his back, and he watches as Max moves up to sit on top of him, slowly and deliberately. Theo swallows, automatically moving his hands to Max's hips, as Max kisses him, pierced tongue claiming his mouth.

Theo's head is spinning. He can't believe how good this feels.

He's still nervous, though, he can't help that, and he thinks about it as he touches Max. He smoothes his hand down over Max's bare back, over those gorgeous wings he knows to be there, wondering if Max can tell just how nervous he is, right now.

At least my hands aren't shaking, Theo thinks, as one digs its fingers into that black, messy hair, and the other makes its way down to the small of Max's back, where Theo knows the tips of those wings are. Slowly, on some kind of instinct, he slips his thumb underneath the hem of Max's boxers, tugging slightly, and he hears Max moan against his lips. The sound is surprisingly satisfying.

Then Theo's thumb slips, though, making the elastic of the underwear snap back against Max's skin with a surprisingly loud sound, and Max flinches.

"Whoa," he says, surprised, and he looks almost comically confused, as he glances over his shoulder. Theo probably would have laughed, if he weren't so embarrassed.

"Shit," he mutters. "Shit, I'm sorry."

Max only chuckles, eyebrows raised as he looks back at Theo.

"Don't worry about it," he says, a small, surprised laugh in his voice. But Theo is shaking his head, actually putting his hand over his eyes, humiliated.

"No," he says, practically cringing. "No, I'm sorry, I just—"

"Hey," Max says, prying away Theo's hand with his own, a chuckle lacing his words. "It's fine."

Theo hesitantly looks up at him, feeling the blush creep up his neck, wanting nothing more than to just vanish, right now. He feels like *such* a *virgin*.

Max only smiles, though, affection and amusement clear in his blue eyes.

"Baby, come on," he says, pushing back Theo's hair from his forehead in a surprisingly tender gesture. "It's fine. Really."

He cocks his head.

"Kind of adorable, actually."

Theo groans.

"Not helping," he says, and Max laughs again. It makes Theo feel all warm inside; he's still not used to hearing Max *laugh*, not like that, and he feels like he's never going to get tired of it.

Max leans down and gives him a chaste kiss.

"Sorry," he says, and Theo just looks at him.

"I just—" Theo starts, feeling utterly ridiculous. He sighs, dropping his voice to almost a whisper. "I just *really* have no idea what I'm doing."

But Max just smirks, taking Theo's hand and kissing it lightly, before moving it down along his body, so that it can go back to tracing his skin, and Theo just looks at him, as he does it. He still feels oddly embarrassed, but he can't help but smile a little, as

Max looks down at him. Max leans in closer, then, pressing his body down against Theo's, and Theo automatically firms his hand against Max's back.

"You're doing just fine," Max murmurs, kissing him on the lips. "Trust me."

There's something about the way he says it. Theo isn't sure what it is, exactly, but it spurs him on, and he pulls Max back against him, as close as he possibly can, kissing him deeply. It only takes a few seconds, before that heat is back, and he actually grabs Max's ass and presses him downward, grinding roughly against him. And Max breathes heavily, moaning deeply as he claims Theo's mouth with that wonderful, pierced tongue.

"You're doing really good," he breathes against Theo's lips. "So good."

The way Max is breathing, the way he touches Theo as though he simply *needs* to touch *all* of him, the way he kisses him as though his survival depends on it... It's all a bit much. It's more than Theo is used to, and he's torn between how terrifying it is in its intensity, and just how *amazing* it feels, as he tries to remember how to breathe.

When he breathes, though, it gets worse, because he's breathing in *Max*; his smell, his exhale, the taste of his skin. It's all *Max*.

He's not sure when his boxers come off, but it somehow happens slowly. Max's fingers are diligent as they tug them off, Theo helping, and before Theo realizes, his underwear has somehow ended up on the floor. He swallows hard, as Max takes off his own, and it hits him; this is the first time he's naked in bed like this, with someone else. Just another thing on a long lists of firsts, it seems.

Theo clings to Max, somewhat nervously, as Max slowly presses down against him, and just like that, there's nothing between them. Nothing but warm hardness and hot skin, and just the feeling of it makes Theo exhale sharply, digging his fingers into Max's dark, messy hair.

"Is this okay?" Max breathes, and Theo swallows hard, nodding jerkily. It is okay. It's *very* okay, albeit completely new and unfamiliar, and he takes a deep breath. Max pulls back for a second, just far enough to look into his eyes, as though making sure, before leaning down and kissing him, slower than before. And Theo's head is spinning again, his hands scrabbling for purchase all over Max's skin.

His eyes are closed, but he opens them when he feels Max move, and he sees him leaning over toward his nightstand. It takes a second, and for Theo to see him opening the small drawer, before he realizes what he's reaching for.

"Um," he says, sounding much more nervous than he intended, but Max soothes him with a look.

"It's okay," he says softly. "It's not for that."

He gets a small bottle from the nightstand, and closes the drawer.

"I mean," he adds, "unless you want to."

Theo swallows, trying to decide if he does want to or not, but Max seems to take his hesitation as confirmation of what he already thinks.

"It's okay," he says again, the smallest, comforting smile on his face, and he kisses him softly. "I thought we might try something else."

Theo looks at him, and hesitates for only a split second, before nodding. He trusts Max. He knows he won't push him into anything.

Max gives him a small nod in return, blue eyes soothing and kind. It still kind of baffles Theo, how someone so snarky and sarcastic can look so incredibly sweet and understanding.

Theo is unsure where to look, as Max squirts some lube from the bottle into his hand; it feels weird to look at the ceiling, but it feels equally weird to look right at him.

He doesn't have to think about it long, though, before Max puts the bottle away and moves his hand downward, slowly and deliberately.

Max looks right at him, and Theo swallows nervously. And then, those fingers wrap around him, and he actually lets out a rather loud moan of surprised pleasure; it's a little cold, but he had no idea that lube could make such a huge difference.

Max watches him intently, as he starts stroking, before taking both of them in his hand, and Theo groans slightly, as he feels Max's hardness against his own, moving just a little bit.

"If you wanna stop, just—" Max breathes, but Theo cuts him off.

"Please, don't," he says, his voice a desperate exhale. "Please, don't stop."

Max's blue eyes widen slightly, as though surprised, but he doesn't deny Theo what he asks for. Instead, he starts moving, thrusting, ever so slowly, and Theo presses his hands against that tattooed back, pressing Max closer against him. It feels so good, the two of them rubbing together, in a delicious mix of wet and friction, and Theo moans deeply, in lack of anything else. He doesn't know how else to express this, doesn't know what else to do. It just feels so good, *so good*.

"So good." He thinks it out loud, and his words are barely a breath, and he's not sure Max even heard them, but it doesn't matter. All that matters is the way Max's body feels, weighing down on his, hot skin on skin, as he thrusts into the tight tunnel of his fingers, rubbing the two of them together. The way Max moans against Theo's skin, planting searing kisses along his throat, his arm actually shaking as it holds him up. Theo gets it; his entire body seems to be vibrating, his skin on fire.

"Shit," he hears Max murmur against his ear, panting, still moving. He sounds completely wrecked. "Oh, god."

Theo doesn't know what to make of it, but the words sound about as desperate as he feels. So he clings tighter to Max, clings to him as they move together, and when he pulls Max's face to his and kisses him, it's like lighting up a powder-keg. Max groans, moving against him with such deliberate determination, and it's only a matter of seconds, before Theo's entire body suddenly tenses up, making him shudder and press his lips against Max's as though his life depends on it.

And just like that, almost taking him by surprise, he feels it, feels that wonderful, amazing release. He's vaguely aware of Max thrusting into his hand just a couple more times, before having the exact same reaction, pressing his body down against Theo, and they breathe together through the climax, for what feels like several seconds.

It's after a few moments of panting and recuperating, afterwards, that either of them says or does anything, and it's Max who does it.

"You're so amazing," he murmurs, kissing Theo's throat, his jaw, his cheek. Theo's eyes are closed, but he can hear the way Max says it as though he's mostly thinking out loud, an almost desperate edge to his voice. "Fuck, you're so beautiful."

Theo swallows dryly, feeling as though he might pass out, and he moves one hand up to card his fingers through Max's black, sweat-damp hair.

"We should do that again, sometime" he murmurs absently, to his own surprise, and Max chuckles breathlessly against his neck. Theo just barely registers how he just made an almost direct reference to what Max said that time, the first time they kissed, behind the school.

"Sure thing," Max says, moving up to kiss Theo on the mouth, and Theo finally opens his eyes, Max's face flushed and his expression pleased, above him. "Anytime."

Theo smiles. He would like that.

CHAPTER 12

COVERS

It's the feeling of being surprisingly cold that wakes Theo up the
next morning.

A slight chill sweeps over his arm, and as he feels the skin
prickle with goose bumps, he slowly opens his eyes, automatically
pulling his arm in underneath the cover. It's nice and warm under
here, and he closes his eyes again, snuggling into the sheets, face
burrowing into the pillow. It smells nice, and he inhales deeply. It
smells familiar.

Theo opens his eyes again as he realizes whose smell it is, and
he groggily looks around. He's in Max's room; he recognizes the
posters and dark color of the walls, in the daylight. And the
sheets smell like him, warm and nice, enough to make Theo curl
up slightly underneath the cover, cocooning himself in its
warmth. He closes his eyes. But it's still cold.

The uncomfortable temperature makes Theo wake up more properly, and when he opens his eyes for a third time, he notices that the bed is empty, aside from him. He looks around again. No Max in sight. And why is it so damn cold?

He looks up at the window, then, the one above the headboard of Max's bed, and has his suspicions confirmed; it's open, just the slightest bit. And Theo swears that there's the tiniest scent of cigarette smoke sifting in through the crack, along with the cold air.

It's with tired reluctance that Theo sits up in the bed, only to feel those goose bumps spread all over his skin, and he immediately pulls the cover up to his shoulders, frowning slightly, sleepy and annoyed. He ends up sloppily wrapping the cover around him, instead, before getting up on his knees and leaning over the bed's headboard, pushing the window open. The cold air hits him in the face, and he groans, squinting.

"Hey." Max's voice is soft, as he notices him, and Theo turns to his right. Max is sitting there, on the roof, back against the outer wall of the house and his knees pulled up. He's fully dressed, a lit cigarette in his hand, and when he sees Theo's disgruntled, tired expression, he chuckles.

"Sorry, babe," he says, flicking some ashes off his cigarette. "Didn't mean to wake you."

Theo doesn't reply, simply lowers his head and rests his chin against the windowsill. The cover is thick and fluffy, wrapped around him all the way up to his neck, over his shoulders.

"What time is it?" he murmurs, voice cracked with sleep, and his eyelids droop slightly, as he looks straight ahead.

"About eight-thirty," Max says, and Theo groans again, frowning.

"Why?"

Max chuckles, grinding out his cigarette against the roof, before moving over to Theo.

"Because I woke up, dying for a smoke," he says, crouching in front of him. "And last night was amazing, and I didn't get a chance to have one, then."

147

Theo looks up at him questioningly, chin still resting on the windowsill, and Max smiles, pierced eyebrow raised pointedly.

"Nothing beats a post-orgasm cigarette," he says, and Theo is reminded of what, in fact, happened last night. Just the thought of it makes him blush and look down, and Max laughs affectionately, moving his hand down to softly card his fingers through Theo's bedhead.

"Don't tell me you're getting all shy on me, now," he says, and Theo groans.

"Yes," he murmurs into the cover. But Max just chuckles quietly, before tugging softly on Theo's hair.

"Come on," he says. "Let's get back inside."

"I am inside," Theo says, looking up as Max straightens slightly.

"Yeah, well, I'm not," Max retorts. "And it's freezing out here."

Theo narrows his eyes at him, and Max makes a little shooing motion with his hands.

"Come on," he says. "Move it, sleepyhead."

Theo groans for the hundredth time, but obligingly backs away, so that Max can climb in through the window. As soon as he's inside, he closes it, and he gets off the bed. Theo practically falls over onto the mattress, still exhausted, cover still wrapped around him like a cocoon, and he watches as Max takes his long sleeved t-shirt off, followed by a pair of black sweatpants. Pretty soon, he's wearing nothing but boxers.

"Alright," he says, climbing into bed. "Move over."

Theo groans indignantly, pulling his cover-cocoon tighter around him.

"No," he mumbles, and Max tilts his head at him.

"Share?" he says, and Theo burrows down deeper, only his head poking out, as he lies there on the bed.

"Get your own," he says, and Max snorts.

"I have my own," he says. "You're just hogging it."

Theo doesn't reply, and Max leans down and kisses his forehead.

148

"Please?" he says, mock innocence and mischief in his voice. He kisses Theo again, closer to his mouth. "Theo?"

He kisses him on the mouth then, properly, warmly, and Theo squints at him as he pulls away.

"Pretty please?"

The sweetness is so obviously a ruse, but Theo still relents, and rolls out of his cover-cocoon, just enough for Max to be able to slip in underneath the cover with him, a smug smile on his face. And although his tattooed skin is cold against Theo's sleep-warmed body, he moves in closer, and Theo doesn't mind, wrapping his arms around his form. Max sighs contentedly, burrowing his nose against the hollow of Theo's throat.

"Now, this is an awesome way to wake up," he murmurs, and Theo hums in agreement. He's still pretty tired, eyes closed, and he could easily fall asleep right now, if he wanted to.

"I mean," Max says, "I've already woken up, but I'm willing to forget about that and pretend this is my first wake-up today."

Theo laughs tiredly, eyes closed.

"You do that," he murmurs, and sighs as he feels Max press a soft kiss against his collarbone. Neither of them speaks for a few seconds.

"I mean it," Max eventually says, softly. "Can't remember the last time I felt this happy about waking up."

Theo opens his eyes, unsure of how to reply to that. It's almost as if Max's words are a physical thing, seeping in through his skin and into his bones, warming him up from the inside, and he has no idea how to convey that feeling.

So he just pulls Max closer and cards his fingers through his hair, planting a kiss against his temple.

"Me, too," he says, hoping Max can hear just how sincere that reply is, and judging from the way he presses himself against him, he can.

Another few seconds of comfortable silence follow, before Theo sighs.

"Maybe we should get up," he suggests, and to his surprise, Max is the one who groans, this time.

"No," he says, nuzzling closer against his boyfriend, and Theo looks down at that messy black hair.

"You've already been up," he points out. "You've even been outside."

"True," Max murmurs against his skin. "But then I came back to bed, and realized what a bad idea that was."

He sighs.

"I've got everything I need, right here," he continues. "I have no reason to get up."

The way Theo's entire body suddenly feels like it's made from warm liquid is unexpected and unfamiliar, as though Max's words have some profound kind of effect on him. But it makes him smile like an idiot, all the same.

"Well, what about breakfast?" he asks, but Max just grabs the edge of the cover and pulls it up over his head.

"I'm willing to make that sacrifice," he says, voice muffled underneath the fabric and stuffing, and Theo actually chuckles.

"What about coffee?" he tries, and for a second, Max doesn't answer, as though deliberating. Then, when the answer doesn't come, Theo crawls in underneath the cover with him, so that they're both hidden underneath it, face to face. Max narrows his blue, makeup-free eyes at Theo's prompt, as though suspicious.

"You drive a hard bargain," he finally says, and Theo sighs, a small smile on his face.

"If it's any consolation," he says, "I don't want to get up, either."

"Then, why suggest it?" Max growls, kissing him on the mouth. Theo tries to ignore the way his whole body tenses up at that.

"Because I'm really hungry," he replies against Max's mouth, between kisses. "And we can't just stay in bed all day."

"Yes, we can," Max purrs, sliding his hand over Theo's bare back. "It's Saturday."

Theo takes a deep breath. God, it's ridiculous how amazing and enticing it sounds to just stay here, all day. But then his stomach rumbles, and the romance kind of dies.

"How about we eat," he suggests, fighting every other fiber in his being that just wants to stay put, "and then we can get back to this?"

Max hums in thought, before pulling way a little bit.

"Fine," he says, with a dramatic sigh. "I suppose I can make that compromise."

They end up having cold leftover pizza for breakfast, and Theo watches as Max makes some coffee, while he leans against the fridge, chewing down a pizza slice. They're both dressed, mostly due to the fact that they're still tired and the morning air is still a bit too chilly, even inside. Max didn't bother putting on a shirt, though, which leaves him wearing only the same pair of sweatpants he wore earlier, when he sat on the roof.

He looks tired, Theo observes, pulling his fingers through his black hair, blinking sleepily. It seems that whatever energy he got from getting up and sitting outside in the cold morning air for ten minutes, has completely vanished, and Theo can't help but smile at the sight of him, standing there, staring at the coffee maker.

Theo finishes his pizza, and makes his way over there, moving up behind Max, who stands with his palms leaning against the kitchen counter. The way he completely relaxes as Theo wraps his arms around him from behind, and then sighs, is immensely satisfying.

"I could really get used to this," Max murmurs, and Theo hums as he presses a kiss against his bare, partly tattooed shoulder.

"To what?" he asks, and Max leans his head back slightly.

"This," he says, moving his hands up to Theo's lower arms, draped over his stomach. He smoothes over the skin slowly with his fingers, and the way it makes Theo sigh contentedly is clarification enough of what, exactly, Max means.

"Oh, that," he murmurs against Max's skin, and Max chuckles.

"You can play innocent with me all you like, Davis," he says, "but you know exactly what you're doing."

Theo smiles against his skin.

"I really don't," he says. "You just make it easy."

He nuzzles into Max's black, messy hair and closes his eyes as he inhales, breathing in the warm, familiar scent of him.

"When it comes to you," he murmurs, without thinking, "all of this is just... easy."

He can't find a better way of putting it. Sure, Max makes him nervous and a bit scared, but at the same time, he makes him so brave. Theo is fully aware of how he would have never dared to do half the things he does with Max, with anyone else, that even though Max makes him nervous, he also wants Theo. He wants him to move closer, wants him to touch him, and when Theo does, he's always kind of surprised at just how much Max seems to enjoy it.

But Max *wants* Theo to talk to him, to be with him, and it makes Theo brave enough to do those things, because he wants it, too.

It just makes it... easy.

Max sighs contentedly, and slowly turns around in Theo's arms, so that they face each other, and Theo's hands are at his back, instead. And he just looks at him, with those dark blue eyes that Theo still isn't quite used to seeing without the black framing of eyeliner, as he moves one hand up to Theo's face, slowly smoothing over his cheekbone with his thumb.

For a few moments, Max looks like he's going to say something, but he seems to decide against it. Instead, he just leans in and plants a kiss on Theo's mouth, and Theo closes his eyes as he kisses him back. It's not until several seconds later that they pull apart, and Max smiles. Actually, it's more of a smirk.

"I think I'd like to go back to bed, now," he says, and Theo can't help but think that that sounds like a great idea.

They do go back to bed, after very briefly considering doing something else, and then deciding against it. What else would they do, anyway? Watch a movie? Study? Just the thought of getting anything at all done is laughable, seeing as how they seem to have a hard time tearing their attention away from each other for more than ten seconds.

So, bed it is, in lack of any better ideas.

Although, curling up underneath the covers in Max's bed, with nothing but warm skin and soft touches and deep kisses to keep them occupied, is pretty much the greatest idea either of them can think of.

"When do you have to be back home?" Max asks, when it's getting close to noon, and Theo frowns.

"I don't know, actually," he says. "Didn't really come up."

It's true; he didn't exactly give his parents much of a heads-up, before he left. All he really let them know was that he was spending the night at a boy's house, and they didn't really question him on that. And they're pretty cool, too. They don't give him curfews or anything, at least not since he turned eighteen.

"Oh," Max says conspiringly, tightening his arm around Theo and nuzzling closer. He plants a soft kiss against his throat. "Does that mean you can stay forever?"

Theo smiles.

"I wish," he says, meaning it. "But I'm afraid I will have to go back home, eventually."

Max groans.

"That's just retarded," he mutters, kissing Theo's bare skin again. "You haven't been here nearly long enough."

Theo closes his eyes as he feels Max's lips against his throat, the warm breath as he murmurs against his skin. It feels good, really good, and he absently notices himself tighten his arm around his boyfriend, slightly.

"Well," he murmurs, eyes still closed, as he trails one hand up along Max's tattooed back. "I don't have to leave *yet*."

He moves over a bit, so that he's lying on his side, properly. They're facing each other now, and Max pulls away the slightest bit to look at him.

"Okay," he says, sounding almost jokingly suspicious, the tiniest smile playing on his lips. "How long can you stay?"

Theo makes a humming sound, thinking, as he moves closer, close enough to brush his lips against Max's, feather-light.

"Don't know," he murmurs, not kissing him, but simply touching those lips with his own, that metal ring lightly brushing against his mouth. "A little while."

Max takes a breath, closing his eyes, just like Theo. Theo can feel his fingers tensing slightly against his waist.

"Long enough for this," Theo nearly whispers, suddenly feeling rather brave and impulsive.

He still isn't used to this, still isn't used to this feeling. It's warm and hot and burning, slowly building somewhere in his stomach, spreading through his body. He's still not quite used to it, but he has gotten pretty used to the way it's a reaction to Max. It doesn't take much, after all, that much he has learned. It doesn't take much for Max to drive him crazy.

"For what?" Max asks, voice raspy and low, and Theo smoothes his hand down along Max's waist, over his stomach, over his hips. He's wearing boxers, but they're thin, and tight enough for Theo to feel the outline of his muscles and his hipbones.

"This," Theo replies, barely audibly, and he can clearly tell what kind of reaction Max is having, right now. It's obvious, he can feel it, as his fingers ghost over the slight bulge in Max's underwear. It gets bigger as Theo touches it, harder, and Max exhales slowly, moving one hand up along Theo's back.

"Well, I can't say I mind," he murmurs absently against Theo's lips, and Theo swallows hard.

He hasn't done this before. Which is odd, he thinks, considering what else they've done, so far. The make-out sessions, all the touching and kissing, even Max going down on him. Not to mention last night. Just thinking about last night is enough to make Theo shiver and tense up in the most amazing way, and for a moment, he forgets all about the fact that he has never actually touched Max this way, before, so deliberately; last night was more in the heat of the moment.

Instead, it makes him brave, and he slowly slips his hand underneath those boxers, making Max almost gasp, as Theo wraps his fingers around him.

Max's hand moves up to Theo's hair, fingers carding through it, pulling him as close as he can without kissing him, and Theo uses every ounce of restraint he has to keep their lips apart from each other. His eyes are closed, though, and he can both hear and feel the way Max is suddenly breathing heavily, gyrating his hips ever so slightly against the pressure of Theo's hand.

Neither of them says a word. Not even Max, who's usually so full of comments and witty remarks. Instead, they're silent, apart from the breathing and the deep moaning now emitting from Max's throat, sounds that make Theo squeeze his eyes shut and move his hand more deliberately, loving the way Max clings to him desperately, as Theo touches him.

It lasts for a while, as Theo takes his time, but eventually, Max can't seem to take much more, kissing Theo as he falls right over the edge. And it's after another few seconds of silence and heavy breathing, that Theo feels Max's hand slip in underneath his underwear, as well, and he swallows hard.

He doesn't open his eyes, though, and he doesn't say a word. He's already hard, and instead, he just lets Max return the favor, as he clings to him, letting himself get lost in this blissful, perfect day, desperately wishing that he could stay suspended in it forever.

♦

Sunday seems to pass unbearably slowly.

Up until this weekend, Theo and Max haven't spent more than a few hours together, at a time, and that has been bad enough. Bad enough for Theo to feel like he's somehow waiting for his next fix of some amazing drug.

This time, though, they spent nearly twenty-four hours together, and as soon as Theo got back home, Saturday night, he

155

could feel his skin practically crawling. He needed Max, needed him there. He *needs* him.

They talked a bit on Sunday, a few texts in between their forced study sessions, for what it was worth. Theo imagines that Max had a much easier time with the schoolwork, but it didn't really help Theo, as he sat there, trying to get it done. It was boring, slow, and so very uninteresting, and all Theo could think about was running back to Max's house and never leaving there again.

But things aren't that easy. There are certain obligations, even outside of schoolwork, and Theo couldn't have gone back there, no matter how badly he wanted to. So he had to wait, all day and all night.

Monday has never felt more welcome.

Cassie is the first person Theo runs into, Monday morning, and she makes sure that he hasn't forgotten about the *Thor* screening that week. And Theo scoffs indignantly; how could he forget?

He doesn't see Max during the first half of the day; they haven't had any classes together, yet. And at lunch, it takes about fifteen minutes of looking around (with Cassie rolling her eyes at him), before Theo actually spots Max, who immediately makes his way over to their table.

"Hey," he says, planting a deliberate kiss on Theo's mouth, before he has a chance to reply. And Theo can't help but kiss him back, a bit more enthusiastically than usual, before letting him pull away.

"Hey," he says breathlessly, as Max sits down next to him. Max gives him a small smile, before turning to Cassie.

"My lady," he says, with a nod, and Cassie nods back.

"Good sir," she replies, and Theo smiles a little at the repertoire the two of them seem to have developed so quickly.

Max turns back to Theo, one hand automatically finding its way to his leg, where it smoothes over the fabric of his jeans. It's an affectionate gesture, more than anything, and it makes Theo feel all warm inside.

"I can't stay long," Max says, obviously sad about this fact, and Theo frowns.

"Why not?" he asks, and Max cocks his eyebrows, looking slightly bored and annoyed.

"Group assignment," he says flatly. "We're meeting up, and sadly, I have to be there."

Theo hopes he doesn't look too much like he's pouting, but apparently, he does, at least judging from the little, teasing smile Max suddenly has.

"You'll survive for a few more hours," he says, giving him a soft kiss and murmuring against his mouth. "Not so sure about me, though."

Theo can't help but smile, and Max smiles back. And Theo gets momentarily lost in those gorgeous, dark blue eyes, back to being framed by the black eyeliner Theo is more used to.

Max leaves after another ten minutes or so, and Theo is sad to see him go. But Cassie is great company, and Theo only glances once at Michael, Hannah and Ben, as they sit across the cafeteria. He hasn't really thought about them, lately.

Theo is lucky enough to see Max again during recess, before the last class of the day. He finds him by his locker, as though he's waiting for Theo, and going up to him and giving him a long, proper kiss suddenly feels so natural, it's ridiculous.

"Still alive, are we?" Max asks, and Theo smiles.

"Barely," he says, kissing him again. "You busy later?"

"Depends," Max says. "If I'm not, does that mean we can hang out?"

Theo cocks his head, and Max chuckles.

"Then, no," he says. "My day's wide open."

"Awesome."

They just stare at each other for a moment, before Cassie nudges Theo slightly in the arm.

"Uh, guys," she says. "What's he doing here?"

Theo and Max both follow her line of sight, and almost immediately spot who she's talking about; he's kind of hard to miss.

Michael is standing further down the half-crowded hallway, talking to someone, Hannah and Ben right next to him, looking oddly tense. It's after another second or so, that Theo recognizes the guy they're talking to; it's Luc, Michael's big brother.

He goes to their school, but he rarely ever shows up, and Theo is more than surprised to see him here. If nothing else, it makes him slightly anxious. Luc has been suspended more than once, for fighting and picking on other students, and Theo knows very well how edgy and easily provoked he can be. And it doesn't help that he's a bit of a fitness freak, who's rumored to even be on steroids, making his volatile personality all the more unsettling.

Theo has never liked him, has barely ever really talked to him, despite being friends with Michael for so long, and he has always made a point of avoiding him. And it has always worked out fine; Luc has never really had a beef with him, anyway.

This time, though, it's different. At least, apparently, judging from the way Michael suddenly tenses up as he spots Theo, looking over at them. Theo frowns, can't imagine why, and then, Luc spots him, too. And he actually looks mad.

"What's he doing?" Cassie asks, but Theo just half-shrugs, confused and just a little bit concerned.

"Don't know," he says. He's about to dismiss it, when Luc suddenly starts making his way over, despite Michael seemingly trying to talk him out of it.

"Shit," Theo murmurs, very quietly. He doesn't know why Luc is coming over here, but it can't be good, and he honestly doesn't want him anywhere near him.

"What?" Cassie says, frowning at him, but Theo doesn't have time to answer, and only has time to catch Max's confused and slightly watchful expression, in the corner of his eye, before Luc is suddenly there.

"Davis," Luc says, as he reaches them. "Long time, no see."

Theo swallows, trying to seem relaxed. Luc isn't really taller than him, but he's bigger, and Theo knows how easy it can be to piss him off, seemingly by doing nothing.

"Hey, Luc," he says. "Good to see you."

Luc flashes a humorless, oddly dangerous smile, one that clashes weirdly with his face; he would be handsome, if he didn't look so bitter and mean, all the time, and despite his dark blond, short hair, he looks a lot like his brother. Although, Michael's face is, in contrast, kind, and well-matched with his personality. Well, most of the time.

"I don't know, man," Luc says, actually taking a step forward, making Theo tighten the grip on his shoulder bag the slightest bit. "See, I've been hearing things. Heard you've been talkin' shit about my little brother."

Theo blinks, honestly confused. He has no idea what Luc is talking about, and vaguely wonders what kind of *shit* he supposedly has been spreading. He wants to glance at Michael, or Hannah, or Ben, all three of them standing half-behind Luc, but he doesn't dare. Instead, he decides to try and get out of this situation, as quickly and as painlessly as possible.

"I really haven't said anyth—" Theo says, just barely bordering on a stammer, trying not to look Luc in the eye, but at the same time making it a point to, as he shakes his head a little bit. He has always been intimidated by Luc, even after he started hanging out with Michael. Because where Michael has a calm air about him, Luc is the opposite, somehow emanating a vibe that makes you walk on eggshells around him.

"And all because of this little shit, too," Luc says disdainfully, cutting off Theo and frowning in Max's direction. Max doesn't look offended, though. Instead, he gets a *wtf*-expression that mostly says something along the lines of *dude, you serious?*

But it still makes Theo mad, uncomfortably so. He's fine with being insulted, he can take that. He's *not* fine about someone insulting Max, even though he's completely sure he can take care of himself.

Michael looks a bit uncomfortable, then, and he glances at Hannah and Ben, who both look equal parts concerned and annoyed.

159

"Luc," Michael finally says, grabbing Luc's arm gently. "Come on, man."

"Whoa, brother," Luc says, with an edge to his voice that makes even Michael snap his jaw shut. "I'm not done, here."

Theo swallows, hoping he doesn't come off as too nervous. He can practically feel Cassie tense up behind him, not to mention Max.

"I'm sorry if I said anything," Theo says, carefully, even though he knows full well that he *hasn't* been saying bad things about Michael, or his friends. "I didn't mean to—"

"That doesn't cut it," Luc says, cutting him off again, shrugging off Michael's hand as he takes another step forward, and Theo tenses up properly, this time, suddenly worried about what he might have gotten himself into. Luc isn't exactly above physical violence, and he can definitely be described as slightly unstable, and pissing him off really isn't a good idea. But Theo doesn't know what else to say, or do. It seems that there is no right way of getting out of this, and he knows that no one, not even Michael, is really keen on trying to make this guy back off.

It's when Luc makes the slightest move to take another step closer, though, that someone actually does do something, and Theo is probably more shocked than anyone, when it happens.

"Alright, we get it," Max says tiredly, sounding bored, more than anything, as he steps forward, practically putting himself between Theo and Luc. "You're a big, strong man, and your dick is huge. Everyone here is perfectly aware of your insecure, little compensation issues. So simmer down, there, okay?"

Theo can't help but widen his slightly, looking at Max incredulously. If Max turned to him, he would see an expression of warning, almost pleading shock, as Theo knows perfectly well how terribly stupid it is to provoke Luc. It's so stupid, that he can't believe Max is actually doing it.

No, he thinks. *No, please don't.*

Then again, Max isn't stupid. He knows perfectly well how touchy Luc can be, everybody does, and that he's really only making matters worse for himself. So why is he still doing it?

Theo turns back to Luc, when he actually seems to puff himself up a bit, a stark contrast to the slim figure of Max, who stays put, hands in his pockets.

"You're starting to piss me off, faggot," Luc says, voice low, as he actually takes a step closer to Max. But Max doesn't really flinch. Instead, he pulls back the slightest bit, more like someone would shy away from something foul-smelling, rather than scary. And he actually smirks.

"Wow," he says dryly. "That's some impressive vocabulary you got, there."

It's an odd sight; Luc is both bigger and taller than Max, who simply stands there, looking up at him, a slightly cocky smirk on his face, almost like he knows something Luc doesn't. And it's obvious that Luc notices that, too; he hates being made to look stupid, which is ironic, seeing as how he isn't, Theo knows that. He's actually pretty smart. He's just a giant, insecure asshole, most of the time, so it doesn't show.

People around them seem to notice Max's jab, too. The whole situation hasn't attracted that much attention, but enough for a few stragglers to stop and observe, some of them actually giggling or laughing at Max's words. Not Theo, though, nor Cassie, not even Michael and the others. Theo would love to enjoy this, sure, but he's too busy worrying about Max actually getting hurt. He knows how rash Luc can be.

"You need to shut up, right now." Luc's voice is low, and laced with warning, enough to make Theo tense up considerably. He turns to Max, who simply gives Luc a sarcastically apologetic look, before lowering his voice to the same volume as his.

"Not gonna happen, I'm afraid," he says, and Theo swallows, turning back to Luc.

Shit.

For a split second, it almost looks as though Luc considers maybe *not* punching Max in the face, but it's rendered moot, when he actually does.

He's a big guy, that much is obvious, and therefore, it doesn't take much to basically knock Max to the ground.

And apart from that, and the collective gasp that follows from the small group of people around them, Theo doesn't remember much. He doesn't remember much between then, and suddenly connecting his own fist to Luc's jaw, and it seems that the only thing that actually snaps him out of it is the sudden, intense pain in his hand.

"Theo!" Cassie's voice is equal parts shocked and worried, and while Theo blinks, disoriented, he feels her hands grip his arm and pull at him slightly, while someone else apparently intervenes and pulls Luc away, so that they're out of each other's reach.

Theo looks up and sees Cassie's face, hazel eyes wide and concerned, before he looks over and sees Max, sitting up on the floor. They catch each other's eye for a split second, before a teacher comes along and makes the group of students disperse, breaking up the confused, drastically altered atmosphere.

And as Theo cradles his hand, head somehow spinning, he can't help but think that this was probably a terrible idea.

CHAPTER 13
CONSEQUENCES

Theo isn't usually one for swearing. He doesn't really mind it, it's just that he has never really gotten into the habit of doing it, himself, so it feels a bit odd.

But right now, all he can think of is a steady stream of curse words, bursting to come out.

He and Max got in trouble. Pretty big trouble. Luc got the most of it, though, getting suspended for what feels like the millionth time (he must be used to it, by now). And Theo, seeing as how he actually hit someone, regardless of the reason, is in a bit of a tight spot.

Both he, Max and Luc were brought to the principal's office within minutes after the *incident*, and while Luc was dealt with pretty quickly, Theo barely had time to think about the whole thing. He just managed to exchange looks with Max, who was brought in before him, and wait with Cassie outside, until she had to go to class, and left. It didn't take long before Max was sent back out, and Theo went inside the principal's office, to receive his punishment.

"Mr. Davis," the principal says, gesturing to the chair in front of his desk. "Please, have a seat."

Theo hesitantly sits down, eyeing the block on the principal's desk; it has *Henry Milton* stamped on it, in brass letters, and Theo shifts uncomfortably.

The principal, Mr. Milton, has his light blue eyes fixed on Theo for a moment, his expression serious. It somehow suits his middle-aged appearance; he's balding, with light gray hair, and with a face that looks made for smiling either kindly or snidely. Dean doesn't really know which would be more accurate; he has only ever spoken to this guy once or twice. He's a stickler for rules, though, and can be a bit of a hardass. Unless everyone does their job, that is, and does as they're told—then he can be downright cuddly.

Theo is really hoping for some leniency, here. Hopefully, Mr. Milton will see his side, and take into consideration that no real harm was done, that the guilty party is pretty obvious, and that that certainly isn't Theo.

"You had an altercation this afternoon," the principal says, lacing his fingers together and placing his entwined hands on the desk in front of him. "Tell me about it."

Theo swallows.

"Uh," he says, eloquently, trying to ignore the way his hand still hurts. "Luc came up to me, and started accusing me of spreading rumors, or something."

"Rumors about what?" Mr. Milton keeps a completely straight, neutral face.

"About his brother," Theo says. "Michael."

"And have you?" Mr. Milton asks. "Spread rumors about him?"

Theo frowns.

"No," he says. "I wouldn't. I don't even know what rumors he was talking about."

Mr. Milton nods. He seems to believe him.

"Then, what happened?"

Theo hesitated, deliberating.

"Michael tried calming him down," he says. "But it didn't help. And then..."

He swallows, thinking about it, and Mr. Milton looks at him pointedly.

"Then?" he says, and Theo replies.

"Then, Max stepped in," he says, and he's not lost on the way his voice suddenly sounds so much softer, as he says it. The gratitude and affection he feels for Max is definitely shining through, right now, and he's almost certain that Mr. Milton can tell. "He stepped in, and Luc punched him. So I punched him back."

Mr. Milton just looks at him for a moment, before his expression softens. Clearly, he can tell what Max means to Theo, just from the way he talks about him, and he sighs. It seems that Theo might actually be getting the rare leniency he's hoping for.

"Well," Mr. Milton says, shifting a bit, as though slightly uncomfortable. "That does corroborate what Mr. Collins said. Although, he was a bit more... *colorful*, in his description."

Theo quirks a small smile at that, he can't help it. Of course Max would have been more colorful about it, as the principal puts it. He can only imagine just how *colorful* he must have been; he does have a way with words, after all.

"Yeah, he does that." Theo can't help the words escaping his mouth, in a low murmur, and he wonders if Mr. Milton caught them. If he did, he doesn't really show it.

"And according to other students present," he says instead, sounding a bit tired, "that is what happened, as well. It seems that there is a unanimous agreement that Luc Cohen is the one to blame, so to speak."

Theo tenses up a bit. He senses a catch.

"But—" *There it is.* "You *did* hit a student. You were, however briefly, involved in a fight, on school grounds. Which makes this a problem."

Theo feels his heart beat a bit faster, anxiously. He tightens his right hand into a loose fist, but winces as he feels his knuckles throb. Seriously, it hurts way more than he thought it would.

"Okay," he says, feebly, and Mr. Milton looks at him for a few moments.

"Mr. Cohen has been suspended," he says, with genuine sympathy on his face. "And normally, I would have you suspended, as well."

Theo tenses up, suddenly very worried, and the principal sighs again, looking tired.

"But this is a first for you," he says. "And you're a good student, you never get into trouble. And from what I can tell, you had a very good reason for doing what you did."

He says that last part with a pointed look at Theo, who feels oddly, emotionally, exposed, as though Mr. Milton can easily see just how much he cares about Max, and that he only wanted to protect him. Which is all entirely true, of course.

"So I'm going to let you off with a warning," Mr. Milton concludes. "And a week's detention. Okay?"

Theo swallows, as his entire body seems to relax with relief. He nods.

"Okay," he says, and the principal nods.

"Alright, then," he says. "I've called your parents, and someone will pick you up. School's pretty much over for the day, anyway, so I'm sending you home."

Theo nods, and Mr. Milton makes a gesture that he interprets as a sign to leave, but as he gets up from the chair and reaches the door, he stops.

"Mr. Davis," the principal says, and Theo turns around to face him. He looks sympathetic, and surprisingly understanding. "Stay out of trouble, okay?"

Theo hesitates for a moment, before he nods, and leaves the office.

He's honestly a bit surprised to find Max waiting for him, sitting on a stuffed bench right outside the office. It's kind of like a waiting room, and Theo slowly makes his way over to Max, whose face lights up a bit as he sees him.

"Hey," he says, holding out his hand, and Theo takes it, as he sits down on the bench, next to him. "How'd it go?"

Theo sighs tiredly, as though a whole bunch of tension is being lifted off of him.

"Fine," he says. "Detention for a week, and a warning. You?"

Max shrugs.

"Nothing," he says. "I didn't really do anything, so they can't really punish me."

"Then, why are you still here?" Theo asks, frowning, and Max raises a pierced eyebrow at him. Theo looks down, realizing it was a stupid question.

Neither of them speaks for a few moments, and then Theo shakes his head.

"That was so stupid," he mutters, and Max must know he's referring to the fight. But still, he simply shrugs, looking unbothered. And then, Theo realizes something.

"You knew he was gonna do that, didn't you?" he says, looking up. "You knew he was gonna hit you."

Max looks at him sheepishly, the tiniest hint of a smirk on his face, as though he's torn between smugness and slight shame.

"Maybe," he admits, and when Theo shakes his head and looks away, he sighs softly. "You weren't supposed to hit *him*, though. That wasn't part of the plan."

Theo frowns, turning to him.

"What did you think was gonna happen?" he asks, and Max half-shrugs, suddenly looking a bit nervous, in that uncharacteristic way of his. The way he sometimes looks, when approaching territory that is too emotional, or just too unfamiliar.

"I don't know," he says. "But the whole point was for you not to get hurt."

Theo just stares at him for a moment, blinks.

"So, you stepped in, *knowing* that he would hurt you, instead?" he asks, shocked at how odd that sounds, at how ridiculous the notion is. But still, to his surprise, Max half-shrugs again, in confirmation. And Theo exhales slowly, as though suddenly overwhelmed by a kind of affection and gratitude he has never really felt before.

And stupidly, he doesn't know what to say. Instead, he just looks down at his lap, stunned.

Max doesn't seem to mind, though. What are you supposed to answer to something like that, anyway?

"You ever done that, before?" Max asks after a little while, and Theo looks up at him. He knows Max's referring to the whole punching-thing, and he thinks about it.

Truth is, he hasn't done that before. The closest he has ever gotten is punching pads and huge sandbags, in the gym. But he has never actually done it to another person, before.

Theo shakes his head and looks down at his lap again.

"No," he says, before glancing back up. "You?"

Max pauses for a moment, then cocks his head.

"I know how to take a beating," he says, the slightest trace of bitterness in his voice, and Theo blinks. He doesn't ask about it, though. Now is not the time.

Instead, he lets his eyes fall on the small cut just below Max's cheekbone. It's not much, although there will probably be a bruise there tomorrow, and it could have been so much worse. But seeing it is somehow painful, and it makes Theo angry.

He's not used to feeling angry, not like this. Not like he did when he somehow thought it was a good idea to attack Luc, a guy who is bigger than him, and not to mention clearly more experienced with causing physical pain in others. They're lucky the whole thing was interrupted, or things could have gotten so much worse.

Neither of them speaks for a few seconds, as Theo absently rubs his right hand, which is still throbbing. Max looks down at it.

"Does is hurt?" he asks, and Theo hesitates for a moment, before nodding. It's kind of embarrassing, but come on—who knew a jawbone could be so damn painful to ram your fist into?

Max holds out his hand, and Theo hesitantly extends his own, letting Max gently take it. He looks down, watches as Max softly runs his fingers over his knuckles. They're not bruised or anything, but they still hurt more than Theo would like to admit.

Max chuckles softly, and Theo looks up at him.

"What?" he asks, and Max keeps his eyes on Theo's hurt hand. He's smiling.

"You punched a guy in the face," he says, and Theo pauses for a moment, before sighing softly.

"Yeah," he says, looking down again.

"You defended my honor." There's something jokingly serious in Max's voice, and Theo looks up at him again. Those blue eyes are on him, this time, and Max's expression is equal parts smug, teasing and serious. It seems he can't really say something like that without having to downplay it, but Theo appreciates the attempt, nonetheless.

He scoffs, looking back down at his hand.

"Yeah, well," he says evenly. "You defended mine, first."

Max doesn't respond right away, but after a few moments, he brings Theo's injured hand up to his face and kisses it, very softly.

"And I'd do it again," he says, and Theo looks up at him. For once, Max sounds and looks completely sincere, and Theo can't help but smile slightly.

"Me, too," he says, and Max quirks a small smile in return. And for a few seconds, they just stare at each other, somehow completely at ease, Theo aware of only Max's touch, rather than the pain in his hand. And he leans in and kisses him, softly, like he's precious. Because he really is. Theo hasn't really been able to grasp that, before, but it's true.

It's after only a second or so of bliss, that the door to the waiting room suddenly opens, and the two of them pull apart, Theo turning around to look. And just like that, the bliss is replaced by something like worry, as he sees who it is.

"Theo," Eric says, and Theo automatically tenses up.

"Dad." The one word is surprisingly tense. His father looks concerned rather than angry, but there is definitely anger there, too.

"You okay?" he says, voice tight, a little bit rushed, and Theo nods, swallowing.

"Yeah, I'm fine," he says. "I just—"

"Good," Eric says. "We're going home."

Theo hesitates, glances at Max, who wearing a completely neutral expression. He's still holding Theo's hand, though, and he squeezes it ever so gently.

"Dad, just—" Theo says, turning back to his father, who cuts him off.

"No," he says, practically pointing at him, as he steps into the room. "I get a call from the school saying that my son got in a fight. My son, who, as far as I know, doesn't do stuff like that. So right now, you're gonna get in the car, and we're gonna go home."

Theo blinks, but gets over the surprise at his father's attitude, pretty quickly.

"It wasn't like that," he says. "It's fine, I just—"

"Theo, I swear to god." Eric's voice is suddenly low, dangerous, and Theo closes his mouth. "You're—"

Eric cuts himself off, then, as he suddenly seems to notice that his son isn't alone, and he lets his gaze wander to Max's and Theo's clasped hands. Then, he looks up at Max. Max, who looks as calm and unaffected as ever, even as Theo's father takes in his appearance, from his black clothes, to his piercings, to his black eyeliner and messy hair.

"Is this him?" Eric says, voice suddenly filled with controlled anger, as he looks at Theo. "This is the guy you've been seeing?"

Theo swallows, glancing at Max.

"Yes," he says. "This is Max. My boyfriend."

Eric seems to start at the word *boyfriend*, as though unprepared for the seriousness of his son's relationship. After all, just a few days ago, Max was *just some guy* Theo was seeing.

Eric smoothes one hand over his mouth, over his dark stubble, as though trying to calm down, and Theo tenses up a bit.

"Get in the car, Theo," his father says, voice low. "Now."

Theo frowns.

"Dad—"

"Now."

"I can't just leave him here," Theo protests, frowning, a bit surprised at his odd choice of words. But it's true; he can't just leave Max here, not after everything, not after he waited for him. And if nothing else, he's pretty sure his parents aren't coming to pick him up, anyway.

"Yes, you can," Eric says, actually grabbing Theo's sleeve and tugging, enough to pull him to his feet. "We're going. Now."

Theo just stares at his father. He doesn't usually act like this, and for a moment, Theo is simply stunned. He registers Max getting up, too, standing beside him, and he feels him hold onto his injured hand. It hurts, but he doesn't want to let go.

"Dad," he says, looking his father in the eyes. They're the same height, almost exactly.

"Son, don't." Eric's voice is resolute, and Theo simply knows that there's no use arguing.

He's vaguely aware of Max's expression, out of the corner of his eye. He looks tense, irritated, like Theo has seen him before. Every time he's had that look, he has done something stupid, something reckless, and the last thing Theo wants is for him to get in trouble over doing something like that, especially concerning Theo's father. But he's pretty sure Max knows better. At least, he hopes so.

Still, though, he decides to pick his battles, and he eventually nods, eyes on his father.

"Fine," he says, and although Eric almost looks like he's about to relax a bit, his jaw is clenched. It's like he's one provocation away from really exploding, and Theo isn't about to risk that.

Theo turns to look at Max, who still has that same expression, the one that made him step in front of Luc earlier, the one that seems to always make him step in and place himself between

Theo and whatever is threatening him. It's tense, and surprisingly hard and serious, more than Theo is used to seeing on Max's face. He squeezes his hand gently, ignoring the pain.

And Max doesn't say anything, neither of them does. Instead, Max just blinks, visibly relaxing a bit, and Theo makes the slightest move to kiss him. He doesn't get to, though. He doesn't get to, because his father tugs on his arm forcibly enough to pull him away, and Theo starts in surprise. He glances at his father, as though asking what the hell he's doing, but Eric just tugs again, harder this time, and Theo stumbles a bit, reluctantly stepping away from Max.

"Now, Theo," Eric bites out, and Theo doesn't resist. Instead, he just lets his father drag him along, heading for the door. He keeps his eyes on Max, though, for as long as he can. He looks oddly angry, as he stays put, unmoving.

But then, to Theo's honest surprise, Max quickly steps forward and takes Theo's face in his hands, planting a hard, deliberate kiss on his mouth. It's brief, and it's rushed, but Theo savors it, until his father tugs on his arm again, dragging him out of the waiting room, leaving Max standing there, watching them go.

The drive home is tense, to say the least.

Neither Theo nor his father speaks for a few minutes, as Theo looks out through the window. He feels angry, surprisingly so. He has never really had a reason to be angry at his father, not like this. Little things, sure, but this... This is different. He can't quite put his finger on it.

"I don't want you seeing that guy anymore," Eric suddenly says, and Theo turns to him.

"What?" he says, frowning, but his dad has got a rather resolute expression.

"You heard me," he says. "I don't like his effect on you."

Theo just looks at him, still frowning, honestly baffled.

"His effect on me?" he says, sounding the slightest bit annoyed. "What's that supposed to mean?"

"Getting into fights," his father retorts, sounding angry. "For example."

"Right," Theo says, suddenly sounding rather sarcastic. "'Cause that was his fault. It's not like he stood up for me, or anything."

"Do you even hear yourself?" Eric turns to him, looking at him for a few seconds, before turning his eyes back to the road. "Since when are you such a smartass?"

Theo blinks. He hadn't really thought of it that way.

"I'm just pointing out what actually happened," he says, still sounding unusually acidic. "Max didn't make me do anything. Luc was the one who started it."

"So you had to fight him?" Eric says, raising his voice slightly.

"I didn't *fight* him, dad," Theo replies, raising his voice, as well.

"No, you just punched him in the face."

"He punched *Max* in the face," Theo exclaims. "What was I supposed to do?"

"Not get involved," Eric says, sounding properly angry, now. "That's what."

"So, you're telling me I should have just let that happen?" Theo says, frowning. "That's it?"

"I'm telling you to *stay out of it*." His father glances at him. "It had nothing to do with you."

"Are you kidding me?" Theo looks at his father incredulously. "It had *everything* to do with me. Luc was gonna kick my ass, and Max knew that, and he stepped in, anyway. He got hurt, because of me."

Theo notices the slight drop in his voice, as he says it. He doesn't like how true it is. He knows that Max made his own choice, and that he can take it, but knowing that he got hurt, simply to protect Theo, makes Theo's heart ache.

"That doesn't make you obligated to get involved," his father says, clearly sticking to his standpoint, and Theo resists the urge to scoff.

"Bullshit," he says instead, angrier than he's used to, barely noticing the way his father practically winces at the way he says the word. It's a pretty mild curse word, sure, but it's still more than what usually comes out of Theo's mouth. "I wasn't *obligated* to, I *wanted* to. You've never felt that? You've never wanted to punish anyone who hurt someone you cared about?"

Theo's father is silent for only a second, but it's long enough for Theo to feel like maybe, just maybe, Eric thinks he has a point. It doesn't last long, though.

"We'll talk about this when we get home," Eric says, his voice suddenly low with controlled anger. "But it still goes. You're not seeing him again."

Theo grits his teeth, angry and anxious, at the same time. He really doesn't like the sound of that, and it worries him. But he knows there's no point in arguing, not right now. So instead, he just stares out the window, waiting for the inevitable fight that will follow, when the car finally stops moving.

CHAPTER 14

CHANGES

Theo doesn't really remember ever being so angry at his parents, before. Not like this. And he's pretty sure that this is the biggest fight with them, that he has ever had.

When they finally got home, Theo had the distinct feeling that his father had somehow given his mother a warning beforehand; she was there, and Theo remembers her looking tense and concerned.

They went right into it, Amy asking Theo what happened, while Eric practically scowled, and Theo tried his best to stay calm. He told her about what Luc had said, what he had done, and how Max had stepped in and pretty much taken the blow that was meant for Theo. And he told her how he had retaliated, by punching Luc in the face and landing himself in the principal's office.

Amy didn't look happy about it, but unlike her husband, she seemed concerned, rather than angry. And for a moment, Theo hoped that maybe she would have a different take on this, that maybe she would disagree with Eric's conclusion of blaming it all on Max and his *effect* on their son.

But she didn't. Despite her obvious concern, she seemed to agree with Eric, to Theo's honest surprise and frustration. And now, after what feels like ages of yelling and arguing in the living room, neither of his parents seem to want to budge.

"You're seriously banning me from seeing him?" Theo asks incredulously, angry and simply baffled at the irrational conclusion. "Because of this? Just 'cause some asshole picked a fight with me?"

"It's not just this," Amy says, as though trying to calm him down. "It's just the final straw."

Theo frowns at her, disbelieving.

"What, exactly, have I done lately to make you say that?" he asks, and his mother sighs.

"Several things," she says. "Your language, for one."

Theo just looks at her, confused.

"My *language*?"

"Have you heard yourself, lately?" Amy says, frowning. "Swearing, talking back. You never even used to raise your voice."

"Yeah, well, maybe I should have." Theo keeps his eyes on her, unwavering. "Seeing as how you don't even seem to hear me, otherwise."

He's honestly surprised at his own behavior, surprised at the way he doesn't back down.

He knows his mother has a point; it's been subtle, so much so that he has barely even noticed it, himself, but he has changed his way of talking. Little by little, he knows that he has stopped flinching at the sound of curse words, started insisting when he knows his opinion deserves to be heard, gotten used to idea of actually saying how he feels, out loud.

He thinks back to when he told Hannah to shut up, and even to today, when he actually faced Luc, unblinking, rather than fumbling and stammering and looking away.

He remembers when that all started. He remembers finding Max behind the school, that day, several weeks ago, and he remembers talking back and arguing with him, shocked at himself, the entire time. That was probably the first time that really happened. The first time he felt like someone wanted him to talk, like someone actually gave a crap about what he had to say, even if they didn't agree.

Max never tells him to shut up, never belittles his opinions and thoughts. Maybe Theo has just gotten so used to that, that he has started doing it with other people, including his parents, something he never would have done before. And maybe, people don't really like that. Especially not when they're all so used to him keeping quiet.

Amy looks taken aback at her son's words, actually flinching slightly, and Eric looks at Theo.

"That's enough," he says sternly, and Theo turns to him. "Don't talk to your mother, like that."

"She's the one blaming someone else, for me suddenly growing a backbone," he retorts, voice more resolute than he's used to hearing from himself. "The one telling me I can't see my boyfriend, the one person who *doesn't* make me feel like I need to shut up, all the time."

Eric looks honestly shocked at those words, an expression that blends with the obvious anger that's still very present, on his face.

"You both are," Theo continues. "You're pissed at me for talking back, when really, I'm just pointing out that this is bullshit."

Both Amy and Eric react at that, ever so slightly, and Theo gets a small feeling that adding another curse word, however mild, probably wasn't the best idea.

"This isn't someone else's fault," he says, trying not to sound too angry. "And it definitely isn't Max's."

"We're not saying it is," Amy says diplomatically. "But ever since you started seeing him, you've been different. Skipping school, going out, talking like this. And now, fighting."

"Then that's *exactly* what you're saying," Theo exclaims, frustration seeping into the anger. "You're blaming him, like he's somehow ruined me, when all he's done is make me *happy*."

He swallows hard, surprised at the sheer conviction in his voice, and he vaguely hopes that it will be enough to make his parents change their minds. But their expressions don't change; Amy still looks concerned, and Eric still looks angry.

"I know you think that, sweetie," Amy finally says, taking a step closer to her son. "But you're young, and sometimes, that means you don't always see what's best for you."

Theo just stares at her, honestly shocked. He doesn't know what to say to that. It's just so irrational, not to mention patronizing, the words coming out of his mother's mouth. And for several seconds, they all just stand there, silent, until Theo heaves a heavy sigh, suddenly feeling very tired.

"Yeah, well," he says, anger and frustration replaced by weary exhaustion. "I may be young, and maybe I don't always know what's best for me. But at least he makes me feel good about myself, which is more than I can say for you two, right now. Or anyone else."

He looks at his parents, both of them, waiting for either of them to say something. But they don't, either because they have nothing to say, or because they're too stunned to. Theo doesn't really care. He's too tired, and he knows he has lost this battle, no matter how unfair it is.

It takes another few seconds, before he turns around and leaves the living room, picking up his schoolbag on the way, and neither of his parents makes a move to stop him, as he climbs the stairs. When he reaches his room, he resists the urge to slam the door behind him, as he enters. The time for anger has passed. Now, there's only tired hopelessness in its place.

Theo isn't sure if his parents simply forgot about it, or if they just deem it irrelevant, but they didn't take his phone. It's still in his pocket, and he takes it out as he sits down on the bed. There's a text from Max, sent only fifteen minutes after Theo left the school with his dad, over an hour ago.

You okay?

And right after that one is another, sent five minutes later.

Blink twice for yes.

Theo smiles, despite himself, and he takes a deep breath.

I'm okay, he writes back. *My parents say I can't see you anymore.*

It doesn't even take a minute, before Max replies.

I figured, he writes. *I don't think your dad likes me too much.*

Theo cocks his head, as though Max can see him.

Sadly, no. My mom agrees with him. I'm pretty sure they're gonna take my phone btw, just a heads-up.

It makes him oddly sad to write that, but he knows it's true; his parents have probably just forgotten about it. They're not used to punishing him, after all, seeing as how he has never really done anything worth punishing him over. At least, not before this.

Who knew that falling in love would be enough?

Theo's phone beeps with Max's reply.

Well, that's just stupid, he writes, and Theo can practically hear the dry tone. *It's not like we won't see each other, anyway.*

I think they just wanna make a point, Theo writes.

I guess, Max replies. *We might be conspiring, you know. Planning to run away together, join the circus.*

Theo smiles, before another text shows up on his phone.

You'd sell popcorn, I'd shove swords down my throat. We could live together in a trailer with four cats and a lizard. It would be awesome.

Theo actually laughs out loud at that, glad that Max can make him smile, despite the fact that they're both in such a huge mess, right now.

That does sound awesome, he replies. *Hopefully we won't have to, tho. Not a big fan of trailers.*

Well, you just don't know how to live, do you.

Theo's smile stays on, and suddenly, he's hit with such an intense sensation, a hollow, almost physical ache in his chest. It's not so much the addition of pain, but more the *absence* of something, and he takes a deep breath, trying to ignore it.

I miss you, he writes, still not quite used to the feeling, like Max is a literal part of him. A part that leaves a huge, gaping void, as soon as it's gone.

I miss you too. The reply eases the pain a little bit, enough to make it more manageable, and Theo sighs, falling back onto the bed, landing on his back.

He supposes he should have seen this coming.

Theo was right; his parents had simply forgotten to take his phone from him. But, seeing that coming, he made sure to write down Max's number and tuck it away in a desk drawer, and he made sure to turn off his phone, before handing it over to his mom. The last thing he wanted was for them to go through his messages, and if nothing else, some vindictive part of him wants to make sure this whole thing won't be so easy for them.

He doesn't come down for dinner, instead stays in his room, bored. His parents have disconnected his laptop, so even though he still has it, he can't go online. It seems that they're desperate to make sure he can't talk to Max, no matter what. But at the same time, he's somehow fine about it, too tired and defeated to be angry. And if nothing else, he knows that he'll see Max, anyway, at school. Hopefully.

Theo is in the middle of watching an episode of *Firefly* on his disconnected laptop, when there's a soft knock on his door. He pauses the episode, computer perched in his lap, as he sits on his bed, legs outstretched and back against the headboard.

"Yeah," he says flatly, half-expecting his mother, but when the door slowly opens, he's surprised to see Riley, peeking his head in.

"Hi," he says, carefully. "You busy?"

Theo folds his laptop shut and puts it next to him, on the bed. He shakes his head.

"No," he says. "Come on in."

Riley seems relieved, and he steps inside, closing the door behind him. Theo can't help but notice that he looks slightly unsure, uncomfortable.

"I talked to mom," Riley eventually says, making his way into the room. "She told me what happened."

He sits down in the chair by Theo's desk, and Theo clenches his jaw for a moment.

"Yeah?" he says, and Riley nods.

"I mean," he adds, "I heard about some of it, at school. Just didn't really believe it."

Theo frowns.

"What do you mean?" he asks, and Riley raises his eyebrows.

"Someone punches Luc Cohen?" he says. "People are gonna talk about it."

Theo shifts uncomfortably. He hadn't thought about that.

"Yeah, well," he says, picking at the hem of his t-shirt. "Not as exciting as it sounds, trust me."

"Still, though." Theo looks up at the small note of pride in Riley's voice. "That was pretty badass."

Theo looks down at his lap, a small smile on his face. Yeah, it probably was pretty badass. A bit, at least.

"Is it true?" Riley says. "That he punched Max?"

Theo looks up at his brother, frowning.

"Mom didn't tell you?" he asks, and Riley shakes his head, looking sympathetic.

"No," he says. "She just told me you got in a fight. She told me Max had been involved, though."

Theo sighs, some frustration creeping into his tone.

"Of course, that's what she said." He sounds bitter, to say the least. It's something he's not used to hearing from himself. "But yeah, it's true. How did you know, if she didn't tell you?"

Riley gives him a small smile.

"Again," he says, "it was all over the school. And actually, most people think it's pretty cool, that you stood up for him like that."

Theo shifts a bit, uncomfortably.

"He stood up for me, first," he mumbles, and Riley nods. Theo can see it, out of the corner of his eye. "And it was worth it, even if it did land me in detention for a week."

Riley smiles, before getting serious again.

"Mom told me you can't see him again," he says, voice subdued. "She said it's for your own good."

Theo sighs in exasperation, leaning his head back against the bed's headboard.

"Yeah, I know," he says tiredly. "It's such bullshit."

Riley chuckles, and Theo looks at him, frowning.

"What?" he asks.

"Nothing," Riley replies, shaking his head. "It's just that you've gotten more... comfortable, lately. Mom mentioned that, too. She doesn't like it. Neither does dad."

Theo scoffs.

"Yeah, apparently, Max has a 'bad effect' on me," he says, and god help him, he actually uses air-quotes.

"I don't think so." Theo reacts at the confident calm in Riley's voice. "I mean, sure, yeah, you've changed a bit since you met him. But not in a bad way. You seem more confident, more relaxed."

He shrugs.

"You seem happier," he says. "Even if that does mean you actually curse now, a little bit."

Theo just looks at his brother, before smiling.

"Tell that to them," he says, shaking his head. "I swear, dad took one look at Max and just... He didn't even give him a chance."

He sighs heavily.

"I knew this would happen. That's why I didn't tell them. I just knew they would react like that, right off the bat. It's like they don't even want to know who he is, what he's like."

"I think they're scared." Theo frowns slightly at Riley's words. "They're our parents, you know. I'm not saying it's fair, or that it makes sense. And I mean, I like Max, I know he's not a bad guy, and I agree that this is bullshit."

He glances at the wall, thinking, with that precocious look on his face.

"But imagine your kid suddenly changing, like you have," he says, "and this random, scary-looking guy comes into his life, at the same time. It's easy to blame him for that, for corrupting your son. I'd probably be scared, too."

Theo considers that for a few moments, staring. He blinks.

"How the hell are you only fourteen years old?" he finally asks, and Riley chuckles, turning back to him.

"I'm just observant," he says.

"Yeah, well, that's pretty insightful for a kid," Theo retorts. Then he frowns. "And Max isn't *scary*."

Riley raises his eyebrows at him pointedly.

"Dude," he says, "he can be pretty scary. Especially if you don't know him."

Theo considers that for a moment, then cocks his head, admitting that Riley has a point. He remembers how intimidating Max was, before he got to know him. Which makes it all the more shocking, how sweet and funny he can be. How sweet and funny and thoughtful and gorgeous and—

Theo closes his eyes, sighing. *Damn*, he's got it bad for this guy.

"But that's the thing, though," he says, opening his eyes again. "He's not bad for me. I mean... I feel *good* about myself, with him. Like I don't have to put up with other people's crap, all the time, like I actually have a say."

"I've noticed," Riley says, a small smile on his face. "But I think mom and dad are a bit too freaked out to deal with that, right now."

Theo doesn't reply. He's angry at his parents, there's no question there. But at the same time, he sort of gets where they're coming from, he gets what Riley is saying right now. But that doesn't excuse anything. It doesn't excuse the way they talked to him, the way they simply blamed everything on Max, or the way Eric literally pulled Theo away from him, at the school. It's not alright, and no matter their reasons, Theo can't really accept his parents' behavior.

He'll just have to wait, instead, hoping that they'll come around. And if nothing else, he is eighteen, which means that he's technically an adult, and they can't really stop him from doing anything.

The matter of him living in their home, though, complicates things. In that sense, they really do have a say in what he does, and Theo doesn't like the idea of going against his parents, either. Because they're his parents, and it feels wrong.

But that won't stop him from seeing Max. Nothing will.

"What were you watching?" Riley asks, gesturing at Theo's closed laptop. "When I came in?"

"*Firefly*," Theo replies, before cocking his head. "Wanna watch?"

Riley gives him a small smile, before getting up from the chair and sitting down next to Theo, on the bed, and his big brother scoots over to make room.

Theo feels a surge of affection for his brother, at how *wise* he actually can be, and he's so glad to have him on his side. And for a little while, as they watch the crew of Serenity kick some ass on the screen, things feel pretty okay, despite everything.

♦

Theo thought it would be simple, going to school. He thought it would be like normal, seeing Max and going about his business as usual.

He may have overstated matters a bit.

Although he is eighteen, and although there were technically no further repercussions of the fight than him getting a week of detention, there has clearly been a slight shift, when it comes to him and Max being around each other. There's nothing the teachers or the school can do, really, but Theo is still uncomfortably aware of people somehow paying more attention to him, now, teachers and students alike.

He doesn't see Max for the whole next day, though, and only knows he has been to school because Cassie has talked to him.

"He asked about you," she says, when they meet up for lunch. "He seemed pissed that you keep missing each other, between classes."

She wrinkles her nose.

"He asked me to pass on a message for you, but I'm not gonna."

Theo just looks at her.

"Why not?" he asks, and Cassie practically cringes.

"Let's just say it was a very physical request," she explains, and Theo can't help but laugh at her discomfort. "But he says hi."

Theo is glad to hear it, but in the midst of it, that ache inside grows just a little bit stronger; he misses Max, he really misses him, and knowing he's around, but not right here, is only making it worse.

When the day comes to an end, Theo has detention, which means he doesn't see Max for the rest of the day. And since his cell phone has been confiscated, he can't really reach him. So, he sits through his detention in restless silence, trying to get some schoolwork done, before he finally gets to go home. It's cold outside, and he misses Max's warmth more than ever, borrowing Riley's phone (with his permission) when he gets home, to send a small text just to say hi. The simple reply is enough to make him smile, and he really hopes he gets to see Max tomorrow.

Theo's wish is granted.

He's on his way out of a classroom, the hallway milling with students, when he feels someone grab his arm. He turns to find Cassie, a conspiring look on her face.

"Your man wants to see you," she says in a low voice, cocking her eyebrows, and Theo automatically looks around.

"Not here," Cassie says, sounding scheming and exasperated, all at once, and Theo looks back at her. She cocks her head toward the front entrance. "He said you'd know."

Theo frowns at her, eyes slightly narrowed.

185

"You're kind of enjoying this," he says. "Aren't you?"

Cassie shrugs.

"Maybe," she admits gleefully. "It's very covert ops."

Theo scoffs, smiling, and Cassie nudges him gently.

"Go get him."

Theo doesn't need telling twice.

Cassie wasn't very explicit in saying where, exactly, Max wants to see him, but Theo has an idea. He makes sure to get his jacket, though, before slipping out through the front entrance and making his way across the schoolyard. The temperature has really dropped lately (it looks like it might even snow, soon) and he shoves his hands in his pockets, as he goes.

The moment he reaches the building on the other side and rounds the corner, he spots him. Max. And for a moment, Theo experiences an odd sense of déjà vu.

Max is standing near the wall, a cigarette between his fingers, and as he hears Theo approach, he looks up. The way he blows out a slow stream of smoke, dark blue eyes sharp, takes Theo right back to the first time he ever bumped into him here, behind the school. The only difference, really, is the expression; rather than looking smug and mischievous, Max's face lights up, and he smiles as he catches Theo's eye.

"Hey," he says, taking a few steps to meet Theo halfway, and as soon as he reaches him, he leans in to give him a kiss. And Theo closes his eyes, exhales slowly, because it's the best kiss, ever.

Then again, he tends to think that about pretty much every kiss they share, no matter what. Maybe *kissing* Max is just the best thing, ever.

Max makes a content humming noise as he pulls away, cigarette still secured between his fingers. He shivers slightly, from the cold or something else, Theo can't really tell, but the way Max smiles tells him that he doesn't really care, anyway.

"I missed you," Max says, moving in closer and tugging softly on Theo's jacket, and Theo automatically places his hands on

Max's waist. He absently wonders how warm that black coat is, if it's enough to keep him warm, through the winter.

"I missed you, too." Theo practically murmurs the words, just staring at Max's face, taking in his features, the black makeup and the metal piercings, the way he smiles at Theo in a way that Theo has never seen anyone else smile at him, before. He moves one hand up to cup his boyfriend's face, gently smoothing over the small cut below his cheekbone; Theo was right, it has left a bruise, but it's really not that bad. He decides to not think about it right now, and instead and relishes the way Max seems to melt against him, as he kisses him, slowly.

Max hums against his mouth in appreciation, and when they pull apart, he just sighs, sounding tired and completely content.

"Man, I've got it bad for you," he mutters, and Theo smiles, vaguely remembering thinking the exact same thing, the other day. "How you holding up?"

Theo moves his hand from Max's face and places it against his waist, again, while Max takes a long drag on his cigarette.

"It's fine," Theo says, sounding tired in a way that suggests it's anything but *fine*. "My parents are really sticking to it. I feel like they're about to pay off the teachers to spy on me and keep me in line."

Max smiles mischievously.

"You mean, to keep you from misbehaving?" he says. "Like surreptitiously meeting your hot, dangerous boyfriend in secret?"

He pulls on his cigarette, cocking his eyebrows suggestively, and Theo chuckles.

"Something like that," he says, tilting his head. "You're not that dangerous, though."

Max looks outraged.

"I can be dangerous," he says in mock indignity. "I'm just... really subtle about it."

Theo laughs, and places a chaste kiss on his lips.

"Sure," he says, as Max drops his burned-out cigarette to the ground and grinds it out with his boot. "If you say so."

187

"Hey," Max says warningly, looking down at Theo's chest, as he tugs on his jacket. He seems to do that a lot, like it has become a bit of a habit, especially when he's feeling unusually shy. Or, at least the closest thing Max can actually get to feeling shy, or modest. "Don't test me."

Theo smiles, watching Max's face, as Max watches his own hands, tracing Theo's clothed chest.

"Yeah, well," Theo says. "Might have to, if this keeps up. There are those very determined to keep us apart."

He says that last part with some dramatic effect, and Max scoffs slightly, with a small smile.

"Let them," he says, a hint of seriousness underneath the cocky tone, his words effortless. "I love you, I'm not giving you up that easy."

Theo's stomach drops. He blinks, and simply stares at Max, who still has his eyes on Theo's front, where he's unnecessarily tugging at the lapels of his jacket.

"What?" Theo finally musters dumbly, in a somewhat stunned murmur, and Max looks up at him.

"Hm?" he says, dark blue eyes slightly wide, eyebrows raised, making him look so innocent that it's obvious he's trying too hard. He has never really been good at looking innocent, of all things.

"You, what?" Theo says, voice slightly steadier, but still stunned rather than disbelieving, and he keeps his eyes fixed on Max's, which keep the same expression. Then, after a few moments, Max visibly shifts slightly, glancing down.

"You heard me," he says, voice low, with a tone that says he was sort of hoping Theo hadn't heard him, the first time. And Theo swallows uncertainly, heart suddenly pounding.

"I did," he confirms. And it takes another couple of seconds of silence, on his part, before Max looks up at him again. He looks uncomfortable. *Really* uncomfortable, actually, and Theo watches, as he practically fidgets, looking down. It's something he has barely ever seen Max do, and he suddenly realizes that he's probably supposed to say something.

"I love you, too," he blurts. And almost immediately, he feels the urge to facepalm in embarrassment; that did not come out as gracefully or smoothly as he had hoped, and he suddenly feels ridiculous.

But Max doesn't seem to notice, or care. Instead, he slowly meets Theo's gaze again, hands still softly gripping the front of his jacket.

"Good," he finally says, looking rather unlike his normal, effortless self. Theo nods, feeling ridiculous, and Max nods back. And then, after what feels like several seconds of tense silence, Theo actually snorts, his face breaking into a smile, and Max looks at him like he's insane, before smiling, as well.

"Shut up," he mumbles, looking down, but for some reason, Theo can't stop laughing. It's a rather silent laugh, making his shoulders shake slightly, and Max looks up at him again. He rolls his eyes, smiling.

"Stop it." His words carry no weight, though, as he chuckles, tugging at Theo's jacket. "I already feel like an ass, you're making it worse."

Theo presses his lips together, trying really hard not to smile, but he can't help it. He's not even sure why; something about the whole situation just makes him want to laugh, and Max seems to get that, at least judging from the way he keeps that unusually shy smile, avoiding Theo's eyes.

Theo takes a deep breath, in a valiant effort to control himself, and Max looks up at him again.

"You done?" he asks, a small smile still on his face, and Theo nods.

"Yeah," he says. "Sorry."

They just look at each other for a few moments, before Max sighs and pulls Theo closer. The kiss he gives him is soft and sweet, and Theo closes his eyes, keeping them closed as Max leans their foreheads together.

"You're making me stupid," Max murmurs. "You know that?"

Theo sighs.

"I very much doubt that," he says. "But I get what you mean."

Max makes a small sound of confirmation, before suddenly letting out a small scoff.

"Fucking Batman," he murmurs, and Theo frowns, opening his eyes.

"What?" he says, and Max pulls away a bit.

"I shouldn't have said anything," he explains, looking into Theo's eyes, "when you came by here, that day. I should have just kept my mouth shut, and we wouldn't be in this mess."

Theo thinks back to the day in question, back when he first caught Max smoking here, behind the school. He remembers it in such perfect detail, and he smiles, almost shyly, at the memory.

"I was so nervous," he admits, and Max frowns. "When you talked to me. I mean, I thought you were a total douchebag, at first, but I was still crushing on you. And you made me nervous."

Max frowns indignantly.

"Douchebag?" he says. "Why?"

Theo gives him an *are you kidding me?*-look.

"You blew smoke in my face," he says pointedly, with a small smile. "Twice."

Max rolls his eyes at the memory.

"Alright," he says, "that may have been douchebag-level behavior. But we've been through this. I thought *you* were the douchebag."

"Still, though," Theo says, cocking his eyebrows.

"Fine, I'm sorry," Max practically whines, leaning in and kissing Theo on the mouth, moving his arms up to wrap them around his neck. "But I think I've made up for it."

Theo makes a doubtful sound, and Max frowns indignantly, lips still pressed against Theo's.

"I have," he says defensively against his mouth. "With blowjobs and orgasms and my generally awesome company."

Theo can't help but chuckle, still keeping their lips locked together, and he smoothes his hands up over Max's back. Somehow, he finds it oddly amusing that just a few weeks ago, he would have blushed and fumbled and been extremely uncomfortable at Max's way of phrasing things. It still kind of has that effect on him, but he's more used to it now, and it's something about Max that he would never want to change.

"Fair enough," he admits, melting as Max lets one hand run its fingers through his hair.

For several seconds, they just stand there, kissing, holding each other, and Theo finds himself feeling eternally grateful at the fact that he did choose this route, that day, all those weeks ago. That he chose to take the route behind the school, rather than another one, on that specific day, at that specific time, when he ran into Max. He's not sure what things would have been like today, if he hadn't.

"I love you." The words escape his lips out of nowhere, slightly muffled against Max's mouth, and for a moment, he tenses up. They only said it for the first time, two minutes ago. Maybe this is way too soon. Hell, maybe Max doesn't even *want* to say it anymore, maybe he has changed his mind.

The way Max tenses up against him, though, in his arms, tells a different story, and Theo absently notices how those fingers tighten their grip on his hair, ever so slightly.

"I love you." There's only a breath of hesitation before Max says it, and when he does, his voice has the same, non-flinching confidence that Theo is used to hearing. And Max kisses him again, not moving his lips away more than a fraction of an inch. "I love you, Theo."

Theo exhales slowly, tightening his arms around Max.

He just knows that he'll never get tired of hearing that.

CHAPTER 15
TIES

To say that everything is a mess right now, would probably be an understatement.

Theo finds himself feeling unusually resentful toward his parents, even though it's been a few days by now, since they had their big fight. Maybe he just figured they would come around, eventually, or at least try to see his side of it. But so far, no luck, and he just feels uncharacteristically annoyed, especially at his mother. He was hoping that she might soften, at least, unlike his dad, seeing as how she's usually the one to back him up and support his choices.

Perhaps this is too much, though, he thinks. If his parents' motives are in fact driven by him suddenly changing so drastically, lately, and for the worse, according to them, this might be too much. Asking them to simply accept it, might be the most he has ever really asked them for, and he's not entirely sure they will be coming around, anytime soon.

Going to school helps a bit, since it's the only way Theo actually gets to see Max, anymore. He doesn't see him that often, though. They get to have lunch together, if they're lucky, and more than once, Theo has only heard from Max through either Riley or Cassie, either when seeing them in halls of the school, or through text messages to their phones (since Theo still hasn't gotten his own phone back). It's not enough, but it's something, and Theo is really glad to have at least some people on his side.

He also still has detention, which means he has to sit around even after classes are done, before going straight home, since he's basically grounded, which only gives him more time to miss Max so *endlessly*.

Nearing the end of the week, though, Cassie reminds him of the *Thor*-screening, and after some arguing with his parents—and convincing them, annoyed, that he's going with a friend, rather than Max—they finally let him go. He's glad; it's a nice break from everything that's going on, and although he could risk bringing Max along, anyway, he and Cassie both agree that it's an unnecessary risk. If Theo's parents find out, things could get so much worse, and Theo honestly isn't about to risk abusing the one piece of freedom he has actually gotten, lately.

Theo's mother drops him off at the movie theater, where he's supposed to meet up with Cassie. It annoys him, to say the least, that his parents insisted on driving him, but he figures it's best not to argue. It's just their way of making sure he's actually doing what he says he's going to do, with who he says he's going to do it with.

Theo spots Cassie waiting outside the movie theater, as his mother pulls up the car, and Amy sighs, killing the engine. She doesn't say anything for a moment, but Theo has a feeling that she wants to, so he gives her the chance.

"Theo," she finally says, "I'm sorry it has to be like this."

Theo doesn't answer, simply glances out the window, absently touching the door handle. He's itching to leave, but somehow, he feels like his mother needs him to listen, for a moment. Unlike with his father, he has a hard time rejecting her, or letting her down.

"I know you must be angry with us," his mother continues, her voice soft and sympathetic. "But we just worry about you. I don't like it, but it's for the best."

Theo still doesn't reply, and Amy tentatively touches his arm, making him look up at her. Her face is kind and thoughtful, and Theo once again blatantly questions her part in this, her way of deliberately keeping him from someone who makes him happy. It just doesn't make sense.

"I'm not trying to be the bad guy, here," Amy says. "I'm only doing this because I care. I hope you know that."

Theo just looks at her, before nodding, and his mother presses her lips together, as though she wants to say something else, but decides against it. Instead, she looks over his shoulder, through the passenger side window.

"Is that her?" she asks, sounding lighter, as through striving for casual conversation.

Theo follows her line of sight, and spots Cassie, her red hair bright against the bleak autumn backdrop. She's standing outside the theater's entrance, slightly huddled against the cold.

"Yeah," Theo says, turning back to his mother, who nods, as she gives him a small smile.

"Okay," she says, as though she knows Theo isn't as alright with this whole thing as he's letting on, right now, but that she's taking what little peace she can get. "Well, don't keep her waiting."

Theo isn't used to things being so stiff and tense with his mother, and as he gets out of the car and waves her off, he can't stop wondering why the *hell* she would go along with this whole thing. Maybe she really *is* worried about him, like parents are, and Riley's word come to him, as he walks over to the theater entrance.

"Maybe they're scared... I'd be scared, too."

194

He doesn't want them to be scared, they have no reason to be, and he wishes they would see that. Then again, if he has changed so much, lately, maybe it kind of makes sense. They don't seem too happy about his sudden burst of rebellion, after all.

"Hey!" Cassie lights up when she spots him, and they hug. "Thought you'd stood me up."

She gives him a stern, jokingly angry look, and Theo smiles, ruffling her hair in a way he knows she hates.

"How could anyone stand you up?" he says, and Cassie smiles smugly.

"Good point," she says, holding out her arm. "Shall we?"

Theo smiles wider, hooking his arm through hers, as they make their way inside.

There isn't that much of a crowd, but that probably shouldn't be surprising. Considering the fact that the movie in question has been out for years, already, and that it can easily be downloaded, if nothing else, most people don't really seem to keen on paying to see it. But the sparse crowd is kind of nice, Theo thinks, as he and Cassie find their seats, popcorn and sodas in hand. It's calmer, devoid of small, annoying children and people who'd rather talk through the whole movie, than actually watch it.

"So, how's it going?" Cassie asks, putting some popcorn in her mouth. The movie hasn't started yet, so they just sit there, waiting, as the theater fills up with people.

"Are you kidding?" Theo says, voice sharp with sarcasm. "It's awesome."

Cassie raises an eyebrow at him, and he cocks his head in apology. He didn't mean to snap at her, and she knows that.

"You know," she says, her voice considering, "I think I see it, now."

Theo frowns.

"What?" he says.

"Nothing," she says. "It's just, that kinda sounds like something Max would say."

Theo's expression relaxes, and he just looks at her.

195

"Not in a bad way," she adds, rather hastily. "I mean, I kinda like it."

Theo just keeps looking at her, as Cassie puts the straw of her soda cup in her mouth and pulls down a huge gulp of Coke, eyes wide and still focused on his. Then, Theo turns away to look at the blank, white movie screen at the other end of the large room.

"If it helps," Cassie adds, "you have that effect on him, too."

Theo glances at her.

"What do you mean?" he asks, and she shrugs.

"Well, he's..." she says, searching for the words. "He's *nicer*, now. Not as abrasive. You know, overall. I mean, he's still pretty bitchy, but... I don't know. Can't really explain it."

She shrugs again, and Theo can't help but quirk a small smile.

"Bitchy?" he asks, and Cassie nods.

"Yes," she says, then rolls her eyes. "Oh, come on, you know he'd approve."

Theo considers that for a moment, before cocking his head in agreement. Max probably would approve. And it's adorable.

"Any word from Michael?" Cassie asks after a little while. "Or Hannah?"

Theo frowns, looking at her.

"No," he says. "Why?"

Cassie shrugs, looking at the big, white movie screen.

"No reason," she says. "It's just too bad you guys fell out."

She looks down at the popcorn in her lap and puts some more in her mouth.

"Especially Hannah," she adds. "She wasn't always like that."

Theo nods in agreement.

"Yeah, I know," he says. "She—"

Then he frowns.

"Wait," he says, "how do you know that?"

Cassie doesn't answer right away. Instead, she sighs and looks up, staring at the screen, slowly putting some more popcorn in her mouth.

"We used to be friends," she finally says, and Theo's eyebrows actually go up, in surprise. "A couple of years ago. Best friends, actually."

She sighs again, looking down at the popcorn again, absently digging through it for a moment, before selecting the right kernel to eat.

"She wasn't a bitch, back then," she says, sounding a bit sad. "She was really sweet. We had a lot of fun together."

Cassie looks back up at the screen, straight ahead.

"Then she met Michael," she says. "And he was cool, and popular, and he seemed to like her. And I guess she decided that she'd rather be friends with him, than with me, the geeky weirdo. I wasn't exactly cool enough to fit in with her new clique."

Cassie lets out a small, almost humorless laugh, before turning to Theo.

"I don't blame Michael, though," she says. "He seems like a nice guy."

Theo nods in sad confirmation.

"He is," he says. "I just think he needs more of a spine, than he has. He tends to let people push him around."

Cassie frowns, clearly surprised.

"Shocking, I know," Theo says. "But when everyone likes you, there's not much room for conflict, if you want them to keep liking you. And if nothing else, with a brother like Luc, I'd probably be pretty reserved, too."

It kind of makes him sad to think about it. Michael *is* a good guy, and he was a pretty good friend, since he and Theo started hanging out, last year. Theo is honestly a bit surprised at him distancing himself so much, just because of Theo being with Max. He didn't really see that coming.

"So, I guess the question is," Cassie says, "is Michael really being a douche about this, or is it just Hannah, acting like she thinks she's supposed to, and Michael just going along because *he* thinks he's supposed to?"

Theo sighs, turning to look at the blank screen.

"Beats me," he says. "The whole thing's turned into a bigger mess than I thought it would."

"Yeah," Cassie sighs, sympathetically. Then she nudges Theo's arm. "But hey, at least you got your man."

Theo smiles then, turning to her, and she smiles back, and Theo can't help but feel really happy and grateful that the two of them became friends.

The movie is amazing, but seeing as how they've both seen it a bunch of times, already, they knew that, beforehand. But still. It's a nice distraction, and Theo is glad his parents let him go. Even if it does piss him off a bit, that he basically needed their permission.

They sit through the credits (*duh*), along with almost everybody else, which is a nice surprise. But then Theo remembers that this is a screening almost entirely attended by proper fans, so it makes perfect sense that they all stay behind for the post-credits scene. And it doesn't matter that Theo and Cassie have already seen it a bunch of times; there's something so calming about sitting in a movie theater, just relaxing. It's a nice break from everything else that's going on, if nothing else, and Theo appreciates every moment of it. He's in no rush to leave.

Eventually, though, he does have to leave, and he and Cassie make their way out of the theater, into the cold night air. Theo is surprised, but at the same time not, to see his dad's 60s' Chevrolet already waiting outside, and he sighs.

"That's my ride," Theo says, turning to Cassie. "It sucks, but I gotta go."

Cassie pouts sympathetically.

"Yeah, well," she says. "I'm glad they let you out for the evening."

Theo grimaces, and Cassie smiles. Then she moves in and hugs him tightly, Theo reciprocating, and he hears her sigh.

"It'll be okay, you know," she says. "It'll all work out."

Theo nods, even though she can't see it, and when they pull apart, she squeezes his arm.

"I had a good time," she says, and Theo smiles.

"Me, too," he says. "Thanks."

"See you at school," Cassie says, and Theo nods, giving her a small wave, as he turns around and makes his way to the car.

He can practically feel the tension emanating from his father, as he slips into the passenger seat, but he doesn't look up, as he closes the car door. He sees his father basically fidget for a moment, before speaking.

"Did you have fun?" he asks, and Theo nods, snapping his seatbelt into place.

"Yeah," he says, unnecessarily fiddling with his jacket for a moment, before looking up at his dad. "It was good."

Eric doesn't say anything. Instead, he just looks at Theo, for several moments, as though wanting to say something, kind of like Amy did, when she dropped Theo off. But he doesn't say anything, and instead, he simply turns his gaze straight ahead, as he puts the car into gear and drives off.

♦

Theo meant it when he talked to Cassie, about Michael and Hannah, and the whole mess that has suddenly appeared. He meant it, and although it has been a while, now, since they stopped talking to him, it still makes him kind of sad. Sure, he's got Cassie, now, and Max, and they're honestly better and more supportive relationships than he has ever really had.

But Michael was the closest thing he had to a best friend for a pretty long time. He helped pull him up from the very depths of insecurity, and if nothing else, Theo isn't sure he even would have dared to even *speak* to Max, without that. He owes Michael a lot, and it makes him sad that they're not friends, anymore.

It's with that thought that Theo is stunned, to say the least, when Michael suddenly approaches him one day, at school.

Classes have just ended for the day, and Theo makes his way out of the classroom, heading for his locker. He only makes it halfway, though, before he feels someone tap him on the shoulder, and he turns around. Michael looks oddly uncomfortable, and Theo resists the urge to just stare at him, in surprise.

"Hey," Michael says, putting his hands in his pockets, and Theo just keeps staring at him. He glances around them automatically; part of him wonders if Hannah is anywhere nearby, seeing this. He hitches his shoulder bag up a big.

"Hey," he replies, and for a second, Michael just nods absently. Then, he clears his throat a bit, glancing away.

"So listen," he says, voice a bit low. "I, uh..."

He looks around, before looking back at Theo, and cocking his head, and Theo goes with him as he makes his way to a more secluded part of the hallway.

"I'm sorry," Michael finally says, after several moments of hesitant silence. "I just—"

He sighs, looking away again.

"I'm sorry about Luc," he says, looking at Theo. "He shouldn't have done that. He was way out of line."

Theo straightens up a little bit. He hasn't really thought about Luc in the past few days, actually. Not with everything else going on.

"I mean, when he punched that guy—"

"Max," Theo interjects, somewhat stiffly, and Michael looks at him for a moment.

"Max," he repeats. "Right."

He looks down.

"I didn't say anything to him," he says. "I didn't blame you, or anything, barely even mentioned you. He just heard about the whole rumor-thing, and I mentioned how you and me were... *whatever*, around the same time. He just jumped to conclusions."

Theo assumes that *whatever* means *fighting*, or *not friends*. Maybe even *one party ignoring the other for no valid reason*. He doesn't mention it, though.

Michael looks up at Theo. His dark eyes look oddly sad, even a little bit ashamed, and it's a look Theo isn't used to seeing on his face. With his handsome features, dark hair and rather impressive physique, it just looks weirdly wrong to see him with any other expression than complete and utter confidence.

"You know how Luc gets," Michael says sadly, almost pleading. "I know that doesn't make it okay, but—"

"No, it doesn't." Theo is almost surprised at his blunt reply. He would be, if he hadn't gotten used to actually speaking up, recently.

Michael, however, looks blatantly surprised, and actually blinks in confused shock, for a moment. Theo can't really tell if that's a good or a bad reaction. And honestly, he finds that he doesn't really care.

"Yeah," Michael finally says. "It doesn't."

He clears his throat.

"And the rumors weren't even that big a deal," he says, half-shrugging. "Just something about me being bad in bed, or some shit. Got blown way out of proportion."

Theo can't help but chuckle a little at that, and Michael quirks a small smile, seemingly relieved.

"You sure it's not true?" Theo asks, eyebrows raised, and Michael gives him an exaggerated look of smug confidence.

"Please," he says. "Who do you think you're talking to?"

Theo cocks his head, a small smile on his face.

"Right," he says. "I almost forgot."

Michael's smile widens a bit, and for a moment, Theo feels just a little bit lighter. It's nice to actually talk to Michael again, even though he feels like they probably won't really be able to go back to the same friendship they had before. Somehow, Theo feels like he has outgrown it, like he won't be able to take the same, submissive place in it, anymore. Which is a good thing. Most definitely.

Michael sighs and looks over at the clock on the wall.

"Listen, man," he says, turning back to Theo, "I gotta go."

Theo nods.

"Yeah, I've—" he says, sighing with slight irritation ."I've got detention."

Michael presses his lips together, a look of sympathy on his face, and a small trace of the apology he gave a few moments ago, knowing his brother is the reason for Theo's detention.

"That sucks," he says, and Theo half-shrugs.

"It's only today left," he says. "So, it's not that bad."

Michael nods.

"Well, good luck with that," he says, and Theo smiles dryly. "I'll see you around."

"Yeah."

Michael claps his hand on Theo's shoulder, before leaving, and Theo just stands there for a moment. He exhales slowly. He definitely feels lighter than before. It feels good.

Detention is just as boring as ever.

It's Friday by now, and Theo can't quite believe that he has put up with several days of this, already. It's just him and a few other students, none of whom he knows, and after what feels like forever, they're finally released, Theo gathering up his things and heading for the door.

Straight home. He can practically hear his father's reminder from this morning, ringing in his head, and he puts on his jacket as he steps outside. The small group of students who shared his plight in detention mill past him, hurrying down the steps of the school entrance, and Theo shoves his hands in his pockets, eyes cast downward.

It's the sudden whiff of cigarette smoke that makes him look up.

"Took you long enough." Theo feels his heart leap, even before he turns to his right, and sees none other than Max, sitting on top of the small stone wall, next to the school steps. His legs are crossed, indian-style, a lit cigarette in his hand, and he tilts his head as Theo spots him.

"Well, sorry about that," Theo says dryly, and Max smiles. "You know, it's kinda creepy, you lurking in the shadows, like that."

The words aren't entirely unfounded; it's already dark outside, and Max's black outfit makes him nearly invisible against the backdrop of bushes.

"I'm not lurking," Max says, grinding out his cigarette against the stone surface, beside him.

"No?" Theo asks, and he can't help but smile slightly.

"No," Max confirms, getting up from where he sits and placing himself at full height, right in front of Theo. "It's called being stealthy."

Theo raises his eyebrows, amusedly.

"Stealthy?"

"Yeah," Max says, moving closer and slipping his hands around Theo's waist. "Like a ninja."

Theo laughs.

"Fair enough," he says, placing his hands on Max's hips, automatically pulling him closer, so that their faces are only inches apart. "Or a vampire."

Max makes a face.

"Vampire is too obvious," he says. "Not to mention overused."

He smiles mischievously, leaning in closer.

"And besides," he says, voice slightly lower. "If I wanted to bite you, I wouldn't have to lurk in the shadows to do it, anyway."

He moves in and places a soft kiss against Theo's throat, just below his jaw, and Theo automatically sucks in a sharp breath.

"I thought you said you were stealthy," he says, voice lowered to match Max's. "Not lurking."

Max practically purrs against his skin.

"Same difference."

Theo huffs out a small chuckle, but then Max nips at neck ever so softly, and he actually closes his eyes for a moment.

"Okay," he says breathlessly, surprised at his lack of voice-control; it's amazing what Max's touch does to him. "Maybe not the right place for this."

Max groans and pulls away.

"Well, can you blame me?" he says, moving one hand up to pull his fingers through Theo's hair. "I feel like I haven't seen you in ages."

He kisses him then, softly, slowly.

"It's been ages," he says, voice low and hoarse, making Theo shiver. "And let's just say that thinking about you in the shower doesn't quite cut it, anymore."

Theo closes his eyes again, firming his grip on Max's hips. It's weird how he used to get so extremely uncomfortable when Max said stuff like that, back when they had just started seeing each other. Sure, he still gets pretty uncomfortable, but the way Max's words would turn him on something fierce, even back then, has since kind of become the dominant sensation, and instead of making him blush and fumble and look away, it makes his entire body heat up.

Theo swallows.

"You can't just say stuff like that," he murmurs against Max's mouth, and he hears Max hum in thought.

"Why not?" he says. "Because it makes you uncomfortable?"

"Because it turns me on."

Max actually pauses a little bit then, even pulls away the slightest inch, and Theo opens his eyes, suddenly afraid he's said something too weird. But then, Max smiles wickedly.

"Well, fuck," he says, his voice low. "Now I really wanna bite you."

He kisses him again, slowly.

"Or, you know," he breathes. "Whatever you want."

Theo takes a deep breath.

"Now's really not the time," he says, trying to will himself to pull away from those wonderful lips, with that hard, metal piercing.

"I really don't care," Max murmurs back, kissing him deeper, and Theo loses his breath for a second. And then he gets it back.

"No," he says, pulling away and shaking his head. "Probably not the best idea."

He can't help but glance up at the school, which is virtually empty now, but still. Max follows his gaze, and sighs.

"Damn it, you're right," he says. Then he turns back to Theo and gives him a quick kiss. "I hate it when you're right."

Theo smiles.

"No, you don't."

And Max smiles back.

"Whatever."

They don't talk more for a few moments. Instead, they just kiss, slowly, keeping it rather chaste and not using any tongue, because Theo honestly feels like he would tackle Max to the ground and mount him, if they did. Which, in itself, is a rather unfamiliar sensation, and one he still hasn't quite gotten used to, yet.

Max has a point, though. It has been ages, and Max isn't the only one who's had to get some kind of tension relief in the shower, every now and then.

"We should go somewhere," Max suddenly says, breaking the kiss, and Theo opens his eyes.

"What?" he says, and Max pulls away a bit, just enough for them to be able to look at each other properly.

"We should go somewhere," he repeats. "Get out of here."

Theo just looks at him.

"Where?"

Max shrugs.

"Anywhere," he says. "Just you and me."

Theo considers that for a moment.

"What, are you serious?" he asks, slightly disbelieving, and Max smirks.

"Dead serious," he says, and Theo just blinks at him.

"What, we're just gonna run off together into the sunset?" he asks dryly, a tiny smile on his face, and Max chuckles, leaning in and placing a quick kiss on his lips.

"That's one way of putting it," he says. "But I was thinking on a more temporary basis. And probably not as ambitious."

Theo narrows his eyes at him, undeniably getting pulled into Max's enthusiasm.

"Like, how?" he says, and Max tilts his head, thinking.

"No idea," he says. "I just need to get out of here."

He kisses Theo again, slower, this time.

"*We* need to get out of here," he says. "If just for a little while."

Theo just looks at him, and after a few seconds, he smiles. He can't help it.

"Well, what did you have in mind?" he asks, leaning closer to Max, who smiles back at him, in that way of his that makes him look like an angel who's been kicked out of heaven. He hums in thought.

"Well," he says. "First off, let's leave here."

Theo raises his eyebrows at him.

"Oh, we're doing this right now?" he says, and Max answers by taking his hand and lacing their fingers together.

"Now's a good a time as any," he says, cocking one pierced eyebrow, and Theo glances up at the school. He should be going home, *straight home*. His parents are pissed and paranoid as it is, and doing anything else than simply going straight home, right now, is not very wise. It's a stupid idea, one bound to get them into trouble, and Theo and Max both know that. Theo definitely knows that.

But somehow he can't think of a single valid reason not to do it, anyway. He looks back at Max.

"Then, let's go."

Max says nothing, only smiles wider, and Theo feels like he would go with him anywhere. He probably would, and for a moment, there isn't the slightest trace of regret, as Max pulls him along with him, leaving the school.

CHAPTER 16
SNOW

"So, where to?" Theo asks, as he and Max make their way along the street.

It's been about fifteen minutes since they left the school, and so far, all they've really done is talk, while walking along, occasionally stopping to pull each other into a spontaneous kiss. It makes Theo feel a bit silly, to be honest, which both he and Max have pointed out a couple of times, so far, but he has decided that he doesn't really care. He has just missed Max so much, these past several days, and he doesn't care if he's being sappy and ridiculous.

"I don't know," Max says, as they reach the park, which is only a few blocks away from the high school. "Didn't really think that far."

Theo cocks his head.

"Well," he says. "I'm fresh out of ideas. We should probably go somewhere, though, it's getting really cold."

It's true; it's colder than it has been in a while, and although Theo loves simply walking here, with Max, the weather will sadly be keeping them from staying out here for too long. And he has no idea what Max had in mind for them to do, or where to go.

"Yeah," Max says, huddling up slightly. "You've got a point."

They enter the park, which isn't very big, but big enough to have an abundance of large trees and several winding, graveled paths, all lined with old-fashioned, wrought-iron streetlamps. It's really cozy, actually, and Theo squeezes Max's hand, as he holds it in his own.

"Well," Theo says. "Why can't we just go back your house?"

Max makes a face, looking a bit uncomfortable.

"Nah," he says. "My parents are home, for once. So, maybe not a good idea."

Theo takes a moment to register that.

"Why not?" he asks, a bit hesitantly, and Max glances at him, a bit sheepishly.

"They, uh..." he starts, clearing his throat a bit. "They don't exactly *know* about you."

Theo blinks, and actually stops dead, making Max almost stumble for a moment, as their hands are locked together.

"What?" Theo says, and Max gets the tiniest hint of anxiety in his eyes, at Theo's expression.

"It's not like that," he says hastily. "I haven't kept it a secret, or anything, I would never do that. And they wouldn't mind, I'm sure of it."

He glances at the ground.

"It just... hasn't come up," he says. "And they haven't asked. So... They don't know."

Theo frowns, trying to wrap his head around this.

"I thought they didn't care what you did," he says slowly.

"They don't," Max confirms, sounding almost a bit sad, looking back up. "And like I said, they wouldn't mind. That's not really the issue. I mean, they've sorta met guys I've been with, before."

He adds that last part with some obvious reluctance, and Theo valiantly tries to ignore the way the thought of Max being with anyone else makes his insides twist uncomfortably. It's not like he doesn't know, though; Max is way more experienced with stuff like that, and Theo has never been under the illusion of anything different. That kind of shallow dynamic was the one even their relationship had at the start, after all.

"Then, why—" he starts, hesitantly, but Max cuts him off.

"Why is taking you home to meet them such a big deal?" he finishes, eyebrows slightly raised, and Theo half-nods in confirmation. And Max sighs. He practically fidgets, glances away, searching for the right words.

"Because it's you," he finally says, black-lined eyes looking back at Theo. "Because you're not like anyone I've met, before. You're not just some guy, you're—"

He takes a deep breath, clearly awkward about explaining this.

"You're *you*," he says dumbly, gesturing at him vaguely. "You're important. And just dragging you home when they're there, just like that, like you're just anybody... It doesn't feel right. Can't really explain it. I just wanna do it right, I guess."

Max looks down at the ground, scuffs at the asphalt with his boot, in an uncharacteristically awkward and timid gesture.

"So," he practically mumbles, "it is a big deal."

He looks up at Theo, almost hesitantly.

"It's a big deal," he says awkwardly, half-shrugging, "because you're a big deal. To me, at least."

Theo doesn't answer him. Max usually has a way with words, but occasionally, like this time, he falls a bit short, and Theo is glad he knows him well enough to interpret what he's trying to say, correctly. He knows what Max means. He just doesn't know how to react to it.

So instead, he just stands there, staring, completely dumbfounded, as Max looks at him, waiting for him to speak. But he doesn't. For several seconds, there's nothing but silence between them, and finally, as usual, it seems to get the better of Max, who clearly isn't accustomed to tense, emotional silence.

"Okay," he says, nodding, trying to sound like his normal, casual self, and almost succeeding. "That was... Yeah."

He presses his lips together, suddenly unbearably awkward, and Theo finally snaps out of it.

"I'm sorry," he mutters, shaking his head, as though to shake off the daze. "I'm sorry, it's just... No one's ever said something like that to me, before. I just need a minute to... to *process*."

He does some awkward gesture trying to illustrate this, which looks ridiculous and ends up making him feel stupid, more than anything.

Max nods. He takes a deep breath, as though he's relieved, and another few seconds pass, without either of them saying anything, and Theo just looks at Max, takes in his face and his features. He has noticed how those dark blue eyes look almost scared, sometimes, when Max tells him something like this. It makes him feel oddly sad, and strangely protective.

"It's okay," Theo eventually says, in lack of anything else, moving one hand up to push that black hair back from Max's forehead. It's a tender gesture that he only dares to use, because Max has done it, in the past. And the way Max almost leans into the touch, ever so slightly, somehow makes his heart ache.

"It's fine." Theo gives him a small smile. "I get it."

He plants a soft kiss on Max's lips.

"And you're important, too," he says, voice low. "You're a big deal."

Max quirks a small smile.

"This is getting way too cheesy," he says, and Theo chuckles, rather than taking offense at Max's well-developed defense mechanism.

"You started it," Theo retorts softly. "And it had to be said."

Max's smile widens, and he scoffs.

"Fair enough."

Neither of them speaks for a few seconds, and they just look at each other, unblinking. Then Max tilts his head a bit.

"I love you." He says it easily, effortlessly, without even blinking, and it makes Theo's heart do a backflip.

"I love you, too," he says, and he could have sworn that Max's heart just did a backflip, as well, at least judging from his expression.

Then, Max clears his throat, breaking the moment.

"Alright, then," he says, turning away and taking a few steps. "Onward."

Theo frowns slightly, still a small smile on his face.

"You know," he says, catching up to Max, "eventually, you're gonna have to do that with a straight face."

Max looks at him, and Theo gives him a look that shows he's only teasing, which makes Max half-smile, almost self-consciously.

"Yeah, well," he says. "I haven't actually said that before."

"Really?" Theo sounds softly disbelieving, and Max half-shrugs.

"Not to anyone but you," he says. "And, to be honest, it freaks me out a bit."

He looks at Theo pointedly.

"So, I'm sorry if saying it takes a little getting used to." He glances down at Theo's hand, entwined with his own, before looking back up at him. "I do love you, though. No question, there."

Theo smiles, actually blushing slightly against the cold, as Max looks straight ahead. It's kind of adorable how he gets so flustered by this. Cool, sure and confident Max. Theo can't help but feel slightly amused by it. And moved, simply because Max is doing it for him, *because* of him.

Theo leans in and kisses him on the cheek, and Max glances at him.

"Then that's good enough for me," Theo says, half-seriously, and Max quirks a small smile.

"Well, good," he says, raising his eyebrows. "Or else I'd have to do all kinds of shit to prove it."

"Like, what?" Theo asks, and Max shrugs, sighing in thought.

"Something rash," he finally says, melodramatically. "Like climb a mountain, or rob a bank."

Theo laughs.

"Well, I'm flattered," he says, with the same joking severity, masking his awkward, actual sensation of feeling flattered. "But bank robbing *is* illegal, and I'm afraid we don't really have any mountains, around here."

Max pulls back indignantly.

"Ye of little faith," he says. Then he looks around, spotting the large statue that's planted in the middle of the park, as they're just walking past it.

It's a piece that some obscure artist made a few years back, with some abstract-looking chunk of rock at the top. There are three stone plateaus leading up to it, fenced off at the bottom by a black railing, and the plateaus serve as giant steps, with water running down them from the top, in the summer. Right now, though, the statue is nothing but a large slab of rock on a pedestal, according to Theo, and he has never quite understood the appeal of it.

"How about that, then?" Max says, pointing at it, and Theo frowns, looking up at the looming landmark.

"What about it?" he asks, and Max looks at him.

"I'd climb that," he clarifies. "Seeing as how there are no mountains."

Theo chuckles.

"Alright," he says, nodding. "Sure."

Max raises his eyebrows at him.

"What," he says, "you don't think I'd do it?"

"That's not what I said," Theo points out softly.

"Oh, but I think it is." Max narrows his eyes, taking a step back and letting go of Theo's hand. "I know what I heard."

He actually takes a few steps backwards, then, before suddenly turning around and grabbing hold of the railing, and Theo starts in surprise.

"What are you doing?" he says, and watches as Max, with surprising agility, heaves himself up onto the first stone platform.

212

"I know what I heard," Max repeats, straightening slightly as he climbs up onto the next level. "And it sounded like a challenge."

Theo frowns, mouth half-open, as his eyes follow Max's ascent.

"What?" he says. "It was not a challenge."

Max reaches the top platform, stands up right in front of the giant rock, and dramatically turns around to point down at Theo.

"It was a challenge, good sir!" he exclaims, lowering that already unusually low and gravelly voice, for dramatic effect.

"It really wasn't," Theo says, a mix of exasperation and annoyed affection both in his voice and on his face. He even smiles a bit. "Come on, get down from there."

"You know," Max says, ignoring him and looking around from his vantage point. "This is actually kind of anticlimactic. Doesn't feel nearly as impressive, from up here."

Theo glances around; the park is virtually empty, except for a few people walking around.

"Yeah, okay," Theo says, looking back up at Max, who's towering on his stone plateau, several feet up. "Maybe you should come down, then."

Max doesn't answer him, but keeps looking around the park. It's dark and it's cold, but it's still somehow pretty, with the old-fashioned streetlights, and the frost that seems to cover every single fallen leaf and blade of grass. It makes everything sparkle, somehow.

"Nope," Max says after a few moments, still somewhat dramatically. "I'm proving my love."

He looks back down at Theo.

"Or, you know," he says, shrugging, "this lame-ass, thoroughly underwhelming version of it."

He sighs, his breath coming out in puffs of steam. Theo can see it, even from where he's standing.

"Okay," Theo says, "I get it. Your love has been proven. Now, please, come down."

Max frowns, as though thinking, before shaking his head.

213

"No," he says, and Theo sighs. "This needs to be more impressive."

"Like, how?" Theo says, shoving his hands in his pockets, against the cold. Without Max's hand in his, it suddenly feels much colder.

"Fuck, if I know," Max says, shrugging. "Like, fireworks, or lightning. Maybe even a choreographed dance number, performed by pirates. Anything."

Theo sighs, huddling against the cold. He wants to be annoyed with Max, somehow, which he kind of is, at the moment. But he can't help but smile and feel all warm inside, all the same. It's almost enough to warm up his cold-exposed skin. At least, until he feels the uncomfortable sensation of something small and cold against his cheek.

Theo automatically blinks, and brings his hand up touch his face. It's wet, and he frowns, before suddenly noticing the reason behind it, as a small, white snowflake lands on his hand. He looks up.

Max has noticed it, too, and he chuckles, looking up at the black sky.

"Something like that," he says, nodding up at the several tiny specks of white, falling out of the darkness, and Theo watches.

It's snowing. Out of nowhere, there is suddenly an endless amount of white snowflakes, quietly falling to the ground, and Theo chuckles.

"Yeah," he says, still looking up at the sky. "Although, I'm pretty sure you can't take credit for making it snow."

He hears Max make a humming noise, and looks at him. Max's eyes are on him, and they narrow slightly.

"Or can I?" he says, pointing at Theo, and Theo raises his eyebrows.

"No," he says, shaking his head, "you really can't."

Max simply smirks, though, lowering his arm.

"Yup," he says, sounding oddly smug. "I made it snow."

"You didn't make it snow." Theo is kind of amused now, smiling. "Now, come on, get down."

214

Max narrows his eyes at him for a few more moments, before seemingly relenting and climbing off the statue. When he reaches the railing, he smoothly leaps off of it and places himself in front of Theo.

"I made it snow," he says, his voice low, a small smile playing on his lips. "I love you so much, I made it snow."

"Sure you did," Theo says, looking at Max, his smile casually mirroring his. Although, he has a distinct feeling that he can't completely disguise the way his heart does a double-take at Max's words. "I'm very impressed."

Max nods in mock seriousness, and he moves in a bit closer.

"You should be," he says, placing his hands against Theo's waist, and Theo hums in agreement.

"Although," he says, cocking his head a bit, as he takes his hands out of his pockets and moves them up to the back of Max's neck. "With that logic, *I* could be the one who made it snow."

Max frowns.

"Don't steal my thunder," he says in mock offense, shaking his head. "Just let me have this."

Theo scoffs lightly, suddenly grinning.

The snow is falling just a little bit heavier now, and it's just cold enough outside for it to stick to the ground. It may be gone, tomorrow, though, but Theo doesn't care. He doesn't care, because right now, it's all perfect, and tomorrow is an entire night away.

He leans in and kisses Max softly, amazed at how that small action can thrill him so much, every single time, and he sighs heavily, content, as he pulls away. He ruffles some white puffs of snow out of Max's messy, black hair, and smiles.

"Okay."

♦

"It's a motel."

Theo and Max have been wandering around for a bit now, just hanging out, talking, but the cold is starting to get the better of them, and somehow, they've ended up outside a motel. It's not the nasty kind, though, Theo observes. It looks really clean, with more of a hotel-vibe, really. But still.

He's not entirely sure why, but it makes him feel oddly tingly and nervous.

"Yeah," Max says, sounding a bit sheepish. "Must admit, not exactly what I had in mind."

He turns to Theo, then, almost a bit worried.

"We can go somewhere else, if you want," he says hurriedly, knowing full well what a checking into a motel implies, and Theo looks at him. "I'm not trying to steal your virtue, or anything."

He adds that last part with some uncomfortable, dry humor, and Theo chuckles.

"Real smooth," he says, turning back to the building. He can practically feel Max's uncharacteristic tension.

"Seriously, though," Max says. "If you're weirded out by the whole motel-thing, it's fine. We can go someplace else."

"Like, where?" Theo looks at him pointedly, and Max just blinks, considering that for a moment. Then he shrugs.

"No idea," he says. "But a motel kind of screams *cliché* and kills the romance a bit, don't you think?"

Theo considers that, looking down at their entwined hands. It's actually really cold, by now, and his fingers are far past slightly numb. He's entirely sure that Max feels the same, but for some reason, neither of them wants to let go of the other.

"Well," Theo finally says. "We can't go to my house. Can't even go to yours. And unless we want to cut this night short, or spend it at a bus stop, this is our only option."

He looks up at Max, almost tentatively, from under his eyelashes.

"And as far as romance goes," he adds, "I don't really care where I am. As long as you're there."

Max just looks at him for what feels like several seconds, blue eyes slightly stunned and almost dazed, like they sometimes get when he looks at Theo. It makes Theo's heart beat just a little bit faster.

Eventually, though, the still unfamiliar feeling seems to get the better of Max, who cocks his eyebrows, a casual smirk on his face.

"Speaking of *cliché*," he says, and Theo rolls his eyes, smiling, as he looks away.

"I was trying to be smooth," he says dryly, and Max chuckles.

"Oh, you're very smooth," he says, kissing Theo's cheek. "I'm all aflutter."

"Shut up," Theo mumbles, but his heart's not in it, and Max laughs again, moving in a little bit closer.

"You've got a point, though," he says. "And if nothing else, I'm freezing my ass off and would really like to get inside."

Theo glances at him.

"Alright, then," he says. "Let's go inside."

It's about as awkward as Theo expected it to be.

The guy at the front desk looks to be in his early twenties, and he raises his eyebrows at the two of them pointedly, when they ask for a room (with a double bed). He doesn't look snide or judgmental, though; it's more of a *nice work, bro*-look, and it makes Theo feel awkward enough to intently look at the flower-patterned, old wallpaper on the opposite wall, rather than straight at the guy. He feels his cheeks heat up, and hopes that they're still flush enough from the cold for him not to notice.

Max, on the other hand, as casually as ever, accepts the keycard and pays for their room, and Theo goes with him as they leave the front desk. The guy leans back in his chair and actually smiles a bit, looking amused, and Theo really tries not to think about it, as he disappears out of sight.

"Well, that was awkward," Theo mutters, mostly to himself, and for a second, he's worried that Max will take offense. But he doesn't. Of course he doesn't.

"Nah," he says, fiddling with the keycard in his hand. "He just knows the main reason two teenagers would check into a motel together."

Theo exhales slowly, glancing up at the ceiling of the hallway.

"Yeah," he says, rather dryly. "Not helping."

Max doesn't answer, only chuckles quietly, as he gives Theo's hand a light squeeze, and soon enough, they've reached their room, which is at the far end of the hall, on the first floor. It's not nearly as tacky as Theo somehow expected; he has never actually spent the night at a motel, before.

There's a big double bed in the middle of the room, a small TV against the opposite wall, and a small, adjoining bathroom, all of which feels very simple, small and underwhelming. It helps ease Theo's nervousness a little bit, somehow.

It' not that late yet, and seeing as how they don't really have anything in particular to do, anyway, they decide to simply wing it.

Theo makes a point to text Riley, since he won't be coming back home tonight. He uses Max's phone, and simply lets Riley know that he's okay and not to worry about him, appreciating the fact that Riley replies simply with an OK rather than a small, precocious lecture on how mad their parents are going to be.

Theo and Max end up going out to get some food, then going to the store to get some snacks, and Theo tries not to glance too long at the condom selection by the counter of the cash register. He's not sure why he does that. Probably for the same reason as he thought about it last time he and Max were about to spend the night together. He can't really shake that thought, especially not when they're spending the night at a *motel*, of all places.

They walk through the cold, back to the motel, hands locked together the whole time. Max smokes a last, evening-cigarette on the way there, and when they arrive inside and make their way past the front desk, the guy behind the counter gives them a nod of recognition, which Max returns with a small salute. When they get back to their room, they end up sitting on the bed, legs

218

crossed, opposite each other, unwrapping the fast food they've bought.

Theo closes his eyes and really savors the bacon cheese burger in his hands, actually letting out a small moan of satisfaction, as he bites into it.

"Whoa, easy there," Max says, and Theo opens his eyes. "I can't handle competition like that."

Theo smiles, still chewing, before he swallows the bite down.

"I don't know, man," he says, cocking his head. "It's a pretty good burger."

Max doesn't say anything, simply smiles. It's a soft smile, a genuinely happy one, and Theo can't help but feel all warm inside, as he sees it.

It's only lately that he has started to realize how Max's smiles really have changed, how his entire expression seems to have changed. Sure, he's still somehow the same bitchy, sarcastic asshole he's always been, but when he's with Theo, that other side comes out, the soft one, the happy one. The one that plants lazy kisses against Theo's throat, when they're close to each other, the one that smiles, instead of just smirking, and the one that likes to snuggle up close, underneath warm covers, when he gets the chance.

That side of Max has come out gradually, and Theo isn't entirely sure that side even properly existed, before, which is somehow a very sad thought.

They don't go outside again, after that. Instead, they just cuddle up on the double bed, watching *Star Wars: Return of the Jedi*, which is the only decent thing on TV at the moment, and share the snacks that they've bought. Eventually, they end up narrating the movie, like a commentary, and it leaves them both in tears from laughing so hard. And the snow falls quietly outside the window, and Theo realizes that he can't think of any place he'd rather be right now, than right here. Right here, in this stupid motel room, watching *Star Wars* on a tiny, crappy TV, eating snacks and laughing, with Max's warm body and soft-smelling skin, only inches away. It's simply all kinds of perfect.

By the time the movie is over, they end up just lying on the bed, on their backs, with mellow music streaming from the tiny speakers on Max's phone, their fingers entwined. Theo looks up at the ceiling. There's a tiny crack, right by the wall, and he studies it for a moment.

"What are your parents like?" he asks, practically out of nowhere, and he feels Max shift slightly, next to him.

"What?" he says, and Theo turns his head to look at him.

"Your parents," he says. "What are they like?"

Max just looks at him, blinks, and then seems to wrap his head around the question.

"They're, uh..." he starts, looking for the words. He frowns. "They're ambitious. I guess that's a word for it."

He looks up at the ceiling.

"They don't really care about stuff that isn't useful." He pauses. "I mean, they probably care about me, they're my parents. But they don't really seem to care about, uh..."

He rolls his tongue piercing between his teeth for a moment, deliberating, a small frown on his face.

"Failure," he finally settles on. "If you don't succeed, you're not really useful, and..."

Max shrugs.

"I think that's why they let me do pretty much whatever I want," he says. "They're never really around. Even when they're at home, and not working, it's like they're not even there. Mostly, they don't really ask me stuff, don't really talk to me about stuff. Except for school, if I do badly, or do well. Then they're all over it."

Theo listens silently, remembers Max mentioning once how his parents really only seem to care about his grades. He also remembers that note he accidentally found in Max's room, when he spent the night there, the one that looked like a torn corner of a math test. It had a nice message from Max's mom on it, and Theo is starting to gather that praise from his parents is something more rare than Max has really let on, before, and that it means more to him than he wants to admit. Why else would anyone keep a note like that?

He doesn't mention it, though. He felt that Max wouldn't want him to know, back then, and he probably still wouldn't want him to.

"So, at least I've got that going for me," Max says, sounding light in the way he tends to do when trying to ease the tension, when things get too emotional or too serious. He turns to look at Theo. "I'm pretty smart."

"Max, you're practically a genius," Theo says, and Max makes a face. It's not the first time Theo has seen him react that way to a compliment on his intelligence, and it still kind of confuses him.

"Thanks," Max says, a bit uncomfortably, glancing away. "I appreciate that. I guess, it just kinda loses its flavor, when it's the only compliment you ever get from your parents."

He looks back at Theo, suddenly.

"Shit," he says, sounding almost appalled. "I didn't mean to put it like that, I'm not trying to be self-pitying, or anything. None of the whole my-parents-don't-love-me-if-I'm-failing-thing, I just—"

"It's fine," Theo interjects. "I wasn't thinking that."

"I just don't wanna be that guy," Max continues. "You know? The poor, pathetic over-achiever—"

"Max." Theo's surprisingly firm tone shuts him up, and they look at each other. "It's fine. That's not what I think about you, I've never thought that about you."

He pauses for a moment, as Max swallows hard.

"I just think it's too bad," Theo finally says, trying to find a good way of putting it. "I mean, you're amazing. And I think it's too bad that there's so much counting on what you do, rather than who you are."

He moves their interlaced hands up to his mouth and kisses the back of Max's hand.

"Because you are awesome," he says, even though that word doesn't quite cut it. "You're amazing, you're... you're just perfect, really."

"I'm really not perfect," Max says, shaking his head, and Theo looks at him.

"Well," he says, "even if you aren't, your lack of perfection makes you perfect."

Max gazes at him for a moment, chewing on his lip. Then he chuckles.

"That doesn't even make sense," he says, shaking his head, and Theo smiles.

"It doesn't have to," he says.

"And it's really cheesy and poetic," Max continues, still shaking his head, and he laughs as Theo nudges him softly.

"I can't help it if I'm eloquent," Theo says. "You're just gonna have to get used to it."

"I'm getting there," Max says, and they just stare at each other for a few seconds. It makes Theo feel slightly ridiculous, and incredibly cliché, but he can't help it.

Eventually, Max sighs, and looks down at their hands.

"You know what," he says, but doesn't wait for Theo's reply. "You're good for me."

Theo doesn't really know what to say to that, but Max saves him the trouble.

"You make me better," he finally says, and Theo blinks.

"Well," he replies then, trying to sound light. "You weren't that bad, to begin with."

Max smiles briefly, humoring him, before turning serious again.

"No, I meant— " he starts, before sighing. "To me."

Theo frowns, and Max looks up at him. He looks a bit unsure, almost scared.

"You make me wanna treat myself better," he says, as though trying to find the right words. "I've never really, um..."

He looks back at their hands, as he absently smoothes over Theo's skin with his thumb, pressing his lips together, considering what to say.

"I've never really cared about myself," he admits, after several seconds of silence. "Never really thought I had to. Didn't really think it was worth it. But... you make me feel like it's worth it."

He looks back at Theo, slowly, hesitantly, and Theo doesn't look away.

"So, I guess," Max says, tentatively, "thanks for that."

Theo doesn't answer him right away, doesn't say anything for several seconds. And Max's expression changes, enhancing that uncertainty again, the one that borders on fear, while Theo just watches. Then, Theo suddenly moves, rolling over and placing himself on top of Max, straddling him. He watches Max's utterly stunned expression, as he leans down and cups his face with both hands, gently smoothing over the fading bruise below his cheekbone, the small cut practically healed.

"It is worth it," he says, his face only inches away from Max's. "*You* are worth it."

He plants a quick kiss on Max's mouth, before pulling away again.

"Don't ever think you're not." He watches Max for a moment, watches those dark blue, slightly widened eyes, those slightly parted lips. He looks surprised, more than anything, and Theo continues, his words slightly rushed. "You're the most amazing person I know, and it kills me that you don't think that about yourself."

Theo takes a deep breath, surprised at his own honesty. He doesn't usually talk like this, not with anyone but Max. And he knows that Max is the same; he would never say these things to anyone else, and he's clearly having a hard enough time saying them to Theo. The whole conversation sounds pretty out of character for both of them, actually, but it's like they've stopped caring; there's no other way of putting any of this, and it needs to be said.

Theo leans down and places his forehead against Max's, inhaling. He closes his eyes, as if that makes this easier to say, for both of them, as if it's not as difficult, if they can't see each other.

"I just—" Theo cuts himself off, hears Max breathe, feels his chest rise and fall underneath him. "I love you so much."

He's shocked as he says it, because he has never said it like that before, with such intensity. But it's completely true, and he needs Max to know that, somehow.

Max doesn't reply right away. Instead, he swallows, moving his hands up to settle on Theo's hips, as though hesitating for a split second. Then, he moves his face up just an inch, just enough for his lips to touch Theo's, and Theo immediately melts into him, reciprocating the kiss.

Max smoothes his hands up over Theo's back, up to his shoulder blades, so he can pull him down to him, pull him closer, and for what feels like several minutes, they just kiss. They kiss, and keep kissing, all warmth and softness and desperate need, but somehow without the urgency Theo has gotten used to. He likes it, though. For once, there's no sex, no desire. Only the need to be close, to touch, and to never, ever let go. He's oddly moved by it, in a way he can't really explain.

"I love you, too." Max's voice is low, slightly thick with what sounds like emotion, and he moves one hand up to smooth over Theo's hair. It's a tender gesture, an affectionate one, and it makes Theo's entire body relax.

"And you're the best thing I've ever had."

CHAPTER 17

HEAT

There are few things in life that feel as amazing as sleeping right next to the one you love.

Theo has learned this, firsthand, and although this is only the second time ever that he has done it, he has already decided that it's one of his favorite things in the entire world.

Max and Theo started dozing off around midnight, lying together on the bed. They then, in some sleepy, fuzzy state, managed to strip down to only their underwear, before curling up underneath the covers to sleep properly, and Theo practically wrapped himself around Max and pressed his body against that warm, partially inked skin.

They both fell asleep almost instantly, and Theo isn't quite sure why he's waking up, now.

It takes him a little while to notice, his head heavy with sleep, and for a few moments, he just lies there, absently touching Max's skin, still not entirely sure if he's awake or dreaming. He doesn't mind, though. He doesn't mind, because whether it's a dream or not, the feeling is simply wonderful.

Max is lying on his side, Theo notices, Theo spooning him, one arm slung over his chest and one leg loosely wedged between his. It's warm and nice, soft and safe, and for a little while, Theo just breathes him in, sleepily inhaling the scent of Max, head still fuzzy and only half-conscious.

Slowly, Theo starts smoothing his hand over Max's bare chest, running his fingers along his collarbone, the hollow of his throat, gently mapping him out with his touch, and he sighs contentedly, nose burrowed into Max's messy hair. He just loves touching him; he can't help it.

It's as if of their own accord that his fingers start moving down along his boyfriend's chest, feeling the outline of his muscles, his bones, fingertips lightly grazing his nipples and smoothing down toward his stomach. Max shifts a little bit, then, and Theo vaguely wonders if he's awake. It's not a very conscious thought, though; Theo is still barely awake, himself.

He moves his fingers toward Max's hand, which is resting against the mattress, and gently strokes his knuckles, softly, slowly, before sliding his palm up along his lower arm. Theo keeps his eyes closed, but he knows the outlines of the tattoos above the elbow, and he automatically traces the skin where he assumes them to be. It's not difficult, after having done it so many times, before.

That's when he feels the hairs rise on Max's arm, prickling under his touch, and Theo inhales deeply, focusing only on that. He still doesn't open his eyes. He doesn't need to. There's only warmth, and skin, and the feeling of those goose bumps underneath his fingers, as he trails softly along Max's arm and up to his shoulder. It makes Theo feel safe and loved, and thrilled, all at the same time, in his sleepy, half-conscious state.

Theo absently moves in closer, presses his chest against Max's tattooed back, feels the heat of his body, against his own. It's enough to make him inhale deeply, eyes still closed. He still feels as though his hand is moving on its own, mapping out Max's skin with soft, slow tenderness, moving down to his waist.

There is the slightest hint of salt on Theo's lips, as he softly presses them against Max's neck. It's a vague taste of warmth and sweat, but Theo likes it, because it's *Max*, and he does it again, slower this time. He's not sure why; it just comes so naturally to him.

He feels Max shift slightly beside him then, against him, and again, he vaguely wonders if he's awake. It's when he settles his hand on Max's hip that he gets his answer; Max's hand moves up to cover Theo's, slowly lacing their fingers together, and Theo inhales deeply.

Yes, Max seems to be awake.

He doesn't seem to be much more conscious than Theo, though, pressing slightly against him, leaning into his body with his own. It's more of a lazy, languid response, and Theo counters by moving in even closer, pressing down gently on Max's hip, with his hand. It makes Max shift slightly, and Theo inhales sharply, as Max's ass presses up against him. *Damn it.* He's not sure if it's because he's still kind of half-asleep, but suddenly, Theo is acutely aware of a very different sensation, one decidedly more intense than the soft, lazy one from a moment ago.

It somehow feels inappropriate. He can't help thinking that, as the pressure of his hand on Max's hip increases just the slightest bit. It somehow feels inappropriate, to lie here, pressing up against Max, when they both seem to be only half-awake, and Theo swallows hard, trying to ignore the way that warmth starts pooling in his stomach, blood rushing downward. He can't do this, just like that, press up against Max, while suddenly imagining all kinds of scenarios in his head. No, he can't do that.

Apparently, though, Theo's body doesn't care, because that's exactly what he's doing.

He's barely aware of his own breath becoming slightly heavier, as he places a slow, open-mouthed kiss against Max's neck. He barely registers how he's suddenly pressing against Max's ass, so slowly and purposefully, boxers straining over his hard-on, and how his hand moves down to trail along the hem of Max's underwear. It just happens, and he hardly has to think about it.

Theo is very aware, though, of the way Max responds.

It's the moan that does it. Just a small hint of one, more of a heavy exhale, but it's enough to make Theo tense up and press more firmly against him. He's certain Max can feel it now, that hardness grinding into his ass, and as Theo trails his hand over Max's lower abdomen, Max grips his hand tighter, fingers still entwined. He slowly steers Theo's hand downward, over the hem of his boxers, and when Theo feels the bulge underneath that thin fabric, he exhales sharply, nuzzling his face against Max's neck.

Max is most definitely awake. He's hard, aroused and eager, and he's hard because of *Theo*, which is somehow more than Theo can handle.

It doesn't take much more than that. Theo starts massaging Max through his underwear, Max's hand still on top of his, which somehow makes it even hotter, especially when Max starts moaning, and emitting low, deep groans from the back of his throat. Theo presses against him harder, grinding into his ass, and he can practically hear his own heartbeat, as he kisses Max's neck, slowly, nipping the skin gently with his teeth. It's so surreal, somehow, like he's still caught in some kind of amazing dream. Everything is heightened, every sense acute, every nerve ending seemingly buzzing with activity.

Max doesn't stop him when he slips his hand in underneath his boxers and wraps his fingers around him. Instead, he bites out a rather loud moan, equal parts surprised and pleased, and moves his hand to Theo's hip, behind him. He moves back against him, pressing and grinding, and Theo grits his teeth, leaning his forehead against Max's shoulder. He can't take this. Everything is burning, building, charged with the memory of every moment that he *hasn't* been able to be with Max, to touch him, for these past several days, and he can't really think straight.

Theo is completely certain that he could come right now, just from pressing against Max and hearing him moan, as he strokes him. It would do the trick, no doubt about it.

But it wouldn't be enough. It wouldn't be enough, and for once, Theo wants more. So much more.

He takes his hand out of Max's underwear, but barely has to say or do anything, for Max to take the hint. Instead, he just pauses for a moment, as Max awkwardly turns around in his arms, so that they face each other. Theo opens his eyes then, finally, but finds that it's too dark to make out Max's face properly.

Not that it matters. It doesn't matter, because as soon as he realizes that those lips are just inches away from his own, he launches forward, claiming them, and Max reciprocates with such eagerness that it makes his head spin.

Suddenly, Max's hands are everywhere. They smooth over Theo's arms, his neck, down over his back and his hips, before grabbing his ass and pulling him closer. Max starts moving against him roughly, drawing a deep moan from Theo, who tries to keep himself from losing control. He's not used to losing control, and he's not sure how to handle it.

But the way Max bites his lip and claims his mouth with that wonderful, pierced tongue, and the way he makes sounds that are simply obscene, is enough to make Theo momentarily forget all about control and trying to keep it. Instead, it makes him brave, makes him bold, and he slips his hand underneath Max's boxers, tugging at them slightly, groaning deeply, relishing the way Max is just as hard as he is.

Max tenses up slightly, sucking in a sharp breath.

"What's gotten into you?" he asks, breathing heavily, voice rough from sleep. It's the first thing either of them has said, since this whole thing started.

Theo lets out something like a growl, planting hard, searing kisses against Max's throat, sucking marks into his neck, pressing him closer, grinding against him, skin burning and heart pounding.

"Want you." The words come out in a breath, almost unintentionally, but as Theo says them, he knows it's all he can really think right now, anyway. "I want you, Max."

He has never said anything like that, before, has never really *felt* anything like that before, not like this, and the response in Max is immediate. He lets out a heavy moan of surprised pleasure, as though his entire physical being has some kind of profound reaction to those words, and his grip on Theo tightens.

"Fuck," he breathes, sounding completely wrecked. "Jesus christ."

He grabs onto Theo's hair then, keeps his head in place so that he can kiss him, pulling at his bottom lip with his teeth and plundering his mouth with his tongue, and Theo lets him. He lets him take control, lets him push, and Theo ends up on his back, Max straddling him and grinding down against him. He lets him take his wrists and push them down into the mattress, lets him kiss his throat and bite his neck, smoothing over the sensitive skin with his tongue. He lets him take him over completely, because it's all he wants, right now. Somehow, it's all he has ever wanted.

Everything is suddenly a blur, a dream-like, intoxicated haze of warm mouths and hot skin, hands everywhere and filthy moans filling the dark silence of the room. Theo slips his hands underneath Max's boxers, grabbing his ass and pushing him down against him, making Max groan loudly, eventually taking those boxers off, completely. Theo's follow within seconds, ending up somewhere on the floor, and before he knows it, Max is moving down along his naked body, planting slow, open-mouthed kisses along his chest and his stomach. He makes his way even further down, and Theo lets out a low groan, as Max's sure fingers wrap around him, making him close his eyes again.

Somehow, he's not surprised when he feels Max's wicked, wonderful mouth swallow him down, but he still emits a strangled moan that sounds dirtier than he's used to, and he instinctively grips the sheets as tightly as he can.

Holy shit.

It's not like last time, like the first time. Maybe it's simply because Theo isn't nervous, this time, or maybe because he knows what to expect. Either way, it's simply *better.* It's better, which in itself is shocking, because he honestly hadn't thought it *could* be, and he barely hesitates, digging his fingers into Max's hair. He doesn't push, instead simply does it to somehow ground himself, as Max takes him apart with nothing but his mouth, and Theo uses every ounce of restraint he has to not thrust up into that warm, wet heat.

He's already getting close. He's already getting so close, but as he feels it, he suddenly decides he doesn't want it. He doesn't want to come. Not yet.

"Wait," Theo breathes, barely able to articulate, and he tugs gently on Max's hair, making him stop what he's doing. He looks up at Theo, who meets his gaze.

"What is it?" Max asks, clearly confused and impatient, with a hint of worry.

Theo licks his lips. He's not sure how to answer, how to put it, so he simply tugs on Max's hair again, softly, just enough to make him take the hint and move back up along his body. As soon as he's close enough, Theo pulls him down into a kiss, and when they pull apart, Max frowns slightly.

"You okay?" he says, glancing down at Theo's body, a hint of concern in those dark blue eyes. For a moment, Theo doesn't understand why he's asking, but then he notices that he's actually *shaking,* if only just a little bit.

"I'm fine," he says, kissing Max again. "I'm good."

"Really?"

Theo licks his lips again, trying to find the words.

"I want—" he starts, but cuts himself off and swallows nervously. "I want to."

Max just looks at him, lips slightly parted, eyes still hungry, but also confused. Theo sighs, almost frustratingly, placing his hand against Max's lower back and pulling him down against him, making them both wince at the unabashed skin-on-skin contact. His other hand is still in Max's hair, and as he pulls him closer, he's acutely aware of the both of them breathing heavier, automatically moving slightly against each other, rutting and grinding.

"I want to," Theo repeats, breath catching slightly at the sensation of Max's hardness against his own, the skin there still wet from that wicked mouth. "I want *you*."

He looks at Max pointedly, and finally, Max seems to catch on. He blinks.

"You sure?" he asks, the soft concern in his voice blatantly pierced by something that sounds like excited hunger, and Theo nods.

"Yeah," he says, pulling Max into a slow, hot kiss. "Yeah, I'm sure."

Theo feels slightly out of it for a few moments, after that. He just feels high, somehow, and it's only made more acute with the realization that they're really going to do this. They're *actually* going to do this, that even though they've done so much else, by now, it still feels like a big deal.

It shouldn't be a big deal, Theo thinks, *but it is*. It's a huge deal, to him it is, and it's actually going to happen. It makes him feel excited and terrified, all at once, like he so often seems to feel, where Max is concerned.

It's after only a few seconds of rather intense making out, that something occurs to Theo, and he pulls away the slightest bit.

"Do you have...?" he asks, hesitantly and a bit awkwardly, trailing off. It only takes about a second for Max to catch on, though, and he gets a rather sheepish look.

"Actually," he says, "I do."

He leans over the bed's edge to retrieve his wallet from the back pocket of his pants, and Theo raises his eyebrows slightly in curiosity, as Max extracts a condom from it.

"I'm not a presumptuous dick, or anything," Max says, voice a bit subdued. "It's just... habit."

He gives Theo a glance, looking almost apologetic, but Theo simply tells himself that it's nothing new. He has known, from the moment he and Max started seeing each other, that Max has been rather busy, when it comes to stuff like this, and that Theo is by far the first guy he has been with. In other words, Max is bound to be prepared.

But Theo doesn't really reply. Instead, he tries to convey it through a look, and watches as Max gets a small, single-use packet of lube from his wallet, as well. Those blue eyes look oddly self-conscious, underneath the obvious arousal.

"Sorry," Max says, throwing away the wallet and putting the condom and lube on the small bedside table. "I hope it's not weird, or anything, I just—"

Theo grabs onto him then and rams their mouths together, effectively silencing him, and when he pulls away, Max looks simply stunned.

"You need to shut up," Theo says softly, his entire body buzzing with impatience. "Right now."

Max doesn't need telling twice. He just looks at Theo like he's somehow seeing him for the first time, like he's nothing short of an epiphany, and the way he kisses him then is enough to make Theo's head spin. He suddenly feels impatient, wants to expedite things, but Max holds him at bay.

"This might take a while," he says, trying to talk normally, while breathing heavily and squirming against the way Theo places open-mouthed kisses against his throat.

"Uh-huh," Theo murmurs absently against his skin, and Max exhales, clearly trying to focus.

"Yeah," he says. "Don't wanna rush it, or it might not work out."

"I don't care," Theo murmurs, kissing his mouth, and Max groans.

"Yes, you do," he says. "Trust me."

He moves one hand up to card his fingers through Theo's hair, which is already slightly damp with sweat.

"And I really don't want to hurt you," he says, slightly softer than a moment ago. "So, we're taking our time. Okay?"

Theo looks up at him, swallows hard, and then nods.

"Okay," he agrees, leaving the matter in Max's much more capable and experienced hands. "I trust you."

Max's blue eyes seem to soften at that, and he leans his forehead against Theo's for a moment, exhaling. He doesn't say anything, doesn't need to. They both know where they stand, here.

Theo watches with some kind of apprehensive fascination, as Max tears open the small packet of lube, watches as he squeezes some into his hand. Max then locks his eyes with Theo's and moves his hand far downward, the other hand nudging at Theo's legs a bit, urging Theo to spread them wide. And he leans in and kisses Theo on the mouth, making him almost completely relax, and sigh against him, while he slowly, carefully, slides a finger inside.

Theo feels his whole body react, tenses up automatically at the unfamiliar sensation. It feels weird, at first, but as Max keeps kissing him, and starts slowly moving his finger, in and out, Theo gradually, eventually, starts to relax again. It's not exactly a downside, when Max leans down and kisses his throat, slowly trailing up along the base of his jaw, the shell of his ear, breathing heavily and making small, somehow comforting noises. Theo isn't sure why, but it really helps, and he closes his eyes, smoothing his hands along Max's tattooed arms, trying to ground himself.

This is Max. This is *Max*, and that fact alone makes everything else irrelevant, enough to make Theo simply become pliant underneath him.

It's after what feels like several minutes, that Theo starts clinging to Max desperately, moaning and panting with pleasure, as Max's slowly added fingers move inside him, eager, yet simultaneously soft and patient, in their persuasion. It honestly doesn't even feel weird anymore; by now, it just feels *good. Really* good.

Why haven't we done this before? Theo absently wonders. Seriously, why have they been putting this off for so long?

Minutes pass, and Theo keeps his eyes closed, trying to even out his breathing, but it's virtually impossible. All he can really feel is Max, touching him and kissing him, his fingers moving inside him and making Theo squirm and moan in a frankly undignified way. But he's barely present enough to care. This just feels *so* good, so amazing, and he doesn't care.

"Ready?" Max's voice is only a whisper, heavy and almost panting, right by his ear, and Theo swallows hard. He opens his eyes and finds Max's blue ones, looking right at him. He nods.

"Yeah," he breathes, trying to string together a coherent word, just barely succeeding, and Max just looks at him, before nodding in response. He looks hungry. Excited, high, even slightly concerned, but most of all, hungry, and it does things to Theo that he barely knows how to deal with.

Theo absently moans in something like disappointment, as Max's fingers pull out of him, and he watches as Max gets the condom from the bedside table, keeps his eyes focused on him, as he tears open the wrapping with his teeth. And Theo doesn't look away, doesn't shy away from the sight of Max putting the condom on, as he kneels between Theo's spread legs. He doesn't look away, because for once, it doesn't feel awkward or embarrassing, but rather arousing as hell, and as though Max notices, he puts the condom on slowly, deliberately, taking his time. When Theo looks up at him, those intense, blue eyes meet his, and *damn*, he's not sure how much more of this he can take.

Max squeezes out the last of the lube into his hand, and then keeps his eyes focused on Theo's as he moves his hand back downward. Slowly, he slides his fingers inside again, making Theo arch his hips and inhale sharply, biting down hard. But he doesn't look away, not once, and Max uses his other hand to hoist Theo's hips up the slightest bit, while he moves his fingers inside him, rubbing and loosening up, making Theo squirm underneath him.

"Theo," Max says, his voice just above a rough whisper, as he leans down so that their faces are mere inches apart. "I don't want to hurt you."

Theo doesn't know what to say to that. He's too busy trying to control himself and simply keep breathing.

"You know that," Max continues, his voice oddly firm and soft, at the same time. He sounds completely sure, and as he speaks, Theo suddenly feels those fingers hit a spot that makes him widen his eyes and bite out a loud moan, feeling jolts of pleasure shoot through seemingly every nerve in his body. Max seems unfazed, although Theo can tell how those blue eyes are suddenly burning, Max relishing the way he's making Theo come undone.

"I don't want to hurt you," Max repeats calmly, while Theo squirms pointlessly against him, trying to make any kind of sound that doesn't sound like a whimper. "So if you're uncomfortable in any way, and you wanna stop, you just say the word. Okay?"

Theo swallows hard, squeezing his eyes shut. He can barely hear what Max is saying; he's too wrapped up in this, too wrapped up in the way he suddenly wants nothing more than to feel Max inside him, *properly*, so much so that he's somehow lost on how Max slowly pulls out his fingers.

"Theo," Max says firmly, voice now heavy with desire. "Okay?"

Theo forces his eyes open then, and he nods.

"Okay," he says, breathlessly and barely audibly, and Max tilts his head a bit, as he looks down at him. There's something familiar in those eyes, something raw and predatory, and Theo realizes where he has seen it before. It's the way Max used to look at him, back when they first started seeing each other, and more than anything, he finds that it makes him harder and more turned-on than ever, which somehow surprises him.

Theo's eyes are locked on Max's blue ones. They don't falter for a moment, Theo's hands absently moving up to those partly tattooed shoulders, as Max moves closer and then slowly pushes in.

It only burns a little bit, less than Theo somehow expected it to, but it's enough to make him groan loudly and tighten his grip on Max's shoulders, and he swears he can feel Max's entire body *shudder*. For a second, Max pauses, as though to collect himself, before slowly pulling out and easing back in, carefully, taking his time. When he finally bottoms out, the moan that emits from his throat is enough to make Theo grit his teeth in some kind of tense, impatient pleasure. He closes his eyes for a moment, breathing deeply, shakily, and when he opens his eyes again, he can see, despite the darkness, that Max looks completely wrecked.

Those dark blue eyes are soft, but burning, and Theo can see the question in them; *Is this okay?* And so he nods, hoping Max can tell just how much he means that. Apparently, he can, because he starts moving then, thrusting slowly, and Theo finds himself moaning along with the movements, gripping Max's shoulders tightly.

He tries to keep his eyes open. He wants to watch those blue eyes, wants to see Max's face and expressions, as he moves into him, breathing heavy and uneven, but he can't. Vision just feels like such a superfluous sense, at the moment, and so he closes his eyes, moving one hand down along Max's back, while the other smoothes over the tattoos on his upper arm.

He can barely think. Everything is suddenly just a haze of heat and warm skin and friction and pleasure, as Max eventually starts moving at a more deliberate, slightly rougher pace. Theo hears downright filthy sounds escaping his own mouth, and Max hears them, as well. Theo can tell by the way he moans and grunts, placing open-mouthed kisses against the skin below Theo's ear, his muscles tensing up and almost shaking.

It did feel a bit weird, at first, Theo must admit, and that much he had kind of expected, to be honest. But any sensation of that has slowly been replaced by what he's feeling right now, this unrelenting, consuming thing that leaves him completely lost.

Theo can soon tell by the way Max starts breathing raggedly that he's getting close, that he's close to the edge and that Theo is the reason. It's enough to make Theo clench his jaw and tighten his grip on Max's body, gripping his upper arm and pressing against his lower back with his hand. He's vaguely aware of Max almost flinching slightly, but he doesn't make much of it. He can't, he's too distracted to.

Theo shifts slightly, hears Max groan at the unexpected friction, and suddenly, everything is on fire. Theo's skin burns, tingles, *crackles*, and he grips Max's arm tighter. This time, he can hear Max suck in a sharp breath through his teeth, but he doesn't slow down. Instead, Max burrows his face against Theo's neck, as he smoothes down over Theo's chest and slowly takes him in his hand, stroking him, along with his thrusts. It's like a shot of adrenaline, and Theo is just completely gone.

He moans against Max's shoulder, squeezes his eyes shut, his grip on that tattooed upper-arm suddenly vice-like, and he moves his other hand up over Max's back. He presses his lower arm across his shoulder blades, across the top of those inked wings, and pulls downward, roughly, enough to make Max bite out a surprised, strangled groan. But he keeps going, keeps thrusting, keeps stroking, and Theo feels like he wants to say something, but he knows that it would somehow break the spell. Instead, he only breathes erratically, his deep, groaning moans quickly dissolving into noises that sound more like embarrassing, desperate *whimpers*, and he tries to keep it together. But it's difficult, and he's so, *so* close.

He doesn't have to keep it together, though, not for long. He doesn't have to, because suddenly, he's tumbling over the edge, skin burning and body tensing up, and Max's mouth is on his, hungry and yearning and wonderful, and Theo just lets it happen, a strangled moan escaping him, as he feels that blissful, white-hot release. And Max thrusts a few more times, eagerly, before going rigid, groaning against Theo's lips, and Theo tightens his grip on him, as if by reflex. Max's groan turns into one that sounds almost pained, then, but it's over in a matter of seconds, and they both slowly, gradually, come back down from their climax.

Theo is panting, head spinning and ears ringing, and he feels somehow disoriented from the onslaught of sensation; he swears his hands felt like they went numb, at some point.

Max moves his hand back up, and places it against the mattress, next to Theo, before burrowing his face back into the crook of Theo's shoulder, breathing heavily. And Theo just stares at the ceiling for several seconds, swallowing dryly. He feels like he might pass out, and he's slowly becoming more aware of the uncomfortable stickiness on his stomach. He doesn't even feel grossed out, though; he's too blissed out to, anyway.

It's a while before either of them speaks, and it's Max who does.

"Shit," he pants against Theo's neck and into the fluffy softness of the pillow. He sounds completely exhausted and somehow confused. "You're stronger than you look."

Theo frowns.

"What?" he says, breathlessly, and Max lifts his head to look at him. He raises his eyebrows tiredly.

"What," he says, practically panting. "You didn't notice grabbing me like you were trying to snap my arm in half? Or apparently trying to break my spine?"

Theo just looks at him, surprised. He knows Max is exaggerating, but still. It suddenly hits him that Max actually *was* flinching and groaning slightly in pain, before.

"Not really," Theo finally musters, hesitantly, with a tiny hint of guilt, and Max rolls his eyes. Then he smiles, though, and actually huffs a laugh.

"Yeah, well," he says, moving one hand up to pull his fingers through Theo's sweat-damp hair. "I think this was worth a few bruises."

He plants a quick kiss on Theo's mouth.

"Actually," he adds breathlessly, cocking his head. "I'm completely sure it was."

Theo smiles softly, and lets out a heavy, deep sigh, trying to slow down his frantic heartbeat.

"Well," he says. "I'm sorry. Didn't mean to."

Max groans and kisses him again.

"Don't be sorry," he says against his lips. "Ever."

Theo kisses him back, smoothes his hands up along that tattooed back, with deliberate softness, this time. He supposes he is rather strong; he just never really uses it outside a gym, and he's sorry to apparently have used it on Max.

He couldn't help it, though. The pleasure was simply incomprehensible, and he didn't know what else to do, than to just cling to Max and never let him go.

They lie like that for a another minute or so, before eventually going to get cleaned up, and then crawling back into bed, still somewhat exhausted. Theo lies down on his back, spread out across the sheets, and Max lies down next to him. They both just stare up at the ceiling for several seconds, neither of them speaking. The only source of light is the small lamp they just lit, on a bedside table, since it's still pitch black, outside. It's just past three a.m.; Theo checked.

"Well, that was awesome," Max eventually says, sounding slightly breathless, and Theo lets out a heavy, very content sigh.

"Yeah," he says, and Max looks down and takes Theo's hand in his own.

"You know," he says, lacing their fingers together and then unlacing them, smoothing his fingertips along Theo's knuckles and joints, mapping out his skin. "This probably makes me sound like a total douchebag... But *man*, I've wanted to do that since the first time I kissed you."

Theo hums in acknowledgement.

"Yeah, I remember," he says, a lazy, satisfied edge to his voice, as Max lightly entwines their fingers again. "You wanted to *fuck me senseless.*"

Max actually snorts in surprise.

"Whoa," he says, chuckling, and Theo turns his head to look at him. Those blue eyes are slightly widened, and there's a blatantly amused and impressed look on his face. He smiles. "The f-bomb, Davis? Really?"

Theo smiles back, feeling oddly satisfied at Max's reaction.

"Yeah, well," he says, "after all the time I've spent with you, can you blame me?"

Max makes a non-judgmental face.

"Fuck, no," he says, before cocking his eyebrows. "Out of curiosity, though. Did I succeed?"

Theo gives him a small, half-teasing smile.

"I'd say that you definitely did," he says, and Max looks at him smugly.

"Awesome," he says, eyes on Theo. Then he shakes his head with a sigh and looks up at the ceiling. "Jesus, I feel like I'm just stripping away your innocence."

Theo narrows his eyes at him, even though Max can't see it, and he keeps Max's hand in his own as he moves up so that he's sitting on top of his boyfriend, instead. He leans down and takes both of Max's hands, gently pressing them into the mattress, on either side of Max's head, lacing their fingers together. Max doesn't even look surprised; he just smirks mischievously.

"Yes, you are," Theo says, leaning in so that their faces are only inches apart. "But only because I let you."

He gives Max a quick kiss, one which Max chases after, in a futile attempt to reclaim Theo's mouth.

"And I only let you," Theo continues, "because I *want* you to."

Max raises his eyebrows, smiling slyly.

"Is that so?" he says, and Theo hums in confirmation.

"Yup," he says. "I'm simply using you for my own, nefarious purposes."

Max narrows his eyes, then.

"Well, damn," he says. "And here I thought *I* was the one corrupting *you*."

"Sorry to disappoint," Theo says, leaning down again to kiss him, and Max tightens his grip on Theo's hands slightly.

"Well, I'm not entirely disappointed," he murmurs as they pull apart a fraction of an inch, and Theo hums against his mouth.

"Yeah?" he says, voice low. "How's that?"

"I got you to say a bad word," Max nearly whispers, a conspiring edge to his voice, one made all the more amusing by the sly smile he wears, as he says it. And Theo smiles, as well.

"Which one?" he asks, his mouth just barely brushing against the metal ring in Max's bottom lip. "Fuck?"

Max makes a satisfied sound in the back of his throat.

"Yes," he purrs, giving Theo a light kiss. "That's the one."

Theo chuckles.

"Fuck," he repeats in a low voice, and Max shudders theatrically, letting out a low groan.

"You don't know what you do to me, babe," he says, and Theo grins.

"Well, that's hardly the worst thing you've made me do," he says. "At least, not after what we just did."

"Nah, that was awesome," Max says lightly, and Theo just looks at him for a moment, completely dazed, wondering how you can be this full of love and affection for another person, and still somehow remain intact. He smiles.

"It was," he says, leaning down and kissing Max, slowly, deeply, but when Max suddenly chuckles, he pulls away the slightest bit.

"What?" he asks, and Max sighs.

"We're gonna be in so much trouble," he says, and Theo smiles, deciding to completely disregard that truth, just for a little while. He kisses Max, instead, breathing him in and savoring this moment, this night, wishing he could just hold onto it, forever.

Because whatever happens after this, it will have been worth it.

CHAPTER 18

NEW

It's the feeling of being poked repeatedly in the arm that wakes Theo up the next morning.

He groans and shies away from the annoying touch, only to have the poking move up along his arm and gently start assaulting his face. He groans again, louder this time, and burrows his face into the pillow, but he poking is relentless, and he finally opens his eyes.

"Oh, good," Max says. "You're awake."

He's lying on his side, next to Theo, head resting on his arm, slightly propped up against the pillows. He's not wearing any eyeliner, and Theo absently remembers him cleaning it off last night, before they went back to sleep. His blue eyes are still intense, though, gorgeous and stunning, in the early morning light.

He stops poking Theo's face with his finger and pulls back his hand, and Theo narrows his eyes at him. But Max just raises his eyebrows innocently.

"Don't give me that," he says lightly. "I had to do something, you were just lying there."

"I was," Theo confirms, voice cracked, and muffled against the pillow. "Because I was *sleeping*."

"And now, you're not," Max says gleefully, earning another groan from Theo, in response.

Max seems to decide on a different tactic, then, and he shuffles closer to plant a light kiss on Theo's cheek. He doesn't say anything, and when he goes for Theo's mouth, Theo automatically kisses him back, very lazily, encouraging Max to move even closer and put his hand by Theo's waist. His hand is slightly cooler than Theo's skin, under the cover, but not by much, and Theo exhales slowly, feeling himself relax. He picks up on just the slightest scent of cigarette smoke, telling him that Max has been awake for at least a few minutes, already, and he finds the smell oddly comforting, mixed up with Max's own.

Theo surrenders then, and he pulls Max to him, half-rolling onto his back, so he can wrap both his arms around his boyfriend and press his bare skin against his own.

"That's more like it," Max murmurs, planting a kiss against Theo's throat. He settles against Theo's body and puts his arm around him, hitching one leg up to half-wedge it between Theo's, and for what feels like a rather long time, neither of them moves. At least, as far as Theo is concerned; he falls asleep again after only a few seconds, savoring the feel of having Max so close, wrapped up in his arms.

It's the sound of Max's voice that wakes him up again.

"I'm gonna take a shower," Max murmurs, and Theo groans as he pulls away and squirms out of his arms. He doesn't open his eyes, as he reaches lazily for Max's warm body, and he feels the shift in the mattress, as Max sits up in the bed.

Then, Theo is stunned awake again, when a soft pillow hits him in the head.

"That means you too, sleepyhead," Max says, and Theo groans indignantly, opening his eyes. Max pulls away the pillow he just used to attack his boyfriend, raising his eyebrows pointedly, and Theo blinks at him sleepily.

"But I'm tired," he says, voice cracked with sleep, and Max shrugs.

"Suit yourself," he says, dropping the pillow and getting up from the bed. Theo watches as Max makes his way over to the small bathroom, can't take his eyes off of him. He's naked, in all his toned, gorgeous and tattooed glory, and he reaches the bathroom door and steps inside.

"I guess I'll just entertain myself," he says casually over his shoulder, before closing the bathroom door behind him. It's only a second or so, before Theo hears the shower come on, and he watches the door, absently holding the pillow Max left behind. He narrows his eyes.

That son of a bitch.

He's still tired, and he yawns as he gets out of bed, but he's not tired enough to go back to sleep. Not when the alternative is taking a nice, hot shower with his boyfriend.

Theo winces slightly as he walks, surprised, but then remembers exactly what they did last night. Or, this morning, he's not sure which it is. Either way, it seems to have left him just a little bit sore, but less so than he somehow expected. It's not that bad, though; by the time he reaches the bathroom door, he barely notices it.

He's just as naked as Max, and therefore has nothing to take off, before stepping into the shower, but he pauses when he catches his reflection in the bathroom mirror. There's a hickey on his neck, and another on his chest, somewhere below his collarbone, and Theo touches them absently. *Hickeys.* He has never actually had that, before. It's not exactly aesthetically appealing, but the fact that they were made by Max somehow makes them so. It's like a mark, like Max branding him as his own, and he likes that, for some reason.

Max doesn't seem the least bit surprised when Theo steps into the shower. Instead, he barely gives him a second to adjust, before grabbing his wrist and pulling him in, so that they both end up underneath the showerhead. Max leans in and kisses him, slowly, and he chuckles as he pulls away.

"What's so funny?" Theo asks sleepily, smiling against his lips, and Max gives him another, quick kiss.

"So predictable," he says, and Theo makes an indignant sound.

"What?" he says. "How do you know I wasn't planning on taking a shower, anyway?"

"Because that doesn't sit well with my ego," Max replies, sliding his hands down Theo's sides. His skin is already slick and wet. "It prefers to think that it's all about me."

Theo groans, smoothing one hand down to the small of Max's back, while the other moves up to cradle his face.

"I hate it when your ego is right," he grumbles, and Max's mouth shapes into a smirk, which disappears as Theo covers those lips with his own.

They haven't showered together before, and Theo finds that it's somehow more intimate than he expected. The hot water, the bare touches, hands moving effortlessly over slick, warm bodies. It's enough to make him close his eyes and pull Max closer, pressing the two of them together, with nothing but wet, hot skin between them, and he lets out a soft moan as he notices the effect it's having. Max is hard, and Theo finds his own body quickly responding in the exact same way.

The soft kisses slowly start escalating, then. Before Theo knows it, Max is pulling him along, as he moves to lean with his back against the wall of the shower. And Theo doesn't object, doesn't say a word, as Max places his hands on his hips and pulls him in, pressing the two of them together, hands suddenly more eager than before. Instead, Theo moans, louder this time, and when he feels Max's wet hardness pressing against his own, he exhales sharply, and moves up his hands to place them against the wall, on either side of Max's head.

He will never get enough of Max. He is his drug, his oxygen, and Theo has simply come to accept that.

Theo is vaguely aware of how brave Max makes him. He has thought about it before, but not like this. Max makes him bold, makes him dare to make a move, to take what he wants, to stand up and talk back, and most of all, he makes Theo dare to touch him like this, everywhere, as much as he likes. He makes Theo dare to put his hands against Max's tattooed back and move them downward, feeling the outline of those muscles underneath his fingers, moving down to that perfect ass, where he simply grabs, and presses their bodies together.

Theo can barely even believe that once upon a time, he was afraid to even touch Max, at all. That first time, that first kiss, when Max pulled his fingers through Theo's hair and slipped his hand into his back pocket, while Theo wanted nothing more than to slide his hands underneath that black, long-sleeved t-shirt and touch Max's skin.

But he didn't. He was too afraid to. And now, here he is, rutting against him, with nothing but soft skin and hot water between them, mouths fused together, that metal ring hard against his lips, and that pierced tongue plundering his mouth and making him see stars.

It's amazing, so perfect, and somehow, it makes Theo feel unstoppable.

It's that feeling that makes him move his hand down over Max's thigh, smoothing over his wet skin, before trailing up along the inside of his leg. Max notices, and moans into Theo's mouth.

"What are you doing?" he asks, but he doesn't sound the least bit objecting or surprised.

"Last night was amazing," Theo replies absently, kissing Max again. "*You* were amazing."

He hears Max groan against his lips, as he moves his hand up to touch him, caressing and stroking, so very slowly. Max is so hard, and feeling it against his fingers feels so good.

"Just returning the favor," Theo continues, and Max chuckles breathlessly.

"I think we've covered that," he says hoarsely, smiling slyly. "I mean, I've literally been *inside* you."

Theo ignores him, and moves down to kiss his neck, using his tongue to smooth over the marks that have appeared there since last night, courtesy of Theo's mouth. Max groans.

"Seriously," he murmurs, moving one hand up to the back of Theo's neck. "What's gotten into you?"

"You," Theo replies, and Max chuckles darkly.

"Oh, that is clever," he says, sounding amusedly impressed, and Theo smiles against his skin, as he hears a smile in Max's voice. "Clever boy."

Theo hums in agreement, before suddenly getting an idea. It's not like it hasn't occurred to him before, but this time, it's different. This time, he really wants to. He *really* wants to, and for once, he's actually going to do it.

Theo has a feeling that Max somehow knows exactly what he's planning, as soon as he kisses him again. Theo makes the kiss deep and slow, stifling Max's moan, as he pushes his tongue into his mouth, more possessively than usual. When he pulls away, he moves his hands up along Max's waist, purposefully, before slowly sliding them down again, settling on Max's hips.

Max doesn't say anything. Instead, he just locks his eyes on Theo, and watches him move downward and plant a slow, searing kiss against his collarbone, making Max hiss a breath through his teeth. And Theo savors that sound, keeps it, moving further down to trail his tongue across Max's wet skin, over his chest, his nipples, and down toward his hard stomach.

Max keeps watching Theo as he moves downward, blue eyes suddenly dazed.

"You're killing me," he says languidly, his hand absently moving along Theo's upper arm, as Theo keeps planting slow, open-mouthed kisses against his stomach. His breathing gets just a bit heavier, and he swallows hard as Theo gets down on his knees.

Max's eyes are burning now, expectant and somehow stunned, and when Theo looks up at him, the two of them don't look away from each other for several moments, somehow caught up in the intense intimacy of the whole situation. Because it somehow feels more intimate than either of them probably expected, and it takes Theo slightly by surprise.

Theo slowly looks down again, as his hand wraps its fingers around Max. And Max lets out a heavy breath, just as Theo parts his lips and takes him into his mouth.

He does it slowly, but the reaction from Max is immediate, and he emits a deep, heavy moan.

"Oh, you are definitely killing me," he says, his voice already completely wrecked, and Theo feels Max's hand find its way to the back of his head. He doesn't push, barely does anything; he just keeps his hand there, absently stroking Theo's shower-wet hair, slowly, almost affectionately, as Theo works him over with his mouth.

It's not that difficult, Theo finds. He has never done this before, and he somehow thought it would be more technical, less spontaneous. But it's not. He barely even has to think about it, simply moves his tongue and lips along Max's length, his hand working over what his mouth can't take, and he closes his eyes at the sounds Max makes, as he does.

He has never heard Max make sounds like that, before. Other occasions have come pretty close, but Theo realizes that this is the first time Max is simply *receiving*, in lack of a better word, the first time with Theo where he hasn't had to focus on anything other than simply the way it *feels*. And, apparently, it makes him moan and pant and utter sounds so obscene and pleased, that it makes Theo so hard, just hearing them.

It's after a little while longer that Max's hand starts pulling through Theo's wet hair, rather than stroking it, gently holding onto it, but not pushing or pressing, which Theo somehow appreciates. He likes this, though, and absently feels like moving his hand down to touch himself. Hearing and feeling Max's reactions to what he's doing is so much hotter than he thought it would be, and he's not quite sure how do deal with that.

Then Max's breathing speeds up a bit, though, and Theo hears him groan.

"I'm gonna—" he breathes, panting, trying to articulate. "Theo. Oh god—"

Theo almost pauses at that. He loves the reaction he's getting from Max, loves hearing him say that, and he loves the thought of making him come. But at the same time, he's not entirely sure he's ready for that. Going down on him is one thing, but taking it? Somehow, that feels like a bit much for his first time, and for a few moments, he wonders if maybe he should stop. He wants to, but at the same time, he really wants to keep going, and he's not sure if—

He doesn't have to think about it any longer than that. Max takes the choice away from him, by grabbing his hair properly and gently pulling him away, and Theo can't help but look up, confused. Max tugs on his hair again, then, making Theo stand up, and before he knows it, Max is kissing him, deeply and hungrily. And Theo is stunned for about a split second, before eagerly reciprocating. He sure as hell doesn't mind this.

Max groans into his mouth, while he moves his hand downward and starts stroking Theo, slowly at first, then faster, and Theo groans in surprise. Again, not that he minds. He really doesn't, and as though by its own accord, his hand moves down and wraps its fingers around Max, who's so hard and so close, and who practically starts thrusting into Theo's hand.

Theo doesn't want to move his mouth away from Max's, not for a moment, but those sounds Max is making... It's enough to make him change his mind, and he pulls back a little bit, just far enough to be able to properly look at Max's face. Those dark blue eyes are lidded and dazed, mouth half-open and panting, and seeing it somehow makes something hot coil tightly in Theo's stomach. He has never watched Max like this, before, never properly *watched* him, as he comes undone, and he finds that it might be the best thing he has ever seen.

Max looks like he wants to close his eyes, squeeze them shut and just let go, but as though he gets that Theo doesn't want him to, he doesn't. Instead, he keeps his eyes fixed on Theo's green ones, watching him watch Max, and Theo feels that heat coil tighter, as their hands move in some kind of uneven unison, bringing them both closer and closer to the edge.

"Come on, baby," Theo finds himself saying, breathing heavily, almost panting. It almost feels like someone else is talking, because that's just not something he would ever really say. "Come on."

He's not sure why he says it, absently realizes how weird and unfamiliar it feels, but he soon finds that he doesn't really care, in the heat of the moment. He doesn't care, because as he says it, Max emits something like a whimper, something Theo has never heard from him, before. And it makes it worth it. It makes it worth it, and he watches intently as the next few seconds unfold, watches as Max teeters on the edge, before falling over it completely, parting his lips and letting out a low, stuttering groan, as he tenses up, and comes over Theo's fingers.

For a moment, everything is suspended, and Theo just watches the expression on Max's face, watches him close his eyes for a second, while his body nearly shakes with the force of his orgasm, and it's enough. It's enough to make that coiled heat build so fast, until it reaches the breaking point, and suddenly, Theo is coming as well, black spots dancing in front of his eyes, and he leans against the wall with his hand, to keep himself from practically collapsing.

It's the most intense, beautiful thing, and it takes several seconds of stuttering, heavy breathing, before Theo comes back to his senses.

"So amazing," he hears Max breathe, and he opens his eyes. He was barely aware that he had closed them. "Gorgeous."

Max looks up at him through heavily lidded eyes, and Theo swallows hard. His arm is keeping him standing, leaning against the wall behind Max, but it's shaking.

"Fuck, I love you," Max says, sounding exhausted, and he pulls Theo in for a slow, languid kiss. "It's retarded."

Theo huffs a tired laugh.

"Well, that's nice," he breathes, and Max smiles.

"Yes, it is," he says, kissing him again. When they pull apart, Theo is too tired to move any further, and so just leans their foreheads together. "The way I feel about you, the way you make me act... It really is retarded."

Theo groans softly.

"Your pillow-talk needs some work," he says, trying to even out his breathing. "But I guess that's part of why I love you."

Max chuckles.

"Well, we're in the shower, so..." He shrugs. "And good thing, too."

Theo smiles at him, absently wondering if Max can tell by the way Theo looks at him, just how happy and blissful he feels, right now. Not that he hasn't told him that, or shown him. He's certain that Max knows.

Theo moves his hand away from the wall, his legs finally steady enough to keep him standing, and he takes a step back, so that he ends up right underneath the showerhead. And Max scoffs, smiling lazily, as he moves away from the wall and into Theo's arms, where Theo feels like he would want him to stay, forever.

CHAPTER 19
RESOLVE

"You sure you're okay?"

It's way past noon, by now, and Max and Theo have finally managed to make their way outside, leaving the motel. It's Saturday, and surprisingly, the snow that fell last night did stick around, which means that there are several children outside, playing. Theo barely notices them, though. He's too focused on the fact that he will have to go back home.

"I think so," he says. They've walked all the way from the motel, and now, they're standing at the edge of Theo's street. He can see his house in the distance, not too far off. He swallows.

"Do I have to?" he practically whines, and Max gives him a small, sympathetic smile. "Can't we just go somewhere else?"

"Well," Max says, "you know I'm all for breaking the rules and fucking shit up."

He sighs, moving one hand up to tidy Theo's scarf.

"But believe it, or not," he says, "I don't like getting *you* into trouble."

He looks up at Theo, blue eyes sincere in a way that Theo still somehow isn't used to seeing them. Theo sighs.

"I know," he says. "And I appreciate it. Not that it stops it from happening, but still."

Max narrows his eyes at Theo's attempt at humor, but doesn't reply.

"I just," Theo says, looking down the street, toward his house. "I've got a bad feeling."

Max follows his line of sight.

"Yeah," he agrees quietly. "But what's the worst that could happen, right?"

Theo raises his eyebrows at him pointedly, and Max cocks his head.

"Fair enough," he relents, remembering how bad it has gotten, so far. Theo is pretty sure he wouldn't be able deal with that for much longer, and especially not if it gets worse.

Theo looks at his house for a few seconds, in silence, before taking a deep, steadying breath.

"Okay," he says, nodding. "I'm going."

Max squeezes his hand, entwined with his own, before reaching up to cradle Theo's face with the other. He kisses him softly.

"Good luck," he says, a hint of his usual cockiness, that Theo knows is there simply to ease the tension. But he appreciates it, nonetheless.

"Thanks."

And with that, they part ways, Max staying put while Theo makes his way along the street. He looks over his shoulder once, twice, and a third time, before reaching his house, and every time, Max is still there. Theo wishes he could have stayed, but somehow, he feels like that would have made the impending confrontation with his parents worse, and he throws Max one last glance, before walking up to his front door. And just like that, Max is out of sight.

Theo lingers for a moment, hesitates, before he takes a deep breath, and opens the door.

It's unlocked, and Theo steps inside and closes it behind him. He can't help but feel like he wants to keep quiet, like he can somehow avoid this whole thing, if he doesn't make too much noise. Which is a stupid, completely ridiculous idea, of course. And if nothing else, he's not as quiet as he thinks; within seconds of closing the front door behind him, he hears footsteps coming from the kitchen. And he takes another deep, steadying breath.

His father is upon him in seconds, looking positively livid.

"Where the hell have you been?" he practically shouts, right in his face, and Theo makes a point of not flinching. He hasn't even taken off his jacket, yet. His schoolbag is still slung over his shoulder. He grabs the strap a bit tighter.

"Out," he says, unable to help but glance away for a second. His father isn't physically much bigger than Theo, nowadays, but he's still his father. And he can be very intimidating when he wants to be.

"Out?" Eric repeats incredulously. "You better have a more decent explanation than that, boy."

"What's going on, here?" Theo looks up at the sound of his mother's voice, as she steps out of the living room. He catches her eye and forces a small, tentative smile.

"Hi, mom," he says, subdued, and he can see the very obvious relief on her face. It only lasts for a second, though, before she presses her lips together, her brow furrowing into a somewhat anxious frown.

"Nice to see you're back," she says, her voice unusually on edge. "Why don't you come inside. We need to talk."

Theo nods, looking down, as his mother makes her way into the kitchen. He glances up at his father, who seems to think better of standing in the hall, yelling at his son. He opts for following after his wife, no doubt planning to stand and yell at his son in the kitchen, instead.

It's after another minute or so that Theo makes his way into the kitchen. It's still early afternoon, but his mother seems to be in the process of cooking something, and Theo isn't really that surprised. She loves cooking, loves baking and making tasty things. She tends to joke that Eric is the housewife, though, since he does most of the cleaning, and can't really cook to save his life, which makes him dependent on her, rather than the other way around.

Theo isn't sure why he's thinking about that, right now. Probably just a defense mechanism, anything to avoid what's to come.

"Well?" Amy says, folding her arms as she stands by the counter, in a true mom-fashion, Theo thinks. "What do you have to say for yourself?"

Screw that, Theo adds, revising. *That* was in a true mom-fashion, almost hilariously so.

Theo takes a deep breath, putting his hands in his pockets.

"I, uh..." he starts, suddenly realizing that he doesn't actually have any kind of contingency plan, here. "I don't know."

His father frowns incredulously.

"You don't *know*?" he says, an obvious, angry edge to his voice. "You deliberately disobeyed, and disappeared for an entire night! And for what? To run off with some delinquent?"

Theo frowns then, but not really in anger. Instead, he finds himself oddly amused and baffled, in a dry, distant kind of way.

"You sure you know the definition of 'delinquent'?" he says, before he can stop himself. "'Cause Max doesn't fit it."

He immediately regrets saying that.

"Don't get smart with me, boy," Eric says, voice low and angry, and he actually points at Theo, warningly. He's closer now, standing right in front of him. "You know what I think about that."

"Yeah, I do," Theo says dryly, unflinching, unable to stop himself. Again. "You keep telling me."

Eric grits his teeth, then, jaw working. He lowers his finger, eyes still trained on Theo's, angry and determined.

"I don't know what the hell's going on with you," he says, voice still low with controlled anger. "But if you're hooking up with this guy, just to prove some kind of point—"

"To you?" Theo says, usually knowing better than to interrupt his father, but at the same time accepting that he seems to be taking a different approach this time, anyway. His eyebrows are slightly raised in disbelief. "You think this is because of *you*?"

"Look, I get that you wanna stir things up," Eric says, an almost patronizing tone in the midst of his anger. He seems to decide on ignoring Theo's question. "And that being with this kid is basically a giant middle finger to me and your mom—"

"Excuse me?" Theo can't help but gape at his father incredulously.

"But I'm not about to let some *guy* mess you up," Eric continues, raising his voice to drown out Theo's interruption. Theo still interrupts him, though.

"His name is Max," he says, enunciating every syllable, his volume starting to match his father's. "And that's not why I'm with him."

"Really?" Eric says doubtfully. It's not even a question, but more of a resolute statement, almost with an edge of sarcasm to it.

"No, dad," Theo says. "Believe it or not, I'm not doing this, just to piss you off."

"No?"

"No! Did it ever occur to you, that maybe I actually *like* him?"

"Well, that's the problem, isn't it," Eric says. The two of them are basically shouting in each other's faces, by now. "You can't even see straight!"

Theo lets out a loud, exasperated sound, glancing away for a moment.

"For fuck's sake, dad," he says, looking back at his father. "Do you even hear yourself?"

It's only after another moment or so, that Theo realizes how that's probably the worst word his parents have ever heard come out of his mouth, and his father just stares at him for a second.

"Do *you* hear yourself?" he says loudly, still sounding angry. "What the hell's going on with you?"

"I don't know!" Theo replies angrily, nearly shouting. "Maybe, if you stopped yelling at me for a second, I could tell you!"

"This is what I'm talking about," Eric says harshly, clearly unaccustomed to, and very frustrated by, his son's new attitude. "Since you met this guy, you've turned into this!"

Eric gestures at his son vaguely, and Theo knows he shouldn't take offense at that, but somehow, he does. He does, because he can hear the utter disapproval and almost something like *disdain* in his father's voice, and he swallows hard.

Amy hears it, too, though, and for the first time since this started, she speaks up.

"Eric," she says, almost warningly, her voice low but firm, probably in an attempt to calm things down. Eric doesn't seem to hear her, though.

"You used to be a good kid," he continues, and Theo is just too stunned—and oddly, embarrassingly hurt—to say anything back. "Now, it's like you're just turning into a punk with an attitude problem."

They're not very harsh words, not really. But knowing that his father means them in the worst way is enough to make Theo feel weirdly subdued, as a result. And he's not the only one who notices Eric's sudden, unfair insult.

"Eric!" Amy exclaims then, louder, this time, and Eric glances at her.

"Amy, don't—" he says, but doesn't get further than that.

"No, that's enough!" Amy's voice is raised, angry and determined, and it makes both Theo and his father turn to her in stunned surprise. Amy never raises her voice like that. Well, almost never. Her rage is more the cold kind, the kind that makes you want to curl up and cower beneath it. Not that this kind doesn't have the same effect. Theo is just shocked, and he glances at his father, whose mouth has snapped shut, eyes on his wife.

"This has gone on long enough," Amy says, voice slightly lower but still tense with anger. "And it's getting ridiculous."

Eric just looks at her for a few moments.

"Amy, sweetheart," he begins, his voice suddenly very soft, but not the least bit patronizing. Amy doesn't seem to care, though.

"Maybe you should go outside," she says pointedly, and Eric sighs quietly.

"I just—" he says, but is once again cut off.

"Now," Amy says, with a tone that leaves no room for argument. "I'd like to speak with our son, for a minute."

The silence that follows is tense and charged, and it drags on for what feels like several seconds, before Eric seems to give in. He sighs heavily and glances at Theo, before leaving the kitchen and making his way out into the hall, where he leaves through the front door. He's going to the garage, no doubt, where he tends to spend hours on end, tinkering with his car, especially when he's upset.

Theo doesn't say anything, just slowly turns back to his mother. She has never been an angry, mean person, not by a long shot, but that somehow makes her anger all the more difficult and odd to handle, when it actually happens.

Amy sighs and places her hand against her forehead for a moment, as though collecting herself, before she looks up at her son. Her eyes are back to their gentle kindness, and she lowers her hand.

"Sorry about that," she says, giving Theo a small, weary smile. Theo just shakes his head in a reassuring gesture.

"I'm just getting very tired of this whole thing," his mother continues. "I mean, it seemed like the right thing to do, at first, keeping you away from that boy. 'Cause trust me, I know what it can be like to fall for a bad boy."

Theo frowns in surprise.

"You do?" he says, and his mother nods, huffing a small, silent laugh.

"I do," she says pointedly. "I was teenager once too, you know."

Theo doesn't reply, instead just presses his lips together in an effort to not smile. Amy sighs.

"It was before I met your dad," she says. "There was this guy, and he was... just amazing. Charming, handsome, funny, like you wouldn't believe. And he had quite the attitude problem. It made him very likeable, but at the same time, it made him a complete ass, that most people had a hard time dealing with."

Theo glances at the floor, trying not to think about how that sounds like a spot-on description of Max.

"I thought I was special," Amy continues, and Theo looks up at her. "Because he picked me. But I wasn't. He was a mean guy, underneath all that charm, and no matter how much I tried or how much I cared about him, that didn't change. Eventually, it started breaking me down. That's when I realized that it didn't matter that I was in love. It wasn't enough, and he would still always be a bad *guy*, and not just a bad boy."

Theo doesn't answer, right away. He doesn't, because he doesn't really know how to respond. All he can think about is how it all suddenly just makes sense.

Of course his parents would be wary about someone like Max, even his mother, who would never be like that, otherwise. And Eric is bound to know about his wife's experiences with guys like Max—the type of guy they *think* Max is—and therefore positively militant in his efforts to keep that type away from his son. It makes sense, and suddenly, Theo feels any ounce of anger at his parents, or at least his mother, disappear.

"Max isn't like that," Theo finally says, carefully, and Amy sighs. She looks concerned.

"Are you sure?" she asks, and Theo nods, without hesitation.

"Yes," he says. Then he shakes his head. "I can't explain it. He's just... He's not like that. At all."

He doesn't mention how the earlier description fits so perfectly, figures it's implied that he's referring to the *bad guy*-description, rather than the bad boy-one, and Amy seems to get it. She looks at him, folds her arms and then brings one hand up to absently fiddle with her necklace, like she always does when she's anxious or worried.

"You care about me," Theo says. "And you worry about me. I get that."

He sighs, trying to find the right words. He can't afford to phrase this wrong.

"But this isn't working." He's not entirely sure he got it right, but there's a certain pleading edge to his voice that he's not doing on purpose, one which he's pretty sure his mother picks up on. It makes her look sad.

"You've done your best to keep me from him," Theo continues, unable to keep the softness out of his voice. "But your best obviously isn't good enough. And it doesn't make sense, either, keeping us apart. You know that, or else you wouldn't be here, talking to me about it."

Amy doesn't answer him right away. She keeps fiddling with her necklace absently, thinking. Then, she sighs.

"Why is this so important to you?" she says softly, as though unable to find any other way of expressing it, and Theo doesn't even hesitate.

"Because he makes me happy, mom," he says. "He makes me feel... *good* about myself. Like I'm worth something, like..."

He sighs, glancing around. Then he shrugs.

"I love him." He looks back at his mother, surprised at the lack of waver in his voice. He has never said that out loud before, not to anyone but Max, and it visibly takes Amy off-guard. "I love him, and I—"

He cuts himself off, taking a deep breath. Then he shakes his head.

"I can't be without him."

His mother doesn't reply for several seconds. She swallows, blinking, clearly taken by surprise at her son's confession, and she doesn't seem to know what to do. Theo is pretty convinced that neither of his parents have really managed to grasp just how important Max is to him, how important they are to *each other*, and he can see his mother feeling pretty much lost, right now.

"You love him?" she finally says, her voice a bit tense. Theo nods, practically holding his breath.

"Yes," he says, without blinking, and his mother exhales slowly, deliberating. Theo swallows, somewhat nervously.

"Well," his mother says, softly. "Riley seems to like him, anyway."

Theo frowns.

"You talked to Riley?" he asks, and his mother smiles affectionately.

"He talked to me," she says. "He doesn't think this is fair. And from what he told me about Max... Well, he seems like a good guy."

"He is," Theo confirms, feeling a surge of gratitude toward his little brother, for backing him up. "He's the best."

Amy smiles.

"And you have been smiling more, lately," she admits. "Especially for someone who's grounded and phone-less."

She adds that last part pointedly, and Theo gets a sheepish look.

"And I suppose that a boyfriend who *improves* your grades, rather than the other way around, is a keeper."

Theo doesn't reply, doesn't even breathe. Then, finally, his mother sighs, as though making a decision.

"Alright," she says. "I'll give him a chance."

Theo tries not to sound like he's gasping for air, when he exhales in relief.

"Thank you," he says.

"I'll talk to your father about it," Amy continues. "But it seems to me like this has gone on long enough. And if this boy means so much to you, I think it's about time I met him, myself."

Theo just nods, trying to compose himself.

"Yeah," he says. "Okay."

Amy presses her lips together, narrowing her eyes a bit.

"You're still grounded, though," she says pointedly. "For the rest of the weekend. And no phone, no internet. Despite everything, you *did* run off without warning, and were gone for almost twenty-four hours."

Theo looks down sheepishly. He had almost forgotten about that.

"Okay," he says, not about to risk making his mother change her mind.

"And the only reason your punishment isn't worse," Amy continues, "is because you had the decency to let us know you were okay."

Theo nods, thankful that he had made sure to text Riley last night.

"Okay," he repeats, before looking up at his mother. She regards him for a moment, before nodding.

"Alright," she says. "I'll talk to your dad. You, run along, and we'll discuss it later."

Theo nods.

"Yeah," he says. Then he steps forward and gives his mother a hug, hoping it will convey his gratitude and relief. "Thank you."

His mother hugs him back, holding him tightly, and it makes Theo feel very safe for a moment, despite the fact that he's almost a head taller than his mother, by now.

"You're welcome," she says, and Theo feels his shoulders relax with relief, as he then leaves the kitchen and makes his way up to his room.

♦

By the end of the day, Theo has another conversation with both his parents.

While he strategically kept his distance after coming home, his mother kept her word and talked to his father, and despite Eric's obvious reluctance, they agree to giving Max a chance. Theo tries hard not to seem too relieved or too excited at the prospect of *not* having to sneak around and go behind their backs, and instead just stands there, nodding, showing that he understands their logic and why they didn't do this, in the first place.

263

Although, Theo has the distinct feeling that if it were up to his father, Theo would have been sent away, or something, anything to keep Max away from him. Eric tends to get like that, kind of obsessive, especially when it comes to something that's important to him, and Theo is glad that his wife is there to balance him out. God knows what he would be like if he didn't have her.

Either way, Theo's parents eventually reach a decision. They agree to invite Max over, to meet him, talk to him, and therefore give him, and his and Theo's relationship, a shot. It's honestly more than Theo hoped for—so much more, considering how prepared he was for a verbal beatdown, when he got home—and he accepts it gladly. He's not about to push his luck, not with this.

The rest of the weekend is somehow easier to deal with, after that. Despite the fact that he's still grounded, and phone-less and such, Theo feels lighter, more optimistic, and he really looks forward to seeing Max on Monday. He would look forward to it, anyway, of course, but it's different, this time. Somehow, with his parents coming around, he feels like everything is suddenly a bit easier again.

Theo gets his phone back on Monday morning, and almost as soon as he gets to school, he runs into Cassie.

"Hey, you little rebel," she says, as he sits down next to her in History class. "I ran into Max. He mentioned your little adventure, this weekend. Care to elaborate?"

Theo glances at her, getting his notebook from his bag.

"Well, good morning to you, too," he says, and Cassie gives him an exasperated look, fiddling with her pen. Theo half-shrugs.

"Yeah, we took off for a bit," he says. "Just for the night."

Cassie starts, making her chair fall forward with a thud. She was balancing it on its back legs, but now she's staring at Theo, hazel eyes wide and intrigued.

"For the night?" she asks. "And what does that mean?"

Theo smiles in awkward amusement.

"It means we spent the night together," he clarifies. "Just hung out."

Cassie nods, deliberating, clearly sensing that he's not telling the whole story. She then glances around the rowdy classroom, which is still filling up with students, before she slides closer to Theo and looks at him pointedly. Theo almost pulls back a bit, at the unexpected proximity.

"Hung out?" she says, before continuing in a conspiring whisper. "As in, getting it on?"

Theo frowns at her, and she cocks her eyebrows suggestively.

"Doing the nasty?" she whispers.

"What?" Theo whispers, amused, and Cassie cocks her eyebrows again.

"Sexytimes?" she suggests, and Theo makes a face.

"Who even says that?" he says, shrugging, still whispering, for some reason.

"Well, did you?" Cassie asks, and they way she stares at Theo, along with the question, makes him just open and close his mouth like a goldfish, unable to answer. And Cassie's eyes widen, her mouth shaping into a sly, satisfied smile.

"Oh, my god, you did," she says, sounding scandalized. She then tilts her chair back again, fiddling with her pen, and Theo isn't lost on the big grin on her face.

"Slut," she adds, and Theo looks at her, meeting her gaze. Her teasing and genuinely affectionate, impressed expression makes him smile, though, and he turns his attention back to the surface of his desk, as the teacher enters the classroom, asking all the students to settle down.

Theo tries to focus, he really does. But for some reason, he can't wipe this sudden, stupid smile off his face.

It's after that first class that Theo finally sees Max. He's actually waiting outside the classroom, sitting cross-legged on the floor with a pair of headphones on, and as soon as he spots Theo, he gets up and takes them off.

He's hard to miss, and he's therefore the first thing Theo sees, when he walks out. He's also the first and only thing on Theo's mind, and it makes Theo immediately stride over to him and pull him into a kiss.

Max doesn't waste a second in reciprocating, pulling Theo close and kissing him slowly, affectionately, making Theo close his eyes and actually hold his breath for a few moments. It's only when they pull apart, that Theo notices Cassie, standing right next to them. She clears her throat.

"Keep it PG, you guys," she says, looking at them pointedly, before turning around and walking away.

"Hi, Cassie," Max calls in mock sweetness, and Cassie just waves as him over her shoulder, as she walks away, leaving Max and Theo alone in a sea of students.

"I missed you," Max says, giving Theo a quick kiss, and Theo grins.

"I missed you, too," he says, and for a few moments, they just stare at each other. That is, before someone bumps into Theo, and snaps him out of it. It's just as well, because he feels like he could just stand there and stare at Max forever, otherwise.

"So, how did it go?" Max asks, as they start walking. He seems a bit on edge, hands in his pockets, and he sort of walks half-backwards, as to keep his eyes on Theo. He sounds the tiniest bit anxious, and Theo is pretty sure he feels kind of guilty for getting Theo into more trouble than he was already in. Even though it really isn't his fault.

"Actually," Theo says, "it wasn't that bad."

Max frowns.

"What does that mean?" he asks, sounding suspicious. "Is that good?"

Theo takes a breath, steadying himself.

"I talked to my mom," he explains, hitching his bag up on his shoulder. "I sorta got through to her, about this whole thing, about you. And, well..."

He shrugs.

"She's giving it a chance." Max just looks at him, before shrugging questioningly, and Theo explains. "She talked to my dad, and managed to convince him."

"And...?" Max really does seem slightly on edge, and Theo resists the urge to smile in teasing amusement.

"And," he says, "you've been officially invited to my house. For dinner."

Max actually stops dead, then, making Theo stop, as well. And then he pulls back a bit, his expression suddenly humorously terrified.

"Wait, what?" he says dumbly, and Theo chuckles at his reaction.

"They want to meet you," he says. "Or at least, my mom does. Not so sure my dad's too happy about it, but it's still happening."

Max blinks, apparently stunned.

"Uh," he says, eloquently. "Dinner? At your house?"

Theo nods, pressing his lips together.

"With your family?" Max continues, eyebrows raised, and Theo hums in confirmation.

"Yeah," he says. "That's the gist of it."

Max seemingly holds his breath for a moment, letting it sink in, before exhaling slowly.

"Right," he says, nodding. "Okay."

Theo looks at him pointedly.

"You alright?" he asks, and Max keeps nodding, making a face that's probably supposed to be reassuring, but which only makes him look oddly nervous.

"Yeah," he says. "First time for everything, right?"

Theo grins, admittedly amused at Max's somewhat terrified reaction, and he takes Max's hand and places a soft, chaste kiss on his lips.

"Exactly."

CHAPTER 20
DINNER

"So, they finally caved, huh?"

Theo looks up at Riley's words. The two of them are sitting in the living room, Theo half-attempting to study, while Riley plays videogames, and they haven't really spoken in the last fifteen minutes. Riley glances at his brother pointedly, though, as he asks the question, and Theo sighs.

"Yeah," he says. "I guess they did."

Theo is honestly a little bit surprised, on some level, that his parents haven't changed their minds, about meeting Max. It's not that they normally would do something like that; he's still just anxious about how they went from completely disapproving, to tentatively accepting. Or his mother did, at least. His dad is still pretty tense about the whole thing.

"Took them long enough," Riley says, eyes back on the TV, thumbs maneuvering the Playstation 3 controller in his hands. "I didn't think mom would be such a hardass about it."

"She had her reasons, apparently," Theo says, not going into it any further. And Riley doesn't ask. "And hey, thanks, by the way."

Riley glances at him, questioning.

"For talking to her," Theo clarifies. "About Max."

Riley quirks a small smile, turning back to the TV. He shrugs.

"He's a good guy," he says. "I figured he deserved a chance."

"Still, though." Theo finds that his voice sounds more serious than he intended. "Thanks."

Riley gives him another glance, before nodding. And that's all they say about that.

"So," Riley says after another little while, a teasing edge to his voice. "You nervous about it?"

"About what?"

"Dinner."

Theo shifts slightly in his seat.

"I don't know," he says. "Shouldn't be, right?"

Riley cocks his head.

"Well," he says, "I would be. I mean, mom and dad practically hated the whole idea until a couple of days ago. Even if they changed their minds, I'd be nervous."

Theo just stares.

"Well, thanks for that," he says sarcastically. "Now, I'm not nervous, at all."

Riley smiles in a typical, teasing little brother kind of way.

"Happy to help," he says, and Theo scoffs.

"Bitch," he mutters under his breath.

"Jerk," comes the reply from Riley, and Theo returns his attention to his studying.

He shouldn't be nervous, right? Max is the one meeting his parents, the one thrown into a situation that Theo is pretty sure he really isn't used to. All Theo has to do is be there. No big deal.

Theo sighs. Tomorrow night. Tomorrow night, Max will be coming over, and they're all going to sit down and have dinner, together.

It should be interesting.

♦

"I don't like this."

Max pulls on his cigarette, glancing at the cold, snow-covered ground. Theo looks at him, a bit apprehensively.

"Yeah, maybe this whole dinner-thing is a bit much—" he starts, hesitantly, but Max cuts him off with a look.

"No, that's not it," he says, almost hurriedly, like he really wants to reassure him. "That's not it, trust me."

He gives Theo a quick kiss on the mouth.

"I want to," he says, before cocking his head, as though revising. "...ish."

Theo gives him a pointed look.

"Ish?" he asks, and Max glances away briefly. He sighs, worrying at his pierced lip.

"Don't get me wrong," he says. "I'm not too excited about the prospect of having a civilized meal with your parents. I mean, I barely even talk to my own parents. How am I supposed to talk to yours?"

He glances at Theo pointedly, and Theo opens his mouth to reassure him, but Max cuts him off.

"But," he says, "I do want to do this. For you. I know it's important, so... Yeah."

He shrugs awkwardly, and Theo lets out a slow breath. It's amazing how Max can still surprise him, somehow. He can be so considerate, so sweet, while still being the same sardonic prick as always toward anyone else, and for some reason, it makes Theo feel all the more special. Because Max wants to do things for him, wants to make him happy. Even though he recoils at the idea of having dinner with Theo's family, simply because of how

270

awkward and unfamiliar it is, he's going to do it tonight. For Theo. Just for him.

"Thank you," Theo says, taking Max's hand, the one not holding a lit cigarette between its fingers. "Really."

Max grumbles.

"Yeah, alright," he says. "Don't get all cheesy on me."

Theo smiles, pulling him in for a kiss.

"Should I wear a tie?" Max asks, frowning, his tone that perfect mix between sardonic and joking, and Theo chuckles.

"No," he says. "I mean, don't get me wrong, I'd love to see you in one. But no. It's just dinner. No big deal."

"You sure?" Max asks pointedly, cocking his eyebrows. "I've got a blue one. Really brings out my eyes."

He widens those dark blue, black-lined eyes, as though to prove this point, and Theo smiles, tilts his head, pushing that black hair back from Max's forehead.

"Well, I'm intrigued," he admits. "How about we save that for a different occasion?"

Max quirks a smile.

"Fair enough," he says, giving Theo a kiss. "I'll just be my usual, charming self."

♦

The day ends much faster than Theo somehow expected, and before he knows it, it's nearly dinnertime.

Amy is cooking, Eric isn't home from work, yet, and Theo is alternating between tidying up his room and getting his hair right. The latter task is frankly ridiculous, though; his hair is rather short and plain, just short enough to *not* be a pain to deal with, so there's really no point in standing in front of the mirror, adjusting every single strand. He doesn't even usually do that. He has never really cared about it, and he has no idea why he's suddenly starting, now.

Maybe he's just nervous. Hell, he *knows* he's nervous. Probably nowhere near what Max is feeling, though, and Theo still can't believe he's actually doing this for him.

Theo can only hope that the night goes smoothly.

It's when the doorbell suddenly rings that Theo practically throws himself down the stairs, while attempting to casually let his mother and brother know that he's getting the door, and he gets a somewhat amused eye-roll from Riley, which he decides to ignore. Instead, he takes a breath, before opening the front door.

"Hi," he says, a bit more hurriedly than he meant to, and Max raises his eyebrows at him.

"Hi," he says, smiling in something like surprise at Theo's apparent fluster. And Theo just stares at him for a moment, before reanimating, and stepping aside.

"Just, uh—" he says stupidly, and Max narrows his eyes as him, while stepping over the threshold. It's snowing a little, outside, and as Theo closes the door, he watches as Max brushes some snow off of his coat. He suddenly doesn't really feel nervous, anymore, but rather excited, in a way he can't really explain.

"How you feeling?" Theo asks, and Max looks up at him.

"I'm good," he says, a bit apprehensively. It's like he's a bit confused by Theo's manner, and Theo deliberately takes a deep breath, calming down. "Just need a minute."

Theo nods, and Max takes off his coat and snow-covered boots. Theo just watches him, feeling his heart rate steadily slow down, until he feels still and completely calm. Just being near Max tends to do that to him, when it's not making his stomach leap and fill up with butterflies, that is. It's like Max centers him, grounds him.

It's when Theo notices what Max is wearing, that his face breaks into a small smile.

"Hey," he says, gently taking a thin, black suspender strap between his thumb and index finger. "Look at that."

Max gives him a small glare.

272

"Don't," he says warningly, but with a certain softness to his voice. "It's not like I dressed up, or anything."

Theo cocks his head.

"I don't know," he says. "You look pretty good, to me."

Max looks at him pointedly.

"I always look pretty good," he says smugly, but in a way that lets Theo know he's just being an ass, on purpose. "But thanks."

Theo eyes him up and down, smiling. Max is right, it's not like he has dressed up, or anything; that wouldn't really be his style, anyway. Instead, he's just wearing his ordinary uniform of a black, long-sleeved t-shirt, and black jeans. The only detail slightly altered is the addition of the suspenders, and Theo can't deny that he loves the way they look on him.

Max takes a deep breath, then, and Theo looks up at him. Those blue eyes look slightly nervous, and he gives him a small nudge.

"Hey," he says. "You okay?"

Max exhales slowly, and nods.

"Yeah," he says. "I'm fine."

Another few seconds pass in silence, and then Max scoffs and shakes his head, a small smile on his face.

"Look at that," he murmurs. "Now, *I'm* new at something, and you're walking me through it. Oh, how the tables have turned."

Theo just smiles affectionately, doesn't mention how he actually kind of likes the fact that for once, Max is the inexperienced one, and Theo is the one who has to calm *him* down. Not that Theo has any previous experience with this sort of thing, either, but at least Max is as new at it as he is.

"Just be yourself," Theo says, absently smoothing those black suspenders between his thumbs and index fingers. "You'll do fine."

Max raises a pierced eyebrow at him, pointedly.

"Need I remind you," he says, "that being myself is what generally fucks things over for me, rather than the other way around."

273

Theo looks up at him, chews his bottom lip for a moment. Then he cocks his head.

"Touché," he says. Then he leans in and gives Max a quick kiss, as Max rolls his eyes. "But it's also what made me fall for you. And it's what made Riley like you, so you've at least got him on your side."

Max doesn't answer right away, instead just looks at Theo, who raises his eyebrows hopefully. And Max sighs.

"Alright," he says. "I'll do my best."

Theo decides to ignore the blatant sarcasm, and instead nods.

"That's all I'm asking," he says. "And you'll do fine."

Max makes a grumbling sound.

"Yeah, well," he says, "I must admit, I'm kinda nervous. Never really 'met the parents', before."

Theo gives him a small, teasing smile.

"Nervous?" he says, having his suspicions confirmed. "You?"

Max narrows his black-lined eyes.

"Yes," he says, pointing at Theo warningly. "And that does not leave this room."

Theo chuckles, but nods, all the same.

"My lips are sealed," he says. "No one will hear of your actual, human emotions."

"Better not," Max grumbles, but quirks a small smile, all the same. Theo kisses him again, trying to be reassuring.

"I love you," he says. "Thanks for doing this."

"Anything for you, babe," Max replies, giving Theo a quick kiss, himself. "I love you, too."

Theo exhales slowly, leans his forehead against Max's for a few moments, as though it will ground him.

"Ready?" he finally says, and he hears Max exhale, as well.

"As ready as I'll ever be," he replies, and Theo gives him one last, chaste kiss, before they make their way out of the hall.

They keep their hands locked together, fingers entwined, and Theo absently notices how Max's grip tightens just the slightest bit, as they step into the kitchen. Amy is already there, by the stove, while Riley is in the middle of setting the dining room table. The dining room is connected to the kitchen, through an open, vaulted doorway, and so he spots Theo and Max right away.

"Hi, Max," he says, making his way back into the kitchen, and just as Amy turns her head to see who her youngest son is talking to, Max replies.

"'Sup, Riley," he says, and Riley gives him a smile, before returning to the dining room, a pile of plates in his hands. Meanwhile, Amy turns around completely, and at least in Theo's eyes, she is visibly startled when she sees Max.

"Hello," she says, sounding awfully relaxed, considering. She turns to Theo, expectantly, as she makes her way across the kitchen, and Theo clears his throat unnecessarily.

"Mom," he says, suddenly realizing all over again how nervous *he* actually is about this. "This is Max."

Max takes a slow, quiet breath, a deep inhale which would probably go unnoticed to anyone but Theo, who knows all of his quirks and mannerisms, by now. It still feels somehow unusual, to see him even remotely nervous about *anything*.

"Good to meet you," he says, extending his hand—his right one, the one not currently locked together with Theo's—and Amy takes it.

"You, too," she says, clearly trying not to stare too much at him. "I've heard a lot about you."

Theo absently realizes that Amy was probably half-unprepared for what Max actually looks like; whatever she's heard has probably been from Eric, or maybe even Riley, and Theo doubts that his father went into much, at least positive, detail. He tries to remember how he himself saw Max, when he first saw him, how his whole appearance was daunting and intimidating, to say the least. Theo often forgets that he's simply used to it now, and that most people would have a harder time seeing past it.

"Really?" Max says, as Amy releases his hand, and she nods.

"Theo won't stop talking about you," she says, almost teasingly, and Theo resists the urge to groan.

275

"Is that so?" Max says, raising his eyebrows as he turns to Theo, who meets his eye.

"Not entirely true," Theo says. "She's exaggerating."

Max sighs, somewhat dramatically.

"Well, I'm hurt," he says, and Theo gives him a glare, which is returned by a surprisingly soft smile. And Amy actually smiles, as she sees it.

"Alright," she says, breaking up the moment. "How about you two help Riley set the table? Dinner should be ready any minute."

Theo nods, and as his mother turns away, he feels Max relax slightly, beside him. He smiles and leans in, planting a kiss against Max's temple, making his boyfriend glance at him.

"Come on," Theo murmurs, and gently tugs Max with him, as they make their way over to help his little brother.

Seeing as how Max and Riley have met before, and hung out, the atmosphere stays rather light, and Theo is glad that Riley is there to help ease the tension and nervousness. He and Max get along really well, after all.

It's when they've just finished setting the table and started bringing out the food, that the front door opens, and Theo tenses up. He looks over his shoulder, in the general direction of the hall, before turning to Max, who looks at him at the same time. They both know who it is, and Theo automatically takes Max's hand as they make their way back into the kitchen.

As soon as they enter it, Eric steps in from the hall.

"Hi, honey," he says, giving his wife a kiss, before spotting his son. His eyes look a bit tense, as they then pass to Max, and a few seconds of slightly uncomfortable silence follow, before Amy steps in.

"Eric," she says, placing her hand on his shoulder. "This is Max."

She looks at him pointedly, and Eric meets her eye, as though deliberating, before he visibly relaxes a bit. Then he turns back to Theo and Max.

"Yeah," he says gruffly, extending his hand, and Max shakes it.

"We've met," he says, the slightest hint of a sardonic tone in his voice. Theo knows he does it automatically, it's just who he is, but Max seems to catch himself at it, and composes himself. He gives a small, slightly dry smile, instead. "Sort of."

Eric doesn't answer, just looks at Max, and for another couple of seconds, it's impossible to tell if he's mad or not. But then, he seems to relax a bit, deciding not to make anything of it, and he simply nods, before turning away.

"I'll be right back," Eric says to Amy. "Just gotta put some stuff away."

"Alright," she says. "Dinner's ready, so hurry up."

Eric kisses her cheek and makes his way out of the kitchen, while Amy gives her son a pointed look, before turning back to the stove. Theo turns to Max, then, who gives him a slightly apologetic look.

Sorry, he mouths, but Theo just shakes his head in assurance, and squeezes his hand. He doesn't need to say that it's fine, because Max knows that it is. Theo doesn't blame him for being himself.

Dinner goes surprisingly well. Amy is open and kind, in a way that gives Theo the distinct feeling that she would rather have done this from the start, than trying to keep Theo away from Max and teach him some kind of lesson. Eric, however, is still a bit on edge, but visibly trying to be welcoming and understanding, and Theo is well aware of more than one pointed look thrown at him from his wife, over the dinner table. Riley, already knowing Max and considering him kind of a friend, by now, seems to do his best to ease any tension, and talks to Max in a relaxed kind of way. Theo really appreciates it; it seems he can always count on his little brother to try and make any situation better, no matter what.

Theo is seated next to Max, Riley sitting across from them, with Eric and Amy at opposite ends of the table, and although Max is the guest of honor, he's not exactly the only subject of conversation. This gives Max and Theo several opportunities to glance at each other, as though making sure the other is still okay about all of this, and every now and then, Theo even squeezes Max's hand under the table, for moral support.

He really appreciates Max resisting the urge Theo knows is there, to say the inappropriate things he always seems to think of, and when Max accidentally drops his fork, he emits a hushed *fuck*, before actually glancing around the table, as though making sure no one heard him. Theo finds it adorable, in lack of a better word, and he catches the way Riley smiles slyly, proving that he definitely heard Max's profanity, although he doesn't mention it, while their parents chat away, oblivious.

It's weird, but Theo can't help but smile, realizing that for once, for the first time since he's met Max, Max is acting as though he actually wants someone to like him. Like this time, he actually *cares*. He cares if Theo's parents like him or not, and it's a completely new side of him, one that Theo hasn't really seen before. Because Max never cares. He never gives a crap if anyone really likes him, or not, and seeing him give a crap makes Theo feel special in a somehow entirely new way.

"So, Max," Amy says, and Max looks up. "You're in Theo's year, right?"

Max nods.

"Yeah," he says.

"What's your favorite subject?"

"Algebra." There's no hesitation in Max's reply, and Theo feels vaguely, vindictively, satisfied at the surprise on both his parents' faces.

"Really?" Amy asks, and Max nods.

"Yeah," he says, before cocking his head. "Well, math, in general. Anything with numbers, really. It just... makes sense."

Riley glances back and forth between his parents for a moment.

"He helped me with my homework, once," he says, and Amy looks at him. "Explained it a lot better than my teacher."

Theo glances at Max, along with Amy, and is half-surprised to find Max looking just the tiniest bit uncomfortable at Riley's words. Theo remembers what he's said about compliments on his

278

intelligence and whatnot feeling a bit weird, but doesn't mention it. And he's not sure anyone else has noticed, anyway.

"Well, that's good," Amy says, sounding surprised, but like she means it, and she turns back to Riley. "A pity that your teacher doesn't seem to live up to his title, though."

She says it jokingly, giving Riley a small nudge.

"Yeah," Riley says, smiling. "Although, Max was a bit of a smartass about it."

He looks at Max, who raises his eyebrows, not the least bit offended.

"Well," he says. "As you know, my smartassery is just one of my many endearing qualities."

He seems to catch himself at maybe sounding a bit too familiar, and he clears his throat a bit.

"But yeah, it's fu—" He cuts himself off, briefly pressing his lips together, before revising. "It's messed up."

Theo tries not to smile. Watching Max trying to censor himself, in any manner at all, is oddly entertaining, and he appreciates the effort.

"I mean," Max continues, "I get the whole ignorant-teacher-thing. Happens to me a lot."

He raises a pierced eyebrow at Riley, pointedly.

"And they don't appreciate my attitude nearly as much as you do."

Riley smiles at that, and Theo gets a warm feeling in his stomach, glad that this is going so well.

Until his father speaks, that is.

"No wonder," he says, voice a bit lowered, almost as though he's torn between saying it out loud and murmuring it to himself. The judgmental undertone of it isn't lost on anyone, though. "That attitude will get you into trouble."

Theo tenses up, watches out of the corner of his eye as his mother gives her husband a pointed, almost angry look, and suddenly, the entire room settles into a tense, awkward silence, which would be enough to make anyone squirm in discomfort.

But not Max. No, Max doesn't get unsettled by awkward tension. He thrives on it.

"As a matter of fact, it does," he says, turning to Eric, who looks up at him. There isn't the slightest hint of intimidation in Max's expression. In fact, he both looks and sounds completely conversational, despite what Eric just said. "See, most people don't like it when you call them out on their shit, and so, my attitude occasionally does get me into trouble. In fact, last time it happened, it kept your son from getting punched in the face."

He doesn't sound accusing, or judgmental, but Theo still notices how pretty much everyone's eyes momentarily flit to the fading, barely visible bruise below Max's cheekbone, and that they all know exactly why it's there. Max, however, still doesn't seem the least bit bothered.

"So, I don't know about you," he says, half-shrugging. "But I'd say it's worth it."

The silence that Max just broke was nothing compared to the one that presents itself now, and Theo finds himself practically holding his breath, as he awaits some kind of reaction. It only lasts for about a second, though, before Max sighs, and turns to Amy.

"Do you have a bathroom?" he asks politely, and she nods.

"Yeah," she says, gesturing toward the hallway outside the dining room. "Down the hall."

Max nods, and gets up from the table, leaving the room and its tense, deafening silence.

Theo just sits there for a moment, before turning to his father, who seems to feel his son's gaze, because he looks at him then. But Theo doesn't even say anything, doesn't really know what to say. Instead, he only manages a look that he knows at least resembles a glare, before he gets up and leaves the room. He swears he can hear Amy reprimanding her husband, as he goes.

The downstairs bathroom is down at the far end of the hall, and when Theo reaches it, he knocks softly on the door.

"Max?" he says, and the door almost immediately opens. Max leans against the doorframe, hands in his pockets. He looks tired, and oddly annoyed, and Theo is almost entirely sure he knew Theo would follow him, so that they could have a brief, private conversation.

"I'm sorry," he mumbles, and Theo sighs.

"Don't be," he says. "It's fine."

"It's not, though," Max retorts softly. "Didn't exactly help my case, and your dad hates me, as it is."

"Yeah, well," Theo says, "he's a dick."

Max just looks at him for a moment, before smiling.

"Aww," he says. "Look at you. All rebellious, just for me."

"Shut up." Theo says it softly, with a small smile, and he takes Max's hand. "He shouldn't have said that. It was out of line."

Max sighs.

"Yeah, it was," he says. "Which was why I couldn't keep my fucking mouth shut."

He smiles bitterly, before exhaling slowly.

"I'm trying, okay?" he says, and Theo nods.

"I know you are," he says. "And I appreciate it."

He gives him a light kiss, the brief touch of lips enough to lend a surprising amount of strength.

"And for what it's worth," Theo says. "I'm pretty sure my mom likes you, at least."

Max smiles, almost smirking.

"Lucky me," he says, before taking on a more serious tone. "She seems nice."

"Yeah."

They don't speak for a few moments, both of them acutely aware of how awkward the whole night has suddenly gotten, and Theo gives Max a small, tentative smile, until Max actually cracks up and starts laughing.

"God, you're adorable," he says, glancing away and shaking his head. "I'm so sorry I fucked up."

"You didn't fuck up," Theo says firmly, not lost on the way Max glances at him approvingly at his use of the curse word, and not lost on how Max, shockingly, has genuinely apologized twice in one conversation. "My dad was being a douche, and if nothing else, they wanted to meet *you*. Not some censored, modest version of you."

Max raises his eyebrows.

"Really?" he says, sounding doubtful. "You sure they're ready for that?"

Theo considers that for a second.

"Probably not," he decides, and Max emits a low, hushed groan. "But you're doing great, so far. And like I said, I think my mom likes you, at least."

Max fiddles with his lip piercing, using his tongue and his teeth, blue eyes locked on Theo's green ones. He seems to be deliberating.

"You know I've got a ridiculously high tolerance for embarrassment," he finally says, matter-of-factly, "so I'm fine with going back in there. I just don't want to make you uncomfortable."

Theo is never going to get used to the reaction he gets when Max says something like that. Seriously, he's *never* going to get over how his heart does a double-take, and how his entire body seems to get all warm and soft, at the mere thought of Max being so considerate, and he lets out a small breath.

"I'll admit it's a bit awkward," he confesses gently. "But it comes with the territory, I guess."

Max just looks at him, as though giving him a chance to get out of this, but Theo knows that's out of the question. How would that look, anyway? Just bailing on this whole night, because his dad doesn't like his boyfriend, which he was already fully aware of?

"Come on," he finally says, tugging on Max's hand gently, and Max lets out a small sigh, before cocking his head, giving in.

"You're the boss," he says, and they make their way back to the dining room.

They finished eating, just before the whole *incident*, and so when Theo and Max get back, Riley is in the middle of clearing stuff off the table. He just gives them both a sympathetic look, before making his way into the kitchen, and Amy soon emerges, starting slightly as she spots them.

"Everything okay?" she asks softly, but pointedly, and Theo nods.

"Yeah," he says, before glancing around. "Where's dad?"

Amy almost rolls her eyes. Almost.

"He'll be back in a minute," she says, clearly annoyed by his behavior at the table, earlier. "There's dessert."

She starts stacking the used plates, and Riley makes his way past her, going for the rest.

"The food was really good," Theo says after a moment, and Max nods, next to him.

"Yeah, it was great," he agrees, sounding somehow softer than Theo is used to hearing. "Thanks."

Amy gives them both a small, appreciative smile, and as she reaches for a plate at the other end of the table, Max surprises Theo by picking it up, himself.

"I got it," he says, almost muttering, before somewhat pointedly adding the plate to the stack Amy has started on, and she looks at him, surprised. The look only lasts for a moment, though; she seems to know better than to make Max feel awkward about offering his help.

"Thank you," she says, instead, and Max just gives her a nod and an uncharacteristically subdued smile, before proceeding to pick up another plate. Amy turns to Theo.

"Theo," she says, "why don't you help me in the kitchen?"

Theo nods, and his mother makes her way out of the dining room. He throws a glance at Max, who now has his back turned to him, and instead catches a softly surprised look from Riley, who gives him the smallest shrug, and Theo follows after his mother, into the kitchen.

Amy is in the process of getting clean plates out, smaller ones, and she starts handing them to Theo, who just looks at her expectantly, while obediently holding the plates in his hands. Finally, she catches his eye, and she exhales quietly.

"He seems nice," she says in a lowered voice. "Very well-behaved."

Theo resists the urge to snort at the description of Max as *well-behaved*. Sure, he has been well-behaved tonight, but it's pretty much the opposite behavior of any other occasion, and Theo is caught between finding it amusing and endearing. Actually, it's probably a mix of both.

"And I'm sorry about your father," Amy continues pointedly, the annoyance at her husband's behavior shining through, again. "That was completely uncalled-for."

Theo gives a small shrug, as Amy adds the last plate to the stack in his hands.

"Yeah," he says, before chewing his lip slightly, thinking. "So... You like him?"

Amy opens a drawer to get spoons, and she looks up at Theo. She opens her mouth to answer, but doesn't get the chance, before Riley makes his way into the kitchen, Max in tow.

"Almost done," Riley proclaims, and Amy gives them both a small nod and a smile, as they put the dirty dishes on the counter and make their way back into the dining room. Max gives Theo the briefest glance, and then he's gone, leaving Theo alone with his mother again.

Theo raises his eyebrows slightly in encouragement, and Amy sighs.

"It's a bit early to tell," she says. "But he seems like a good guy. Sweet, helpful."

Theo is glad, not to mention surprised, that his mother seems to see through whatever hard exterior Max generally projects, and it's relieving. But he still fidgets a bit.

"So—" he starts hesitantly, but his mother cuts him off.

"Relax, Theo," she says, getting some spoons and putting them on his stack of plates. "I only met him about an hour ago, which isn't enough time to learn a person's entire character."

She closes the drawer and looks at her son pointedly, as Theo presses his lips together, resisting the urge to ask again. And then, she gives the smallest hint of a slightly amused smile.

"But so far, so good," she says, voice low. "And I'd say you two have my blessing."

She gives him a peck on the cheek, and Theo can't help but suddenly grin stupidly, just thoroughly happy at his mother's words, and she narrows her eyes at him.

"Now, go," she says, deliberately nudging him toward the dining room. "Set the table. We're having pie."

The atmosphere is considerably lighter, now, and when Theo makes his way into the dining room, he gets a small smile from Riley, as he goes into the kitchen with the last of the dirty dishes. Theo turns to Max, then, who slowly makes his way over to him, hands in his pockets. Theo gives him a small, teasing smile.

"Did you just help clear the table?" he asks pointedly, with a tone that matches his smile.

Max nods slowly.

"Yeah," he says with a small smile, and with an expression that says *I know, right?* "I may be a dick, most of the time, but even I have my moments."

Theo chuckles, putting down his small stack of plates on the table.

"I'm very impressed," he says, and Max raises his eyebrows, jokingly offended.

"You should be," he says, moving in closer so that he stands right next to Theo. "I'm not exactly in my element."

Theo glances up at him then, and straightens as Max hooks his finger through one of the belt loops of his jeans, gently pulling him closer.

"So," he says, voice low and conspiring, "do we have a verdict?"

Theo glances toward the kitchen.

"Yeah," he says, dropping his voice to the same tone as Max's. "I think you passed."

Max smiles, almost smugly, and Theo swears he looks just a little bit more relaxed.

"Good to know," he says. Then he just looks at Theo, keeps his eyes on his, with a slightly adoring expression on his face, and

Theo is once again struck by how amazing it feels to be looked at like that, especially by Max.

Theo is half-surprised when Max leans in and kisses him. He does it softly, in a slow, chaste touch of lips, and it's enough to make Theo close his eyes for a moment. Mostly, he's just a bit surprised that Max is doing it here, right now, when Theo's whole family is around, but he appreciates it, nonetheless. It grounds him, it makes all those butterflies kick in again, and he feels his shoulders relax a bit.

When Max pulls away, he doesn't say anything. Instead, he just gives Theo a small smirk, before pointedly picking up half the stack of plates and proceeding to set the table. And Theo can't help but smile.

By the time they're done, Theo's father returns. Theo isn't sure if anyone else would be able to tell, but he looks downright uncomfortable, like he would much rather not be there, and perhaps he even feels bad about what he said, earlier. Either way, he gives both Theo and Max a nod, as he sits down at the table, and Theo exchanges a glance with Max, before they sit down, as well. Riley emerges from the kitchen a moment later, carrying the pie, and pretty soon, they're all sitting down for dessert.

It's weird, but the atmosphere is now somehow more relaxed and more tense, all at the same time, and Theo notices how Max is just a tiny bit more comfortable, at this point. It's true, this isn't exactly his element, and Theo can tell how uncharacteristically off he is. But he's making an effort, which is all Theo is asking for.

Amy seems genuinely interested in Max and what he's like, which Theo appreciates. Then again, he still has the feeling that she would have preferred this approach, from the start, rather than keeping Max away. Eric stays silent, seemingly resisting the urge to say anything bad or judgmental, and therefore opting to keep quiet, altogether. Theo supposes that that's better than repeating what happened, before.

After a while, Riley starts asking Max about his piercings. He seems intrigued by them, and Theo remembers him asking about them the first time he met Max. Theo honestly can't blame his interest; he really likes them, himself, after all.

"Did they hurt?" Riley asks, and Theo catches a glimpse of a slightly worried look on his mother's face, like she's afraid Max might take offense at a question like that. However, Max doesn't seem bothered, in the slightest, and she relaxes.

Max cocks his head.

"A bit," he says. "Just for a little while, though. They heal pretty quick. The tattoos are worse, they itch like crazy."

He says it conversationally, but Theo isn't lost on the straight-up shocked expressions on everyone's faces. They range from Amy's honest surprise, Riley's intrigued surprise, and the downright pissed surprise with Eric, who thankfully doesn't voice it. Maybe it's the pointed look from his wife that does it, but he keeps his mouth shut.

Theo looks around the table, remembering how no one here probably is aware of Max's tattoos, seeing as how it hasn't really come up, when Theo has told them about him. He suspects that they weren't really ready for it; the piercings are enough, especially for someone so young, but tattoos are worse. They're permanent. At least, that's what his parents would vehemently point out, and Theo would probably agree with them, if it concerned anyone else. With Max, he can't imagine him without tattoos, despite his young age. It's like they're part of his skin, like they're gradually revealed, as time passes, rather than added on.

"Tattoos?" Riley finally asks, pausing with a bite of pie halfway to his mouth, and Max glances around the table. He doesn't look so much uncomfortable, as a bit stunned at the reactions, and he settles down after only a moment.

"Yeah," he says slowly, almost hesitantly, as though expecting someone to yell at him. "I have a few."

Riley nods, absently eyeing Max up and down, as though trying to see said tattoos. Amy and Eric still haven't said anything, and Theo just sits there, trying not to be uncomfortable about the whole thing.

"Where?" Riley asks, and Max half-shrugs.

"Arms, mostly," he says. "And my back."

"Small ones?"

Max almost looks a bit sheepish, for a moment.

"Not exactly," he says, and Riley's eyebrows go up a bit, along with Amy's. Eric is still silent, seemingly grinding his teeth, by now.

"Can I see them?" Riley asks, actually sounding very interested, and Max frowns, glancing around the table. Spontaneously, he would probably have no problem whatsoever with showing his tattoos, right now, even though that would involve taking his shirt off, but he seems to read the situation well enough to know that it wouldn't exactly be appropriate.

"Maybe some other time," he finally says, looking back at Riley, and it seems to take Riley a moment to get it. He then glances at his parents, and nods, looking a bit sheepish.

"Sure," he says, taking a bite of his pie, and Max hesitantly mimics him, glancing around the table. Amy's expression is still somewhat shocked, but she seems to be doing her best to not make a huge deal out of it. Eric is, as well, by simply not saying anything; Theo knows he would be all over it, if he could.

"They're really cool, though," Theo says, in an awkward attempt at being helpful, and everyone turns to him. "Not tacky, or anything."

Max quirks a small, amused smile.

"Thank you," he says, giving Theo a pointed glance, and Riley rolls his eyes, as though disgusted by the sweetness of their whole dynamic.

"What do they look like?" he asks, though, and Max looks over at him. He raises his eyebrows, in a jokingly formal expression.

"I'm glad you asked," he says, his tone matching his expression, and he proceeds to describe his tattoos.

Theo watches his mother's expression of restrained, neutral interest, while his father just sits there looking disapproving (although, everyone seems to be ignoring him, at this point). Riley looks positively intrigued, and when Max gets to describing the wings, Riley's eyes actually widen, while he expresses how cool it sounds, and Max points out that Theo was actually there to keep him company, when he had them finished. Theo can't help but smile at the memory; that whole day somehow caused a shift in their relationship, taking it to a whole new level, before they even realized that they were in a relationship, in the first place.

The rest of the night runs rather smoothly, Max getting visibly more comfortable as time goes on. By the time dessert is finished, he, Theo and Riley move into the living room, while Theo's parents insist on cleaning up. Without his parents present, the whole thing is completely relaxed, and the three of them hang out like they have before, although with Max keeping himself in check and *not* touching and kissing Theo as much as he's used to and as much as he would probably like. Not that Theo minds; he's just glad that the night has gone well, and that despite the awkward incident from before, it all worked out for the better.

Max ends up showing Riley his tattoos, causing the fourteen-year-old to just stare in awe, especially at the wings, and Theo can't help but smile. It kind of resembles his own reaction, the first time he saw them, and Riley starts asking all kinds of questions about it, keeping a rather enthusiastic conversation going, for a pretty long time.

It is a school night, though, and Max eventually has to leave. He says goodbye to Riley, as well as Theo's parents, somewhat awkwardly thanking them, getting a smile and a friendly goodbye from Amy, and a gruff reply and slight frown, from Eric. Theo walks him to the door, where the two of them linger for a minute, while Max puts his coat and stuff on.

"Well," he says, as Theo watches him, hands in his pockets. "How did I do?"

He says it jokingly, but Theo can tell he's a bit anxious about it, underneath it all, and he smiles.

"You did good," he says, stepping closer and moving his hands up to the lapels of Max's black trenchcoat. "I'm proud of you."

Max just looks at him, a surprised look of affection on his face, one he quickly tries to hide with surprised amusement.

"Well, damn," he says. "Not sure I'd go that far."

"I would," Theo says, giving him a small kiss. "I know this whole thing was less than ideal for you, and you did it, anyway. So, yeah."

Max nods slowly, putting his hands on Theo's waist.

"I'm glad I did," he says. "You know, awkward dad-confrontation aside."

Theo knows that Max normally wouldn't have had a problem with said confrontation, and that he was only bothered by it because it was with Theo's father. Again, Theo gets the distinct feeling that for once, Max *actually* wants someone to like him, and he has proven that, this whole night, by being so much more subdued and polite than he would normally be. Not to mention censored, which Theo still somehow finds hilarious and adorable.

Theo leans in and kisses him again, slower, this time, taking his time. He feels Max reciprocate, and for several seconds, they just stand there, kissing. They keep it chaste, though, and eventually, they have to pull apart.

"See you tomorrow?" Max says, moving toward the front door.

"Definitely," Theo replies, and they exchange a small smile and another kiss, before Max steps out into the snow and Theo closes the door behind him. And as he does, Theo lets out a slow, deep exhale, feeling more optimistic than he has in a long time.

CHAPTER 21
GIFTS

It's amazing how different it feels, now.

Even though Theo hasn't for a second *not* been happy with Max, it somehow feels so much lighter and better, now that his parents are okay with it. Well, at least his mother is; Eric still seems a bit opposed to the whole thing, only begrudgingly accepting his son's relationship, really.

Riley seems happy about it, though. After the dinner, Theo didn't really ask their father anything about Max, and his impression of him, but Riley wasn't so subtle. He wanted to know what Eric thought, wanted to know if his opinion had changed, now that he had actually talked to Max, properly. Eric was rather reluctant to answer, as though knowing that he would end up saying something bad, and therefore earning another reprimand from his wife. Theo ended up giving Riley a look that asked him to back off, at least for now, and Riley obligingly left their father alone, leaving Eric to sneak out to the garage, while Theo, Riley and their mother cleaned up. No one seemed to mind.

Cassie was thrilled to hear about how the dinner had gone. Theo told her over lunch, at school, while Max joined them, and every now and then, she would tease them both about how adorable and awkward the whole thing seemed to have been. It made Theo smile, and Max humored her, and overall, Theo was just happy that the dinner had gone so well, at all, embarrassing moments aside.

The following couple of weeks, time goes by rather quickly, with a whole bunch of schoolwork suddenly piling on, and it's only around the middle of December, that Theo realizes that Christmas is coming up. He's not the only one, and so he, Max, Riley and Cassie end up taking a trip to the mall, to shop for gifts.

Max isn't really into it, not really into Christmas, but he comes along anyway, mostly because Theo wants him to. He even goes the extra mile and pulls Theo into a kiss, under one of the several mistletoes that are scattered around the mall, at Christmas time, much to Riley's chagrin, Cassie's amusement, and Theo's happy embarrassment.

Cassie and Riley haven't actually met before, but they hit it off immediately, and Theo and Riley find some nice stuff for their parents, pretty early on. They pick out a new toolbox for Eric (knowing that he needs one, and deciding on it, despite Max's and Cassie's teasing about how cliché a gift it is), and a new set of brushes and oil paints for Amy, who's artistic and often laments about how she never has the time to paint, anymore.

It's while Theo is paying for Amy's gift, that Cassie notices Riley drift off toward a different section of the store, and she nudges Theo.

"What's he doing?" she asks Theo, who looks over his shoulder, while he waits in line. Riley is browsing along the jewelry and accessory section, looking slightly awkward, and Theo glances at Max, who raises his eyebrows.

"He doesn't happen to have a lady friend, does he?" he says, and comprehension dawns on Theo's face.

"Actually, he does," he says, before turning to Cassie, who just looks at him.

"What?" she says, and Theo cocks his head toward Riley. Cassie takes the hint and looks slightly indignant.

"Oh," she says, "so *I* have to help him out, just 'cause I've got a vagina?"

Max makes a sound of mock sympathy.

"Aw, don't say that," he says, patting her shoulder. "I'm sure it's the prettiest vagina in all the land."

Cassie downright glares at him, but Max just gives her a mischievous, and simultaneously innocent smile, clearly enjoying her reaction. Cassie just rolls her eyes then, and sighs.

"Fine," she says begrudgingly. "For the girl."

"Thanks," Theo says, but Cassie just mumbles and shakes her head, as she makes her way over to Riley, who looks slightly lost among all the feminine accessories. Theo and Max watch, as Cassie talks to him, and eventually, their suspicions are confirmed; from what Theo can tell, Riley actually *is* looking for a Christmas gift for Ellie, and might be in need of some help.

"Who's the girl?" Max asks, and Theo glances at him, before turning back in his little brother's direction.

"Ellie," he replies. "Our neighbor. They've known each other forever, and Riley has had a crush on her for quite some time."

Max nods.

"And is it reciprocated?" he says, and Theo half-shrugs.

"I think so," he says. "I mean, from what I can tell. Honestly, I think she might have had a crush on him, for even longer. Pretty sure she wouldn't mind, if he finally made a move."

Max makes a small, almost impressed sound.

"What do you know," he says. "Little dude's got game."

Theo's turn in line comes up, and he pays for Amy's gift, before making his way over to the wrapping station, figuring that they might as well. Riley isn't done yet, anyway, and he and Cassie seem to be in the process of selecting a piece of jewelry.

"What do you want for Christmas?" Theo asks Max, as he wraps his mother's gift, and Max's brow furrows slightly.

"What do you mean?" he says, sounding genuinely confused, and Theo glances at him pointedly.

"For Christmas," he clarifies. "What do you want, as a gift?"

Max just blinks.

"Like... from you?" he says dumbly, and Theo quirks a small smile.

"Yeah," he says. "From me."

Max takes a few seconds to answer, actually shifting a bit.

"I don't know," he finally says. "Haven't really thought about it."

Theo cuts up some string to tie around the Christmas-wrapped package, glancing at Max.

"Well, I wanna get you something," he says, and Max frowns again.

"Why?" he asks, and Theo shrugs, tying a knot with the string.

"Because I want to," he says. "You're my boyfriend, I wanna get you a gift."

He looks at Max, suddenly a bit scared that maybe exchanging gifts is a bit too much, despite how far they've already come in their relationship. But Max's expression looks confused, rather than annoyed, and it calms him down a bit.

"You don't have to get me anything," Theo says, shaking his head comfortingly. "I—"

"No, I want to," Max says, a bit hurriedly, and for a moment, he gets that uncharacteristically shy, almost nervous look that Theo still isn't used to. "I mean, I wanna get you something. I just... I didn't really know it was a *thing*, you know?"

He glances at the floor, before glancing away, avoiding Theo's eyes.

"But yeah, I'd like that," he says, looking back at Theo. "And I kinda have to, now, especially if you're getting me something."

He says that last part with obvious, cocky sarcasm, and Theo smiles.

"Awesome," he says, giving Max a light kiss, and Max gives him a small smile, before helping out with the rest of the wrapping.

Riley and Cassie eventually make a purchase, and Theo eyes Riley's gift approvingly as he shows it to him; it's a necklace, a simple, silver chain with a small, matching pendant of a bird.

"Good choice," Theo says, handing it back to Riley, who puts it back in his bag, looking a bit awkward about it.

"And I didn't even pick it out," Cassie says, a bit proudly. "He didn't really need my help."

"Yeah, I did," Riley grumbles, gratefully. "There's so much stuff, and I don't want it to be too much, or awkward, or anything... She might not even like it. Girls are weird."

"I hear ya," Max says, and Cassie punches him in the arm. He rubs his arm gently, turning to her, but gives her nothing but a small, annoying smirk, and Cassie shakes her head. Theo can't help but smile a bit, at their almost sibling-like squabbling, and by the time he's done wrapping Amy's gift, the two of them are still play-fighting, as they all make their way out of the store.

"Max," Riley says after a while, nudging Max. "Come on, let's go."

Max frowns at him, almost suspiciously.

"Why?" he says, and Riley raises his eyebrows pointedly.

"Because Theo's gonna get you a Christmas present," he says, "and you can't be there, when he does."

Max looks at Theo.

"Wait, what?" he says, but Theo only has time to shrug, before Riley has grabbed Max's coat and tugged on it.

"Come on," he says, with complete ease, and Max goes with him.

"Wait, that means I have to get you something," Max tells Theo, as he backs away, with some measure of sarcastic annoyance.

"Don't worry, I'll make sure it's good," Riley promises his brother, before Theo can reply, and Cassie does a salute.

"I've got this end covered," she says, and Riley gives her a nod of mock seriousness, before he and Max turn around and make their way in the other direction. Cassie turns to Theo, who just stands there for a moment, somehow just so happy about the easy familiarity of the whole situation that just unfolded.

"So," Cassie says, and he turns to her. "What are you getting him?"

Theo sighs.

"I have no idea," he admits, and Cassie purses her lips.

"Alright," she says. "We'll think of something. Come on."

They're practically at the center of the mall when they start off, and they spend the next half-hour or so browsing in different stores, trying to think of what would be a suitable gift. Theo quickly finds a gift for Riley, and he and Cassie continue on their quest to find something for Max.

"I want it to be something small," Theo tells Cassie, as they stroll through a shop full of alternative clothes and accessories. He's not sure how they ended up here, but they've been pretty much everywhere else, already. "Something simple. I mean, we haven't really been together that long, and I don't want it to be too big, or anything."

He thinks about how although he and Max haven't officially been together for more than a couple of months, it feels like they've known each other forever, and that he has never felt this close to anyone in his entire life. He's pretty sure Max feels the same way, regardless of how long it's been, time-wise.

But still. He wants to keep the gift simple, just symbolic, more than anything.

"Well," Cassie says, trailing her fingers along some t-shirts hanging on the wall. "What does he like?"

Theo shrugs.

"A bunch of stuff," he says, fiddling with a price tag on a beanie. "And none of it narrows it down, really."

He discards the beanie and looks around.

"I want to get him something that suits him," he says, thinking out loud. "Something ordinary, but also something that stands out, sort of. I want him to know it's from me, you know? Or something, I don't know."

He feels like an idiot, unable to phrase it properly, but Cassie seems to get it.

"Okay," she says, nodding. "So, kind of like a memento of you?"

Theo cocks his head.

"I guess," he says, and Cassie hums to herself, browsing along the wall.

"Something he wouldn't get himself," she murmurs, "but something that he would like. Something that stands out enough to remind him of you..."

Theo feels like Cassie's got a train of thought that he's not really managing to follow, but he doesn't have to think about it for much longer, before she suddenly stops dead.

"Something like this?" she says, picking something out and holding it up in front of Theo, and he just blinks, looking at it. Then he gently takes it from her, turning it over in his hands.

"Yeah," he says softly. "Something like that."

It's a bracelet, made from dark brown leather, a little over an inch wide, with a vague, black imprint of spread wings, as well as a dark silver buckle. It's not much, nothing special. But still. As Theo looks at it, he feels like it's somehow the gift he's been looking for, despite its simplicity. It's dark enough to not look out of place with Max's black attire, yet still different enough to stand out. And it's small, simple, not a big deal. Just something that Max can keep with him, as a memento, as Cassie put it. Just a symbolic gift.

"You like it?" Cassie asks, and Theo nods, eyeing the bracelet.

"Yeah," he says. "It's kinda perfect, actually."

He looks up at Cassie.

"Thanks," he says, and she smiles.

"Happy to help," she says, and Theo purchases the bracelet, deciding to wrap it when he gets home.

They meet up with Max and Riley about half-an-hour later, sitting down at a small café on the second floor of the mall, and Max slides into the seat next to Theo.

"I have fulfilled my boyfriend-related Christmas obligations," he says, after giving Theo a kiss. "You know, the non-dirty kind."

He cocks his eyebrows suggestively at that last part, making both Cassie and Riley cringe, on their side of the table.

"Really, guys?" Cassie says, squinting in disgust. "Here?"

"What?" Max says lightly, leaning back slightly in his seat, just as entertained as usual, at their reactions. "We're all adults."

He glances at Riley, and makes a face.

"Well," he says. "Close enough."

Riley just raises his eyebrows and looks at Theo, who just shrugs as if to say, *isn't he adorable?* Riley really doesn't seem to think so, however, which is funny, in itself.

"What did he get?" Cassie asks Riley, turning to him, and Riley glances at Max and Theo. He looks at Cassie.

"I'll tell you later," he says.

"But it's good?"

"It's good."

Cassie seems satisfied with that reply, and takes a sip of her tea. Both she and Theo have been sitting here for a little while, so they've both got something to drink.

"What about you?" Riley asks Cassie, and she glances at Theo pointedly.

"Yeah," she says, looking at Riley, nodding. "His is good, too."

Riley nods in return, and Theo just watches the two of them, for a moment, before turning to Max, who gives him a look of bemused suspicion, which mirrors Theo's.

"Well, that was weird," Max says lightly, before shrugging out of his coat and dumping it on the seat. "I'm gonna get some coffee. Anybody want anything?"

Both Theo and Cassie decline, but Riley requests some hot cocoa, which Max says is his treat, and he goes off to get some. By the time he comes back, they all end up sitting there for the better part of an hour, just hanging out. Max half-heartedly tries to peek inside Theo's bag, where his purchases are, but Theo stops him and hands the bag to Cassie, who skillfully hides it by her seat. As a pre-emptive measure, Riley does the same with his bag, which apparently holds his gift for Theo, as well as Max's, and soon, Cassie starts asking Riley about Ellie, making him blush slightly in discomfort. But he talks about it anyway, and it's obvious that he really likes Ellie, making Cassie smile and give him some girl-tips.

Theo is just smiling to himself, slightly unfocused, when Max plants a kiss on his cheek, and he turns to him.

"What?" Theo says dumbly, mostly in surprise, but Max just smiles at him. It's a small smile, an unusually soft one, and he lightly brushes his fingers against Theo's hairline, as though he just wants to touch him.

"Nothing," he says, blue eyes sincere. "You just look happy."

Theo doesn't reply. Instead, he just leans in and kisses Max slowly, softly, in a way that undoubtedly proves that he really is.

♦

By the time Christmas rolls around, Theo is sad to learn that Max will be going away for the holidays. Apparently, he and his parents are going to visit some cousins, as they do almost every year, and he'll be gone until New Year's Eve.

"But then, I'll be back," he promises. "And we can at least spend New Year's together."

He narrows his eyes slightly.

"Unless you've got plans?" he says, and Theo smiles at him.

"Now, I do," he replies, giving Max a kiss.

They're at Theo's house, for once, sitting on his bed, and Max is going away tomorrow. Theo's parents aren't home from work, yet, and the two of them are taking this opportunity to exchange Christmas presents, in privacy.

"Now, bear with me, here," Max says, as he hands over his gift. "I barely ever give presents, and I've *never* gotten a present for a boyfriend or anything, before. So... Just keep your expectations low."

Theo looks at him pointedly, and he wants to say something that reprimands Max for putting himself down, like that. But he doesn't, because he knows that Max knows that. And if nothing else, he knows that Max's view of himself has gradually started changing for the better, and comments like that from Theo isn't going to help.

"I'll try to reign myself in," Theo says dryly, handing over his own Christmas present, and Max gives him a small smile of approval, at the blatant sarcasm. "I'd say the same thing, too, by the way. I've never really done this, before."

It's odd how gift-giving puts one under enough stress, as it is, and yet getting a gift for a boyfriend can be so much worse. But Theo wants to give Max something, and he knows that Max realizes that, which kind of takes the pressure off.

"Moment of truth, then," Max says in a low voice, with a melodramatic edge, and Theo huffs a small laugh, as he eyes Max's gift. Max looks up at him. "I'll go first."

Theo gives him a small smile, and watches as Max opens his present.

As the paper goes, he gets to the small box inside, only to open that and find the bracelet, and Theo finds himself practically holding his breath, awaiting a reaction. He suddenly realizes how nervous he feels about the whole thing.

But Max doesn't make him wait long. Instead, he eyes the bracelet for a moment, turning it over in his hands, before smiling, and he looks up at Theo.

"It's so colorful," he says, with obviously joking concern, and Theo rolls his eyes, making Max lean in and kiss him. Theo kisses him back, and when Max pulls away, he looks so happy, somehow, that it takes Theo almost by surprise.

Max glances at the bracelet.

"It even has wings," he says, without an ounce of sarcasm, a smile still on his face. He looks up at Theo again. "I love it. Thank you."

Theo is slightly taken aback by Max's expression, and he feels those butterflies in his stomach, making him smile.

"Well," he says quietly. "You're welcome."

Max just keeps smiling, and it's only after a few seconds, that he takes a steadying breath and nods at the gift in Theo's hands.

"Alright," he says, sounding oddly tense. "Your turn."

Theo obliges, looking at the gift, while Max puts his new bracelet on.

It's rather small, the package about the same size as the one Theo gave Max, and he resists the urge to shake it, like one spontaneously wants to do with every wrapped thing. Instead, he carefully peels away the tape and the wrapping paper, as opposed to Max, who used the different approach of simply tearing the paper off, and eventually, he gets to a box, inside. He turns it over, eyeing it, before opening it.

There's a ring inside. It's a rather plain ring, rather wide and heavy-looking, the color of pewter, and Theo looks up at Max, who is worrying slightly at his bottom lip.

"It's not a *ring* ring, or anything," he blurts, suddenly coming off as very nervous and uncomfortable. "It's just a... It's a ring."

He shrugs awkwardly, glancing away.

"Riley said you'd get it," he mumbles. "That you wouldn't freak out, or anything."

Theo just stares at him, before looking at the ring again. He turns it over in his hand, eyeing it, before deliberating, and deciding that his right ring finger is probably the best fit. And so, he slips in on, and he can see Max glancing at him, apprehensive hope on his face.

Theo looks up at him, and he smiles. Max barely has a chance to smile back, before Theo has attacked him, pushing him back onto the bed, and before Max can object, he's kissing him, with impatient, adoring determination.

"Thank you," Theo murmurs, making Max chuckle against his lips.

"So, not freaking out?" he says, and Theo shakes his head, with a small sound of confirmation.

"Definitely not," he says, and Max smiles, moving his hands up to Theo's face, to pull him closer.

"Good to know," he murmurs, and Theo shifts his weight a bit, so that he's lying half-on-top of Max, allowing him to smooth his hand up underneath Max's shirt and feel his skin. It makes Max inhale deeply, small goosebumps prickling underneath Theo's fingers, and he lets out a small groan.

"You know," Max says against Theo's mouth, hands trailing down along his body, "I'm gonna be gone for a week."

"That's a long time," Theo murmurs absently, planting a few kisses by Max's jaw.

"Yeah," Max agrees. "Not sure how I'm gonna manage."

Theo quirks a small smile.

"That makes two of us," he says against Max's skin. "Not much we can do about it, though."

"Oh, I'm sure we've got time for a quickie," Max says conspiringly, and Theo almost groans.

"I'm sure we don't," he says, his voice betraying just how badly he would want said quickie, but that they simply can't. "My parents are gonna be home any minute."

"So, we'll make it under a minute," Max says, sliding his hand in underneath Theo's jeans and down over his ass. "It's been forever."

Theo can't argue with him on that; they haven't really had the chance to do more than make out, these past couple of weeks. With the lack of time, due to schoolwork, and Theo's dad still not being entirely comfortable with the relationship, restricting their time together a bit, the two of them haven't really been able to hang out as much. And they haven't been able to spend the night together, either, not since the motel, so all they've really been able to do lately is enjoy the occasional handjob and very heavy makeout sessions. Once or twice, they've gone further, but every time, they've been interrupted, and it has started driving Theo insane.

In other words, Max *definitely* isn't the only one feeling frustrated.

"I know it has," Theo says, breathing slightly heavier, as he feels Max getting hard underneath those black skinny jeans. "And I really want to, you have no idea. It's just not a good time."

"It's never a good time," Max says, his breathing matching Theo's, and Theo is barely surprised when he feels Max grind against him roughly, his hand still underneath Theo's pants, grabbing his ass.

Theo lets out a low moan, and he can't help himself. He *needs* Max, needs him like oxygen, and it's enough to make him press down against him, his own hard-on straining against his jeans. It just feels so good, and he relishes the way Max's pierced tongue slides into his mouth, making him groan and grind against him roughly. It feels *so* good...

It's the distinct sound of the front door opening that makes Theo freeze and snap his eyes open. He listens for a moment, before realizing, with a heavy, disappointed sigh, that it is indeed his mother, who's come home from work. And for once, Riley was out of the house, over at Ellie's, giving Theo and Max the privacy they never manage to get in this house. So much for that.

Theo looks down at Max, who's practically panting underneath him, and those dark blue, black-lined eyes are looking right at him, shining with aroused impatience. And then, Max lets out something between a heavy sigh and a bitter laugh.

"Longer than a minute," he says, and Theo chuckles, dropping his head to lean it against Max's shoulder. He feels Max pull his fingers through his hair, and he exhales deeply.

"I'm gonna miss you," Theo says, his tone a mix between sad and frustrated, and Max lets out a small huff, smiling.

"I'm gonna miss you, too," he says, and he kisses Theo's hair. "Merry Christmas."

♦

The week goes by faster than Theo thought it would.

Ellie really liked her gift, apparently, and she got Riley a *Hellboy* graphic novel, which Theo is pretty impressed with, seeing as how Riley doesn't exactly flaunt his fanboyish love for the comic book in question, and therefore she must really know him and what he likes.

Both Amy and Eric liked their gifts, as well, and Riley started playing the videogame Theo got him almost immediately. Theo is glad to have made such a good choice, since Riley was immersed in it within the first twenty minutes.

Riley got Theo the special edition Blu-ray box set of Christopher Nolan's *Batman*-trilogy, and Theo is thrilled to be able to add it to his collection, despite having seen all three movies a bunch of times, already.

Theo doesn't see Cassie for the holidays, but she sends him an e-card, depicting a very disgruntled-looking cartoon version of Loki, from *the Avengers*, dressed up as Rudolph the reindeer, by a very amused Tony Stark. It definitely makes Theo laugh.

Missing Max is nearly unbearable, and only made manageable thanks to the very frequent texts and pictures being sent back and forth between him and Theo. Most of them detail how much they miss each other, and how sick Max is of hanging out with his relatives, none of whom he really likes, but it doesn't matter. Theo just needs to know he's still there, and that he's coming back, so that he doesn't have to go completely out of his mind.

Max isn't exactly shy with letting Theo know just *how* he misses him, either. Apart from the affectionate stuff, there are one or two texts detailing how Max has thought about Theo while in the shower, apparently causing him to come twice in twenty minutes, and picturing that is more than Theo can deal with, to be honest.

Ever since Theo met Max, and ever since they started getting (very) physical, Theo has found himself inappropriately aroused, far too often. And now especially, with Max gone and Theo only being allowed fantasies about him, it's even worse. That started after that night, though, he remembers, the one at the motel. Theo simply can't get it out of his mind.

He wants to do it again. He wants to have sex with Max again, over and over—anything more than a handjob would do, at this point, and as he takes a late night shower, two days before Max's return, he can't stop thinking about it.

He can't stop thinking about Max's lips against his own, hands smoothing over his body. Skin slick with sweat, the feeling of Max's hot mouth swallowing him down, that pierced tongue driving him crazy. Feeling Max move inside him, thrusting and panting, groaning deeply against Theo's ear, making Theo squirm and moan with pleasure. He even thinks about going down on Max; he hasn't gotten the chance to do that again, after that time in the shower. He's somehow surprised to find that he really wants to do it again. He *really* wants to.

Coming in the shower, while muffling his own moans, picturing every possible scenario involving Max, isn't nearly as good as the real thing, but it's good enough. It'll have to be, Theo thinks, if he's going to survive another two days.

♦

When the day before New Year's Eve finally arrives, Theo is so glad to see Max that he feels like he wants to rip his clothes off, right then and there. That is, he would, if his parents weren't present, and Riley wasn't studying at the kitchen table, as Max comes over to their house.

Max can't stay long, though; he needs to help out his parents with some stuff, and he just came over for a little while, simply because he wanted to see Theo. Theo is indescribably happy to see him, and despite (or perhaps, *because* of) the frankly unbearable frustration they both seem to feel at seeing each other, they don't retreat to Theo's room. Neither of them says it, but Theo is pretty sure that Max knows as well as he does, that if they were to be alone together right now, they wouldn't be able to stop themselves.

So, to play it safe, they hang out in the living room, and before Max leaves, they double-check their plans for New Year's Eve.

Michael has invited them both to a New Year's party at some other guy's house, where pretty much everyone is going to be, apparently. Cassie is invited, too, and Theo can't help but think that it's a nice gesture, especially since he and Michael don't hang out, anymore.

Riley is spending New Year's with his friends (including Ellie, Max teasingly points out), and Eric and Amy are going to a party across town. Theo realizes that this is probably the first time he's actually looking forward to New Year's Eve; last year, he spent it at some party with Hannah and Michael, and he left early. All the years before that, he didn't really do much, at all. So this should be a nice change.

Before Max leaves, he pulls Theo into a deep, slow kiss, as they stand in the hall. Both Theo's parents, and his little brother, are well out of earshot, but Max still makes sure they're not around, before leaning in by Theo's ear.

"Good thing we weren't alone," he whispers. "Or I swear, I would've slammed you up against the wall and given you the best blowjob of your life."

Theo involuntarily lets out a small, frustrated moan, barely audible, but Max clearly notices the way he grits his teeth and grips Max's coat tightly.

"Stop it," Theo growls, and Max gives him a small, mischievous smile.

"Or, you'll what?" he says, his voice just above a whisper, and he nips at Theo's bottom lip gently, with his teeth, making Theo suck in a sharp breath. "Just giving you something to think about, later. God knows, it's what I'll be thinking about."

He pulls away slightly, and Theo looks at him, certain that Max can see just how unbearably turned-on he is, right now. Max quirks a small smile, blue eyes burning.

"See you tomorrow," he says, and they share one last, searing kiss, before Max walks out the front door.

That night, Theo's mind is filled with the images Max has just put there, and he must admit, the effects of it put every other orgasm he's had that week to shame.

CHAPTER 22

MIDNIGHT

It's not like Theo hasn't been to a party, before. He has, more than once, even though he generally doesn't like it much.

This time, though, it's a tad different.

Max and Theo meet up with Cassie, and they go to the New Year's Eve party together. When they get there, the party seems to be in full swing, and the music and shouting can be heard from the street, making Theo feel a little bit apprehensive. Cassie shares his reservations, but Max coerces them inside, and they end up having a pretty good time.

Michael is there, and Theo is grateful that they can still be friends, and on good terms. Hannah is there, too, and while she still seems rather apprehensive about Max, and Theo's relationship with him, she's much kinder about it than Theo expected her to be. She even says hello to Cassie, who is visibly surprised, seeing as how she and Hannah aren't exactly best friends anymore, like they used to be. Theo wonders if Michael has talked to Hannah about the whole thing, or if she has simply warmed up to it, but either way, he's glad.

There's alcohol at the party, lots of it, and although Theo has been drunk before, he finds himself feeling a little bit out of place. It's nothing compared to Max, though, as he moves through the crowd; people blatantly stare at him, with a mix of suspicion and recognition, but as usual, Max doesn't seem to care. He's as comfortable as ever (which he tends to especially be, when making others uncomfortable), and soon enough, he oddly blends right in. He's not one to waste time on people who don't like him, anyway, and he mostly hangs out with Theo and Cassie, instead.

It ends up being a rather fun night, and later during the party, Theo is pleased to see Cassie talking to some brunette, clearly flirting, and apparently getting somewhere with it. She's twirling her red hair around her finger, the other girl giggling and smiling, gradually moving in closer and closer, and Theo nudges Max, nodding in Cassie's direction. Max makes a face, looking very impressed.

"Nice," he says, taking a drink of his beer. "Respect."

They don't see much of Cassie, after that, and Theo finds himself drinking more than he expected. Max does, too, and more than once, he simply grabs a hold of Theo and pulls him into a corner, practically shoving his tongue down his throat. Not that Theo exactly minds, but he can't help but feel that it's a bit too public for him to be entirely comfortable, despite the very intoxicated state everyone is in.

It doesn't make Max's persuasion any easier to resist, though. The moment Theo feels those hands on him, those lips against his own, he can feel himself melt and become pliant against Max's body, leaving him breathless, and pretty much moments away from ripping Max's clothes off, right there. It's not a feeling Theo is used to, not in a place and time like this, but he likes it. It feels drunk and urgent and eager, and he has to force himself to pull away, more than once. He can even feel himself getting hard, and that's as far as he's willing to go, at this point; his self-control is precarious, at best, and there are people everywhere.

It's later on that Max seems to decide something needs to be done, and he simply grabs Theo's wrist and drags him up the stairs. They're both pretty drunk, at this point, and apart from the slight disorientation, all Theo can really focus his attention on right now, is how hot Max's ass looks in those jeans.

There aren't quite as many people on the second floor, and Max tries a random door, which appears to be locked. When he tries a second one, though, it opens, and he pulls Theo with him inside. It's only when the light has been turned on and the door has been locked behind them, that Theo realizes that they're in a bathroom.

Not that Theo even manages to mention this, before Max grabs onto him, fierce, slightly dazed determination in those dark blue eyes.

Theo actually gasps when Max kisses him. Not because he's doing it, but because of *how*, as he actually grabs onto Theo's sweater and promptly steers him backwards, until Theo feels the wall pressed up against his back. He barely even has a chance to react, and when Max pulls away, Theo just stares at him, eyes wide.

"What?" he says, breathlessly, and Max tilts his head.

"What?" he mirrors innocently, and Theo blinks at him.

"What are you doing?" he asks, while Max eyes him up and down. One hand is deliberately moving downward now, down toward Theo's crotch.

"I have no idea what you're talking about," Max murmurs, and looks up again at Theo, as he presses with his hand against the bulge in Theo's pants. And Theo exhales sharply.

"Really?" he says, startled and suddenly very turned-on, all at the same time. "Here? Right now?"

Max quirks a small smile at his outraged tone.

"Yeah," he says, his smile simply predatory. "Why not?"

"Because we're in someone else's bathroom, for one," Theo replies, his voice lowered to almost a whisper, slightly husky, slightly less inhibited than usual. "It's not exactly appropriate."

Max utters a low groan that sounds more like a growl.

"You know what's not appropriate?" he asks, voice low, as he moves his mouth closer to Theo's. "This, right here."

He grabs Theo's crotch pointedly, and Theo stifles a pleased groan.

"Max," he says. "Really not a good time."

"Really?" Max says, cocking his eyebrows. "You're the one who's had a boner for the past half-hour, or so."

He kisses Theo softly, and Theo widens his eyes in surprise and slight panic at Max's information. It's not like he hasn't been aware of said boner, but still; the thought of everyone else noticing makes him feel positively mortified.

Max smiles mischievously at his discomfort.

"Relax," he says. "It didn't show, or anything."

He moves one hand up to gently grip Theo's chin with his fingers, while smiling at him wickedly.

"I just know your expressions," he says, still smiling. "It's written all over you."

Theo swallows hard, trying not to think about how *hot* this whole situation is. It wasn't exactly planned, and although he has indeed been much more keyed up around Max, lately (and when he's alone, just *thinking* about Max), he didn't actually expect to be able to do anything about it, right now. And if nothing else, they're not alone. For the first time while doing this, they're not alone in the house, they're even at someone *else's* house, and it makes Theo feel so much more tense.

Max watches his expressions, watches Theo squirm slightly against him, Max's hand slowly massaging him through his jeans. It makes Theo close his eyes for a moment, before opening them again and looking straight into that intense, dark blue. Max looks amused, somehow, hungry and intrigued. There's a slightly dazed, drunken look to those eyes as well, mirroring Theo's own, and it's enough to make Theo even harder. Max smiles slyly at him.

"Look at you," he murmurs. "Pinned against the wall, people right outside the door, and a hot guy feeling you up."

He chuckles. There's something dark about it, something that makes Theo's heart race.

"Yeah," Theo says, a bit breathlessly, to his own surprise. "Probably not the best idea."

"Oh, but I think it's a great idea," Max says, moving both hands down to slowly undo the fly of Theo's jeans, blue eyes on Theo's the whole time. "You need it."

Theo doesn't stop him. He's honestly shocked at himself for not stopping him, because the timing of this whole situation is just weirdly *wrong*, and completely out of place. But it just feels so *good*, and Max's hands feel so good, as they tug at his jeans the slightest bit, just enough for Max to slip one hand underneath them and massage Theo, with nothing but a thin barrier of cotton in between.

Theo involuntarily moans, but then snaps his mouth shut. He can't do this, can't make a sound. Not when they're at someone else's house, and there are several people right outside. Anyone could come in, for god's sake, it doesn't even matter that the bathroom door is locked. And it doesn't matter that Max touching him right now is the hottest thing, ever.

"See?" Max nearly whispers, leaning in so that his lips are just by Theo's ear. "You're so tense."

He plants a soft kiss by Theo's jaw.

"Fuck, I missed you."

Theo actually closes his eyes, then, trying not to breathe too heavily. The walls aren't exactly paper-thin, and the music is so loud he can feel its vibrations, but still. He has never had to be quiet with Max, before, so he's making a point of not really doing anything, at all, just in case.

"Really not a good time, Max," he breathes, his voice-control already compromised, head slightly dazed from the alcohol, but Max just plants a soft kiss against his throat.

"I'll make it quick, I swear," he murmurs. "I know all your sweet spots, remember?"

311

As if to enforce this, Max slowly slips his hand underneath Theo's boxers and wraps his fingers around him, and Theo has to grit his teeth to keep himself from groaning loudly.

"I'll make you come, in no time," Max says, a small, amused smile in his voice. "Promise."

He starts moving his hand, then, stroking slowly, and Theo tilts his head back, leaning it against the wall, parting his lips in a low, weak moan.

"That's it," Max murmurs in his ear. "Let me take care of you."

Theo swallows hard, keeps his eyes closed. What the hell is happening? What the hell is Max doing, and why the *hell* is this so hot and making Theo feel so turned-on that he can't even see straight? It's ridiculous. And it feels so damn *good*.

Max starts kissing his neck, slowly, and Theo moans quietly. If they were alone, he would be moaning much louder right now, especially as Max starts stroking him faster, while planting slow, searing kisses against his skin. And when Max moves his other hand down to Theo's ass, and slips his hand underneath his underwear, touching his bare skin, Theo actually groans in pleased surprise, making Max pull away a little bit. Theo opens his eyes.

"We're gonna have to do this quietly," Max says, looking at Theo pointedly, blue eyes slightly unfocused, and Theo notices how he's stopped stroking him. "Alright?"

Theo just looks at him, swallows hard. His entire body is buzzing, desperate for Max's touch, for him to continue what he's started.

"Don't stop," Theo hears himself murmur, and he swears he can see a glint of hungry arousal in those dark blue eyes.

"I won't," Max says. "But you need to be quiet. Can you do that?"

Theo knows that Max is just teasing him, that he's savoring every moment of making Theo pant and come undone, like this, and that he couldn't really care less if anyone hears them. And on some level, it annoys Theo. But right now, all he wants is for Max to keep going, his hands completely and annoyingly still against his skin.

Theo nods, and Max gives him a small nod, in return.

"Good," Max says, and he keeps his eyes on Theo, as he slowly starts stroking again. And Theo bites back a deep moan of pleasure, Max keeping his eyes on him, as he grabs his ass, pressing him a bit closer, one hand stroking him faster and faster.

Theo closes his eyes again, tilting his head back, breathing steadily to keep all those euphoric sounds suppressed, while he places his hands on Max's hips. His fingers slowly dig into that black shirt, lips parting as Max's pierced tongue pushes into his mouth, and soon, everything starts spinning. Theo isn't quite sure if it's the alcohol, or the excitement, or just the sensation of having Max touching him like this, when they could easily be interrupted any minute, but it's simply *fantastic,* and he never wants it to stop.

In a matter of seconds, Theo is losing his mind, digging his fingers into Max's black, messy hair, his other hand firmly placed against his hip, gripping so tightly that it just might leave bruises, but Max doesn't seem to care. Instead, he just keeps going, keeps touching and stroking, moaning into Theo's mouth, and suddenly, everything just stops. Suddenly, everything is just suspended in one wonderful second, as Theo feels that blissful release, and he has to actually cling to Max to keep himself from falling over.

He's only vaguely aware of Max pulling away, and he slowly opens his eyes to look down. It seems that Max, while Theo was too blissed-out to notice, grabbed a washcloth lying nearby, to make sure that they didn't make a mess anywhere, and Theo watches as Max glances at it apprehensively.

"Not sure I thought this through," Max murmurs, sounding intoxicated. "I was gonna make it last longer, go down on you and stuff... Guess we got a bit overeager."

He chuckles as he looks up at Theo, nodding at the washcloth in his hand.

"We should probably just throw this away."

Theo lets out something between a groan and a sigh, weirdly not feeling even slightly disappointed at the blowjob he apparently just missed out on, to be honest.

"Seriously?" he says breathlessly. "Not only are we in someone else's house, in their bathroom, now we're ruining their stuff?"

"Oh, come on," Max says, looking around for a place to put the used-up and stained washcloth. "Worth it."

Theo rolls his eyes, while slightly clumsily zipping up his pants and making sure there are no traces of his activities anywhere on him. He is a bit drunk, though, and absently feels like he wouldn't really trust his own judgment and observational skills right now, anyway. But still.

"I guess," Theo murmurs, before leaning back against the wall, feeling immensely satisfied, and Max turns to him. He's not the same level of drunk as Theo, probably much more so actually, and he smirks mischievously.

"Oh, I just love corrupting you," he says smugly, and Theo scoffs, as Max spots a trashcan and drops the stained washcloth into it, before closing the lid.

"Fuck you," Theo murmurs affectionately, and Max gives him an approving glance.

"Now, there's an idea," he says, and Theo just looks at him for a moment, a slight frown on his face.

"Huh?" he says dumbly, and Max moves in closer, putting his hands on Theo's hips.

"Fucking me," he says, with a completely straight face, as usual. He leans in closer, his piercing brushing against Theo's lips, and Theo mirrors Max and puts his hands on those hips, feeling them move slightly closer to him. "I like that idea."

Theo doesn't reply. Instead, he just swallows hard, eyes half-open and looking straight into Max's stunningly blue ones.

"You do?" he finally says, voice low and a bit hesitant, and Max hums in confirmation.

"I do," he says, in that unusually low, smoky voice. He gives Theo a light kiss. "Having you inside me, making me moan... Can't say I haven't thought about it."

He kisses Theo again, but Theo just feels somehow too stunned to reciprocate properly. Max doesn't seem to notice, though; he's oddly dazed and unfocused, and Theo is reminded of the fact that he has been drinking. Theo has, too, but not as much as Max, and it's getting increasingly obvious. Not that Theo really minds.

"You fucking me," Max murmurs, moving one hand up to Theo's face and slowly sliding his pierced tongue along his bottom lip. It makes Theo shiver. "Yeah, I've thought about it. It's made me come, thinking about it."

Theo makes a low, strangled sound. Alright, he might be used to Max's way of talking, by now, but he still has some trouble with this. Mostly because it still makes him uncomfortable, while it simultaneously makes him so very turned-on, and he swallows hard, tightening his grip on Max's hips.

"You want that?" he hears himself say in an intoxicated murmur, and Max groans against his mouth.

"Yes, I do," he replies, moving in closer and pressing up against Theo. "I really do."

He kisses Theo again, slowly, deeply, and Theo swears he's getting hard again, just from hearing Max say these things. And this kiss isn't helping, neither is the alcohol, and god help him, he feels like he just might give in to Max's wish, right here and now, regardless of the circumstances, and regardless of the fact that he has never done it before. He just really wants to. Suddenly, he really wants to do it, to take Max like Max did with him, that night at the motel, and he absently slides his hands down to Max's ass, pulling him closer.

He could do it. They could, they could do it right now, and Theo wouldn't care about the consequences. All of a sudden, it's all he can think about.

That is, until Max suddenly jerks away, blue eyes wide.

"What?" Theo says, but Max doesn't reply. Instead, he claps his hand over his mouth, eyes dazed, unfocused, and slightly panicked, and it only takes another second for Theo to catch on.

"Oh," he says, surprise coloring his tone, and he glances around quickly, before using his hands to steer Max over to the toilet, where he opens the lid. And almost immediately, Max falls to his knees and throws up.

Theo just stands there for a moment, confused, before shaking his head, as though trying to sober up. *Oh.* Well, that was unexpected.

He doesn't dwell on it, though. Instead, he crouches down beside Max, and gently rubs his back, trying to be of some kind of comfort, and after a little while, Max takes a deep, heaving breath. He groans.

"I'm sorry," he mumbles, leaning over the toilet seat, and Theo sighs softly.

"It's fine," he says. "Don't worry about it."

Max just groans again.

"No, I'm gross, and I totally killed the romance," he says, before looking up at Theo. Those blue eyes are still dazed, his face pale, and he looks positively pitiable. "Thanks, though."

Theo quirks a small smile, still gently rubbing Max's back, not mentioning how they both probably know that the previous atmosphere wasn't so much one of *romance* as one of *drunk, hormone-fueled passion.*

"You're welcome," he says softly, and he gets the tiniest, affectionate smile, in return.

It takes another few minutes before Max feels better, during which Theo thinks about what they were actually doing, earlier. Before the very sudden, and almost hilariously abrupt mood shift.

He was ready to do it. Seriously, he felt completely ready to do it, to have sex with Max, to simply take him, right here and now, in this bathroom, in someone else's house. It feels a bit surreal, and on some level, he's glad it didn't come to that. He's pretty sure he wouldn't have wanted the first time to be in a place like this, not like that, and he's pretty sure Max wouldn't have wanted that, either. He's somehow glad that the whole thing was interrupted.

Not that he's glad Max isn't feeling well, and puking his guts out, but still.

Eventually, Max feels better, and Theo gets a washcloth (a different, *clean* washcloth), soaks it in cold water, and holds it against Max's forehead. His skin is clammy, and he glances at Theo, while sitting on the floor and leaning against the wall, a somehow confused, almost suspicious look mixed in with his affectionate expression.

"You're still here," he murmurs, so low that Theo can barely hear him.

"Of course, I am," Theo says, using the cold washcloth to gently dab Max's face. Max actually closes his eyes a bit, letting out a soft sigh.

"That feels really good," he mumbles, nearly slurs. "I've never had anyone take care of me like this, before."

"No?" Theo asks, and Max very slowly shakes his head, as though to keep himself from making any sudden movements, lest he throw up again.

"No," he says. "Not that I usually get shitfaced and throw up, but it happens. And when it does, I'm usually alone."

Theo doesn't reply right away. Instead, he's hit with a sense of sadness he has felt before, one that makes him want to pull Max as close as he can and make sure he never has to feel any kind of loneliness or pain, ever again.

"How you feeling?" Theo asks after a while, and Max groans, opening his eyes.

"Like shit," he practically slurs. "But better."

Theo gives him a small, fond smile, one which Max tiredly returns.

"Maybe we should leave," Theo suggests, and Max frowns.

"But it's not midnight, yet," he says hoarsely, and Theo checks his phone. Sure enough; it's not even eleven o'clock.

"So?" he says, putting his phone back in his pocket, and Max keeps his frown.

"It's New Year's Eve," he says tiredly, and Theo sighs.

"I don't care," he says. "We're getting you home. Come on."

Max weakly protests a few more times, complaining about how they need to do New Year's *properly,* but Theo still manages to get him off the bathroom floor and out into the hallway outside. As soon as he exits the bathroom, Max's arm slung over his shoulders and Max leaning against him, he's met with looks that range from concerned, to confused, to somehow impressed, and he manages to navigate through the crowd and down the stairs.

Cassie spots them as they make their way to the front door, and Theo explains to her that he and Max are leaving early, making her pout slightly.

"But it's not even midnight, yet," she points out, and Theo cocks his head.

"Yeah," he admits, "but we're making that sacrifice. You staying?"

Cassie makes a face, looking a bit mischievous, actually.

"Well," she says, "I think I've got a pretty good shot at a New Year's kiss with that girl I've been talking to, so..."

Theo raises his eyebrows slightly.

"The brunette?" he asks, and Cassie nods. Theo gives her an impressed look. "She's hot."

"So hot," Max agrees drunkenly, and Cassie smiles at him.

"Yeah, I know, right?" she says, looking up at Theo. "Well, happy new year, guys."

She gives Theo a kiss on the cheek, before doing the same with Max, and she gives them a sly smile.

"Wish me luck," she says, before hurrying off through the crowd to find the girl she was talking about.

Theo watches her go, a fond smile on his face. He and Max then make their way into the hall, where they soon find their coats, and quickly make their way out the front door.

It's freezing outside, and Theo immediately feels himself sober up quite a bit. Max, however, isn't responding quite the same way.

"I'm sorry," he says, leaning slightly against Theo, but no longer with his arm over his shoulders, as they make their way along the street outside the house. "I don't usually drink so much. I think someone spiked my drink."

Theo raises his eyebrows slightly.

"Someone spiked your alcoholic drink?" he asks pointedly, with a small, teasing smile. He knows that *spike* can refer to a number of things here, but Max seems to forget that, and groans.

"Well, you can spike it with *more* alcohol, can't you?" he retorts lazily, and Theo cocks his head.

"I suppose," he says. Then he takes Max's hand, lacing their fingers together, as he plants a soft kiss by Max's temple. "But it's fine, either way. Don't worry about it. I'm just glad you're okay."

Max sighs heavily, and by the time they're about a block away from the house, at a rather quiet part of the street, he suddenly stops walking. Theo stops, as well, and turns to look at him. Max seems to deliberate for a moment.

"I love you," he eventually nearly slurs, and Theo quirks a small, fond smile.

"I know," he says, placing himself in front of Max, so that they're face to face. "I love you, too."

But Max just shakes his head then, looking down at Theo's chest, rather than his face, while moving up his hands to grip Theo's jacket..

"No," he says, sounding oddly determined. "No, you don't understand."

He exhales sharply, frowning, as though thinking of what to say.

"I *really* love you," he settles on, "*so* much."

He tugs on Theo's jacket slightly, a strange, almost pained expression on his face, eyes still fixed on Theo's chest.

"And you—" he swallows hard. "I'm a mess. I'm not... *good*. And you're still here."

He moves his hands to Theo's shoulders, as he says it, his upper arms, touching his chest experimentally, as though checking to see if Theo is still actually corporeal, still real.

"It doesn't make sense," he murmurs, and Theo feels a confused, somehow sad, frown settle on his face.

"Hey," he says, moving one hand up to Max's face, so that he can tilt it upwards, finding those blue, drunken eyes with his own. "I'm not going anywhere."

Max grits his teeth slightly, and Theo is honestly shocked to see that those eyes are a bit glossy, shining with actual, impending tears, and he just stares for a moment, somehow confused. Then, he pulls Max closer and puts his arms around him, feeling him lean into him and reciprocate the embrace.

"You *are* good," Theo says, moving one hand up to stroke Max's hair, as he feels his boyfriend pretty much cling to him, fingers digging into his jacket. "You're amazing. You're the best thing that's ever happened to me, and I want to be with you."

He kisses his hair.

"I'm not going anywhere."

"But why?" Max's voice sounds oddly thick, now, slightly muffled against the scarf around Theo's neck. He sounds confused, almost angry, and Theo swears he can hear those tears threatening to spill over. "It doesn't make any sense. Why would you want that?"

"Because I love you," Theo says softly, without hesitation. "Plain and simple."

Max emits a muffled sound that's halfway between a groan and a sob, and he grips Theo even tighter.

"But I'm a wreck," he says, sounding more emotional than Theo has ever really heard him, before. "I can barely function, and you make it better, and that scares me, okay? It fucking scares me."

Max exhales heavily, almost shakily, face still burrowed against Theo's neck.

"I'm a complete fuck-up," he says, voice muffled, and Theo sighs softly.

"But you're mine," he says, pulling his fingers through that black, messy hair, stroking it softly. "And you're not a fuck-up. You're not. And if nothing else, I'm not exactly perfect."

"Yes, you are." Max's reply is immediate, tired and sincere, and Theo feels like contradicting him. He knows that he's not perfect, even Max isn't perfect, just like *no one* is perfect, and that's the beauty of it. Loving someone and being loved in return, despite such an array of imperfections; that's what makes it beautiful. And he knows that Max would normally agree with him, being the rational, cynical person that he is.

But right now, Max isn't being rational. He's baring his heart to Theo, along with its deepest insecurities, and even if Theo somehow managed to get over how emotional and intimate that makes all of this, and how emotional and downright moved it makes *him*, he wouldn't contradict Max. Not right now. Instead, he sighs softly, again wishing that he could somehow wrap Max up and keep him safe from everything, forever, and make him realize how amazing he really is.

"Let's get you home, okay?" he says after a few moments, softly pulling away from Max so that he can look at him. Those blue eyes are still glossy, but it doesn't look like there will be any actual crying involved, at the moment.

Max groans, both looking and sounding positively exhausted, and oddly sad.

"I don't wanna go home," he says, shaking his head, still holding on to Theo. "I wanna be with you."

"Max—"

"Don't make me go home." Max looks at Theo, almost pleadingly. "Please."

And immediately, Theo decides to obey his wish. Because if he can, he wants Max with him always, all the time, and tonight is no exception.

"Okay," he says, pushing Max's hair back in an affectionate gesture, giving him a small smile. "Come on."

Theo's house is empty, when they get to it. With Riley at a friend's house, and with Theo's parents both away for the night, it's oddly quiet, especially in contrast to the celebrations outside, and in neighboring houses.

Max has sobered up a bit by the time they step into the hallway and out of the cold, and he seems to be mostly exhausted, now. Theo makes a point to get them both a big glass of water, before they make their way upstairs, to Theo's room.

"We left too early," Max murmurs tiredly, as he flops down onto Theo's bed, fully clothed. "It's not right."

"You can barely stand," Theo retorts, nudging Max slightly so he can get to the blanket that covers his bed. He tugs on it, making Max groan as he has to shift his weight. "And we're not missing anything."

Max sighs heavily, eyes closed.

"Guess not," he nearly slurs, and Theo watches him for a moment, deliberating, before he quirks a small smile, and lies down beside him. He pulls the blanket over both of them, and as Max notices, he cracks those blue eyes open a little bit. He moves in closer, putting his arm around Theo and making Theo shift slightly, so that he's lying more comfortably. He glances down at his boyfriend, whose eyes are closed again, his face nuzzled against the crook of Theo's neck. Theo just looks at him for a few moments, tightening his arm a bit around Max, using his other hand to smooth over his hair.

It's oddly quiet, and they just lie like that for a few minutes, until Theo hears a loud bang, and looks up.

There's a window to side of his bed, a few feet away, and through it, he can see that the black night sky is suddenly lit up with fireworks, sparks of green and red and gold scattering among the stars. He glances at the alarm clock on his nightstand; sure enough, it reads midnight.

Several more fireworks go off, and Theo hears loud voices in the street, whooping and shouting in celebration. His room is dark, apart from the light of the lamp beside his bed, so the bright sparks of the fireworks outside are projected on the walls, just slightly.

Max stirs then, a little bit, no doubt disturbed by the cacophony outside the window.

"'Sit midnight?" he slurs, not opening his eyes, and Theo nods.

"Yeah," he says softly, and Max hums in reply, before another few seconds pass.

"Happy new year, Theo," he eventually murmurs, cracking his eyes open again just the slightest bit, only to lean in and plant a soft, clumsy kiss on Theo's mouth. And Theo nearly chuckles, as Max pulls away and puts his head back on Theo's shoulder, closing his eyes and nuzzling against the crook of his neck. Theo just looks at him, pulls back a stray tuft of black hair from his face, and smiles.

"Happy new year, Max," he says, and kisses his forehead, Max's presumably sleeping form warm and relaxed against him.

Theo settles against the pillows with a sigh, arms around Max, eyes on the window, watching the fireworks. The whole thing is oddly peaceful, and he's pleasantly aware of his boyfriend, sleeping soundly and breathing deeply, right next to him.

It may not have been the New Year's Eve he imagined, he thinks, definitely not, with far too much drinking and incoherent talking and hooking up in weird places. It's not what he had in mind.

But it's still the best New Year's Eve he has ever had.

CHAPTER 23
BUILD

The next morning, Theo is awake before Max.

It's not surprising, really, considering what shape Max was in when he pretty much passed out last night, and Theo yawns tiredly, as he blinks against the harsh light of the winter morning.

It seems that both of them slept this way, fully clothed, cuddled up together underneath a blanket on Theo's bed, and although Theo's limbs are stiff from staying in pretty much the same position all night, he's happy. He's happy, because this is the first time in weeks that he has woken up with Max by his side, and he can't help but smile as he notices it. He can't help but smile, as he notices that black, messy bedhead, resting against the pillows, Max's face nuzzled against the crook of Theo's neck, one hand softly gripping the fabric of Theo's t-shirt.

Theo just stares at Max's sleeping form for a few moments, before his stiff joints get the best of him, and he squirms slightly, shifting onto his side. Max barely seems to notice, and Theo makes sure the blanket doesn't slide off him completely, tugging it up over Max's shoulders, making Max curl up just a little bit, in his sleep. And Theo keeps looking at him, too blissful to even bother feeling weird about it.

Will he ever get tired of just looking at Max? Regardless of the circumstances, Theo can't seem to help it, his eyes searching every part of Max's face, from those cheekbones to those gorgeous, blue—at the moment, closed—eyes. That lip piercing, the metal stud in his left eyebrow, and that smooth skin that's really only coarse when there's dark stubble scattered across those cheeks and that jaw. The way he looks so sweet and safe, when he sleeps, his expression devoid of any kind of cynical sarcasm.

Theo barely wants to blink, because he can't stop looking at Max.

He can't, because good god, he is just *so beautiful*. He's so beautiful, and Theo can hardly believe that this wonderful, amazing person is *his*.

Theo is slightly surprised when he suddenly hears Max speak, and he blinks a little.

"Theo," Max murmurs, barely moving his lips, eyes still closed.

"Yeah?" Theo says, his voice soft.

"Are you staring at me?"

Theo hesitates for a moment.

"Maybe," he gets out, and Max cracks open one stunningly blue eye.

"Should I be creeped out?" he asks, voice cracked from sleep, and Theo quirks a tiny, almost shy smile.

"Up to you, I guess," he says, and Max seems to consider that for a moment, before smiling sleepily.

"Well, to be fair," he says, "I've done it, too."

Theo feels a faint sense of surprise, but still somehow accepts it, right away. He does, because he loves the idea of Max being unable to stop staring, too. And no, he doesn't care about how creepy that sounds, at least not right now.

Max opens both eyes then, just squinting, really, and reaches out to pull Theo closer. Theo lets him, and soon, they're tangled together under the blanket, foreheads touching. Max gives Theo the smallest kiss, and Theo reciprocates, too happy to even care about the morning breath, Max sighing contentedly, as he nuzzles up closer.

It's amazing, really, how Max never would have done this, only a few months ago. Back then, just the prospect of being this close seemed to terrify him, and Theo is immensely happy that that has changed.

"How you feeling today?" Theo asks, with the slightest, teasing hint in his voice, and Max groans.

"Hungover," he mumbles. "Not to mention, embarrassed."

"Why?"

Max pulls back a little, just far enough to give Theo a tired, pointed stare that says *seriously?* Theo gives him a small smile.

"It wasn't that bad," he says, but Max doesn't seem to believe him.

"Really?" he says, doubtfully. "'Cause I vaguely remember being a bit of a pain."

He frowns then, running his tongue over his teeth, behind his lips. He looks thoughtful, and then stops.

"I threw up, didn't I?" he says, sounding somehow bored, and Theo presses his lips together, which is answer enough for Max, who sighs. "Awesome."

He thinks about it for another moment, remembering.

"And you were there that whole time?"

Theo nods, and Max groans, lowering his head and shimmying down along the bed, just far enough to allow him to bury his face against the hollow of Theo's throat.

"I'm sorry you had to see that," he says, his voice muffled against Theo's skin. "And I said some stuff, too."

"Yeah, I know," Theo says, moving one hand up to stroke Max's hair. "I was there."

"I can't believe you heard all that," Max continues, as though Theo hasn't said anything. "Fuck, I was such an idiot."

"I wouldn't say that," Theo says. "You were just... unusually honest."

Max doesn't reply for a few moments, moving his hand up along Theo's back and softly gripping his t-shirt.

"I know what I said," he says quietly. "I remember everything."

Theo stays silent.

"And I meant it," Max continues. "All of it. I just..."

He sighs heavily, his warm breath pleasant against Theo's neck.

"I just don't usually talk like that," he says, and Theo kisses his hair.

"I know," he says. "Do you remember what *I* said?"

Max seems to think about it for a moment, before he nods.

"I meant it, too," Theo says. "And you really don't have to feel embarrassed."

It's after several seconds of silence, that Max lifts his head and looks up at Theo, their eyes meeting. He looks tired, exhausted really, but most of all, he somehow looks small. Vulnerable. It's enough to make Theo pull him closer and nuzzle against his skin, for once not the least bit eager to get the clothes off either of them. He doesn't want that, not right now, and neither does Max. Right now, Theo just wants to lie here, and hold him, and feel Max's steady breathing, matching his own.

By the time they actually get up, it's almost noon. They both clean up and brush their teeth (Max, especially, borrowing an unopened, spare toothbrush of Theo's), and from what Theo can tell, neither Riley nor his parents are home yet. And sure enough, when he and Max get downstairs, there's no one around.

Max goes outside for a quick smoke, before the two of them fry up some eggs, with a side of soda and painkillers, and Theo is hit by just how good this feels, for some reason. It's so easy, so comfortable, like they wake up together every day, and he can't resist the urge to give Max a kiss every chance he gets. And Max smiles, scoffing at him, but does nothing, really, to stop him.

Later on, Theo is sitting on the couch in the living room, watching an old episode of *Torchwood,* when Max shuffles in, looking exhausted. He has made a cup of coffee, Theo sticking to his glass of water.

"I don't deserve this," Max grumbles, rubbing his temple with his free hand, coffee in the other, as he makes his way over to the couch. Theo just smiles at him.

"Sorry, babe," he says. "Karma."

Max just glares at him, before putting his mug down on the coffee table. He sits down with a huff.

"I don't care," he says, squinting slightly, as he lies down on his back, head in Theo's lap. "I should not be so vehemently punished for drinking alcohol. The embarrassment that comes with it should be enough."

Theo hums in agreement, moving his hand down to pull his fingers through Max's mussed, black hair. Max looks up at him, blue eyes still framed by last night's eyeliner. It's barely even smudged, just a bit smoky, as usual.

"I've had worse hangovers, though," he says, moving his hand up over his head to gently take Theo's, and Theo lazily laces their fingers together. "This isn't half-bad."

Theo gives him a small smile, before Max rolls over onto his side, his head still in Theo's lap. Theo's fingers keep carding through his hair, slowly, softly.

"Any New Year's resolutions?" Theo asks after a little while, and Max sighs.

"Not really," he finally says, before letting out a small chuckle. "Quit smoking, maybe?"

He glances up at Theo.

"How about that?"

Theo thinks about it. Honestly, he hasn't even thought about that, before. Somehow, smoking just feels like such a big part of who Max is, and it has been from the moment they met, so Theo kind of has a hard time imagining him without it. But still...

Max cuts off his train of thought.

"A little unoriginal, I guess," he says, settling back against Theo's lap, and Theo looks down at him.

"Well," he says. "I'm not a exactly a big fan of you shortening your lifespan, anyway."

Max grunts.

"Yeah," he says. "It is a nasty habit."

He looks up at Theo, a small smile on his face.

"I look hot, though," he says, and Theo smiles.

"Maybe less so," he says, "when you're so aware of it."

Max laughs, clearly picking up on Theo's teasing tone.

"Hard not to be," he says cockily, lowering his gaze again, and he lets out a content sigh, as he settles back against Theo.

"How about you?" he asks after a little while, and Theo thinks about it, before shaking his head.

"Nope, can't really think of anything," he says. "Can't really think of anything else I *want*."

Max pauses.

"Anything *else*?" he asks, to clarify, and Theo can't help but smile softly at him, even though Max is looking away, and can't see.

"Yeah," he says, his hand still pulling through Max's hair, and he can practically feel Max leaning into his touch. "I have everything I want."

Max seems to hesitate then, as though scared to hope what Theo might be referring to, before he slowly looks up again. He swallows.

"I don't think I want anything else, either," he says after a moment, and Theo smiles, as if to give Max the confirmation he needs, that he indeed *is* what Theo is referring to. And he can feel Max relaxing a bit, as though put to ease.

"Good," Theo says quietly, before Max looks away again, and Theo turns his attention back to the TV.

They stay like that for a while, Theo's fingers in Max's hair, and Theo feels himself relax, as Max moves one hand up along his knee, to his thigh, where Max is resting his head. He does is slowly, his fingertips brushing lightly against the fabric of Theo's jeans, trailing up along his leg. It feels nice, but when the pressure of Max's hand becomes just slightly harder, and starts sliding up the inside of his thigh, Theo takes a deep breath. His free hand, the one not in Max's hair, curls into a loose fist, against the couch.

He's not entirely sure what happens then, but soon, his muscles are tensing up a bit, as Max's hand softly starts rubbing his leg, slowly, moving further up. And when Max actually plants a soft kiss there, Theo swallows hard. It's a very light kiss, he can barely feel it through his jeans, but just the knowledge of it is enough to make him close his eyes for a moment, and take a deep breath.

Max doesn't say anything, and neither does Theo, as Theo's hand slowly tightens its grip on that black hair, before moving down along Max's neck, his shoulder, down over his chest. Max only lets out a soft groan, as Theo slips his hand underneath his shirt, moving down, tracing the hem of his underwear with his fingers; it's just visible above the waistline of those jeans.

This is stupid. Sure, they tend to get pretty physical with each other, whenever they get the chance, but this is ridiculous. It might be due to their lack of personal time, lately, or the fact that they're just so comfortable with each other now (not to mention, practically *addicted* to each other), but somehow, Theo barely even hesitates to do this. It doesn't matter that they're on the couch, in his living room, in the middle of the day, because *damn it*, he just really *wants* this.

Theo is suddenly reminded of last night, when Max pulled him into the bathroom and pressed him up against the wall, hands all over him and those wonderful lips against his mouth, touching and stroking him until he saw stars, and he grits his teeth. It doesn't take much. It doesn't take more than that memory to make him hard, and he leans his head back against the couch. He swallows, absently trailing his fingers along the hem of Max's jeans, before simply moving down to his crotch, and he

330

feels, with so much more satisfaction than he should, that Max is hard, as well.

This seems to distract Max. He lets out a surprised, soft moan, and Theo looks down at him, as Max's hand stops moving and starts absently gripping Theo's thigh, instead. Theo increases the pressure of his hand, and soon, Max rolls over onto his back again, giving Theo easier access. And *god*, he looks so hot right now, spread out like this, head in Theo's lap, breathing heavily, as Theo touches him. His eyes are closed, and Theo keeps massaging him through his jeans, absently wanting to unbutton them so that he can get underneath, but Max is already moaning and grinding against the pressure of Theo's hand, making Theo even harder.

Jesus, he has missed this. He wants Max so badly, so badly it *hurts,* and all he can think about is making him moan like this, making him breathe his name, making him come, with that expression that Theo loves, and he keeps touching him, slowly and with hard, practiced determination. And Max moans, one hand absently touching Theo's arm, the other gripping the edge of the couch, mouth half-open and eyes closed, and Theo can't stop watching him, watching him as he gets closer, and closer—

The sound of a key in a locked door has never been more unwelcome, and Max seems to notice it almost before Theo does.

He groans, a drawn-out, pained sound that sounds almost like a sob, and Theo automatically whips his hand away, at the interruption. Max frowns, eyes still closed.

"Oh, you have *got* to be fucking *kidding* me," he practically hisses through gritted teeth, before covering his face with his hands, another anguished groan escaping his mouth.

Theo can't do anything but silently, and frustratingly, agree with him.

It's after a moment of panic that Theo realizes that his hard-on can't be seen, thanks to Max's head resting in his lap, and that Max's is hidden, as well, thanks to his jeans doing a pretty good job of keeping it down, and he tries to relax—and think of anything, other than the sounds Max was making, just moments before their untimely interruption.

Theo looks up as he hears someone step into the living room, and is relieved to see who it is.

"Hey, guys," Riley says, seeming a little surprised, and Max drags his hands down over his face, so he can see him properly.

"Hi, Riley," he says, with a sarcastic and cheeky smile on his face, no doubt channeling his frustration at being interrupted. "Whatcha doin'?"

Riley hesitates, just stands there for a moment, before figuring that he probably did just interrupt something. He narrows his eyes.

"You guys weren't doing anything weird, were you?" he says, and Max flops his hands down on the couch.

"You know," he says lightly, "we were just about to bang, on this couch."

Riley makes a disgusted face.

"Gross," he says, but Max is unfazed, simply pointing a finger gun at him and winking, making a clicking sound. And Riley looks at Theo, keeping his expression, but Theo just raises his eyebrows at him, turning back to the TV. He's not sure he would be able to lie, and he definitely isn't sure he would be able to admit to Max's words being almost entirely true.

"Whatever," Riley says with a small shudder. "I'm going upstairs."

"Hey, Riley," Theo calls, and his brother looks at him. "How did it go?"

Riley frowns.

"How did what go?" he asks, and Theo gives him a pointed look.

"New Year's," he says. "Ellie was there, right?"

And suddenly, Riley is practically blushing, glancing away and avoiding Theo's eyes, at any cost.

"Yeah," he mutters. "So?"

"And," Theo says, drawing out the word. "How did it go?"

Riley looks up at him again, frowning, and Max lets out a sigh.

"What my beloved is trying to say," he says, making Theo's heart skip a beat at the endearment, "is, did you get any New Year's action?"

Riley looks away again, and Theo knows they've hit home.

"Did you kiss her?" he asks teasingly, in a big-brotherly way, designed to make Riley as uncomfortable as possible, and Riley actually blushes properly, now.

"I might have," he mutters, clearly embarrassed. "She sorta kissed me."

Theo gives him a genuinely impressed look.

"Nicely done, little brother." He smiles. "How was it?"

Riley glances at him.

"It was fine," he says, shrugging. "I mean, it was good."

Theo and Max give him matching looks of encouragement, and Riley sighs.

"Okay, it was really good." He looks at the floor, clearly uncomfortable. "Can I go now?"

Theo gives him a formal nod.

"You may," he says, and Riley practically runs up the stairs, leaving Theo with a big grin on his face.

"Aww," Max says. "Good for him."

Theo is so used to hearing sarcasm from Max, that he doesn't immediately pick up on the sincere undertone of the statement.

"Yeah," he says, thinking about how that was probably Riley's first kiss, as far as he knows. "Finally."

There's no point in picking up where Theo and Max left off, after that. Instead, they learn, after twenty minutes of trial and error, that they need to actually sit with a pillow between them, lest they make out some more and probably rip each other's clothes off, right there. It's not as fun, granted, but with Riley home, neither of them wants to risk it. Not to mention the fact that Theo's parents could come home, any minute, and they're really not in the mood for that.

It's horrible, though. Theo can barely glance at Max, without thinking of just what they could be doing, right now, and he's painfully, irritatingly reminded of just how long it has been since they could really *be* with each other. He can practically feel his body screaming to press up against Max and do all kinds of dirty things.

Max eventually leaves, before Theo's parents get home, and their goodbye kiss in the hall is so much more charged than it should be.

"You do realize," Max murmurs against Theo's mouth, as his hands slip into the back pockets of Theo's jeans, "that we might die, if we don't do something about this?"

Theo groans, while uselessly, and only halfheartedly, trying to pull away from Max, as those hands pull him closer.

"I'm pretty sure it isn't fatal," he says, and Max makes a small noise of doubt.

"I don't know," he says, giving Theo a light kiss. "I feel like I'm going through withdrawal."

"I know what you mean." Theo keeps his hands firmly planted on Max's waist, resisting the urge to move them to more inappropriate places.

Max doesn't seem to care, though, and he moves in closer, practically grinding against Theo, kissing him more deeply than a moment ago. And Theo groans, pulling away.

"No," he says, and Max gives him a kiss.

"Yes," he purrs, and Theo has to use every ounce of restraint he has, to pull away from Max properly and take his wrists, only to pull those eager hands out of his back pockets.

"Max, no," he says, a small smile on his face, and Max practically pouts, as Theo takes Max's wrists and press them against his chest. Max looks down at his trapped hands.

"So cruel," he says, looking back up at Theo, who just raises his eyebrows.

"Another time," he says, giving Max a light kiss. "Alright?"

Max seems to consider that for a moment, before he rolls his eyes.

"Fine," he says, exaggerating the petulant tone, making Theo's smile widen.

"Okay," Theo says, and he actually turns Max around and pushes him gently toward the door. "I'll see you soon."

Theo opens the door, and when Max is outside, he turns around.

"Love you," he says, giving Theo a kiss, and Theo wonders if he'll ever get tired of hearing that.

"Love you, too."

CHAPTER 24
RELEASE

"Best night *ever.*"

Cassie enunciates every syllable, as she leans across the table toward Theo. Her hazel eyes are wide, and he raises his eyebrows at her.

"Sounds like someone got lucky," he says, and Cassie gives him a cross between an embarrassed grin and a sly smile.

"I don't get lucky," she says. "I'm just that good."

Then she looks a bit sheepish, though, and revises.

"Well, actually," she says. "I'm not that good. Stuff like that never happens to me."

She cocks her head.

"So, yeah, guess I got lucky."

Theo just chuckles, shaking his head as he stabs some peas with his fork, trying to drown out the school cafeteria-chatter around them, as Cassie tells him about her New Year's Eve.

"So, what happened?" he asks, looking up at Cassie, who gets a slightly dreamy look on her face.

"Well," she says, "we talked all night. We kissed, at midnight. And she walked me home."

She glances down at her food, following Theo's example of stabbing some peas, while he eats his.

"And she kissed me goodnight," she continues. "And we exchanged phone numbers."

She looks up at Theo, cocking her eyebrows, as she moves the fork-impaled peas to her mouth.

"Her name's Emma," she says, smiling. "And she's amazing."

She chews on her peas, and Theo gives her an encouraging look.

"Are you gonna see her again?" he asks, and Cassie shrugs.

"Well," she says, mysteriously. "We've texted a lot, and we're hanging out tomorrow. So... Yeah."

Theo gives her a nod, eyebrows raised.

"I'm impressed," he says, before looking down at his plate and continuing, in an undertone. "Slut."

Cassie looks indignant, but smiles as she scoffs in offense.

"Excuse you," she says. "We have done nothing questionable."

"Yet," Theo points out, eating some peas, and Cassie folds her arms.

"I'm a respectable lady, I'll have you know," she says. "It's gonna take more than a date to get in my pants."

"But she will get in your pants," Theo says, mouth full, looking at her and pointing with his fork.

"Hopefully," Cassie says, and Theo cocks his head.

"So," he says, chewing. "Slut."

Cassie just glares at him, but when he grins at her teasingly, she can't help but shake her head and smile back.

It's when Riley passes by near their table, that Theo straightens in his seat.

"Riley," he calls, and his brother stops, turning to him.

"Yeah?" he says, tray of food in his hands.

"You seen Max?" Theo asks, and Riley cocks his head toward the general direction of the cafeteria's entrance.

"Yeah," he says. "He's at the nurse's office."

Theo frowns.

"What?" he says. "Why?"

Riley shrugs, clearly not the least bit worried.

"I think he hurt himself," he says, and although Theo hears the complete ease in his tone, it doesn't seem to matter. Instead, *hurt* is the only word he manages to register, and before either Riley or Cassie can stop him, he has gotten up from the table and left the cafeteria.

It's not far to the nurse's office. It barely takes five minutes before Theo is there, and the first thing he sees is Max. He's sitting on a gurney, legs dangling over the edge, holding something up to his face, and Theo doesn't linger in the doorway for more than a split second.

"Max!"

Max looks up at the sound of his voice, and almost sheepish expression mixed in with the surprise, almost as though he was hoping that Theo wouldn't actually hear about this and come find him. The expression disappears almost immediately, though, and Theo doesn't make much of it.

"Hey, babe," Max says, cocking his head suggestively. "'Sup?"

But Theo isn't having it.

"What the hell happened?" he says, making his way into the room. Max half-shrugs.

"I ran into Luc," he says, head tilted back, and he says it with such glee that Theo can't actually tell if he's being sarcastic or not.

"Luc?" he says, frowning, confused, and Max just half-shrugs again, almost as though he's hoping that's the end of it. But it isn't, of course, and Theo just looks at Max, who eventually sighs.

The nurse glances between the two of them, before pointedly steadying Max's hand, as it holds a small, slowly reddening cotton ball up to his nose. Then she turns around and leaves them alone, walking into the other room.

Max looks at Theo, head still tilted back.

"I went outside for a smoke," he explains, sounding bored, more than anything. "Luc was there, for some reason. He saw me, and long story short, apparently felt like punching me again."

Theo sighs.

"Jesus," he says, carding his fingers through his hair in an anxious gesture.

"Don't worry," Max says dryly, removing the cotton ball from his nose and glancing at it, before putting it back in, the bleeding apparently still not halted. "Some guys stopped him, and he's still suspended. He wasn't even supposed to be here. And you'd think he'd be over that whole emasculating-thing I did. I mean, come on, it was weeks ago."

Theo doesn't reply. Instead, he just drops his arms to his sides and looks at Max, letting out a heavy exhale, lips pressed together. He reaches out to take Max's chin, gently.

"Let me see," he says, but Max just pulls away softly.

"It's fine," he murmurs, and Theo frowns at him.

"Max, you're bleeding," he says sharply.

"It's a nosebleed," Max points out. "Doesn't count."

"Max—"

"I'm fine, really," Max says, both his voice and expression trying to be reassuring. "I can take a beating, it's okay."

"Yeah, you said that, last time," Theo says, frowning, sounding almost annoyed, as he remembers how those were Max's almost exact words, outside the principal's office, back then. "What does that even mean?"

Max sighs quietly then, pressing his lips together, as though instantly regretting saying that. Then he relents.

"It means that Luc isn't, by far, the first one who hasn't appreciated my charming and unique self," he says. He takes out the cotton ball from his nose again and looks at it. It's tainted

339

with his blood, and he lowers his chin, as he continues in a murmur. "And kids can be real assholes."

Theo blinks, taking it in, before realizing what Max means.

"Wait, you were bu—?" he starts, but Max immediately cuts him off.

"Please, don't say 'bullied'," he says, looking positively appalled, and Theo pauses.

"Why not?" he asks, hesitantly.

"Because the word implies that I'm a victim," Max replies. "And I'm not. Never have been."

He shrugs, glancing at the bloody piece of cotton in his hand, before looking back at Theo.

"I mean, sure, I used to get beat up every now and then. But *victim*?" He scoffs and tosses the now apparently redundant cotton ball into the trashcan beside the gurney. "Fuck that."

Theo isn't quite sure how to respond to that. He's honestly kind of surprised; he can hardly imagine anyone having the balls to pick on Max, who could level your self-confidence to the ground with just a condescending smirk. Not that he ever really does that.

Then again, maybe Max wasn't always like that, wasn't always like *this*. Maybe he's like this now, simply because other people made him this way. Theo knows that being picked on and bullied (despite Max's apprehension at the word), really affects a person, and it can turn out one of two ways; either it hardens you, or it breaks you. Clearly, Max went for the first option.

Max sighs, as though he's just had a refreshing nap, rather than a punch in the face.

"I'm starving," he says, and he looks up at Theo, as he hops off the gurney. "What's for lunch?"

Theo just looks at him, unfamiliar with the somehow hard expression he can feel on his face. It seems to be enough to make Max feel just slightly uncomfortable, though, as he stands in front of Theo.

"What?" he says, and Theo pauses.

"Were you gonna tell me?" he says, voice subdued, rather than annoyed, and Max glances away for a moment.

"I guess," he says, half-shrugging as he looks back at his boyfriend. "Just never came up."

"What about today?" Theo asks. "Were you gonna tell me about that?"

Max sighs then, glancing up at the ceiling. It almost looks like he's rolling his eyes.

"Maybe not," he admits, and Theo bristles.

"Why not?" he says, and Max looks at him.

"Because it's not a big deal," he says. "And I knew you'd react this way, and I didn't want to get you into trouble again."

"What's that supposed to mean?" Theo says, frowning. Sure, he appreciates Max's honesty, here, and Max is right about Theo most likely having done something stupid to Luc, if he had been there (like hitting him again). But still.

"Look, I'm sorry, okay?" Max says, a bit softer, and Theo is entirely sure that he means it. "I just—"

He throws up his hands lamely.

"It's not a big deal."

"Yes, it is," Theo retorts, his voice slightly raised, and when the school nurse actually glances over at them from her desk in the other room, he lowers his tone, self-consciously. "It is a big deal, alright? I don't want you to get hurt. And if I do get into trouble because of that, that's on me, not you."

Max just looks at him, an unreadable expression on his face, and then he sighs, taking Theo's hand.

"Fuck, you're way too good to me," he says, looking down at their entwining fingers, and Theo shakes his head.

"I'm really not," he says, and when Max looks up at him again, he gives him a soft smile.

"You know," Theo continues, a lighter tone to his voice. "I bet you could get a note, and go home early."

Max quirks a small smile.

"Where's the fun in that?" he says, and Theo cocks his head.

"I could go with you," he says, and Max's smile widens.

341

"You'd do that for me?" he asks, and Theo gives him a soft kiss.

"You know I would," he replies, and Max narrows his eyes.

"Alright," he says, eyeing Theo up and down. "Come on then, you little rebel."

It's not that hard to get out of school, Theo has realized.

Max does indeed get a note from the nurse, and Theo manages to get a hold of Cassie, asking her to cover for him, and she agrees to it (while rolling her eyes). After that, Theo just gets his stuff from his locker, and as everyone else gets ready for class, he meets up with Max, and they make their way home.

Max's parents have left for work, already, both of them working late today, so the moment he and Theo step inside the front door of Max's house, Theo knows he's done for.

The door has barely shut behind them, before Max is pulling Theo to him, kissing him fiercely, and Theo barely even hesitates, before getting caught up in the sheer urgency of it, tugging at Max's coat pointedly. Max takes the hint, and it's in a series of awkward, fumbling, multi-tasking moves, that they manage to get their jackets and stuff off—lips barely ever leaving the other's—and make their way into the living room.

The choice of room is mostly out of convenience, but Theo isn't about to complain. Not when Max practically shoves him down onto the couch and climbs on top of him, pushing his tongue into his mouth, making Theo inhale deeply, sharply, closing his eyes.

Those hands are everywhere, within seconds, and it doesn't take long before Theo is groaning into Max's mouth, pressing against his back with his hands, slowly moving his hips against Max's, as he grinds down against him. The way Max tugs on his bottom lip gently with his teeth is enough to make his head spin, and he moves one hand down over Max's ass, pressing the two of them even closer together. He feels, with some satisfaction, that Max is already as hard as he is.

"Maybe we should move," Theo says, barely able to articulate, through the heavy breathing and the intoxicated haze, and Max groans.

"No time," he says, punctuating his words with a particularly deep kiss that makes Theo lose his breath for a second.

"Let's just go to your room," Theo insists, using all the self-control he has to form words. "I think that might be a good idea."

Max groans again, and it's only with what seems like extreme reluctance, that he pries himself away from Theo.

"Fuck, you're probably right," he says, but it takes another few seconds for Theo to actually get up, since Max keeps distracting him with kisses and hungry sounds.

Climbing the stairs is a challenge; the two of them seem torn between impatience at actually getting to Max's room, and impatience to touch each other, so they end up stopping every five seconds to make out, before managing to actually tear away from each other and keep moving.

By the time they actually reach Max's room, Theo's entire body is buzzing, screaming for contact with that warm, tattooed skin and those amazing, soft lips, and he surprises himself by actually grabbing Max and practically pushing him down onto the bed.

Max looks surprised, hungry, and amused, all at once, as he looks up at Theo.

"Holy shit," he murmurs with a small smirk, which Theo covers with his mouth, as he climbs on top of Max and presses his body down against him.

Theo is pretty sure he hasn't felt like this before, this excited, this impatient. The only time that comes close, was when he and Max spent the night at that motel, and he couldn't see straight, because he just *needed* Max so badly. He had it bad, that time.

This time, it's worse.

Max fumbles slightly as he tugs at Theo's dark green Henley, pulling it over his head, and it thrills Theo, for some reason. Because Max never fumbles, and Theo can't help but find his sudden lack of smoothness oddly satisfying, as he tosses the discarded shirt to the floor.

Theo goes for Max's black, long-sleeved t-shirt moments later, but then decides to slow down a bit. It's difficult, but the way Max sucks in a sharp breath through his teeth, as Theo pushes his shirt up and trails slow, open-mouthed kisses up along his stomach and chest, makes it totally worth it. And the way he actually moans, as Theo lets his tongue smooth over those kisses, paying extra attention to his nipples and feeling his heart pound frantically in his chest, is enough to make Theo close his eyes and inhale deeply, taking in the scent of Max's warm skin.

He's so hard he can barely think, at this point, and if nothing else, he can think of very few things that would be as satisfying as hearing Max make the noises he's making right now.

"Oh, you son of a bitch." It's a low murmur, almost as though it's uttered between gritted teeth, and Theo looks up as Max says it. Max's eyes are closed, and for a few moments, Theo just watches that frustrated, ecstatic expression, as his tongue keeps giving Max's nipples the attention he seems to enjoy, and Max lets out a low moan, moving one hand up to grab onto Theo's hair.

Well, Theo thinks absently, oddly satisfied. It seems that he has found another one of Max's sweet spots.

Max's patience seems to be wearing very thin, however, and he uses his grip on Theo's light brown, messed-up hair, to pull his face up to his own. The kiss he gives Theo then seems to send a sharp surge into Theo's very core, and for a moment, he can barely even think.

Max is nearly panting when he pulls away, keeping Theo's face only an inch away from his own.

"You're torturing me, and I hate you," he practically growls, and Theo can't help but give him a small, uncharacteristically mischievous smile.

"Yes, I am," he says, moving his hands down to Max's chest, and up underneath the partially removed, black shirt. "And no, you don't."

Max only groans, but releases Theo's hair to allow his boyfriend to pull his shirt over his head. Theo throws the garment aside, and doesn't waste another second, before claiming Max's mouth with his own.

They have only just gotten started, but Theo's heart is already pounding so hard it's almost uncomfortable, and he straddles Max, as Max's fingers impatiently undo the fly of his jeans, making sure to touch and linger, as they do. Theo moans hoarsely, clenching his fist against the mattress of the bed, while Max tugs at his pants, urging Theo to take the hint. And Theo does, somewhat awkwardly getting the rest of his clothes off and throwing them on the floor, before straddling Max again, his hard-on now straining almost uncomfortably against his tight-fitting boxers.

Max's hands move down to undo his own pants, but Theo beats him to it, grabbing his wrists pointedly and forcing them away, which leaves Max looking confused for a split second, but he gets the point. Theo doesn't even look up, as he starts kissing his way down along Max's stomach, which heaves slightly, as his breathing quickens.

Theo is almost surprised at his own dexterity, as he smoothly unzips Max's fly and tugs his pants down over his hips, all the while planting searing kisses against his skin. He hears Max make a sound that's like a cross between a moan and a gasp, when Theo's mouth wanders down over the stretched cotton of his underwear, ghosting over the hard bulge and letting his tongue wet the fabric just a little bit. And Max's hands grab the sheets in anxious fists, and move up to absently smooth over Theo's lower arm, as Theo skims his hands along the hem of Max's boxers, slipping his fingers underneath.

Theo has no idea what he's doing. He has never done it like this before, never really taken charge like this, and he hesitates for barely a split second, before suddenly feeling his insecurity rapidly being drowned out by something that feels like pure *hunger,* and he decides.

He decides, and he smoothly pulls Max's underwear down, before slowly letting his tongue swipe along Max's hard length.

And Max lets out a deep, surprised moan.

"Jesus, fuck." He sounds completely wrecked, hips arching up the slightest bit, as though automatically wanting to thrust into Theo's mouth, and Theo pulls up a little bit, not letting him. Instead, he looks up at Max, watches him clench his jaw and let out a noise that sounds more like a groaning, pained growl, more than anything, as Theo takes him into his mouth. And for some reason, the whole thing is immensely satisfying, Theo slowly working Max over with his tongue, actually closing his eyes.

He doesn't get to keep at it for very long, though; it's only after what feels like a minute, that Max actually grabs onto his hair, somewhat urgently.

"Theo," he gets out, his voice not mustering more than a heavy, strained breath. "Wait."

Theo slows down, and Max picks up on his confusion.

"I'm not gonna last," he musters, sounding almost desperate. "And I don't wanna come, yet."

Theo stops completely, then, and he looks up at Max, who meets his eye. He looks somehow frantic, high, and Theo moves up along his body.

"Okay," he says, unconsciously turning it into a vague question, and Max keeps his fingers in his hair, pulling through it restlessly.

"I wanna do it right," he says, breathing heavily, and the pointed look he gives Theo doesn't take more than a second or two, to interpret.

"Yeah," Theo says, nodding, sounding more eager than he meant to. "Yeah, me too."

Max doesn't even have time to reply, before Theo is kissing him, pushing his tongue into his mouth and feeling those piercings, as he does. God, he just loves those, for some reason.

Max seems almost surprised at Theo's enthusiasm, and he grabs his hair tighter, eagerly reciprocating the kiss, arching up slightly to pull him closer, and it seems like only a matter of seconds, before those black jeans are off, as well as both boys' underwear. And the feeling of Max's bare, warm skin is the best thing Theo can possibly imagine.

They keep touching each other, hands everywhere and mouths fused together, before Theo starts feeling like his entire body is vibrating from impatience, and Max reaches toward his nightstand. He's in an awkward position, though, and ends up cursing under his breath, as he has to actually pry himself from Theo, to reach it.

Not that Theo really takes his attention off him; even as Theo tears himself from his boyfriend and rolls over onto his back, so that Max can sit up and open the drawer of his bedside table, he doesn't take his eyes off of him. He doesn't take his eyes off of that gorgeous, toned body, with those tattoos dancing over his muscles, the wings on his back looking oddly real, as he moves. Theo reaches out and touches them, gently at first, but then with more impatience, and Max has barely gotten out a condom and some lube, before Theo is pulling him back down onto the bed, from behind.

"Fuck, I'm gonna come right now, if you don't slow down," Max says with a sly smirk, putting the stuff on the bedside table. But Theo barely pays attention, and isn't the least bit averse to Max saying that, anyway.

"I want you to," Theo murmurs instead, pulling Max into a kiss, as they end up on their sides, facing each other. His hands are already trailing all over Max's body, over inked skin, as well as clear, and Max groans, pulling Theo closer, underneath the covers. The feeling of that hardness against his own is enough to make Theo lose his breath, for a moment.

"I want you to come," he murmurs against Max's mouth, stealing another kiss. "I want you to fuck me."

The reaction in Max is palpable, and for a split second, Theo is worried he has said something wrong. Until Max speaks, and any doubt in Theo's mind is blown away.

"What did you say?" Max says, his voice suddenly heavy with pure, raw hunger.

"I want you to fuck me," Theo repeats, with barely any hesitation, vaguely aware of how extremely uncomfortable he would normally be about saying something like that. But right now, he isn't. He really isn't, and it feels like the only thing he can really think of saying, right now, anyway.

He just really wants this. He *wants* it, he *needs* it, and he feels like he has been without it forever, like it's the only thing he has been able to think about, for weeks. Which is half-true, to be fair. He can barely even believe how he has survived, for this long.

Max tightens his grip on Theo's body, and lets out a deep, low groan, pulling away just enough to lean their foreheads together.

"Baby, you can't talk like that," he says, and that gravelly, rough tone is more noticeable than ever, making actual goosebumps appear on Theo's warm skin. "You're driving me crazy."

"Good." The one word is firm, almost defiant, and as if to prove his point, Theo kisses him, while moving his hand down to wrap his fingers around that smooth hardness, and Max moans against his mouth in pleased surprise.

"Jesus," he murmurs, gritting his teeth as he pulls away. "I swear, you're killing me."

Theo doesn't reply. He doesn't need to, because Max is already twisting around to reach the lube on his bedside table, and when he turns back, Theo watches as he squeezes some into his hand. Then those dark blue, black-lined eyes are on his, and he feels his entire body tense up in the most amazing way.

As Max puts the bottle of lube back on the nightstand, Theo hitches one leg up over Max's hips; they're still on their sides, facing each other, and when Max looks back at him, Theo feels that anticipation grow stronger, his hands absently smoothing over that wonderful skin. And Max doesn't take his eyes off Theo's, as he moves his hands down between Theo's legs, and further back, taking his time.

When he slowly slips a finger inside, after some gentle coaxing, Theo lets out a dirty, low moan, squeezing his eyes shut, and he can feel Max tense up, in response.

Holy shit. *Holy shit.* It's just as good as he remembers it, even more so, now that he knows what to expect, and Theo focuses on trying to keep his breathing even, as Max keeps teasing, rubbing, slowly moving his finger in and out.

God, Theo had no idea how much he really missed this.

By the time Max has added more fingers, his pace slightly more eager, now, Theo is a moaning, squirming mess. Max moans helplessly, as Theo kisses him, and Theo suddenly feels like he won't be able to take this, much longer.

"Max," he pants, pulling away a fraction of an inch. "Now."

Max seems only the slightest bit taken aback.

"You su—"

"Now," Theo repeats, sounding oddly desperate, which he would normally feel a little embarrassed about. "Please."

That's all Max needs to hear.

Theo can't imagine how he could ever feel awkward about seeing Max prep himself; watching him put a condom on, slowly and deliberately, as though he knows Theo likes it, is oddly arousing, and Theo licks his lips absently. When Max turns to him, though, and gently pushes against Theo's hip, to get him onto his back, Theo shakes his head the slightest bit.

"No," he says, and Max just looks at him, confused, but soon has his unasked question answered, as Theo gives him a pointed, slightly nervous look, and rolls over. He shifts, so that he's lying with his back against Max, and as Max realizes what he means, Theo can hear him exhale sharply, as though seeing Theo in this position is incredibly hot. And it's weird, just how satisfying that is.

Max's hand is almost tentative, as it smoothes over Theo's hip, down along his thigh, before moving up to his ass, and Theo lets out a small breath of surprise, as Max slips a finger inside, before adding a couple more. It feels amazing, hitting all the right spots, and Theo closes his eyes, gripping the pillow tightly. Then Max moves his hand away, and he hitches up Theo's leg a little bit, before lining up, and slowly, very slowly, pushing in.

The reaction is immediate.

Theo lets out a moan, one that Max mirrors, and by the time Max bottoms out, Theo is gritting his teeth and burrowing his face into the pillow. *Jesus christ.*

Max doesn't bother asking if Theo is okay; the way Theo reaches back with his hand and softly smoothes over Max's lower arm is confirmation enough. Max shudders, before pulling out a bit, and slowly starting to move, carefully controlling weeks of pent-up sexual frustration and longing, as he does.

It's amazing, even better than last time, and with every thrust, Theo moans, Max planting kisses against his neck and trailing down over his stomach, with his hand. And with every movement, Max groans deeply in the back of his throat, his hand moving up to keep Theo's hips firmly in place, as he moves inside him, pushing and grinding. It's enough to make Theo feel like everything else in the entire world has disappeared, disintegrated, blown away by the sheer sensation of having Max so close, moving into him and making them both lose their minds with pure, reckless abandon. It doesn't take long, before he hears Max's breath starting to stutter.

Theo isn't sure why, but just hearing Max's groans turn into heavy, panting breaths in his ear, is enough to make his heart race, that familiar heat coiling in his stomach, and he moves his hand back to press against Max's hip, as he moves. Max moans deeply, and he rains kisses across Theo's neck and shoulder, trying to stay in control, while he moves his hand down between Theo's legs and starts stroking him, slowly at first, and then faster, in time with his motions. The feeling of it makes Theo bite out a loud moan, as he squeezes his eyes shut, his focus zeroing in on the feeling of Max's hand against him, the feeling of him thrusting inside him.

And within seconds, he's just losing it.

He's almost surprised when it happens—almost. It hits him like a freight train, and suddenly, Theo is coming, hard and fast, and he nearly cries out, pretty certain that Max's name is in there, somewhere, while Max keeps moving, keeps thrusting, faster and harder. It's the most amazing feeling, and when Theo feels Max tense up against him, he angles his head back, so that he can reach Max's mouth, in a clumsy, but incredibly hot kiss, and for what feels like several, blissfully long seconds, they ride out the climax, together.

It takes a while for Theo to come back down. His hearing is somehow muffled, from the ringing in his ears, and lets his head fall back to the pillow, exhausted. Max tries to catch his breath, planting a soft kiss against Theo's shoulder, as he moves his arm up across Theo's chest, pulling him closer in a surprisingly tender embrace, considering how rough he was being, only seconds ago. And Theo lets out a slow, tired exhale.

"I love you," he murmurs, and Max lets out a soft chuckle.

"That's nice of you to say," he says lightly, panting a bit. "You know, when I'm still inside you, and all."

Theo smiles to himself and gives Max a lame smack with his hand, which is still resting against Max's hip. And Max chuckles again.

"Alright, fine," he says, hugging Theo tighter and kissing his neck, then moving up to kiss his cheek. "I love you, too."

He adds those last words in a whisper, just by Theo's ear, and Theo closes his eyes for a moment, his whole body feeling like it's made of jelly. He can't help but smile.

Getting cleaned up isn't that much of a hassle, and when Theo comes out of the bathroom later, Max is already in the process of getting dressed.

"That seems unnecessary," Theo says in mock petulance, nearly pouting as he makes his way over to his boyfriend, who just throws him a small smirk.

"Yeah," he says sympathetically. "But it's the middle of the day, which I honestly forgot about. And I just have this weird habit of actually wearing clothes, during the day."

He frowns a bit at that last part, as though thinking to himself how weird that is, and Theo just shakes his head, smiling. He has already put his boxers back on, and he figures that Max has a point; he does actually feel a bit weird about wandering around half-naked, right now. Maybe it does have something to do with it not being nighttime, the cover of darkness absent.

"Fair enough," Theo says, following Max's example and picking up his pants from the floor. He has only just managed to pull them on, though, when he sees Max pick up his black, long-sleeved t-shirt.

"Oh no, you don't," he says, snatching up the shirt from his boyfriend's grip. "You're almost completely covered up, already, you gotta leave me with something."

Max raises his eyebrows, mouth falling open, as Theo pointedly eyes those bare, tattooed arms with obvious glee.

"You can't just take my stuff," Max says in a mock accusatory tone. Theo just smiles, though.

"I can," he says, holding the shirt behind his back. "I just did."

"Give it back," Max says, stepping closer, but Theo just shakes his head.

"No," he says.

"Theo."

"Nope." As if to accentuate this, Theo holds the shirt up in the air, over his head, when Max attempts to take it from him, and Max rolls his eyes. He's smiling a little, though.

"What are you, twelve?" he says, but Theo just smiles, and when Max makes another attempt at retrieving his shirt, Theo throws it away and captures Max in his arms. He kisses him firmly on the mouth, and it takes only a second for Max to relax against him. He hums contentedly.

"I'm so glad I got punched in the face, today," he murmurs, and Theo pulls away. Then Max cocks his head, as though he realizes how dumb that sounds. "Alright, maybe not *glad.*"

He moves one hand up to pull through Theo's hair.

"But I got to go home early," he says conspiringly. "And we got to spend some time together."

Theo can't help but smile at that.

"Yeah," he says. "That was fun."

Max smiles wickedly, then.

"I bet you think so," he says, and Theo frowns for a moment, before remembering the stuf he said, in the heat of the moment. And he groans, looking down at the floor.

"I can't believe I said that," he mutters, feeling oddly embarrassed, and Max hums in confirmation.

"Yeah, you were very... *enthusiastic*." He smiles wider. "Never knew you had it in you."

Theo glances at that smug face, before groaning again, and placing his forehead against Max's shoulder.

"Shut up," he mumbles. "I can't believe I did any of that, it's not exactly like me."

"Well," Max says, a fond, amused smile in his voice. "Can't say I'm complaining."

Theo tentatively looks up at him, and Max cocks his eyebrows suggestively, making Theo roll his eyes. He smiles.

"You're such an asshole," he says, and Max laughs, pulling him in for a kiss.

"And you love it," he says, and Theo must admit that he does, as he kisses him.

Theo is too wrapped up in the moment to really notice the soft, rattling sound coming from downstairs, but Max isn't, apparently. He noticeably tenses up, and looks toward the open door of his bedroom, which leads out into the hallway by the stairs. Theo looks at his boyfriend, and is surprised to find that those blue eyes have actually gone wide, as though he's on edge, and listening very intently.

"Max?" Theo tries, but Max doesn't respond.

Then, after a few seconds, Theo hears it.

"Max!" Someone calls from the bottom floor. It sounds like a woman. "You home?"

Theo is slightly stunned at the weird mix of panic, surprise and confusion he suddenly feels, and he watches Max, as his expression changes. Instead of alert, he looks tense, all of a sudden, as well as a little bit frantic, and slightly concerned.

Max swallows hard, looking at his open bedroom door, and Theo glances in the same direction.

"Who's that?" he asks, a bit hesitantly, and Max exhales slowly. His expression is clearly uncomfortable, and a little bit worried, when he replies.

"That would be my mom."

CHAPTER 25

INDIFFERENCE

Theo really shouldn't be surprised, but for some reason, he is.

Sure, Max's mother suddenly coming home, when she should be at work, is definitely a surprise, but come on—who else would it be?

Max seems rather anxious about it, though. Or perhaps *anxious* is the wrong word. It's more something along the lines of *tense*, his eyes fixed on his open bedroom door.

"Your mom?" Theo asks dumbly, and Max lets out a small sigh, turning to Theo. He doesn't have a chance to reply, though, before his mother's voice is heard again.

"Max?" she calls, but Max apparently ignores it, cocking his head, in reply to Theo's question. And Theo raises his eyebrows at him.

"Well, now what?" he says, unconsciously lowering his voice, and Max just shrugs. Then he looks over at the window above his bed, and gives Theo a pointed glance, which Theo returns with a bored glare.

"Are you serious, right now?" he says, his tone flat, but Max just shrugs again.

"Well, I don't know," he says in a low voice, sounding unusually stressed. "It's just a thought."

"I'm not sneaking out through the window," Theo practically hisses at him.

"Well, do you have a better idea?" Max retorts, and Theo looks at him in slight disbelief.

"Yes," he says, voice still lowered. "I could just, you know, *meet* her."

Max looks slightly surprised at the hinted sarcasm, but doesn't seem to mind.

"Or not," he nearly whispers in response, still coming off as slightly on edge. "We've talked about this."

"Yeah," Theo agrees. "But you've met my family, since then, and we've been together for a while, now. I think it's about time. And if nothing else, what am I supposed to do? Just hide up here, while you pretend I don't exist?"

"That's not what's happening here," Max points out, sounding both defensive and comforting, as though desperate to make sure that Theo doesn't think he wants to hide him. "It's just a bit sudden."

Theo gapes at him.

"Sudden?" he repeats. "It's not like you haven't had a boy in your room, before."

He chooses to ignore that annoying twinge of stinging jealousy he feels in his gut, as he says it.

"Well, yeah, but not like this," Max says, to Theo's slight surprise, and then continues in a blatantly sarcastic tone, his voice lowered to practically a hiss. "And I don't know about you, but I feel a bit weird about introducing my first boyfriend to my mother for the first time, after fucking him in my bed, just ten minutes ago."

Theo just blinks at him, slightly taken aback at Max's way of phrasing what they were doing earlier, before figuring that that *was* exactly what happened, and that Max tends to talk like that, anyway. Theo is just used to him softening such descriptions, when it comes to Theo and what the two of them do in bed, together, and he's not offended, not like he used to be.

And then he realizes what Max just said.

"Your first boyfriend?" he can't help but ask, rather softly. He knows that he is, at least going on what Max said back when they first labeled their relationship as such; he said he had *never really been anyone's boyfriend, before*. Still, though. Hearing him say it like this is surprisingly satisfying.

Max just rolls his eyes, clearly anxious.

"Is that really relevant, right now?" he hisses, and then starts, as his mother calls his name again.

"Max?" she says, her voice carrying up the stairs, and Max sighs sharply, eyes on Theo.

"Come on," Theo says, cupping Max's face and giving him a deliberate kiss. "Let's just get dressed, and go downstairs."

"You sure now is a good time?" Max says, half-serious and half-sarcastic.

"Now's a good a time, as any," Theo says, sounding so much more confident than he actually is. "It'll be fine."

Max looks doubtful, but apparently decides to give in, and Theo isn't about to argue.

They get properly dressed in a matter of seconds, and as they make their way through the hallway outside Max's bedroom, Max throws Theo a glance; he looks oddly scared. Theo doesn't say anything, though. Instead, he just takes Max's hand and squeezes it gently, before nodding toward the staircase pointedly, as if to say *go ahead, I'm right behind you.*

It seems to make Max relax at least a little bit.

Theo isn't quite sure, but perhaps his uncharacteristic lack of nervousness right now is due to Max's equally uncharacteristic abundance of it. He seems to unconsciously squeeze Theo's hand, as they make their way down the stairs, and Theo trails slightly behind him, as they go through the hall and into the kitchen. He can hear someone opening the fridge, and when he and Max stop in the doorway, she seems to hear them.

"Hey, honey," she says, and pulls back to close the fridge. "I just—"

The woman stops dead when she spots the two of them, clearly surprised, a bottle of juice in her hand. Her expression gives her open, kind face and sort of vacant look, along with her blond, pulled-back hair and pink hospital scrubs. She looks to be in her forties, and she really looks like she's in the middle of a work shift, more than anything.

"Hello," she says, slowly making her way over to the two of them. The surprised expression on her face is fading, and her gaze passes between Max and Theo, before settling on her son. "I wasn't aware you had someone over."

Max squeezes Theo's hand the tiniest bit.

"Yeah," he says, sounding oddly subdued. "This is Theo."

Theo is vaguely surprised at Max introducing him right away, but he doesn't mention it. Instead, he only glances at him, before looking up at his mother, who meets his eye.

"Theo," Max's mother says, as though sampling the name, in a rather neutral tone.

"He's my boyfriend."

This time, the reaction is more noticeable. The woman looks at her son, her expression a strange mix of surprise, disbelief and just the slightest hint of something that Theo thinks looks an awful lot like amusement. She flicks a glance toward the hall by the front door, where she no doubt now remembers seeing an extra set of outerwear, next to her son's, which told her he was home, in the first place.

She turns back to Max.

"Boyfriend," she says, halfway between a question and a slightly doubtful statement, and she gives Max a pointed look.

There it is again, that amusement. It bothers Theo, for some reason.

Max grits his teeth slightly, but Theo isn't sure anyone else would be able to tell.

"Yeah," he says, his tone flat. "Boyfriend."

The look the two of them exchange then is odd, one that Theo isn't used to seeing between a parent and their child. Then again, after a moment or so, he recognizes it; it's almost the same look he knows he gave his parents, when he and they were having their first Max-related argument. It's a look of slightly annoyed defiance.

It's after another second or so of silence, that Max's mother takes a breath and turns to Theo, a lighter expression on her face.

"Well, in that case," she says, holding out her hand. "I'm Jeanine, Max's mom."

Theo hesitates for a moment, a little bit unsettled by the weird atmosphere, but he keeps his eyes on hers, as he politely shakes her hand. Jeanine gives him a small smile, but it's a tight one, with no real affection behind it.

"What are you doing home, already?" she says then, releasing Theo's hand and turning to her son, who just half-shrugs lamely.

"We got out early," he says, and although Theo's parents definitely would have wanted an elaboration on that, Jeanine doesn't.

"And how did the test go?" she asks. She doesn't seem to have to specify *which* test, exactly, because Max seems to know what she's referring to.

"Nearly a full score," he says, but there's no hint of satisfaction in his voice. And when Theo sees Jeanine's expression, he can see why. She looks at Max pointedly, almost like a parent would look at a small child, as if to say *are you sure?* There's something oddly condescending about it, and it makes Theo bristle.

"Nearly?" Jeanine asks, and Max gives her the smallest of nods. Jeanine just looks at him for another moment, before sighing softly. She doesn't give him any further reply, as she turns around and makes her way to the kitchen counter.

"I just came home to get this," she says, picking up a Tupperware container. "Can't forget dinner, when you're working 'til midnight."

She gives Max a small smile that implies a shrug, but he doesn't reply, and Jeanine jingles a set of keys in her hand. She's wearing an open jacket over her pink nurse's scrubs, as well as shoes, which implies that she really is home only very temporarily, and she starts making her way past them, into the hall.

"I'll see you later," she says, leaning in and giving Max only the slightest brush of a one-armed hug. He barely responds, only nods, and Jeanine glances over her shoulder, as she makes her way to the front door.

"It was nice meeting you," she says, looking at Theo, and he gets the impression that she wants to add his name, but that she chooses not to. Instead, she just gives them both a small wave, before leaving, and closing the door behind her.

Theo is pretty sure he has never felt so uncomfortable about something so mundane, in his entire life, and for several seconds of silence, pierced only by the sound of Jeanine driving off, he just stands there. Then he turns to Max, who's just looking straight ahead, an oddly tired, tense expression on his face. Theo squeezes his hand, making those blue, black-lined eyes turn to him.

"Well," Theo says a bit awkwardly, in an attempt to lighten the mood. "At least, she doesn't seem to hate me. My parents would have freaked."

Max knows that he's referring to the time before Theo's parents accepted Max, and he knows just how true Theo's statement is; an unfamiliar boy in their home, just like that, wouldn't exactly be welcome.

Max gives Theo a small, humorless smile.

"Yeah," he agrees. "Although, honestly, I kinda wish she would, too. I kinda wish my parents would actually get mad at me, once in a while. Or happy, or excited."

He looks over at the front door.

"Most of the time, they just... ignore me."

Theo is struck by the way Max's voice suddenly sounds very small, and for a moment, he's torn between surprised sadness and unfamiliar anger.

He knows what's it's like to be ignored.

For most of his life, before he befriended Michael, he was ignored by pretty much everyone but his family, and he knows how that feels. He knows how being ignored somehow makes you doubt your own existence and importance, to the point where you almost wish someone would yell at you, for no reason. Because at that point, a negative reaction is better than no reaction, at all. At least, if you get yelled at, you exist, and you matter enough to make someone else waste emotion on you.

Theo doesn't want Max to feel that way. And being ignored by strangers is one thing, but being ignored by your family is another thing, entirely.

Theo hesitates for a moment, unsure of how to best comfort Max, who seems oddly deflated and sad about the situation that just took place. He settles for moving his hand to Max's hip and pulling him a bit closer to his side, and planting a kiss against his temple.

"That's their loss," he hears himself say, somewhat unintentionally, and Max looks at him.

"You have a habit of saying the right thing," he says with a small, almost shy smile, narrowing his eyes. "You know that?"

Theo cocks his head, in an unsuccessful attempt to look casually smug, and he ends up smiling, instead.

"I have an idea," he says, pulling Max closer, so that he can put his hands on his waist. Max definitely isn't lost on the way Theo is blatantly trying to distract him and cheer him up, but he seems to just accept it, granting a small, genuine smile of his own.

"And what's that?" he asks, while Theo plants a kiss against his forehead.

"We should get some pizza," Theo says, moving his lips to Max's cheekbone, where he kisses him. "And we should watch bad movies. And maybe even make out."

Max scoffs.

"Like I'm that easy," he says in mock, smug offense, and Theo hums against his skin, planting a kiss by his eyebrow, just below the piercing.

"I would never do you the dishonor," he says, in equally mock seriousness. "Just some well-behaved movie-watching, then."

"And pizza," Max interjects, and Theo smiles against his skin.

"And pizza," he agrees. "*Daredevil*, maybe?"

Max makes a pained, oddly impressed sound.

"Oh, that is bad," he says, sounding a little appalled, and Theo nods.

"It really is," he confirms.

"We must watch it."

"Yes."

It's only much later, in the middle of watching Ben Affleck run around in red leather, on the TV, that Theo actually realizes what Max was worried about earlier. Why he was anxious about Theo meeting his mom.

Theo just sort of assumed that perhaps Jeanine would be angry about it, or that Max was simply nervous about introducing his boyfriend to her. Now he realizes that Max's mother reacted exactly the way Max feared she would, in a way Theo didn't quite account for; *indifferently.* Jeanine just didn't seem to care that her son had a boyfriend. Hell, she even seemed a bit doubtful and amused by it, which still irks Theo, when he thinks about it, and she didn't even seem to remember Theo's name, within moments of meeting him. Then again, she didn't spare him more than a glance and a handshake, after all, before basically dismissing him entirely.

From what Theo can tell, that's pretty much the normal way for Max to interact with his parents; briefly, shallowly, and with quite some distance. They ask about his grades, maybe some other small stuff, and Theo can't help but notice how Jeanine's reaction to Max's *nearly full score* was neither good nor bad. It just wasn't really there, just a little sigh, like it didn't really matter and she didn't really care. And from what Max has told him, Theo suspects there would only have been a proper reaction if Max's score had been either at one hundred percent, or very low. Anything in between seems to be deemed unworthy, somehow, as if the silence should be enough to make him want to do better.

"I'm sorry," Max says after a little while, slumped against Theo, on the couch. Theo looks down at him.

"For what?" he says, and Max shifts.

"For putting you through that," he explains. "I mean, I saw it coming, and I was kind of expecting my mom to not take it seriously."

He sighs.

"Like I've said before," he says. "My parents have sort of met guys I've been with, just not like that. I guess she just doesn't think you're any different."

Theo only has time to feel an uncomfortable pang of jealousy in his stomach, before Max seems to realize the bad phrasing.

"That came out wrong," he says, sitting up so he can look at Theo, properly. He looks a bit apologetic, and a bit worried. "I just mean that they've seen me with other guys. I think they're pretty aware of my... previous habits."

It's obvious that he doesn't want to talk about it, about the looser lifestyle he used to have, and Theo somehow appreciates that.

"I was afraid my mom wouldn't take you seriously," Max continues, a bit softer. "That she wouldn't take *us* seriously, like you're just some random guy. I guess I was right, and I'm sorry. That's why I kept putting it off. I hated the thought of putting you through that."

He sighs frustratingly.

"God, I just get so sick of it, sometimes."

Theo just looks at him for a few moments, before leaning in to kiss Max on the mouth, closing his eyes during the brief touch of their lips.

"It's fine," he says, moving his hand up to smooth over that black hair, pulling his fingers through it and settling at the back of Max's head. "It's done. And we did good."

Max scoffs, a small smile on his face.

"Yeah, I guess we did," he says, absently trailing his hand along Theo's chest, softly. "It was a bit anticlimactic, though."

Theo chuckles.

"Yeah," he agrees. "But I still haven't met your dad, so there's always that."

"Oh yeah," Max says. "His way of seeing things is pretty much identical to my mother's, so that should be fascinating."

The sarcasm is obvious, and it makes Theo smile. He already has his arm around Max, and he pulls him in a bit closer, kissing the top of his head, which seems to be enough to make Max simply relax against him. They sit like that for a little while, then, not speaking.

Until Theo starts thinking about what happened earlier that day, the reason they went home early, in the first place. And he can't help himself.

"Hey," he says softly, and Max hums in confirmation. "About today, what Luc did..."

He can already feel Max tensing up, next to him.

"Why haven't you told me about that, before?"

He knows that Max knows what he's referring to; there aren't exactly that many options as to what it could be. He knows that Theo is asking about the reason for him being so calm and dismissive about actually being punched in the face, simply because he *knows how to take a beating,* and Theo can feel him shift slightly.

"Because it's over," Max replies after a little while, eyes on the TV. "It used to happen, doesn't happen anymore, and I don't like talking about it."

364

Theo swallows, looking down at his boyfriend. He's leaning slightly against Theo, and there's no real tension in his body, to match the tense subject. So Theo tentatively tries again.

"Okay," he says gently. "I'm just asking, 'cause—"

"Why do you wanna know?" Max asks, glancing up at him, and Theo hesitates.

"Because I want to know you," Theo replies. "That's all."

Max looks at him for a little while longer, before looking back at the TV, sighing. Then he straightens a bit, so that he's sitting next to Theo, rather than slumping against him.

"There's not much to tell," he finally says, looking at Theo, shaking his head slightly. "Some guys kept picking on me, taking my stuff, beating me up. It lasted for a couple of years, but it's over now."

Theo doesn't reply. He wants to say something, but he doesn't know how. Max seems to notice, and answers his unasked questions.

"It got pretty bad, for a while," he says, and for the first time, some painful discomfort shines through. "But then it stopped. And the guys who did it were a grade above me, so they graduated last year, anyway."

"How did it stop?" Theo asks, absently trailing his fingertips along Max's shoulder, very softly. He's only half-aware that he's doing it, and he's not sure Max notices it, either; they tend to touch each other like that all the time, one way or another.

Max seems to think about it for a moment, before sighing, apparently gazing at the half-eaten pizza on the coffee table. Then he seems to decide.

"You know why I got these?" he asks, tapping his shoulder lightly, to indicate the tattoos on his back. "The wings?"

Theo thinks about it for a moment, realizes that he has never actually thought about it much. He has mostly been a bit baffled by the fact that Max is so young, and has them, at all. Finally, he shakes his head, and Max pauses.

"It was actually an escape kind of thing," he says, before looking down at his hands. His brow furrows a bit, as he deliberates.

"I mean, these guys... They were assholes." He shakes his head a little, and his voice has a slightly somber tone to it, uncharacteristic for him. For some reason, there's no sadness, though. "They beat me up, made me feel like complete shit. And no one really seemed to do anything about it, or even really notice. It messed me up a bit."

He exhales.

"But then," he says, "after a pretty long time of on-and-off bullying, in lack of a better word, I just decided that I'd had enough. The ones who did that to me, *they* were piles of shit. Not me. And I just wanted to leave it all behind me, rise above it. So I did."

It's obvious that Max is uncomfortable about using the word *bullying*, and Theo thinks of what he said earlier about it implying that he's a victim, when he really doesn't see himself as one.

Max looks at Theo, blue eyes oddly determined, without a trace of sadness or self-pity.

"I chose to change," he says. "I chose to deprive them of the satisfaction that came with hurting me. I chose to stand up. And these wings remind me of that. They remind me that I'm better than them, and that I can just rise above the bullshit, if I want to."

He sighs, and Theo just looks at him, waiting, processing his words.

"I decided to get them just before I turned eighteen," Max says, a slightly lighter tone to his voice. "Which probably wasn't the best idea, to be honest. That was actually one occasion when my parents *almost* got properly involved. Even Gavin asked me about it, asked if I was sure. But I insisted, and he did them for me. Afterwards, I actually kinda freaked out a bit, wondered what the hell I'd gotten myself into, 'cause I mean, they're *huge*."

Max scoffs lightly, a small, rueful smile on his face.

"But then I remembered why I wanted them, in the first place," he says. "And if nothing else, I figured I was stuck with them, anyway. So, I just went with it, saw it through."

He looks straight ahead for a few moments, seemingly deep in thought. Then he turns back to Theo, whose eyes and attention are completely focused on Max.

"The wings make me feel strong," Max eventually says. And again, there isn't a trace of sadness or self-pity in his expression. "Powerful, sort of. I know it was probably a bad idea, to get tattoos that big, so young, but I don't regret it now. I was in a bad place when I got them, but it was worth it."

He cocks his eyebrows a bit then, looking a bit smug and impressed with himself.

"Not to mention, they look fucking awesome."

Theo chuckles.

"They really do," he agrees, leaning closer so that he can press his lips against Max's throat. "Why else do you think I have sex with you?"

Max makes a thoroughly offended noise and makes a move to get up, but Theo grabs him and pulls him into his arms, laughing as Max curses at him, and raining kisses all over his face. And right now, Theo honestly couldn't be happier.

CHAPTER 26
REFUGE

"I just don't understand what I'm doing here," Cassie says, folding her arms.

"It's mandatory," Theo replies, flipping through a brochure lazily. "Everyone has to go."

"Yeah, I get that." Cassie sighs, a bit irritably. "But sex-ed is all condoms and avoiding pregnancy. I don't need that."

"And why's that?" Theo says, sounding bored, skimming through page after page depicting drawings of ovaries and testicles.

"Because when I get laid," Cassie says pointedly, "there are no penises involved."

Theo frowns and looks up at her.

"Well, that's just no fun," he says, and Cassie punches him lightly in the arm.

"Just *try* to wrap your gay little mind around the concept," she says, and Theo raises his eyebrows at her pointedly.

"You do realize that we're both equally gay?" he says, but Cassie just glares at him.

"You know what I mean," she says acidly, and Theo smiles a little, as Cassie turns her attention back to the podium.

They're sitting in the school's assembly hall, surrounded by a whole bunch of students from other classes, and awaiting a guest lecturer who's apparently going to tell them all about sex and its components. Not that most people here need it, being a bunch of horny teenagers, but Theo supposes that it's good that they're being taught, anyway. God knows, there's a shitload of myths that need to be debunked, even in this day and age.

He turns back to his brochure, which was handed to him when he entered the assembly hall, and reads some interesting facts, before looking back at Cassie. She's still staring straight ahead.

"You okay?" Theo asks, and Cassie glances at him.

"Yeah, I'm fine," she says, a bit too quickly, before turning her gaze back to the podium. And Theo frowns.

"This isn't just about penises, is it?" His question has a hint of humor, but he still earns a glare from Cassie. When she doesn't reply, he nudges her arm. "Hey, talk to me. What's up?"

Cassie seems to hesitate, before sighing.

"Remember Emma?" she says, and Theo thinks back.

"The hot brunette from New Year's?" he asks, and Cassie nods.

"That's the one." She sighs. "We've hung out a few times, and I mean, I'm into it. But she seems a bit... put off."

Theo frowns.

"What do you mean?"

Cassie shrugs.

"I don't know," she says. "Maybe I just read the signs wrong? I know she's not straight, at least, that much she's told me. And I like her."

"So, what's the problem?"

369

"Well, when we hang out," Cassie starts, "it's like we both want something to happen, but neither of us does anything. You know?"

Theo thinks about it.

"So," he says, "nothing has happened since New Year's? Physically speaking."

Cassie shakes her head.

"No," she says, and Theo considers this, before sighing.

"Have you tried making a move?" he says, and Cassie frowns a little, before turning to him.

"Like... kissing her?"

Theo shrugs in confirmation, and Cassie glances away.

"Not really," she admits. "I guess I kinda assumed she would, you know."

Theo resists the urge to roll his eyes.

"Well," he says, "maybe you need to do it. I mean, she obviously likes you. Give it a shot."

Cassie nods slowly.

"Yeah," she says. "I think I'll do that. Thanks."

"Don't mention it," Theo murmurs, flipping through his sex-ed brochure some more.

"Hey, where's Max, by the way?" Cassie asks, and Theo automatically looks around, even though he knows he's not there.

"He's in the other group," he explains, vaguely disappointed at not seeing Max, as he looks around, slumping in his seat. "They've got this after lunch."

For efficiency's sake, all the students were divided up, and Theo is a little sad that he and Max ended up in different groups. But at least he gets to sit with Cassie, which really is good enough.

The lecture isn't very long, and surprisingly interesting and informative. It's always fun to watch several students squirm uncomfortably in their seats, if nothing else, while the proper use of a condom is demonstrated, for instance. Either that, or they try really hard not to look too interested, and they end up just looking around shiftily, while the lecturer moves on to talk about STDs and teen pregnancies.

By the end of it, there are free condoms handed out, and brochures and stuff, and Cassie grabs a handful of condoms, as she and Theo pass by the table.

"What are you doing?" Theo asks tiredly. "You don't even need those."

Cassie gives him a slightly indignant look, and then pops his shoulder bag open, shoving the fistful of condoms inside. Theo barely has a chance to look at her accusingly, before she grabs a bunch of single-use packets of lube as well, which are also being handed out freely, in a small basket, and tosses them into his bag, as well.

"There," she says, shutting his bag again, before he has a chance to stop her. "You need them more than I do. *Way* more, I'm guessing."

She cocks her eyebrows pointedly, and Theo just frowns at her, with a shrug.

"Why are you projecting your sexual frustrations onto me?" he says, and Cassie actually laughs.

"Oh, sweetie," she says, patting his shoulder. "I don't need to project anything. It's all over you, already."

Theo glares at her, but she just walks past him, still smiling.

"Uncool, man," he says, in lack of anything else, and she's laughing again, by the time he catches up with her.

♦

It's incredible, really, how dark it gets outside, now. Despite it only being around seven p.m., it's pitch black, and Theo can't help but feel like they're having dinner in the middle of the night, at his house.

"Theo?" Amy calls, as she prepares the food, by the stove. He turns to her. "You mind getting the plates?"

Theo gives her a nod of confirmation, stacking some plates in his hands, before setting them down on the kitchen table. This is usually where they eat, rather than the dining room, seeing as how they're only four people. But Eric isn't home yet; he has gone out with some friends, apparently, so it's just Theo, Riley, and their mom.

"Where's your brother?" Amy asks, and Theo shrugs.

"Beats me," he says. "You sure he's not over at Ellie's?"

Amy frowns a little.

"Why would he be there?" she asks, and Theo gives her a non-committal, but highly suggestive look.

"No reason," he says innocently, and his mother narrows his eyes suspiciously.

"Is there something I should know?" she asks, and Theo raises his eyebrows a little, as he gets some glasses for the table.

"You mean, besides the obvious?" he says pointedly, and Amy frowns. She looks like she's about to say something, and she opens her mouth to most likely start interrogating her oldest son about his younger brother's whereabouts, but she doesn't get the chance. Theo's phone rings, vibrating in his pocket, and he holds his finger up in a silencing, and jokingly patronizing gesture. Amy just gives him a bitchface that reminds him of Riley's, but he only smiles; it's fun to tease his mother, sometimes.

Theo gets his phone out of his pocket, and frowns as he sees the caller ID, while simultaneously feeling his stomach flutter for a moment. He brings the phone up to his ear, and answers it.

"Hello?" he says, and when he hears the reply, he's not surprised. It still makes him feel all warm inside, though.

"Hey, babe." Max's voice is clear on the other end. "It's me."

"Hey," Theo says, unable to hold back a small smile. "What's up?"

"Oh, nothing," Max says, over-nonchalantly. "Just calling to talk about life, global warming, the scandalous casting of Ben Affleck as Batman."

Theo frowns a little, amused, and that's when notices that Max sounds a little out of breath. He can even hear the vague crunching of what sounds like boots on snow, in the background, and his frown deepens.

"Are you outside?" he asks, and he hears a small huff from Max.

"Uh, yeah," he says, drawing out the reply. "That may also be why I called."

Theo's eyebrows go up a little now, instead.

"What?" he asks, and Max sighs. Now that Theo is aware of it, he can practically hear how Max is huddled up slightly against the cold, as he walks.

"I was wondering if maybe I could come over?" he says, hesitance clear in his voice. "And by that, I mean preferably *stay* over. If possible."

Theo can't help his spontaneous, confused reaction.

"What?" he says again, but Max doesn't take offense; he seems to know how sudden this request is. "Why?"

"Remember how I kinda wished my parents would actually get mad?" Max says, a bit too lightly, and Theo nods to himself, remembering his first meeting with Max's surprisingly indifferent mother, the other day.

"Yeah," he says, a bit hesitantly, and Max makes a small noise.

"Well," he says, "they got mad."

Theo straightens a little and looks over at his mom, who politely ignores him. But still, he takes the call into the dining room, where he can't be as easily overheard.

"What do you mean?" he says, when he's alone. "What happened?"

Max lets out a small groan.

"We actually fought," he says, with sarcastic approval. "Can you believe it? I swear, voices were raised, even."

"What do you mean, you fought?" Theo says, frowning. "About what?"

"You," Max says bluntly. "Indirectly, at least."

Theo makes a confused face, one he knows Max can't see, anyway.

"I don't get it," he says, and Max sighs tiredly.

"Me neither, honestly," he says. "One minute, it was fine, and the next, everyone was yelling, and I left. So, here I am."

373

Theo thinks about that for a moment. If it were up to him, he would invite Max over in a heartbeat, but sadly, there are certain restrictions that come with living at home.

"Just give me a sec," he says, and he hears Max murmur something in reply, as he covers the mouthpiece of his phone, making his way back into the kitchen.

"Hey, mom," he says, and Amy looks up. "Can Max come over?"

She frowns a little, as though confused.

"Of course," she says. "It's a bit late, though, isn't it?"

"Yeah," Theo says tentatively, aware of the oddness of his request. "Actually, can he stay over?"

Amy hesitates, absently stirring a pot of what Theo suspects is some kind of meat sauce.

"Theo—" she begins, but Theo cuts her off.

"He just needs someplace to stay," he says, almost pleadingly, not wanting to go into too much detail. "Just for tonight."

His mother looks at him, seems to consider it for a moment, before letting out a sigh.

"Alright," she says. "But it's a school night, so... You know."

Theo presses his lips together, suddenly a bit awkward, not sure what his mother is referring to or what he's supposed to reply.

"Yeah," he says, tapping his phone absently. "Sure thing. Thanks."

Amy gives him a smile that suggests she found that last exchange about as awkward as he did, and Theo makes his way back into the dining room.

"Max?" he says into the phone.

"Still here," Max replies, and Theo lets out a small sigh.

"We're good," he says. "You can stay over."

Max's sigh of relief is very noticeable.

"Thanks," he says, and he sounds like he means it.

"No problem," Theo says. "Where are you?"

"Uh," Max says, as though looking around. "Not too far. A couple blocks from your house."

"Okay," Theo says. "You, get over here. I'll see you in a bit."

"Sure thing."

When the doorbell rings, less than fifteen minutes later, Theo is happy to find Max waiting outside, and he doesn't waste a second in pulling him in through the door.

"Hi," Max says, a bit tentatively, as Theo closes the door behind him. His black coat and black hair are both covered in snow, and Theo can't help but brush some of it off.

"How long were you outside?" he says, surprised at the concern in his voice, and Max cocks his head.

"About an hour," he says. "Give or take."

Theo blinks, suddenly very aware of the way Max is actually shivering a bit.

"What?" he says. "Why?"

"Well, I didn't call you right away," Max says, shrugging. "I figured it was a weird request, anyway."

Theo sighs and kisses him on the mouth, that piercing cold against his lips.

"I don't care," he says, tugging on Max's coat, so that he'll take it off. "You can always call me. Anytime."

Max looks at him fondly.

"Yeah, I'm trying to wrap my head around that," he says, and Theo gives him a small smile.

"Good," he says, before brushing some more snow out of that messy hair. "Now, come on. You're just in time for dinner."

Theo's not sure if it's due to the absence of his father, or simply due to the fact that Max has been over at his house enough for Amy to get used to him, but dinner goes very well. They set another place for Max, and as they eat, Theo can't help but feel pretty happy about how easy it all is. His mother is smiling, talking to Max in a very relaxed manner, and Max seems more relaxed, too, compared to the first time he was here. He still tries to censor himself a bit, but he's definitely not as tense, if at all. He makes sure to thank Theo's mom for letting him stay over, though, and she politely refrains from asking the reason behind the request, in the first place.

Riley is glad to see Max, but seems to regret this, when Max starts asking him about Ellie. Amy ends up chiming in, suspicious from what Theo said earlier, and eventually, Riley admits that yes, he and Ellie are sort of a thing, now. Which causes both Max and Theo to *aww* at him and ruffle his hair, to Riley's great chagrin, and to Amy's amusement.

After dinner, Max and Theo start making their way upstairs.

"Thanks for dinner," Max says, a bit awkwardly, and Amy gives him a small smile.

"You're welcome," she says. Then she looks at Theo. "Do we need to get out some extra sheets?"

She seems to realize the weirdness of her question, as soon as Theo does, and he glances briefly at Max, before shifting slightly, on the spot.

"Uh, no," he says, so blatantly awkward. "I think we're good."

It takes Amy another second, though, before really catching on, and she nods, glancing away. Theo swears he can see her blushing a little bit. She seems to have forgotten that Theo and Max most likely sleep in the same bed.

"Oh," she says, clearing her throat unnecessarily. "Right."

She keeps nodding, and Theo nods back, while Max just stands there, eyebrows raised and looking way more amused than he should at the whole, awkward exchange.

"Okay," Amy says, making a vague shooing gesture. "Off to bed, then."

Theo lets out a small sigh of relief, and he and Max make their way up the stairs.

"That was adorable," Max says smugly, as they enter Theo's room and Theo closes the door behind them. Theo just glares at him.

"Well, I haven't exactly had a boyfriend sleep over, before," he says, a bit snippily. "Shut up."

Max just chuckles, and Theo pulls him into his arms, groaning as he plants a deliberate kiss on his mouth.

"I am really glad to see you, though," he says, slightly muffled against Max's lips, and Max hums in approval, putting his arms around Theo and pulling him closer.

"Ditto," he says, and Theo just kisses him for a few more moments, before pulling away a bit.

"So," he says. "You wanna tell me what happened, exactly?"

Max looks a little apprehensive, and then sighs.

"How about I tell you tomorrow?" he suggests, and Theo nods.

"Okay," he says. "Tomorrow, it is."

CHAPTER 27

SNOW DAY

It's the feeling of black hair tickling his face that wakes Theo up, the next morning.

It honestly kind of surprises him a little, that he usually ends up being the big spoon, when Max sleeps next to him, like this. Somehow, it makes him feel like Max is something vulnerable that needs to be protected, and that Theo does this, simply by keeping his arms around him. He wonders if Max sees it that way, too. Maybe it's just a coincidence that they tend to end up like this.

Regardless, Theo finds himself being not the least bit bothered by that black, messy hair, as it tickles his face. Instead, he nuzzles closer against it, breathing in, and tightens his arms around Max's form, that tattooed back pressed against his bare chest. He can hardly think of anything better than this, right here, and he's not about to complain.

For reasons that should be obvious, they didn't really do anything, last night, besides sleep; Theo wasn't really comfortable doing anything more *advanced*, knowing that his entire family was home, at the time.

His father came home late, and although Max and Theo had withdrawn to Theo's room, by then, Amy is bound to have told him about Theo's late-night visitor. And although Theo is half-certain that Eric wouldn't have let Max spend the night, just like that, he's pretty sure that even Eric wouldn't just throw him out. And if nothing else, Amy can be very persuasive, when it comes to her husband. Theo just hopes that his dad won't be pissed about it all, today.

Despite how awesome it feels, Theo doesn't have very long to savor the feeling of lying here, with Max; seemingly minutes after he wakes up, his alarm goes off.

Max groans, shifting in his arms, and Theo can't help but smile a little.

"'Morning," he says, planting a kiss against Max's neck, and Max groans again.

"What time is it?" he slurs, that rough voice cracked from sleep.

"Seven-thirty," Theo replies, and Max lets out yet another groan, more annoyed than before.

"God, why?" he says, while Theo reaches over to his nightstand and presses the snooze-button. The beeping immediately stops, and Max relaxes in his arms, letting out a sigh, this time.

"We have to get up," Theo points out, nuzzling closer again. "School, remember?"

Max makes an annoyed, whining sound.

"I don't wanna," he says, sounding like a ten-year-old, and Theo smiles.

"Me neither," he replies. "But we have to."

Max seems to consider that, for a moment, before twisting around in Theo's arms, so that they face each other. He gives Theo a kiss, and neither of them seem to care about the morning-breath, too soft and sleepy and happy to bother.

"Fine," Max says petulantly. "You and your stupid responsibilities."

"Hey, I don't make the rules," Theo points out, smoothing over Max's hair with his hand. Those dark blue eyes are squinting sleepily, at the moment not framed by black eyeliner, since Max washed it off, last night.

"I know," Max says, giving Theo a light kiss. "Still pisses me off, though."

Theo can't help but agree with him, but still, to their great annoyance, they do have to get up, and five minutes later, Theo is in the middle of getting dressed.

He hears Riley making his way down the hallway, outside his room, and he hears the distinct sounds of his parents moving around in the kitchen, downstairs. If he's not mistaken, they're leaving for work early today, and he's half-hoping that at least his father will be gone, by the time he and Max get around to having breakfast.

Theo is tidying up the bed a little, when he notices that Max is over by his mirror, a full-length one, that hangs on the wall. He's already dressed, and seems to be in the process of putting on eyeliner. Theo frowns.

"Wait," he says, referring to the eyeliner, "you had that with you?"

Max half-shrugs, keeping his attention focused on getting the lines right.

"In my pocket," he admits. "For emergencies."

Theo raises his eyebrows.

"Emergencies?" he says, a bit pointedly, and Max looks at him, in the mirror.

"Well, this doesn't exactly happen by accident," he says, gesturing to his face, more specifically, his eyes. "I tend to carry one around, just in case I end up in this situation."

Theo quirks a small smile.

"So, you carry makeup around, just in case you need to apply it?"

Max holds something up, and Theo can see that it's what looks like a small, black-tipped stump of a pencil.

"Just a tiny one," Max says innocently. "Like I said, for emergencies."

Theo scoffs lightly, with a smile.

"You're such a girl," he says, as Max goes back to applying his makeup.

"Said the bottom," Max retorts softly, and it takes a moment for Theo to get what he just said, making him glare into the mirror, actually blushing slightly. Max catches the look, but only gives him an amused, oddly fond smirk, in return.

"And besides," Max continues, smudging the eyeliner ever so slightly, while Theo straightens the covers of the bed. "It's important to me. I feel naked, without it."

He looks over his shoulder, at Theo.

"Imagine going out without a shirt on," he says. "It's kinda like that."

"Yeah, I get it," Theo says, realizing that he actually does. To him, who thinks Max looks amazing and gorgeous and hot, pretty much whenever, it doesn't really matter whether he wears makeup, or not. But at the same time, Max's look, all of it, including the eyeliner, is what makes him *Max*, and Theo would never change a single thing about it.

"And, by the way," he says, making his way over to where Max is standing, a bit surprised at his comfortable way of talking about this. "I've only been the bottom, twice."

"Out of all the two times, we've actually had sex," Max says, but there's not an ounce of accusation in his voice. There's only slight amusement, and he glances at Theo in the mirror, with a small smile. "Not that I'm complaining."

Theo sighs, and wraps his arms around Max's waist, from behind.

"I'm almost complaining," he mutters, planting a kiss against Max's neck. "Not about the bottom-thing, but the twice-thing."

He sighs again, leaning his chin against Max's shoulder, and Max gives him a fond, sympathetic look, in the mirror. Then, he gives him a small, wicked smile.

"Well, glad to see I'm not alone in that," he says. Then he tilts his head a little, putting the small cap back on his pencil, makeup now applied and ready. "And if it's any consolation, I'd be happy to blow you right now, if you want."

Theo is only briefly shocked at the way Max says that like he's talking about making a sandwich, before he remembers that that's nothing new; Max even tends to exaggerate it, simply because he knows what kind of effect it has on Theo. But Theo still reacts, and for a moment, he just tenses up, swallowing hard, his face heating up, as he feels the blood flow rapidly move downward. Max notices all of this, without a doubt, but all Theo can muster is: "Uh..."

And then, just as Theo's libido vaguely thinks that *yes, we probably have time for that*, there's a knock on the door, and he actually jerks.

"Yeah?" he says, a bit more discomposed than a moment ago, and he hears his mother's voice from the other side of the door.

"Just making sure you're up," she says. "Dad and I are leaving for work."

"Okay," Theo says, and as Amy seems to hesitate for a second, he gets the impression that she wants to say something else, but feels too awkward to, like she's reminding herself that her son isn't actually alone, in there.

"Alright," she says instead. "Bye."

"Bye."

Theo hears her footsteps disappear down the hall, and he exhales slowly, turning back to his reflection. And Max is wearing the meanest little smirk.

"What?" Theo says, but Max just shakes his head, pocketing his eyeliner.

"Nothing," he says, stepping away from the mirror, so that Theo's arms drop from his waist. He turns to Theo, then, blue eyes amused. "I just like getting you all flustered."

Theo vaguely remembers Max saying that before, ages ago, when they sat on his roof, long before they actually fell in love. Then again, he's pretty sure he was in love with Max from the start, and just didn't want to admit it. And for all he knows, Max was already half in love with him then, too.

"You're a bad person," Theo says softly, but Max just chuckles, and kisses him slowly on the mouth.

"And you love me, anyway," he says, and Theo smiles a little.

"Yeah," he admits. "I do."

Max leaves for the bathroom, and while he's gone, Theo is surprised to hear his cell phone *ding* with a text message alert. He frowns, but picks up his phone. It's a text from Cassie, and he opens it.

I've got two words for you, it says. *Snow day.*

Theo just stares at his phone for a moment, before reanimating and moving over to the window, where he pulls up the blinds. It's only after a couple of seconds of squinting at the white light outside, that he actually notices the weather, and he widens his eyes a bit; it's snowing. And not just snowing, but everything seems to be covered in the stuff, maybe a few feet deep, by the looks of it. Huge, white flakes are rapidly falling to the ground, and Theo notices the snow plow driving around in a seemingly futile attempt to keep the roads clear, as new snow just keeps piling on. This weather is bound to cause some mayhem later, he thinks, at least on the roads, and he feels a bit sorry for his parents, who have already left.

But still, Theo can't help but smile.

Really? he texts Cassie back, and her reply is immediate.

Really, she confirms. *It's on the school website.*

Theo double-checks this information, and is unreasonably happy to find that Cassie is indeed right. The smile on his face widens into a grin, and he makes his way into the hallway outside his room.

"Hey, Riley!" he calls, and his brother pops his head out of the kitchen.

"What?" he responds, and Theo leans against the railing of the staircase.

"Snow day, dude," he says, and Riley quirks a smile.

"I know," he says. "Ellie just told me."

Theo's eyebrows go up.

"Oh, she did, did she?" He can't keep the teasing tone out of his voice, and he can see Riley blushing, even from where he's standing.

"Yeah, she did," Riley confirms petulantly. "I'm going over there, actually."

Theo's eyebrows go, if possible, even further up.

"Really?" he says, and Riley fidgets.

"Well, her parents are at work," he says, clearly awkward about saying it. "So—"

"Say no more, little brother," Theo says, a smug look on his face. "I'll hold down the fort, here."

Riley frowns at him, but when Theo cocks his eyebrows suggestively, he instead makes a disgusted face.

"Ew," he says. "Gross, Theo."

"I didn't say anything," Theo says in mock offense, throwing his hands up, but Riley just shakes his head.

"Didn't have to," he replies. And with that, he goes back into the kitchen, and Theo smiles to himself, fiddling with the phone in his hands, before going back to his room.

The moment Max returns from the bathroom, Theo snatches him up into his arms, earning a look of surprise, to say the least.

"Whoa," Max says, as Theo kisses him. "Why are you so cheery, all of a sudden?"

Theo hums against his mouth.

"Rumor has it," he says, "that school's cancelled, today."

Max pulls back and looks at him.

"What do you mean?" he says.

"Snow day," Theo explains, and Max looks at him suspiciously.

"*Confirmed* rumor?" he asks, and Theo nods.

"Yes," he assures him. "Confirmed."

Max seems to think about this for a moment, eyeing Theo up and down, before he makes up his mind.

"Well, in that case," he says, immediately tugging on the hem of Theo's shirt, while giving him a deliberate kiss. "No need to get up, is there?"

Theo can't help but laugh, and he lets Max pull his beige Henley off, before reclaiming his mouth. Then he hears Riley's voice from downstairs.

"Theo!" he calls. "I'm going, now!"

"Alright," Theo yells toward the stairs, frozen in his position of cupping Max's face and trying not to think too hard about Max's hands against his waist. "You behave, you hear me?"

Riley doesn't reply, but his grumble can be heard all the way upstairs, before he leaves through the front door and closes it behind him. And both Theo and Max laugh, before resuming their activities.

They both seem to feel that clothes are completely redundant, at the moment, and they tug them off of each other, while stumbling over to the bed. By the time they crawl back underneath the covers, they're wearing only underwear, and Theo simply savors the feeling of skin on skin. He's never going to get enough of that, never going to get enough of Max's warmth, the way he smells, the way he tastes, and the way direct contact with him makes the most amazing rush surge through Theo's body.

They don't talk. Instead, they just kiss and touch and occasionally laugh, for no apparent reason, just drunk on each other, and weirdly, Theo doesn't even want more, right now, despite Max's previous, rather inappropriate suggestion. He suddenly just wants this, wants to hold Max against him, wants the pure innocence of it all, in a way he can really only relax into when they're alone.

It's when they've rolled around and ended up with Theo practically lying on top of Max, that Theo remembers something; the reason why Max is here, in the first place. The room is silent and calm, now, and when he decides to ask about it, he does it as lightly as he can.

"Hey," he says softly, absently trailing his fingers along Max's hairline, down along his neck, his shoulder. "About last night..."

Max sighs a little, and his blissed-out expression turns slightly more somber.

"What about it?" he asks, full well knowing the answer. Theo hesitates.

"You wanna tell me what happened?" he says, and Max doesn't answer right away. Instead, he just keeps looking at Theo, as though trying to decide what to say, and whether to actually tell him, or not.

Then Max seems to decide, though, and he sighs heavily, before nudging Theo ever so slightly. Theo takes the hint and rolls off of him, and Max then surprises him by sitting up. He doesn't get out of bed, or anything, though. He just sits up, so that all Theo can see is the back of his head, and those inked wings and tattooed arms. There's something heavy about it, about his posture, in a way Theo hasn't seen before.

"Uh," Max starts, sounding uncharacteristically subdued. "My dad got a job."

Theo frowns, confused, as he rolls onto his back, tucking one arm under his head.

"Your dad has a job," he says, and Max cocks his head the tiniest bit, in confirmation.

"Yeah," he says, not looking at Theo. "And you know how his job has him traveling a lot?"

Theo nods.

"Yeah," he adds, when he remembers that Max can't see him. It makes him feel oddly unsettled when Max has his back to him, like this, but he's pretty sure it's only because Max has a hard enough time as it is, talking about sensitive subjects; the lack of eye contact makes it easier. Theo can't really stop himself from reaching out with his hand, though, to softly trail along those tattooed feathers, with his fingers.

"Well," Max continues, "he got a permanent position somewhere else, pretty far from here, actually."

Theo isn't sure why, but he doesn't like the sound of that. It makes him feel tense and unsettled.

"So, he has to move," Max says, his voice oddly heavy. "Along with my mom. And me."

Theo's hand stops moving, stops trailing that inked skin.

"They told me last night," Max says, now clearly more bothered by this than he's letting on. "And I told them I didn't wanna go."

He lets out a small huff of bitter laughter.

"They were surprised, apparently," he says. "They said they didn't think I would care. And I guess that a few months ago, I wouldn't have, but... It's funny how things change."

He moves his hand up to rub the back of his neck, uncomfortably, while Theo just lies there, stunned.

"Who knew you would indirectly be the cause of my first, proper fight with my parents."

Theo blinks.

"Me?" he asks dumbly, and Max lets out a small sigh.

"Why do you think I want to stay?"

Max sighs again, tilting his head back, as though looking at the ceiling.

"They said that it shouldn't be such a big deal," he continues, bitterness seeping into his voice. "Actually, they said 'how important can that boy be'. And that's a direct quote, by the way."

Max moves one hand up to rub against his forehead, in an uncharacteristically troubled gesture.

"And I said that if they actually talked to me, once in a while, they'd know." He swallows hard. "But they didn't buy it. They just told me to get over it, that it's just a phase, anyway."

He lets out a humorless laugh.

"They actually said *phase*," he says dryly. "Like out of some manual for cliché parenting. Can you believe it? So yeah, I got pretty pissed. And when it comes to arguing with my parents, it was probably the third time ever, with actual yelling involved."

Theo stays quiet, lets Max speak, and Max sighs again, sounding frustrated and oddly broken, all of a sudden.

"See, the thing is," he says, "this really doesn't feel like a phase. And even if it were a phase, I wouldn't care, 'cause it actually makes me *happy*. And I've never really been happy before."

He puts his face in his hands, then, not in sorrow, but in some kind of pained frustration.

"I don't wanna give that up," he says. There's a slightly unusual, emotional edge to his voice. "Not just like that."

Theo doesn't answer him right away, can barely even react. He's still trying to process what Max just told him, still trying to comprehend what this means.

Max is going away, that's what this means. It means that Theo won't see him anymore, and as that thought sinks in, Theo suddenly feels a hollow, pitch-black ache in his chest. It's a surprisingly physical sensation, more like the absence of something, rather than added pain, and he remembers when he had that exact feeling for the first time, after his father had basically pulled him out of school and told him he could never see Max again. It seems so long ago, now, but this sensation is eerily similar. Only this time, it's much worse, much more intense, and he actually takes a deep breath, almost as though he's gasping for air.

He can't lose Max. He *can't*. Like Max says, he doesn't want to give this up, not just like that.

Theo sits up then and places himself behind Max, before wrapping his arms around him. He can feel the warmth of Max's bare skin against his own, as he locks his arms across his chest, pulling him close. He presses a kiss against Max's shoulder.

"They're not taking you from me," he says, his voice low. He's a little surprised at the soft conviction in his tone, and Max lets out a small huff of laughter.

"How possessive of you," he says lightly, with some smugness to his words, in his usual attempt to decrease the level of emotion. But Theo doesn't respond. He just keeps Max there, arms locked around him, and after a few seconds, he can feel Max's body relax, as he lets out a small exhale.

"I know," he says somberly, moving his hand up to gently hold Theo's forearm. He smoothes the skin over with his thumb. "I don't want them to, either."

"I'm not letting them."

Theo's voice still has that conviction, now with the smallest edge of anxiety.

"I'm not so sure you have a say in the matter," Max says softly. "And neither do I."

"Yeah, well, I don't care." Theo is suddenly aware of some anger seeping into his voice.

"You should," Max says. "I mean, what am I gonna do? Sure, I'm eighteen, but I can't exactly afford my own place. And yeah, we're graduating soon, but they're moving in like, a month. There's still time to enroll me in another school, even if it is pretty late in the game, so there's nothing stopping them, really. Doesn't matter that it's impractical and stupid."

Theo is surprised at how soon the move is happening, and oddly surprised at how angry he suddenly feels at Max's parents. But then, he realizes he's too tired and sad to be angry, and he lets out a frustrated groan, as he leans his forehead against the crook of Max's neck.

"This is such bullshit," he says, and Max makes a small sound of agreement.

"I know," he says, calmly. "It really is."

"How can they do that?" Theo says, his words slightly muffled against Max's skin.

"Well," Max says lightly, again trying to lighten the mood, "they are my parents. I'm economically kinda dependant on them, to live."

"We could get a place," Theo suggests, but knowing that it's a stupid idea.

"And pay for it, how?" Max says gently, showing that he has clearly thought about the option, already, which is somehow enough for Theo. Knowing that Max wouldn't mind living together, and the way he sounds a bit sad, as he refutes the idea, makes Theo feel a little bit better.

"Maybe you could stay here, at my house," he says, this time with an obvious tone in his voice that says he knows he's overreaching. And Max smiles a little, sympathetically, Theo can tell.

"I'm pretty sure your parents wouldn't be okay with that," he says, and Theo sighs, knowing full well that he's right. There's no way in hell his parents would agree to letting Max actually *live* here, even if only until graduation. "And I wouldn't exactly want to impose on anyone else."

Neither of them says anything for a while, after that, but then Theo moves his head to rest his chin against Max's shoulder.

"Run away and join the circus?" he says, and this time, Max actually laughs.

"Oh, that would be awesome," he says, and Theo smiles, moving his face up to nuzzle against Max's black, messy hair. "We could finally implement the trailer-idea. And finally get those four cats."

"Don't forget the lizard," Theo adds, and Max laughs. Then Theo frowns a little. "You remember that? Sending me those texts?"

"Of course, I remember," Max says, a bit softer than Theo would have expected, referring back to when Theo was dragged out of school, and just before his parents took his phone and grounded him. "I think I've reread every text-conversation we've had, at least ten times."

And Theo swears that he can feel his heart do a literal backflip, no matter how physically impossible that may be, and his breath actually hitches a little bit. He takes a deep breath, his nose nuzzled against Max's hair, and he closes his eyes, as he inhales that wonderful, familiar scent, a smile inevitably creeping into his expression. It's ridiculous, but hearing Max say that, even this far along in their relationship, is the best thing, ever. It makes him feel downright *giddy*, in lack of a better word, especially considering that he has reread their text-conversations more times than he would like to admit, himself.

"I love you," he murmurs, unintentionally. His voice is a little bit muffled, and he kisses Max's hair, his arm tightening its grip around his body. "So much."

He can practically feel Max's entire body relaxing against him, every muscle softening and becoming pliant, in his arms. He lets out a soft sigh, as Max blindly moves his hand back to touch Theo's face.

"I love you, too." His words are soft, in a way that Theo has only now gotten used to hearing from him. Compared to the harsh, abrasive tone he always seems to use with anyone else, and used to have even with Theo, the sheer tenderness of it is oddly moving.

They just sit like that for a few seconds, until Theo lets out a heavy sigh, absently planting small kisses against the back of Max's neck, and on his shoulder.

"It'll be okay," he says, not entirely believing his own words. "We'll work it out."

He's pretty sure Max doesn't believe it, either, but they both have the decency not to mention it. Instead, Max just nods, before turning his head, so that he can kiss Theo on the mouth.

"Okay," he says, and at least for a moment, everything feels like it will be.

CHAPTER 28
PLAY

Despite the rather heavy news Max just delivered, both he and Theo seem to feel that it would be a waste of a perfectly good snow day to dwell on it. They opt for ignoring it, instead, at least for now, and by the time they're dressed again and have had some late breakfast, the mood is once more considerably lighter.

Max doesn't want to go back home, for obvious reasons, and Theo figures that he should just as well stay where he is, anyway. Theo's parents aren't home, so it's not like it would make such a difference, if they went to Max's house.

It's around noon that Max starts itching for a cigarette, after holding off for a pretty long while, and he decides to step outside.

There's a back door that faces the backyard, and despite only having to stand right outside for a couple of minutes, it's nearly cold enough to need pretty much every layer of winter wear, so

Max properly wraps himself up. Theo, in lack of anything better to do, decides to join him, and the minute he steps outside, he feels that oddly pleasant winter chill. It's not windy, instead it's completely still, but the snow is still falling rapidly, and in fat, white flakes. Theo swears the snow is visibly deeper now, than it was this morning.

He turns to Max, looks at him.

"Is it worth it?" Theo finds himself asking after a while, as he watches Max take a pull on his lit cigarette. And Max glances at him, before glancing at the cigarette, getting what Theo is referring to. He half-shrugs.

"Probably not," he admits. "Can't seem to stop, though."

Theo chews his bottom lip.

"Why not?" he asks, and Max shrugs again, with a small sigh, eyeing the cigarette between his fingers.

"Don't know," he says. "I mean, I didn't used to care. I figured, what's a few years off your life, right?"

He looks up at Theo.

"Never really saw a reason to quit."

His expression is almost completely neutral, but Theo just stares at him, as Max turns away again, looking out over the snow-covered yard. He takes another pull on the cigarette, and Theo swallows.

What's a few years off your life? he thinks, oddly surprised at his own, sudden shift in mood. What kind of reasoning is that? Maybe Theo has simply been blind to it, before, but suddenly, hearing Max say that is almost physically painful. *Of course a few years matter,* he wants to tell him. *Of course you shouldn't ignore it, let alone actively contribute to taking those years away.*

But he doesn't say it. He doesn't say it, because he feels like now is not the time, somehow.

Still, though. Sometimes he forgets how Max sees himself, and sometimes he forgets that Max hasn't just changed Theo, but also the other way around. Max has given Theo confidence, some kind of strength, which Theo honestly thinks about almost every day, and he's happy and grateful. He owes Max so much.

But Theo forgets sometimes, that these past few months, Max has slowly gained an actual sense of self-worth, which he didn't have before. He has slowly started seeing himself as valuable and worthwhile, and that makes Theo happy, because that's exactly what Max is, and that's exactly how Theo sees him.

Max hasn't really known that before, and maybe, the same ignorance has led him to believe that the effect of those cigarettes doesn't matter. That it doesn't matter that they might make him sick, and actually kill him, in the long run. And Theo hasn't even noticed, because Max smoking is so much hotter than it should be, and it's something that he has fond memories of, ever since he first found Max behind the school, and they kissed for the first time. Theo honestly loves that about Max, so this is, indirectly, on him too.

Suddenly, Theo wants to just pluck that cigarette away from Max's mouth and make sure he never touches it, again.

He doesn't, though. He doesn't, and instead, he takes a few steps away from the door and crouches down. There's a small roof above the porch by the door, so the snow isn't too deep here, and he gathers up some snow in his hands, making his fingers almost immediately turn a shade of pink, from the cold. Then he starts shaping the snow into a ball. The snow is perfect for it, crunching and creaking between his fingers, and he smiles a little, as he stands up. He turns to face Max, who narrows his eyes at him.

"What are you up to?" he asks suspiciously, tapping away some of the last ashes on his cigarette. And Theo just keeps his smile, looking down at his snowball.

Then he looks up, and without warning, throws the snowball at Max's chest.

The look on Max's face is priceless; it's a mix of confusion, utter shock, and a hint of *what the fuck*, and he looks down at his chest. The scattered snow leaves a sharp contrast against the black coat, and he slowly looks up at Theo.

"Did you just throw a snowball at me?" he asks, sounding disbelieving and a bit surprised, and Theo just cocks his head, a casual expression on his face, before crouching down to gather up more snow in his hands.

"And you're seriously gearing up for another attack?" Max continues indignantly, in the same tone of voice, but Theo still doesn't answer him, shaping the snow into a ball. He only catches a glimpse of Max's slightly panicked expression, before he hurls the snowball at him, this time getting a more noticeable reaction.

"Dude, seriously," Max says, actually taking a step back, but Theo doesn't relent. Instead, he just smiles at him mischievously, and Max glares at him for a moment, before rolling his shoulders a bit.

"Fine," he says defiantly, flicking the cigarette away and gathering some snow from the ground. "If that's the way you want it."

Theo barely has time to get more snow, before Max's snowball hits him in the shoulder, and he immediately retaliates, this time hitting Max in the arm.

"I swear, I will *tackle* you," Max threatens, gearing up with another snowball and advancing on Theo, while Theo stumbles backwards and nearly falls over. The snow is much deeper away from the roof, and it takes him a moment to reclaim his footing. Max doesn't relent, though. Instead, he hurls another snowball at Theo, who expertly ducks, making it fly over his head, and he backs away a little bit more.

"You talk big," he says, gathering up some more snow, with a rather amused smile on his face. "But you're gonna have to catch me, first."

Max tilts his head, both him and Theo now knee-deep in snow and getting gradually covered in a thin layer of the white flakes that keep falling from the sky.

"Really?" Max says. "That's your line? You know it's a challenge, right? Not to mention a rather unoriginal one."

"That sounds like excuses, to me," Theo retorts pointedly, before throwing another snowball at his boyfriend, who just barely manages to dodge it.

"Oh, hell no." Max practically murmurs it, but Theo can still hear him, and he actually laughs out loud when Max practically lunges at him, snowball in hand. Max tries to grab him, and his fingers brush against the sleeve of Theo's jacket, but Theo manages to get away, and the impromptu snowball fight quickly turns into a chase, more than anything.

The snowballs keep flying, though, and Theo is barely even aware of the way his fingers are actually going numb from the cold. Instead, he keeps throwing, keeps dodging, and staggers a little whenever Max actually manages to hit his mark. Before he knows it, he's covered in snow, and so is Max, which is kind of an odd sight; the black of his clothes and hair looks rather stark against the white background.

It's the sound of a window opening that makes Theo look up.

"Hey!" The voice is familiar, and Theo turns toward the house next to his own. Sure enough, Riley is sticking his head out through a second story window of Ellie's house, and Theo and Max both stop what they're doing to look up at him.

"What are you doing?" Riley calls, and Theo holds up his prepared snowball, pointedly.

"What does it look like?" he yells back, before lowering the ball again and tossing it between his hands. "You should try it. Or are you too old for that?"

He adds that last part with a smug little smile, and Riley looks a bit annoyed, for a moment. Then he turns around, though, as if he's talking to someone, and after a few seconds, he turns back to Theo.

"Hang on a minute," he says, sounding a bit bored, before closing the window. Theo just raises his eyebrows, looks at Max, who simply shrugs, and after another second or so, Max quickly throws his snowball at Theo. It hits him square in the chest, and Theo jerks back, dramatically offended.

"Hey, that's cheating!" he exclaims, but Max is already backing away, a sneaky smile on his face.

"That sounds like excuses, to me," he says pointedly, and Theo narrows his eyes. But Max is already dodging, by the time

Theo's snowball actually flies through the air, making it land in the deep snow, instead.

It's after another few minutes of snowball-fighting, that Theo notices Riley come walking around the corner of the yard. And to his surprise, Ellie is actually with him.

"Hey," Theo says, smiling. "Caved, huh?"

"I may have convinced him," Ellie says, with a dimpled smile, her blond, slightly curly hair half-hidden beneath a knitted hat. Riley glances at her self-consciously. He's already a bit taller than Ellie, both of them fourteen years old, and Theo can only imagine what the height difference will be when he actually hits a proper growth spurt, in a couple of years. But still, he looks oddly small and shy, next to her, which Theo reluctantly finds adorable.

"Good job," Theo says, impressed, and Ellie smiles at him easily. She has been living right next door for as long as Theo can remember, after all, and while she and Riley have been friends that whole time, Theo has come to see of her kind of as a little sister.

"Alright," Max chimes in, rolling up a snowball in his hands. "Riley, you have five seconds, before I throw this at you."

"What?" Riley practically sputters. "What for?"

Max shrugs.

"Call it a pre-emptive strike," he says, and then counts silently to himself, before throwing the ball at Riley's chest. And Riley just looks at him, stunned.

"Come on, little dude," Max says, backing away and gathering up material for another snowball. "Show me what you got."

And with that, the snowball fight is back in full swing.

Ellie and Max haven't actually met before, but they get along easily, and they even gang up on Theo and Riley for a little while, making the brothers run for cover. It's a snowy massacre, and after a few minutes, Theo makes a point of actually getting some gloves for him and Max; his fingers are dangerously numb, by now, and he knows his boyfriend agrees.

By the time they're all too exhausted to actually run around in the snow, anymore, Ellie starts building a snowman, which Riley helps her out with. And soon enough, Max and Theo pitch in, as well, eventually creating a snowman that stands as tall as Ellie, with sticks and rocks for arms and a face. Riley laments that they don't have a carrot for the nose, but they make due with a bigger rock, which has the pointed edge of what might pass for a slightly stunted nose.

Eventually, Riley and Ellie return to Ellie's house, causing Max and Theo to smile at Riley teasingly, to his chagrin. Then Ellie takes his hand, though, and Theo is very amused to see his little brother blush, as she does it.

Max is standing slightly behind Theo, as Theo watches them go, and after a little while, he nudges him.

"Hey," Max says, and Theo turns to him. "You ready?"

Theo frowns.

"For what?" he asks, and Max cocks his head.

"I said I was gonna tackle you," he says, matter-of-factly, and Theo's eyes widen a little.

"What?" he says dumbly, and then reacts when Max takes a step forward. "No wait, Max—"

He barely gets the words out, before Max suddenly lunges his body against him in an *actual* tackle, knocking Theo down into the soft, fluffy snow. Max ends up on top of him, and Theo groans a little, but can't help but laugh.

"Oh, man," he says. "Uncool. Just, not okay."

Max only chuckles, though, looking way too satisfied.

"I warned you," he says, and Theo sighs.

"Yeah, but now I've got snow inside my collar," he says, suddenly very uncomfortable at the cold sensation against his skin. "Not to mention, snow everywhere."

Max glances down at himself and lets out a small groan.

"Yeah," he agrees. "Me, too."

He leans down and gives Theo a cold, soft kiss.

"Maybe we should get inside."

Theo nods and gives him a quick kiss in return.

"Sounds like a plan."

They get up from the ground and make their way inside, Theo glancing back, only to see the backyard's tranquil look completely destroyed from their past hour or so of actual *playing*. And in the middle of the mayhem stands the snowman, quickly getting another thin coat of snow, which keeps falling from the sky.

It's only when Theo actually starts taking his jacket off, that he notices just how cold he is. He wasn't exactly dressed for playing in the snow, and neither was Max, so they're both half-shivering by the time they've gotten everything off. And it seems that the snow on them has melted into their shirts and jeans, and into their shoes, and Theo pulls Max to him to rub his hands against his cold upper arms.

"Come on," he says, both of them shivering a bit. "Let's get warmed up."

The quickest and best way to get warmed up is to get the wet clothes off, so they end up stripping down to their underwear and hanging the wet clothes in the bathroom, before Theo digs through his closet for anything that Max could borrow. He ends up handing him a dark green Henley (one of his favorites), and Max takes it.

"Thanks," he says, eyeing it a bit warily.

"Yeah," Theo says, sounding a little self-conscious. "Don't have much to choose from, I'm afraid."

Max cocks his head, as if to say that it's fine, and Theo gets out a pair of black sweatpants, as well. He and Max are very nearly the same height, and they're both in pretty good shape, but where Theo has a slightly stockier build, Max is a bit more toned and slim, which means that most of Theo's clothes will probably be a little too big for him, anyway. So it doesn't really matter what he picks out.

"It's perfect," Max says, with a small smirk, putting the sweatpants on. Theo is a little sad, as usual, to see those tattoos covered up, as Max puts on the sweater, but he knows he and Max are both too cold to walk around half-naked, right now.

Theo puts on a pair of jeans and a t-shirt, with a hoodie over it, and as they both make their way into the kitchen to make some coffee, he can't help but eye Max up and down. He can't help it, because honestly, this is the first time he has seen him wear any other color than black.

Max notices, and as they sit at the kitchen table, he narrows his eyes at Theo, while holding a hot cup of coffee in his hands.

"What?" he says, and Theo half-shrugs.

"Nothing," he says, taking a sip of the beverage. "It looks good on you."

It's true, the dark green Henley does look good on him. Maybe it's just the dark shade of the color, an easy transition from black, but it really does suit him.

Max glances down at himself.

"Yeah," he mutters, tugging at the shirt a little. "Too much color, though. Not sure how to feel about that."

Theo raises his eyebrows, and nudges Max's foot with his own, under the table.

"Well, maybe we should take it off, then," he suggests, a little surprised at his own words, and judging from Max's expression when he looks up at him, he is, too.

"Yeah," he says, voice dropping a little. "Maybe we should."

It's only a matter of minutes, before they're back in Theo's room, grabbing and kissing, all warmed up and therefore all for taking their clothes off. And it's only a matter of moments, before they're in Theo's bed, Max's borrowed Henley tossed to the floor, along with Theo's hoodie. Max straddles him, as Theo lies on his back, and Theo helpfully arches up a little, to make it easier for Max to pull his t-shirt off, before Max takes both Theo's hands in his own and presses them down into the mattress.

Theo is vaguely, happily aware of the dark leather bracelet around Max's wrist, the one with the black, imprinted wings, and the way his own ring feels on his finger. It's weird, really, how happy those details make him, and he kisses Max even deeper, wanting him even closer. This is all that matters.

"We should have sex," Max suddenly says, sounding breathless and almost comically eager, and Theo just blinks up at him.

"Yeah," he says after a moment, nodding, extremely aware of how both he and Max are already hard. "We should."

Max hums in approval, kissing him again, and Theo shivers, as those hands smooth down over his chest.

"Do you have...?" Max murmurs, trailing off, and Theo is about to say *yes*, before he realizes something.

No, he doesn't. He doesn't have any lube, and he doesn't have any condoms. He's just so used to being at Max's place, where that stuff always seems to be readily available, that it hasn't even occurred to him that he doesn't actually have any, himself.

So, Theo somewhat awkwardly hums against Max's mouth, in a hesitant sound, calling for his attention, and Max pulls away a little.

"What?" he asks, and Theo cocks his head a bit, making Max frown. Theo answers him, feeling weirdly embarrassed.

"I, uh..." Theo says, glancing at the nightstand, for some reason. "I don't have any."

"You're kidding." Max sounds disappointed, more than anything, and Theo looks up at him, shrugging.

"Why would I have any?" he asks, and Max shrugs back.

"I don't know," he says. "Why *wouldn't* you have any?"

Theo frowns at him, with a *are you kidding me*-look on his face.

"This may have slipped your mind," he says, with a surprising amount of sarcasm, "but I was a virgin, until pretty recently. I haven't exactly needed it, before."

Max looks like he's about to say something, but then catches himself, thinks about it, and then cocks his head.

"Fair enough," he says, before sighing.

"Well, don't you have any?" Theo asks, and Max looks at him.

"I don't exactly carry that stuff around," he says, but Theo just raises his eyebrows, pointedly.

"You did, the first time," he retorts, and Max makes a vague, non-committal gesture.

"Well, yeah," he admits. "But I had *been* carrying it around for a while, already. I haven't exactly refilled my wallet-supply."

He says that last part with some amount of sarcasm, and Theo feels a slight twinge of jealousy, for some reason.

"Why not?" he asks, and Max glances away.

"Because I haven't needed to," he says, referring to him previously being *prepared* for such situations, in lack of a better word. "Not since I met you."

"But you used to?" Theo says, despite himself, and Max looks at him. He looks oddly uncomfortable, all of a sudden, and Theo *knows* that he's not comfortable talking about this.

"Maybe," he says. "Yeah."

"Like... A lot?"

Max sighs, sounding almost frustrated, along with that uncharacteristic discomfort.

"Do we really have to talk about this, right now?" he says, and Theo, due to some kind of masochistic curiosity, doesn't take the out that Max is giving him.

"I'm just asking," he says instead, and Max sighs heavily, before pulling back and sitting up straight, still straddling Theo.

"Fine," he says, reluctantly, eyes on Theo. "Yes. Happy?"

No, Theo wants to say. No, he's not happy. Actually, Max's reply does nothing but make that involuntary twinge of jealousy suddenly grow ten times bigger and stab Theo right in the gut, and he swallows hard. He has managed to ignore it for weeks and weeks, but it's kind of hard to, when it's unintentionally thrown in your face, over and over again. Max's mother's reaction to her son's relationship didn't exactly help, or the general reaction from his parents; they figured that Theo was *just another guy,* after all.

But Theo nods. And neither of them says a word for what feels like several, long seconds.

"Why would you ask that?" Max eventually says, not sounding the least bit accusing or hurt. He just sounds a little confused, and Theo glances away, somehow unable to look right at him.

"I don't know," he mutters, suddenly feeling oddly exposed and uncomfortable and ridiculous, and as if Max notices, he sighs softly. He leans down and places his elbows on either side of Theo, against the bed.

"Hey," he says gently, using one hand to trail his fingers along Theo's hairline, very tenderly. "You know that doesn't matter, right?"

Theo looks back at him then, and those blue eyes look almost sad.

"I know," Theo says, his voice almost a whisper, and Max just looks at him for a few moments.

"I haven't exactly been good," he says quietly, trying to sound light and joking, but only coming off as sad, which he seems to notice. "And yes, I have been with other guys. Other... people, actually."

He glances away, and Theo vaguely remembers that conversation they had on Max's roof, so long ago, when Max mentioned how Beth was into him. And when it came to whether or not he swung that way, he said he *had tried it, once or twice,* but that it wasn't his thing. At the time, he didn't seem too bothered about telling Theo stuff like that, and Theo was barely jealous, because he figured that Max wasn't his, anyway, and never would be.

This time, though, it's different. This time, Max looks almost ashamed, ashamed about being with people that *weren't* Theo, guys or not, and suddenly, it makes Theo feel sad.

"I know that," he says, and Max looks back at him, almost hesitantly. "And no, it doesn't matter."

He takes a breath.

"I just used to feel like you wouldn't want me," he admits, "because I wasn't... *experienced.*"

He quirks a tiny smile at the use of the word, one which Max tentatively mirrors.

"And sometimes, I guess I just forget that just because you were my first, doesn't mean I was yours." Theo swallows. "By far."

Max sighs softly, that sad look mingling with one of pure, adoring affection, now.

"You are my first, though," he says, smoothing his fingers over Theo's hair. "In every way that counts."

He gives him a soft kiss.

"I've never been with anyone like you, before," he says. "No one's ever treated me the way you do. And I've never felt as good about myself, like I do with you."

He cocks his head a little, as though aware of how cheesy and chick-flicky this all sounds.

"So yeah," he says, "I've had sex before. Lots, actually. But none of them were you."

He looks at Theo pointedly, and that look somehow completely negates the heavy, jealous pain that Theo feels in his chest at those words, and his discomfort slowly evaporates.

"And I wasn't in a very good place, when all that went down," Max admits, a bit more somber. "I'd like to erase some of it, if I could. It wasn't good for me."

He just looks at Theo, then, scanning his face with that dark blue gaze, somehow avoiding his eyes.

"You're good for me."

Theo doesn't immediately respond. He knows that only a couple of weeks ago, he would have had a harder time dealing with this, but now, somehow, with everything that's happened, he doesn't. And especially after what Max told him earlier, about him moving, which he really doesn't want to think about more than necessary.

Max waits for a moment, before giving Theo a slightly anxious, soft look.

"Okay?" he says, tentatively, almost with some hesitation, and Theo nods.

"Yeah," he says, and he means it. "It's okay."

As if to enforce his words, he reaches up to press his lips against Max's, and Max almost immediately melts against him, in a slow, hot kiss. It's almost as if it makes every doubt in Theo's mind evaporate, and he slowly smoothes his hands up along Max's back.

Then, out of nowhere, he remembers something.

"Wait a minute," he says, and Max pulls away, confused. He almost looks the tiniest bit worried, like he's afraid Theo might have changed his mind.

"What?" he asks, and Theo nudges him slightly, making him climb off of him.

"I might actually have some," Theo says with a sigh, and he gets out of bed and makes his way over to his schoolbag, which is lying on the floor by his desk.

Max waits, as Theo digs through the bag to find what he's looking for, and when he does, he silently thanks Cassie for somehow being psychic and simply *knowing* he would need this in the near future. He takes a single-use packet of lube in his hand and tosses it over at the bed, and Max catches it effortlessly. He looks down at it, raising his eyebrows, and he gives his boyfriend a pointed look. Theo feels his face heat up, for some reason, like he's embarrassed.

"Blame Cassie," he mutters, picking out some of the condoms his best friend also shoved into his bag, on that occasion, and he makes his way back over to the bed.

Max cocks his head, eyeing the small packet of lube in his hand.

"Blame her?" he says. "I'm sending her a fucking fruit basket."

Theo gives him the tiniest little slap at the back of his head, a light nudge, more than anything, and Max smirks.

"What?" he says, looking up at Theo, who puts the condoms down on his nightstand. "She's being a good friend. What can I say?"

He shrugs, and Theo glares at him. He's standing beside the bed, and Max just looks at him, long and hard, before licking his lips.

"And you know," he says, his already rough voice just a bit lower, as he puts the lube down on the nightstand and gets up on his knees. "It would be a waste not to honor that."

He places himself in front of Theo, who can quickly feel himself getting hard again, just from Max kneeling on the bed like that, talking in that smoky voice. And it doesn't exactly help, when Max moves his hands down to Theo's jeans and starts undoing his fly, that blue gaze tilted upward, to catch Theo's eye.

"It would be downright disrespectful," Max continues, and Theo absently moves his hand down to smooth over Max's hair, the back of his neck, down along his bare shoulders. He's not sure what's happening, right now, but he sure as hell doesn't mind. He doesn't mind the way Max keeps his eyes on his, as he unzips Theo's fly and slowly tugs his jeans down a little, or the way he leans in closer and slowly starts placing open-mouthed kisses against Theo's stomach. Theo really doesn't mind.

"'Disrespectful' is a bit strong," Theo says, "don't you think?"

He's aware of how he already sounds a bit breathless, but he doesn't care. In fact, Max seems to like it, smiling a little against his bare skin, eyes now averted.

"You caught me," he murmurs slyly, his warm breath trailing down along Theo's stomach, along with the softest sweeps of his tongue. "I'm just trying to get in your pants."

Theo lets out something between a groan and a chuckle.

"Bonus points for subtlety," he says, and Max chuckles, smoothing his hands down along Theo's body, before directing his attention to the now very noticeable hard-on in his underwear.

"Subtlety was never really my strong suit, anyway," Max says, moving his lips downward, kissing his way to the hem of Theo's boxers. Theo gasps lightly, as Max pulls the underwear down. "Who has time for that shit."

He adds those last words in a barely audible murmur, and suddenly, Theo's mind just goes blank. He closes his eyes and lets out a small breath, as he feels that tongue against him, those lips eager and gentle, all at once, and that hot, wet mouth downright heavenly, as Max swallows him down. Theo tries to calm his suddenly frantic pulse, and lets one hand trail along the bare skin of Max's shoulders and neck, while the other moves up to stroke his hair. Because he actually strokes it, gently; there's no urgency, no tugging or pulling. At least, not yet.

Theo can't help himself. He opens his eyes and looks down at Max, who's focusing every ounce of his attention on Theo, eyes closed and small sounds escaping him now and then, while he uses both his hands and mouth to drive Theo crazy. Theo swallows hard, his breath hitching at the amazing sensation, and for what feels like a rather long time, he just stands there, completely wrapped up in the way Max's mouth feels, like he simply can't get enough.

He can, though. He's just not there yet, and he wants to draw it out.

Max seems a little surprised when Theo gently tugs on his hair, and those dark blue eyes are downright sinful, when they look up at him. He doesn't say a word, though, doesn't object when Theo gently pushes against his shoulder, wordlessly asking him to lie down. Instead, he simply does as he's told, while Theo takes his pants off properly, along with his underwear, and Max isn't far behind. Within seconds, his clothes have joined Theo's on the floor, and before long, the two of them are underneath the covers, hands everywhere and lips locked together, with nothing but bare skin between them.

Theo doesn't say anything, and neither does Max, instead filling the afternoon air with hot, hungry sounds and eager touches. After a little while, Theo awkwardly reaches for the lube Max put on the nightstand, and presses the plastic packet into Max's hand, hoping to convey the message. He's pretty sure he does, but Max doesn't really respond to it, right away.

"Actually," he says, and that sly tone of his voice makes Theo look at him. They're both lying on their sides now, facing each other, and Max eyes the small packet of lube in his hand. Then he looks up at Theo pointedly, before slowly leaning into him and pushing gently, until Theo ends up on his back. And Max straddles him, before leaning down, hovering above Theo, and giving Theo a rather great view of that partly tattooed, naked body. He opens the lube, and while Theo watches, speechless, he squeezes some of the thick liquid onto his fingers, before tossing the packet aside, unceremoniously.

Theo thinks he knows what to expect, is kind of prepared for it, but Max surprises him by moving his hand back over his own body, rather than down to Theo's crotch. Then his expression changes, and it takes Theo a moment to realize that Max is actually touching himself, using his own, slick fingers to prep *himself*, rather than Theo. And for a second, Theo just stares.

"Max—" he says, but is cut off.

"We don't have to," Max says, a bit hurriedly, like he's worried about pushing Theo into something he doesn't want, as it's pretty obvious what he's prepping himself *for*. He starts moving his hand away, but before he can stop what he's doing, Theo grabs his arm, keeping his hand right where it is.

"That's not it," Theo says, breathing heavily. "I'm just—"

He swallows hard.

"I've never done that, before." He tries not to sound nervous, failing miserably, and he tries not to come off as scared about getting the whole thing wrong. An endeavor which he fails equally miserably, of course. "I wouldn't know what to do."

God, he sounds pathetic. But he's just so unprepared for this that he can feel himself freaking out a bit, and Max looks down at him, his expression excited and somehow comforting, all at once. He leans down a bit, planting a soft kiss on Theo's lips.

"You don't really have to do anything," he nearly whispers, and Theo slowly releases his arm in favor of smoothing up along his waist. "Just let me."

Theo swallows hard again, as Max gives him another kiss. He shouldn't be nervous. Hell, they've done pretty much everything else, already, what difference would this make?

Well, actually, he figures it's a pretty huge difference. Because this is one aspect of sex he still doesn't have any experience with, whatsoever, and that's downright scary.

He nods, though, because he wants it. He wants what Max is offering, wants to be inside him, and he has wanted it, in the back of his mind, ever since Max first suggested it in that bathroom on New Year's Eve. Just this morning, he was honestly thinking about it, and Max knows that, has most likely been thinking about it too.

So Max gives Theo a small nod in return, before going back to what he was doing, his expression changing and his lips parting in one pleased moan after the other, as he does it. And Theo lies there, on his back, watching Max hover above him, touching himself, and he feels himself becoming almost painfully hard, at this point.

This is new. This is new, and it's exciting and terrifying, all at once.

It's after a little while, when Max is nearly leaning his forehead against Theo's, panting and groaning from the pressure of his own fingers, that Theo really has to fight the urge to touch himself. It's all he can think about, Max an irresistible, flushed epiphany above him, and he swallows hard, digging his fingertips into Max's thighs, instead.

"Theo," Max eventually breathes, and Theo makes a small sound of confirmation. Max isn't satisfied, though, and he lifts his head a little, to motion vaguely toward the nightstand. It takes another second for Theo to get it.

"Oh," he says, a bit stunned. "Right."

His hand seems reluctant to obey him properly, fumbling for a condom, and when he finally gets a hold of one, it takes him three tries to actually open the wrapper. *Shit.* He remembers being nervous the first time he and Max had sex, and every other thing they did before that, but this is different. He's not sure why, but he suddenly feels like there's pressure on him to perform, now, pressure that simply wasn't there before.

Max looks a little impatient, but he doesn't say anything, letting Theo take his time, putting the condom on. That takes two tries, and as Theo curses internally at his own lack of smoothness, right now, Max leans down and kisses his neck, slowly and hungrily. And Theo closes his eyes for a moment, suddenly more eager than a minute ago, as he finally gets the condom on.

"We're good?" Max practically pants then, and Theo nods, making Max pull his fingers out and steady himself against the mattress. He gives Theo a slow, searing kiss, before straightening, almost sitting up completely, eyes on his boyfriend, before taking Theo in his hand, and slowly moving into position. And within the next couple of seconds, Theo's mind goes completely blank.

He actually holds his breath, and he's not sure why. Maybe it's just the intense overload of sensation, as Max moves, pulls back up, before slowly moving down again, pushing Theo inside. Maybe it's the way that tight, wet heat feels around him, as he bottoms out, the way Max lets out a deep, guttural moan, moving one hand down to rest against Theo's chest, as though to steady himself. Theo has no idea, but whatever the reason, his entire body is suddenly burning, and he finds himself staring at the ceiling, letting out his held breath in a surprisingly sharp exhale.

His heart is pounding, his fingers tightening on Max's hips, and suddenly, he's breathing again. His breaths are shallow and quick, though, surprise and utter pleasure mingling together, his mouth half-open, as he tries to wrap his head around the sensation.

Max seems to notice his reaction—of course, he does—because he leans forward then, the slight shift making Theo let out a surprised moan.

"You okay?" Max asks, sounding oddly breathless and impatient, and Theo swallows hard, nodding jerkily, as he stares at the ceiling.

"Yeah," he breathes, barely audibly, and Max touches his face, making him meet his gaze. Theo immediately reacts; those dark blue eyes are shining, excited and hungry, and it's enough to make Theo instinctively tighten his grip on Max's hips.

"Are you sure?" Max says, articulating so much more clearly than Theo feels capable of, right now. And he is sure. He's very sure, he's just momentarily stunned by this feeling, the amazing sensation of having Max on top of him like this, of being *inside* him, and those intense, blue eyes staring right into his soul.

"I just—" Theo says in a labored breath, cutting himself off and letting out a very quiet groan, as Max shifts again. "It just feels really good."

He's a mess, already. He would be embarrassed of his own behavior, if he weren't so incredibly caught up in this, caught up in the feeling of it all. And he watches, with some satisfaction, as Max licks his lips, clearly affected by Theo's reaction.

"Yeah," Max says, and as if to accentuate this, he moves up a little bit, before sliding back down, making Theo grit his teeth and let out a small moan. "It really does."

His breathing is heavy now, blue eyes intoxicated, and he leans in closer to give Theo a soft, hungry kiss. It's like the best kind of drug, the touch of his lips shooting surges of chemicals through Theo's entire body, and he closes his eyes, absently loving the feeling of that metal ring against his mouth. Then, Max pulls up again, making Theo gasp, before he pushes back down, and Theo squeezes his eyes shut, trying to make sense of this overload of sensory input.

Max straightens, sitting up to make his movements easier, and Theo just lies there, his hands on Max's hips and smoothing over his skin, eyes closed and seemingly every muscle in his body working to stay in control. He wants to *move*, wants to feel more of that hot, amazing friction, and he finds himself absently thrusting his hips upwards, very lightly. Max seems to take the hint, though; his pace picks up a little bit, and Theo is blissfully aware of every single groan, pant, and labored breath that escapes that wonderful mouth. It might just be the best sounds he has ever heard, and he swallows hard, trailing his hands up along Max's naked body, as far as he can reach. And, as usual, although he wants to keep his eyes closed, he also wants to watch Max. He *always* wants to watch Max.

As Theo opens his eyes, he's hit by the realization that Max is simply *gorgeous*. Sure, he has always known this, and he never really stops being awed by it, but this is different. Seeing Max on top of him like this, moving and moaning, so obviously enjoying the feeling of having Theo inside him, is more than he can really handle, and it's after only a few seconds of watching him, that Theo suddenly sits up.

Max is a bit surprised, that much is obvious. But he doesn't do a thing to stop Theo, as Theo wraps his arms around him, one hand moving up to the back of Max's head, so that he can keep him in place, as he kisses him. Instead, Max keeps moving, reciprocates by grabbing onto Theo, who then surprises them both, by falling back down onto his back, and taking Max with him.

Theo isn't entirely sure what he's doing. This just feels so good, so *unbelievably* good, and he firmly places one hand against the small of Max's back, his other arm pinning Max against him by pressing against his shoulder blades. Max is stunned, in lack of a better word, when Theo then suddenly uses all of his weight to simply roll over, taking Max with him, so that Max ends up on his back. Theo is vaguely grateful that his bed is big enough; it would have been quite the mood-killer if they had just rolled over the edge.

Max's blue eyes are wide, with an expression that's as blatantly shocked as it is aroused, as Theo looks down at him. The two of them are still firmly locked together, Theo's arms slowly loosening their grip around his boyfriend, and he's oddly pleased to find that he managed this whole thing while only just barely pulling out. He's still inside Max, still inside that glorious, tight heat, and he swallows hard, moving one hand to trail down along Max's thigh, and he slowly pushes inside until he bottoms out again.

"Holy shit." Max's stunned, intoxicated murmur is barely audible, and as Theo uses his hand to hitch his leg up slightly, Max actually grabs onto his hair and brings Theo's mouth down to his own. The kiss is burning and impatient, and Theo groans, as he slowly, almost tentatively, starts thrusting.

How the hell did this happen? How the hell did he end up like this, pinning Max down and pushing into him, rather than lying on his back and letting Max do his own, amazing thing? Theo has no idea. But right now, that's the last thing on his mind. Instead, he fights the impulse to just pound into Max, hard and fast; that's not how he wants to do this. He wants to make it last, he doesn't want to hurt him, and he tries to think of how Max usually does it, how he does it slowly and deeply, at first, before speeding up. And as Theo implements this, he notices, with great satisfaction, that he's apparently doing it right.

At least, judging from the way Max moans against his mouth, breathing heavily, one hand gripping Theo's hair so tightly it almost hurts, and the other practically digging its nails into Theo's back. It's like he's surprised at the intensity of his own sensations, pulling away from Theo's mouth to bury his face against his neck, moaning and breathing hard and fast through gritted teeth, while Theo moves one hand up to pull his fingers through that black, messy hair and hold Max against him. Max practically clings to him, and it's when his breathing suddenly starts to stutter, guttural moans slowly turning into quick, shallow breaths, that Theo decides to pick up the pace.

Oh god. It's like his entire body is burning, buzzing, bursting with this onslaught of sensation, all of his focus zeroed in on the way Max feels, body pressed against him, hot and tight around him, those amazing, wonderful noises coming out of Max's mouth.

Theo pulls back a little bit, just enough be able to put more force behind his thrusts, and he looks down at Max, whose hands are now desperately smoothing over Theo's body, aimlessly, mouth half-open and eyes slightly wide, chest heaving rapidly. Theo can barely even comprehend how hot it is, and when Max suddenly tenses up, his entire body going rigid, Theo feels that tight heat constrict around him, making him actually gasp.

And just like that, Max is coming, expression blissed-out and beautiful, and Theo feels his hips starting to stutter, as he thrusts once, twice, before freezing and being simply overwhelmed by his own amazing, white-hot release. It seems that making Max come was all he needed; he's not even sure if it's the physical sensation of it or the emotional one, but either way, it definitely did the trick.

When it's over, Theo doesn't actually move for several seconds. He's too busy marveling at how incredibly, fucking *amazing* this is. All of it. Every moment, every breath, every touch, and every single awkward, uncoordinated movement. Just...

Sex. Just *sex*—sex with *Max*—is the most mind-blowing, remarkable thing. Theo can't believe how he was ever even slightly averse to the idea of it. He can't really imagine ever *not* doing this, ever *not* feeling Max against him this way, hot and flushed, muscles limp with utter and complete satisfaction.

Perfect.

When Max suddenly makes a noise, Theo is pretty sure he's trying to say something, even though it only comes out as a small, exhausted moan, and Theo pulls back a little, practically collapsed on top of his boyfriend. He holds himself up with his arms, so that he can look at Max, properly.

Max looks oddly stunned, lips slightly parted and dark blue eyes dazed, as they gaze toward the ceiling, rather than Theo's face.

"Huh?" Theo asks, his voice a tired breath. And Max blinks, swallowing dryly. He looks positively shocked, at this point.

"Fuck," he eventually says, breathlessly. "Jesus fucking christ."

Theo swallows hard, suddenly oddly worried.

"Was that—" he starts, before trying again, his breathing still kind of heavy. He tries not to sound too self-conscious or nervous, but he doesn't really succeed. "Was that okay?"

Max exhales sharply, almost in disbelief.

"Well," he says, still completely breathless. "It may have been the hottest sex I've ever had, in my life."

He turns his gaze to Theo, then.

"So, yeah," he says. "It was okay."

Theo's immediate reaction of pleased shock is quickly mingled with doubt, and he frowns, disbelievingly.

"Really?" he says, sounding more confused than he intended, and Max exhales slowly.

"Really," he confirms, slowly trailing along the hot skin of Theo's arm, which is tensed up and nearly shaking. "I mean, you taking charge, like that."

He eyes Theo's naked chest, his arms, and he scoffs, with a small, affectionate smirk.

"You keep surprising me," he says. "I like that."

He looks back up at Theo, blue eyes sinful and sly.

"It's unbelievably hot, you know."

As a matter of fact, no, Theo doesn't know that. But then again, he loves it when Max does that, so maybe it's not such a surprise that Max agrees.

Still, though. Theo has never seen himself as that type of person, before. The type of person to just take control like that, and in bed, no less.

"Well, I'm glad to hear it," Theo says, giving Max a light kiss, and Max hums.

"How did you learn to do that so well, anyway?" he asks, eyes narrowed in mock suspicion, but with a hint of genuine curiosity. And Theo glances away, suddenly a little embarrassed.

"From you," he admits in a reluctant murmur, referring to the technique he just used, and Max looks genuinely surprised, before smiling.

"Well damn, I am good, aren't I?" He says it in a blatantly smug way, and Theo glares at him. He can't keep that expression for more than a moment, though, before it's erased by a smile, and he kisses Max, slowly and adoringly.

"Yes, you are."

CHAPTER 29

DANCE

"You're kidding!"

Cassie sounds blatantly shocked, but after a moment, her entire expression takes on a hint of sympathy, as she looks at Theo.

"No," Theo says, fiddling with a pen between his fingers. "I wish I were."

They're sitting in the living room at Theo's house, trying to get some studying done, and Theo has just told her about what he learned from Max the other day; Max is leaving, moving away, just a month from now.

"But that's bullshit," Cassie exclaims. "They can't do that!"

Theo huffs a bitter laugh.

"That's what I said," he says. "Doesn't seem to matter, though."

It's not that he and Max haven't tried to think of a solution. Theo even brought it up with his parents, albeit very carefully, but didn't even try to ask if Max could stay with them. He knows that they would say no. He just knows, and honestly, he can't blame them. And as far as the living-together-idea goes, that's a bust, as well.

"You know what," Cassie says after a while, pointing at Theo with her pen. "We should get a place together. All three of us. It could be like a sitcom-type deal."

Theo chuckles.

"That does sound awesome," he admits. "But the issue of actually *paying* for it still stands. None of us have jobs, and no potential of actually getting one that pays well enough, until after graduation. It's just not doable. It sucks, but it's the truth."

Cassie thinks about that for a moment, before groaning loudly and falling back onto the couch. She's sitting cross-legged, facing Theo, which leaves a large stretch of furniture behind her to fall back on. And when she lands, she lightly punches the cushions, in irritation.

"It's not fair," she says. "Whatever happened to 'true love prevails', and all that crap?"

Theo raises his eyebrows a little.

"Who's taking this harder," he says, knowing his lack of anger is simply because he has started getting used to the idea, "me or you?"

Cassie groans again, dramatically covering her face with her arm.

"I can't help it," she says. "I'm a hopeless romantic. Your pain is my pain."

"Yeah, well," Theo says, nudging her leg slightly with his pen. "I'm not the one going all Scarlett O'Hara about it."

"You should," Cassie replies in a tired, dramatically broken voice. "It's very cathartic."

"I can see that."

Cassie lifts her arm so she can look at her friend, who simply raises his eyebrows at her, before she sighs and sits back up. She slouches a little.

"I'm sorry," she says, combing through her hair with her fingers, the red strands messed up from being pressed against the couch's cushions. "It just sucks, you know? I mean, I know how you guys feel about each other, and you've been through a lot of shit, already. Just seems unfair that you should be separated, after all that."

Theo sighs, looking down at the notepad in his lap and tapping it with his pen.

"Yeah," he says solemnly. "I wish there was something we could do about it, but I'm pretty sure we're fucked, in that department."

Cassie huffs a small laugh, and Theo looks up at her.

"What?" he says, but she just shakes her head.

"Nothing," she says. "Just still not quite used to you actually cussing."

Theo gives her a small glare, before smiling a little.

"Blame Max," he says, looking back down at his notes, and as he thinks about his boyfriend, there's now some dread and sadness mixed in, along with the fuzzy happiness.

Cassie seems to notice, and she nudges him gently.

"Hey," she says, and he looks up at her. "It'll work out. Everything's gonna be fine."

Theo sighs a little, fully aware that it doesn't sound any more convincing, coming from Cassie, rather than himself. But still, he appreciates the effort.

"Speaking of," he says lightly, in a desperate attempt at changing the subject. "How's your love life going?"

Cassie groans a little, looking down and picking at the corner of her notepad.

"I don't know," she says, referring to Emma. "I mean, I took your advice. I kissed her, and she kissed me back, and it was... awesome."

She gets a dreamy look on her face for a moment, before sobering up.

"But I don't know," she repeats. "I really like her, I'm just not sure I'm *feeling* it, you know?"

Theo nods.

"Yeah, I get it," he says.

"I mean, maybe we're just not meant to be," Cassie says, shrugging. "She's amazing, though, and we have so much fun together."

"Well, maybe you're just better off as friends, then?" he suggests, and Cassie shrugs again.

"Yeah, maybe," she says. "Just a little bummed about it, I guess. But we'll see. Who knows, right? Maybe I'll even ask her to the dance."

Theo frowns, then.

"Dance?" he asks. "What dance?"

"The Winter Dance," Cassie replies, as though Theo is a little stupid for not being aware of it. "You know, next week?"

Theo racks his brain, before shaking his head, and Cassie sighs in exasperation.

"Really?" she says. "There are flyers, all over school. How can you have missed it?"

Theo shrugs.

"It's every year," Cassie points out. "Every winter."

"Well, I've never exactly had reason to go, now have I?" Theo retorts. "A year ago, I was pretty much invisible, remember? The Winter Dance was kinda the last thing on my mind."

Cassie cocks her head, a slightly apologetic look on her face.

"Sorry," she says. "But you must have noticed it?"

Theo shrugs.

"Honestly," he says, "I just stayed away from all of that. It was only after Michael and I started hanging out that I even really noticed it was a thing. You know, seeing as how girls would constantly come up and ask him about it."

Theo isn't lost on the obvious trace of bitterness in his voice, and neither is Cassie.

"Well," she says, a conspiring edge to her voice. "At least you've got someone to ask, this time."

Theo frowns at her.

"Who, Max?" he asks incredulously. "Are you serious?"

"Yeah," Cassie says, shrugging, as though she's personally offended at Theo's tone. "Why not?"

"Can you even imagine him going to a *dance*?" Theo points out. "Because I can't."

"Well, if you ask him—"

"I'm not going to," Theo says, cutting her off. "I'm not about to put him through that."

Cassie pouts a little.

"You could always just ask him," she says, but Theo just gives her a look.

"Don't get me wrong," he says, "I'd like to go. If nothing else, because he's leaving soon, and it would be... I don't know, *fun*. Nice."

He sighs.

"But I'm pretty sure he wouldn't want to," he says. "And I'm not about to guilt-trip him into it, by asking."

Theo looks down at his notepad, scratching the back of his head with his pen.

"So, yeah," he says. "Let's just drop it, okay?"

And Cassie, being the good friend that she is, drops it. Instead, they focus on their homework, while Theo tries not to think about the fact that Max will only be around for a few more weeks, and the way just the thought of that makes his heart sink.

♦

Cassie isn't the only one sad about Max moving away. When Riley hears the news, Theo is surprised at how bummed he is about it, and even Amy seems sad. Eric, however, doesn't say much about anything; he barely ever even mentions Max, as though the whole thing still makes him uncomfortable, and generally, he isn't around whenever Max visits their house.

And Max's visits have become a bit more frequent, lately. Theo suspects it's because he doesn't want to be home, right now. His parents still work a lot, and still work late, and especially his dad goes away for a couple of days at a time, to set up for his new position at the company he works at, while Max's mother has taken time off more often to prepare for the move.

"She's already started packing," Max explains, as he lies on his back, on Theo's bed, tossing Theo's miniature Mjölnir between his hands. "She even seems excited about it. They both do."

He sighs, and Theo watches him from his desk, where he has been sitting for the past half-hour, finishing some homework.

"And they still don't get why I'm pissed." Max sounds simultaneously annoyed and tired, and he closes his eyes for a moment. "I swear, I feel like I wanna kill something."

Theo doesn't immediately reply. He can't say that he doesn't share Max's sentiments, because he most definitely does. It's just that where Max is still in the stage of anger, Theo has started slipping into the sad stage, where he just feels heavy and full of empty sorrow, at the very thought of Max going away.

Max stops tossing the tiny hammer between his hands and instead flops it down onto the bed, where it bounces a little, before settling against the sheets. And Theo gets up from where he sits, sighing as he makes his way over there.

"Hey," he says, and Max opens his eyes, squinting up at his boyfriend. "Not in the house. If you're gonna kill something, go outside, where you're less likely to make a mess my mom will hate you for."

Max just blinks, before his face breaks into a soft, almost dopey smile.

"I'll keep that in mind," he says, and Theo tentatively smiles back, as Max reaches up and takes his hand. He doesn't even have to ask, for Theo to crawl into bed with him, curling him by his side and placing his head against his chest, and for several seconds, they just lie there. Max's fingers trace circles into the fabric of Theo's t-shirt, and Theo takes a deep breath, inhaling that wonderful, familiar scent that makes him feel all warm and happy and safe. He barely notices the way he automatically moves his hand across Max's stomach, searching for his touch, and Max immediately obliges, lacing their fingers together.

"I really don't want you to go," Theo suddenly says, a little embarrassed at how downright pathetic he sounds. But Max doesn't seem to think so. And if he does, he doesn't mention it, instead just sighing softly as he plants a kiss on the top of Theo's head.

"And I really don't want to," he says, before they lapse back into silence, the only sound being their steady breathing, and the vague noise of the TV, downstairs; Theo can barely hear it, through the closed door of his room.

"Hey," Max says after a little while, nudging his boyfriend. "I talked to Cassie."

"Yeah?" Theo says, and Max nods; he can feel it.

"Yeah," he confirms. "She told me you guys hung out the other day. And she told me about a certain Winter Dance..."

He says it a bit hesitantly, and Theo glances up at him. Those dark blue, black-lined eyes look a little questioning, their expression pointed, and Theo sighs, settling back against Max's chest.

"What about it?" he asks, and Max shifts a little.

"Well," he says, that hesitance still in his voice. "She told me that you didn't want to ask me."

"Only because I knew you wouldn't want to go," Theo points out, trying not to sound like a douche about it. Then he pauses, thinking. "Why? Did you... Did you want to?"

He asks it with pretty obvious apprehension, and Max sighs, half-shrugging awkwardly, as well as he can, with Theo resting against him.

"Maybe," he finally says. "I mean, sure, I'm not a big fan of dances and stuff like that, but... I'm leaving soon, and..."

He clears his throat a little.

"Feels like maybe we should go," he says. "You know, if you want to."

Theo blinks, honestly surprised, and he looks up at Max.

"Really?" he says, frowning a little, and Max looks blatantly awkward, and maybe even a little shy.

"Yeah," he says, before continuing in some haste, as though trying to fix any awkwardness he may have just caused. "But only if you want to. Either way, I get it. It's fine."

Theo thinks about that for a moment, and then shifts a little, propping himself up on his elbow, so that he can look at Max, properly.

"You'd go to a dance with me?" he says, sounding doubtful and confused, at the same time. "A *school* dance?"

Max glances away, almost rolling his eyes.

"Look, I'm sorry I brought it up, I just—"

"Are you kidding?" Theo says a bit hurriedly, making Max look back at him. "No, that's not it. I'd like to go, I just—"

He clears his throat, picking at the fabric of Max's black, long-sleeved t-shirt.

"I just thought you weren't into that."

"Well, I'm not," Max admits. "But when it comes to you, I've realized I'm into a lot of things I wouldn't normally care about."

And *damn*, that shouldn't make Theo smile like an idiot, but it does, and for a moment, he just stares at Max, pretty sure that his joy is written all over his face. He nods.

"Then, yes," he says. "I would like to go to the dance with you. You know, if you're asking me."

Max quirks a small smile, clearly relieved.

"I am," he says. And Theo nods again, stupidly.

"Cool," he says, and after another second or so of staring, he leans down and kisses Max on the mouth.

"But I'm not wearing a tux," Max says. "And I'm not getting you anything. And also, I will be bringing booze."

Theo can't help but laugh, leaning his forehead against Max's, moving one hand up to smooth over his cheekbone with his thumb.

"I can live with that."

◆

By the time the night of the Winter Dance actually comes around, a few days later, Theo is both anxious and a little excited. Anxious, because he has never been to one of these things, before, and excited, because he's going with Max. Max, who would never in a million years do anything like that. Max, who usually detests pretty much everything involving other people.

Max, who does all of that anyway, just for Theo.

As Theo gets ready to leave, he can't help but think about the reason for Max actually taking him to the dance. Despite Theo kind of wanting to go, he's also fully aware that Max is taking him mostly because he'll be leaving soon. He's leaving soon, and he wants to make Theo happy, and while that thought makes Theo smile, it also makes his stomach twist in uncomfortable knots.

He doesn't want Max to go. He *really* doesn't want him to go, and ever since he told him about the impending move, it's like every single day, every single moment, has been counting down to it. They've been ignoring it, though, pretending that it's never going to happen. They've just gone on like normal, like Max won't be leaving only two weeks from now, like they won't be separated and not see each other again.

Because that's probably what'll happen. It's not that Theo doubts Max's feelings for him, or his own feelings for Max, and he knows that they would do their best to make it work... But he also knows what it's like, when someone moves away. Before you know it, they've got a new life, with new people, and Theo can't exactly expect Max to cling to him, if he ends up somewhere else. Even if Theo knows that he, personally, will cling to Max with everything he's got, he would never ask Max to do the same.

But tonight isn't about that. Tonight is about having fun, and *not* dwelling on the fact that Max is leaving. In other words; more denial.

So Theo gets ready, grateful for the casual theme of the dance, which means he doesn't have to actually wear a suit. He settles for something halfway between casual and formal, though, with dark jeans and a button-up shirt, along with a black blazer and a grey tartan tie. It's an outfit Hannah picked out for him what feels like ages ago, when they first started hanging out and she basically gave him a makeover, and he must admit, it looks pretty good. He remembers her referring to the color of the shirt as *light eggshell*, whatever the hell that means—it's just *white*, who cares what kind?

When Theo makes his way downstairs, his mother immediately spots him; he's half-sure that she was waiting for him, ready to pounce.

"Look at you," she practically trills, a huge smile on her face. "All spruced up."

"Spruced?" Theo says doubtfully, and his mother cocks her head.

"Yeah," she says. "Or whatever you want to call it."

She eyes him up and down, looking positively gleeful, as she leans against the railing of the staircase. Theo huffs a breath, throwing up his hands.

"What?" he asks, but his mother just shrugs innocently, shaking her head.

"Nothing," she says. "Just, you all dressed up, going to a dance. And with a boyfriend, no less."

She adds that last part with a teasing, motherly smile, and Theo actually feels like he might blush a little.

"It's not a big deal," he says, but Amy just keeps smiling.

"It is," she says, growing a little bit more somber. "With all the stuff going on, it's nice that you two can go out, have some fun."

She gives her son a sympathetic smile, and he knows she's referring to Max moving. Like he needs to be reminded of that. Amy shrugs.

"It's just nice."

Theo gives her a small, affectionate smile, and he nods.

"Yeah," he agrees.

Thankfully, Amy spares him the humiliation of posing for a picture, or anything along those lines, although he can hear Riley snicker from the living room, at the way their mother bothers her oldest son, fussing with his clothes and adjusting his hair. It's only when Theo sees a car pull up outside, that he manages to escape, and his mother gives him a hug and a kiss on the cheek, before he leaves.

Cassie is the one to pick him up; Max doesn't have access to a car (and Theo has a feeling that he wouldn't want to borrow one from his parents, anyway), and annoyingly, Theo's father's car is out of commission. Apparently, it's in need of some repairs, so Theo couldn't borrow it, which kind of sucks.

So, he, Max and Cassie ended up deciding that they might as well go together.

"Well, look at you," Cassie says, as Theo slides into the front seat. "All dapper."

"You literally can't see anything but my pants," Theo points out, as he snaps his seatbelt into place. Cassie makes a face.

"True," she says, Theo wearing a jacket and a scarf over his outfit, and his hair looking the exact same as always. "But I'm assuming you're rocking all kinds of hot, under there."

She gestures at Theo, and he laughs.

"Ditto," he says, because he frankly can't deduce anything besides Cassie's coat and the fact that she seems to be wearing black tights. Her hair is slightly curled, though, half-pulled back, and it's clear that she spent just a little bit more effort than usual on her makeup.

They arrive at Max's house within minutes, and Cassie has to honk pointedly, before he comes outside.

"Took you long enough," Cassie says, as Max gets into the backseat. He sighs.

"Yeah, well, I'm here, aren't I?" he says dryly. "Don't get your panties in a bunch."

Cassie just shakes her head at that, and as she pulls back out onto the street, Theo turns back to look at Max.

"Hey," he says, and Max leans forward slightly.

"Hey," he says back, before kissing Theo, although they only have a second or so, before Cassie glances at them and actually smacks Theo lightly in the head.

"Alright," she says. "Everyone says *hey*, and everyone is happy to see each other. Moving on."

Theo glares at her as he settles back in his seat, before he retaliates by smacking her very lightly in the shoulder. Cassie gapes at him.

"Whoa," she says, flicking her eyes back to the road. "Driver! Not cool!"

Theo just smiles, though, because he knows she's not really mad, and the mood is very light and happy, by the time they arrive at the high school. The dance is to be held in the gym, which is the only room big enough to accommodate it, and Cassie parks behind the school building. As they make their way to the dance, Max reaches for Theo's hand, and he automatically takes it, glancing at him. It's weird, but he swears Max looks *happy*. Happier than usual, that is, in a kind of light, almost excited way.

Emma is waiting for Cassie when they arrive, and she, Theo, and Max get properly introduced. They all hand in their coats and jackets, and Max lets out a low whistle, as Cassie reveals the peach-colored, sleeveless dress underneath her coat. It has a slightly flared skirt, goes halfway down her thighs, and she smiles shyly and actually does a small curtsy, at Max's implied compliment.

"Why, thank you, good sir," she says, and Max bows his head.

"M'lady," he says, taking her hand and kissing it. Cassie beams at him, while Theo notices how Emma is looking at Cassie like she's the most stunning thing she has ever seen, and he smiles a little.

"We'll see you inside," Cassie says to Theo, and he nods, as she lightly takes Emma's hand and enters the decorated hall, where Theo can already hear music and raised voices, talking. Max leans in, while he shrugs off his coat, Theo already having handed his in.

"I thought you said they had decided to be 'just friends'," Max says, air-quotes implied, and Theo nods.

"Yeah," he says. "Why?"

Max makes a disbelieving sound.

"Yeah, that's not gonna work." He sounds highly doubtful. "At least not tonight. But hey, good on her. She's probably gonna get laid."

Theo huffs a small laugh, and he turns to Max, who's handing in his black trenchcoat. And he blinks, before his eyes actually widen a little.

"Holy shit," he murmurs, honestly surprised, and Max turns to him.

"What?" he says, and for a moment or so, Theo just stands there, opening and closing his mouth, like a goldfish.

"Nothing," he eventually sputters. "It's just..."

He gestures vaguely at Max, who's made the same choice as Theo, of staying halfway between casual and formal, in black skinny jeans, a black button-up shirt, and a black, pin-striped waistcoat. He's even wearing a tie, although a red one, rather than the blue one he mentioned, once (and frankly, Theo has a hard time imagining blue going with Max's color scheme, regardless of how beautifully it would most likely bring out his eyes). Along with the ensemble are those black Dr. Martens, and that black eyeliner, and for a while, Theo just stares, mouth half-open.

He stares for quite a while, apparently, because Max looks at him pointedly, seemingly halfway between impatient and slightly self-conscious, and Theo snaps out of it, blinking.

"Uh, I just—" he swallows, looking up to meet Max's eyes. "It's just that, this might be the hottest thing I've ever seen."

He's slightly surprised that he says it out loud, but he can't stress enough how true it is, and Max actually looks a little surprised, for a moment. He glances down at himself, before looking up at Theo, narrowing his eyes a little.

"You sure about that?" he says, and Theo licks his lips, thinking about a reply. Then he decides to not say anything, though, and instead moves in and takes Max's face in his hands, planting a kiss on his lips.

The kiss is slow and hot, that metal piercing in Max's bottom lip hard and familiar against Theo's mouth, and Theo closes his eyes, baffled at the sheer intensity of it all. He can feel Max actually hold his breath, and when they pull apart, those blue eyes look dazed and slightly out of it. Then Max blinks, and he nods jerkily.

"Okay, yeah, I believe you," he says, and Theo smiles, before they make their way inside the gym.

The entire hall is filled with blinking, colorful lights, occasional snowflake decorations, and there are so many people, dancing and talking and drinking what Theo is pretty sure is non-alcoholic drinks, and *hell*, there's even a disco ball. He takes it in for a moment, and looks at Max, who is standing right next to him. And Max has pretty much frozen, eyebrows raised, apprehensively looking around the huge room, and Theo squeezes his hand.

"You okay, there?" he asks, with a small smile, and Max doesn't immediately reply. Instead, he puffs up his cheeks, filling them with air, before exhaling in a huff. He cocks his head, making a face.

"Yeah, sure," he says dryly, eyes still scanning the crowded room. "Just... Not really my thing."

Theo smiles a bit wider, and leans in to kiss Max on the cheek.

"Come on," he says, and tugs Max along with him into the room.

They find Cassie and Emma again, and they talk a little, before they make their way over to the drinks' table, where they find that *yes*, the drinks are most definitely non-alcoholic.

"Well, that sucks," Cassie laments, and both Theo and Emma agree.

"Wait, hang on," Max says, slipping his hand into his pocket and taking out what Theo immediately recognizes as a hip flask, pewter colored and plain. He raises his eyebrows slightly, as

Cassie excitedly holds out her drink for Max to pour some liquor into, and Emma gets some, too. When Max turns to Theo, Theo holds out his drink, as well, albeit with the same facial expression. Max notices it, of course.

"What?" he says, shrugging. "I told you I'd be bringing booze."

Theo just smiles, and thanks to the added contribution of Max's self-provided drink (which Theo is pretty sure is nothing but pure vodka), the night quickly takes a more entertaining turn.

They don't do much dancing. Theo doesn't do any, actually, while Cassie and Emma both occasionally run off when the music changes, often while exclaiming *I love this song!,* or something along those lines. Meanwhile, Theo and Max mostly just hang out, choosing kissing, in favor of talking, and drinking from Max's flask. They mix it in with their drinks, at first, but eventually just decide to skip that step altogether, instead making them both squint at the burning sensation of the undiluted vodka going down, directly from the source.

It's fun, though. The night is actually more fun than Theo somehow expected, and Max is still in that weirdly good mood, which Theo isn't about to question anytime soon. Theo even spots Michael and Hannah, who are apparently there together (Theo interprets this as Michael *finally* getting the fact that Hannah has sort of been into him, from day one), and who are apparently surprised at seeing Theo there. They still say hi, though, both of them eyeing Max a bit apprehensively, and Max waves and smiles in such a blatantly mock-adorable way that it makes Theo laugh. Then again, it might all be due to both of them getting pretty drunk, at this point, and neither Michael nor Hannah seem to mind, anyway.

The night draws on, and Theo disappears to go to the bathroom for a few minutes. When he returns, he finds Max sitting at the edge of the dance floor, by a table, by himself. He doesn't look sad or lonely, though; Max is the kind of person who looks like he revels in being alone, in a way that basically dares anyone to come near him, and he looks confident and sure, more than anything. Theo envies that.

"Hey," Theo says, as he walks up to him, and Max gives him a smile. It makes Theo's heart leap, and he's not entirely sure if that's just because of the way he feels about Max, or due to the alcohol he's been drinking. Then again, it's probably a little of both.

"Hi there," Max says, and Theo looks over at the dance floor. He can see Cassie and Emma in the crowd, having the time of their lives, apparently, and when he sees the way Emma moves in closer, eyeing Cassie up and down like that, he can't help but think that Max was probably right about her intentions, before.

He turns back to his boyfriend.

"Come on," he says taking Max's hand and tugging on it a little. Max smiles.

"What?" he asks, and Theo swings his hips pointedly, in a way that would normally make him feel completely ridiculous. Max raises his eyebrows.

"Are you having a seizure?" he asks, amused, but Theo just squints at him, shaking his hips a bit more obviously, as if daring Max to make fun of him. Which he does, of course.

"Okay, what's that even supposed to be?" Max says, while Theo releases his hand and carelessly starts doing something that looks like a move from *Greased Lightning*, making Max groan and squint in something like amused discomfort.

"What?" Theo says, staying true to his moves, adding in some more hip-shakes, which are completely out of time with the music. "Am I embarrassing you?"

"Now, there's a challenge," Max says, still smiling. "You're just embarrassing *yourself*, really."

"Then dance with me," Theo says, not really dancing anymore, just mostly flailing around, and Max chuckles.

"God, you're a fun drunk," he says affectionately, and Theo looks at him pointedly.

"So are you," he says. "Which is why you should dance."

431

"I'm not dancing," Max says resolutely, and Theo narrows his eyes at him.

"Really?" he says, and as if to enforce his words, he turns around and does a little booty-shake. Max smiles wider, stifling a laugh.

"I'm not dancing," he says, shaking his head. "No way."

Theo raises his eyebrows at him pointedly, as he stops moving.

"You sure?" he says, and Max folds his arms.

"Very sure," he says, a small, fond smile on his face. "Completely sure."

Theo leans down and places one hand against the backrest of Max's chair, half-trapping him.

"Really?" he says, and Max chuckles drunkenly, nodding.

"Really," he confirms.

"Not one little dance?"

"Theo," Max says, blue eyes locked on Theo's green ones. "I am not dancing. You couldn't pay me to get up there."

Theo narrows his eyes, pressing his lips together.

"Why not?" he asks, and Max lets out a small sigh.

"Because I hate dancing," he says. "And you know that."

"Yeah, but we're *at* an actual dance," Theo points out, and Max leans forward a little, bringing their faces closer together, and moving up his hand to cradle Theo's face.

"Babe, I love you," he says, "but I don't dance. I'm sorry, that's just how it is."

Theo sighs, a little disappointed, but it's really not all that bad. He's not a big fan of dancing, either; it's mostly the mood of the place, the general atmosphere, that gives him the idea, and it's not like he's good at it, anyway. And if nothing else, he's pretty sure Max knows that it really doesn't mean all that much to him, so it's all good.

"Fine," he says, relenting. "But you're gonna have to make it up to me later."

Max glances away with narrowed eyes, humming in thought.

"Actually," he says, looking back at Theo with a wicked smile. "I think I've got just the thing."

Theo frowns at him, confused, but Max saves him the trouble of asking what it is, by covering his lips with his own. And for a moment, Theo just savors it, leans into the kiss and closes his eyes. Then he pulls away a little.

"You're talking about something other than a kiss, I'm hoping," he says. "'Cause that's not gonna cut it."

Max chuckles against his mouth.

"I've got something a little better in mind," he says, pressing their lips together in a brief touch. "Promise."

Theo jerks back.

"Really?" he says, honestly a bit surprised, and Max cock a pierced eyebrow at him.

"What?" he says. "You think I can't pull it off? Please, give me some credit."

"No, I just—" Theo narrows his eyes at him, almost suspiciously. "I'm curious."

Max lets out a small sigh.

"Later," he says, getting up from his seat and taking Theo's hand, pulling him along with him, as he leaves the table. "Until then, please accompany me over to this dark, secluded corner."

Theo eyes his boyfriend in mock suspicion, as he lets himself be dragged along.

"I don't know," he says apprehensively, glancing over at the crowded dance floor. "Why would I do that?"

"Because," Max says, pulling Theo closer and pointedly trailing his touch down over his ass, slipping it his hand into his back pocket. "I may not be big on dancing, but I've got other talents."

As if to point this out, he leans in and plants a slow, searing kiss against Theo's throat, smoothing it over with his tongue, and Theo feels thousands of goosebumps prickle all over his skin.

"Oh, that," he murmurs, closing his eyes briefly, his hand tightening its grip on Max's. "Why didn't you say so?"

433

Max hums against his throat, and Theo hears a smile in his voice when he speaks.

"Let's just go over there, and you can grope me in the dark," he says. "Like a proper teenager."

And Theo doesn't need telling twice. It doesn't take any more persuasion from Max, before Theo has followed him to the far corner of the huge room, and pressed him up against the wall. He's vaguely aware of how he never would have done anything like this, a few months ago; it's amazing, really, how little he has come to care about what other people might think. And he can't help but think of just how many times he has had this thought, since he and Max started seeing each other. He's still not quite over how insecure he used to be.

They keep at it for what feels like ages, occasionally pausing to take a drink from Max's hip flask, before resuming their activities, their hands all over each other, lips practically glued together, as well as trailing over any skin they can reach. After a little while, Theo starts to feel the endorphins mingle together properly with the effects of the alcohol, his head pleasantly fuzzy and his motor skills just slightly less precise. It feels pretty amazing, and the way Max moans against his mouth and grinds against him isn't exactly helping; Theo can feel that he's hard, even through those tight jeans, and he's completely sure that Max can feel him having the exact same reaction.

Theo barely even notices what's going on around them. He's only vaguely aware of the loud music, the raised voices of people talking, and the colorful, flashing lights. He's in his own little bubble—*their* bubble, his and Max's—and nothing seems to be able to break through.

Which is why he's more than a little surprised, when he feels someone tap him on the shoulder.

Theo starts, and pulls away from Max's lips to look and see who dares interrupt him, right now. And he's met with a very awkward expression, gracing Cassie's face.

"Sorry," she says, looking uncomfortable, and a little scared that she might actually get punched in the face. "I didn't want to interrupt you guys. I *really* didn't."

She adds that last part with great exaggeration, and she looks a little grossed-out for a moment.

"I mean, you're basically a zipper-tug away from having sex, so I just—" She interrupts herself, shakes her head and squeezes her eyes shut, as if to get the image out of her head. "No. Sorry."

She clears her throat, and looks back up at Theo, who's still basically pinning Max against the wall, his hands frozen in the middle of grabbing his ass and pushing in underneath that button-up shirt. *That totally hot button-up shirt*, Theo thinks. *And that tie. And that pin-striped waistcoat that's just begging to be—*

"What do you want?" he says, blinking and trying to refocus. Cassie isn't exactly *blurry*, at least not *yet*, but he still feels a little out of it. And besides, all he can think about right now is how Max's hands feel on him, one digging its fingers into his hair and the other pausing on its way down to his crotch.

"I just wanted to let you know that I'm leaving," Cassie says, a bit hurriedly. "With Emma."

She gestures over her shoulder, and Theo spots Emma standing a few feet away, apparently waiting on her date. Then he looks back at Cassie.

"What happened to 'just friends'?" he asks, remembering what Max predicted earlier, and Cassie gets a sheepish look.

"Well," she says, shrugging innocently, "that's apparently a bit harder to maintain, than we thought, so..."

She cocks her eyebrows pointedly, and Theo quirks a small, affectionate smile.

"Alright," he says, freeing one hand to nudge her, shooing her away. "Go on, get to it."

"You sure?" she says, sounding half-serious and half-joking, while she looks over at Max, who gives her the flirtiest, drunk smirk Theo has ever seen.

"Hey," Theo says pointedly, snapping his fingers in front of Max's face. His boyfriend just looks at him though, eyebrows raised as he turns that flirty smirk on him, instead.

"What?" he says. "I'm just being supportive."

Theo just shakes his head. He's not exactly jealous, and he has no reason to be, so it's not that. But somehow, he just doesn't want his or Max's attention directed anywhere else for longer than three seconds, right now, lest they stop what they're doing, and he's deprived of those amazing lips and those wonderful hands and that hot body and—

"Yeah, you should go," Theo says, turning to Cassie, who looks a little bit traumatized at the intensity of the way her friends are apparently looking at each other.

"I really should," she says, backing off. "You two, have fun."

"Yeah, you too," Theo replies, but his words are slightly muffled, cut off as Max pulls his face closer and kisses him, out of nowhere. And Theo closes his eyes, letting out the smallest moan.

"Behave," Cassie calls, from what sounds like a few feet away, and Theo just makes a vague, waving motion with his hand, not tearing himself away from Max for one moment. "Make good choices!"

And with that, Cassie is gone. At least, as far as Theo can tell, since his entire world has once again narrowed down to one thing; *Max.*

"Told you," Max murmurs smugly after a little while, between kisses, hands back to trailing all over Theo's body. "And you know, maybe we should follow their example."

Theo hums against his mouth.

"And go where?" he asks, not even opening his eyes. *God,* his heart is beating so fast, his blood pumping.

"That's kinda where my idea comes in," Max replies, and Theo half-pauses.

"What do you mean?"

Max makes a small, apprehensive noise.

"I may have arranged for us to have somewhere to go," he says, almost reluctantly, and Theo pulls away.

"Wait, what?" he asks, and Max looks sheepish, drunk, and very aroused, all at once. He chews his bottom lip for a moment, before reaching into his pocket and pulling out what Theo quickly identifies as a keycard. And it takes another second, before his alcohol-addled brain puts the pieces together.

"Is that what I think it is?" he asks, half-pointing at the card, and Max cocks his head. Theo blinks. "You seriously got us a room?"

Max rolls his eyes, clearly a little uncomfortable.

"I may have," he admits, avoiding Theo's eyes. "You know, out of practicality, or whatever..."

Theo is a little stunned for a moment, and then he smiles.

"Oh my god," he says, a little teasingly, a little drunk. "You got us a room."

Max groans as Theo gives him a kiss.

"So what, if I did?" he says, discomfort blending with awkward annoyance, which is all very uncommon for him. "What about it?"

"I never would have pegged you for such a romantic," Theo teases with a smile, kissing him again, and Max lets out another groan.

"Not exactly romantic," he points out. "Also, mention it again, and die."

"I'm willing to take that risk." Theo kisses him again, moving one hand up to cup his face. "And I'm *very* willing to take you up on your offer. Even if you did refuse to dance with me."

This time, the sound coming out of Max's mouth sounds more like a moan, and Theo can feel him smile.

"Good," he says. "And I promised I'd make up for that, didn't I?"

CHAPTER 30
BURN

It's only a matter of minutes, before Theo and Max have gotten their coats and left the school. They notice how Cassie's car is still parked outside, which Theo appreciates; no one should drink and drive, and he's glad Cassie is sensible enough to get that.

Max has a cigarette, while they walk, and it doesn't take long before Theo realizes where they're going. By the time they reach the motel where Max has booked a room, he recognizes it as the motel they stayed at that night, so long ago, back when everything was messy and difficult, and Theo's family wouldn't even accept Max.

Back when Max and I had sex for the first time. Just the thought of that makes Theo shiver, in a way that has nothing to do with the cold winter night.

It's pretty obvious that there's a school dance tonight, at least judging from the much larger number of cars that fill up the motel parking lot, than last time Max and Theo were here. And when they get inside, the guy behind the front desk—thankfully, a different guy than last time—doesn't even look surprised, just looks bored, more than anything, and Theo and Max just slip past him, already armed with a keycard.

They make their way along the first floor hallway, and it's only when they reach their room that Theo realizes something.

"Wait," he says. "Is this the same room as last time?"

Max hums and looks away pointedly.

"Maybe," he says, slowly swiping the keycard and opening the door, and Theo looks at him.

"Alright," he says, "you can't honestly tell me that *that's* not romantic."

Max doesn't answer him, though, and is spared the trouble, when they hear the obnoxiously loud sounds of kissing. They look over their shoulders, and sure enough, a girl and a guy are making their way down the hall, grabbing and practically slobbering all over each other, and judging from their age and outfits, Theo is entirely sure that they've just come from the Winter Dance. They don't even seem to notice Theo and Max, though, and instead just keep grabbing and kissing and moaning, as they open the door to the room right next to Max's and Theo's, step inside, and shut the door behind them.

Theo looks at Max, who nods slowly.

"Tasteful," he says, before he and Theo make their way inside their room, closing the door and effectively shutting out the world.

Theo looks around the room, and feels a small smile on his face, as he takes off his jacket. The room looks exactly the same as last time, which he supposes it totally normal for a motel, but still. It makes him feel all warm and happy inside, as he thinks about that night, about everything that happened. Everything from the fast food to the impromptu *Star Wars* commentary, to the amazing sex that followed. Not to mention the shower they had, the next morning.

"Do you approve?" Max asks after a little while, and Theo turns to him. His trenchcoat is off, and tossed over the armrest of a chair, along with Theo's jacket.

"I very much approve," Theo says, before smiling a little. "And again, you can't tell me this isn't romantic. I mean, really, there's just no other way of looking at it."

Max groans.

"Don't remind me," he says. "And I have my moments, you know. Just don't tell anyone."

"Don't tell anyone that you're a big softie?" Theo says. "That you like cuddling and spooning, and that you booked the same room where you took my virginity, for tonight?"

He says it a bit teasingly, amusedly, but Max just groans again, as though embarrassed.

"Alright, we get it," he says. "Now, do you wanna fuck, or not?"

Theo raises his eyebrows at him.

"Excuse me?" he asks, and Max shifts a little, clearly a bit awkward, despite the alcohol they're both still feeling the effects of.

"You heard me," he says, his confidence slipping just the tiniest bit, while Theo starts making his way over to him.

"I did," Theo says, now narrowing his eyes. "It almost sounded as though you're expecting to get laid."

"Well, yeah," Max says, Theo moving in closer. "I went through a lot of trouble for this, you know."

"Uh-huh." Theo eyes Max up and down, only stopping dead when he's standing right in front of him.

"I mean, I even got the same room," Max continues, trying to catch Theo's eye, but Theo is busy trailing his gaze down along Max's throat, his chest, down over that red tie and that gorgeous, pin-striped waistcoat. "Which, you know, was romantic, like five seconds ago."

Theo just hums in reply, and Max frowns a little.

"What?" he asks, and Theo tilts his head a bit, eyeing Max's chest.

"I'm thinking," he says.

"About?"

Theo licks his lips.

"About whether or not I should take this off," he says, tugging lightly at Max's waistcoat.

"How so?" Max asks.

"Well," Theo explains. "On one hand, it's extremely hot, and I'm not sure I ever want you to take it off, again."

He exhales slowly.

"But on the other hand," he says. "Getting you naked is pretty much the best thing in the world. And yet, neither of these choices is required to actually have sex."

He's a little surprised at his choice of words, but he's pretty certain it's thanks to the alcohol that he chooses them, at all, and it feels good to say it, especially when he notices the way Max tenses up a bit.

"Well," he says, that rough voice a bit lower. "That's quite the conundrum, you got there."

Theo hums in agreement, slowly starting to unbutton the pin-striped waistcoat.

"But I'm thinking that taking it off might be best," he murmurs, looking up at Max, whose eyes are suddenly alight with excitement. He still looks at Theo softly, though, hungrily, as though he wants to eat him alive, but also wants to slowly savor every bite, and Theo can feel his pulse speed up just at the thought of that.

"Probably," Max murmurs in agreement, and for a few seconds, they just stand there, looking at each other, and Theo's fingers have managed to undo all those buttons, by the time either of them does anything.

It's Max who does it, leaning in and kissing Theo on the mouth, and just the sheer intensity of it has Theo fall apart, within moments. Before he knows it, Max's hands are everywhere, and his tie is being pulled off, along with his blazer,

441

and his hair is being tugged at and messed up, while he shimmies that waistcoat off of Max and reciprocates the kiss with rather extreme eagerness. It doesn't take long before the rest comes off, too, Max muttering about how there are *too many fucking buttons*, and Theo can't help but agree, as he undoes Max's tie and tosses it to the side. There are *so many buttons*, but it's *so worth it*, when Theo *finally* gets to that tattooed skin, underneath, and he's kissing and touching, and Max's hands and mouth are everywhere, and everything is just a haze of hormones and alcohol.

By the time they finally make it over to the bed, Theo is undoing the fly of Max's jeans, and Max moans weakly against his mouth.

"How do you wanna..." he asks, trailing off, but Theo already knows what he wants.

"I want you to do it," he practically breathes against Max's lips. "Like the first time."

And Max inhales deeply, a bit shakily, and he nods.

Eventually, *finally*, their pants come off, and they're in the bed, underneath the covers, and Theo's skin is on fire, his hands trailing everywhere, as though he simply can't get enough of Max and the way he feels, the way he smells, the way he tastes. Like he simply can't get enough of *this*, and he kisses Max, roughly, pulling him even closer, as if that were possible. They're both so hard, already, and Theo moans, as Max moves his hand down to wrap his fingers around him.

"Have I ever told you how much I love this?" Max murmurs against Theo's mouth, as he practically lies on top of him. "Having you, like this?"

"You might have mentioned it," Theo replies, pulling Max closer and attempting to silence him with a kiss.

"I do, you know." Max manages to pull away enough to speak, pressing short, sweet kisses against Theo's mouth. "I love it. I love *you*."

Theo groans, digging his fingers into Max's hair, as Max starts stroking him.

"I love you so much." Max's words are a murmur, and Theo is slightly stunned at how incredibly sincere they sound, that pierced bottom lip pressing against his mouth. "So much."

Theo lets out a moan, as Max moves down to kiss his throat, smoothing over the skin with his tongue.

"Theo." The way he says the name is enough to make Theo squeeze his eyes shut, clinging to him. Max says it softly, reverently, and Theo exhales sharply.

"I love you, Max." His words are little more than a breathless moan, and he grabs Max's hair to pull his mouth back up to his own, kissing him fiercely. "I love you, I love you."

Theo feels like he could keep saying it forever, but he doesn't. He says it with his lips, instead, with his hands and his tongue, and the way Max eagerly reciprocates leaves no doubt in his mind about just how mutual those feelings are.

Theo realizes that this is just foreplay, that they're only building up to the really good stuff, but *god* it feels so good. He moves his hand down and starts stroking Max, who moans in pleased surprise, and it's only a matter of seconds, before they're practically panting into each other's mouths, gradually losing their minds and grinding against the pressure and the touch of eager fingers.

"We should really slow down," Max breathes, seemingly reluctantly moving his hand away from Theo's crotch. "I'm not gonna last."

"Then, hurry up," Theo practically pants in response, still touching, stroking, making Max groan against his neck.

"Wouldn't that be counter-productive?" Max says, sounding strained, and Theo plants hungry kisses against his jaw, his throat.

"Just do it, Max," he says, with a desperate edge to his voice. "Just do it. I want you."

Theo can't believe the words coming out of his mouth; it seems that any sense of modesty just completely goes out the window, when he's in a situation like this, and Max sure as hell doesn't seem to mind.

443

"God, you're so fucking hot, right now." The words are no more than a heavy breath, forced out through Max's half-parted lips, and he groans, as he kisses Theo, pushing that wonderful, pierced tongue into his mouth. He makes sure to gently take Theo's wrist, though, moving Theo's hand away from his crotch, and Theo makes a soft whining noise of disappointment.

"Babe, I'm not kidding," Max says, kissing him. "I'm not gonna last. We need to slow down."

Theo knows he has a point, knows how right he is. But *damn*, he just really wants this, *needs* it. He needs it, just like simply *needs* everything about Max.

He nods jerkily, though, and Max pulls back to meet his gaze.

"At least I came prepared, this time," Max says, smirking at him, and to prove his words, he awkwardly gets out of bed and makes his way over to his coat.

"I did too, you know," Theo says, already sounding exhausted, and Max looks over at him.

"Really?" he says, and Theo nods.

"Yeah," he confirms, thinking of how he actually slipped a condom and a small packet of lube into his jacket pocket, before he left home. "Didn't want to risk it, again. Figured I might as well."

Max gives him a wicked, weirdly affectionate smirk, as he makes his way back to the bed, and Theo just watches him as he moves, watches that gorgeous body and that beautifully tattooed skin. He half-sits up as Max puts a small packet of lube down on the nightstand, along with a condom, and he takes his hand.

"Now, you need to get back down here," Theo says, pulling Max into a kiss, as he leans down. "Right now."

And Max is happy to oblige.

It's amazing how everything seems to move at hyper speed, but in slow motion, at the same time. Theo can still feel the effects of the alcohol, and it's just the right amount; enough to make him tipsy and light-headed and all fuzzy and warm and reckless, but not enough to make him unfocused and actually

444

keep him from getting hard. That would have been a let-down, if anything.

Before long, Max is touching him again, but this time, those slicked-up fingers are sliding in and out of him, rubbing and loosening up, and Theo is moaning loudly, shamelessly, clinging to that amazing body and kissing and biting the skin with his teeth. He feels so impatient, so eager, like all of this is just preparations that, annoyingly, need to be dealt with, and Max is making all kinds of happy sounds, already panting and moaning and seemingly losing his mind. Before long, he leans down, just by Theo's ear.

"Babe, you ready?" he breathes, the impatience clear in his voice, and Theo nods eagerly, eyes closed.

"Yes," he pants. "God, yes."

That's all Max needs to hear.

It's only a matter of seconds, it seems, before Max has gotten a condom and put it on, and by the time he starts pushing into Theo, Theo is a panting, moaning mess. It feels amazing, but it's so *slow*, and it's driving him crazy, his entire body on edge.

"Come on, babe," he breathes, pointedly moving his hands down to Max's ass, as if to push him in further, faster, and Max groans at the unexpected pressure.

"Oh god," he bites out, allowing Theo's hands to persuade him, before he slows down again. And Theo lets out a noise of impatience.

"Just *move*," he says, in a way he would normally be a little embarrassed about, sounding equal parts desperate and completely intoxicated by the whole thing.

For a moment, Max looks like he's about to say something. He doesn't, though. Perhaps he hears the sheer pleading in Theo's wrecked voice, or perhaps he just wants this just as much as Theo does, but either way, he takes Theo completely by surprise, when he pushes in all the way, in one, deep thrust.

And Theo makes the most undignified sound, a strangled moan that matches the way he suddenly clings to Max, pulling him closer, deeper, groaning against his neck. And he's sure that

Max is about to ask if he's okay, so he stops him, pressing their lips together in a searing kiss. And Max doesn't ask. He doesn't ask, because Theo is so beyond okay, and Max just feels *so good*, and when he starts thrusting slowly, Theo honestly wonders how the hell he manages to survive whenever they do anything like this, together. Because it's like dying, like slowly dying from a complete, extraordinary excess of amazing emotion and sensation, and this time is no different.

Max was right, though; they should have slowed down a bit. Rather than going on for a long time, slowly and then faster, the pace picks up pretty quickly, and Theo feels that familiar heat coil in his stomach, the sensation building and building, until he can't make any sound but incoherent moans and pants and happy noises. Max matches them, moving into him with deliberate, deep thrusts, and before long, they're both falling over the edge, out of nowhere, Theo suddenly coming hard and fast, even without Max touching him; just feeling him inside seems to be enough. And Theo clings to it, savors it, revels in it, as they ride it out together. It's just all kinds of amazing, and Theo closes his eyes as Max kisses him, deeply and desperately, pressing their bodies together, skin hot and slick with sweat.

It feels like ages later, that they actually stop, and by then, Theo just feels like a soft and thoroughly satisfied mess, like they could just as well stay like this, forever, suspended in time.

They don't, though. Instead, they eventually pull apart, and after cleaning up a bit, they return to bed and curl up together under the covers, still somewhat sweaty and exhausted. Theo pulls Max to him, Max placing his head against his chest.

"Theo," Max murmurs, as Theo moves his hand up to stroke his slightly damp hair. He hums in acknowledgment, and Max swallows dryly. "You're the most amazing person I've ever met."

Theo looks down at him.

"Ditto," he says, and kisses the top of his head. "We should get you tipsy more often, you say such lovely things."

Max smacks his hand against Theo's chest lazily, and Theo chuckles. Then they just stay like that for a few seconds, before Theo notices something that he didn't notice, earlier.

There's a distinct banging sound, coming from the wall behind the headboard of the bed, and they turn to each other, frowning. Max then glances at the wall, before he seems to get it.

"Oh, you gotta be kidding me," he says, as it's pretty obvious what's causing the noise. The banging is rhythmic, but fast, and along with the sound of a girl moaning loudly, there's not much room for interpretation.

"Are they—" Theo says, glancing at the wall. "Have they been going at it, this whole time?"

"Think so," Max says. "Not that that's a good thing, at this point. He doesn't really sound like he knows what he's doing."

Theo frowns at Max.

"Well, he's going way too fast, for one," Max says, gesturing vaguely at the wall, putting on a mock know-it-all expression, almost like he's narrating a documentary. "He's been going on like that since they started, so she's probably pretty numb, by now. And if nothing else, she's faking it."

"How can you tell?"

"Because lady parts need more than just the in-and-out," he says dryly, sounding a bit bored concerning the subject. "And also, last time I heard moans like that, I was watching porn, which is saying a lot."

Theo just looks at him, narrowing his eyes in a mix of half-joking doubt and amused suspicion. Max just shrugs.

"What?" he says. "It's not my favorite kind of porn, but it'll do. And besides, female anatomy isn't *that* hard to figure out."

"Says the gay guy," Theo points out, and Max rolls his eyes, a bit self-consciously, before regaining his expression of slight boredom.

"Exactly," he says. "I'm objective. And I've actually tried it, remember? Back before I knew I was a gay guy. Not exactly my cup of tea, but if I learned anything, it's that sex with a dude is just *way* easier. And way more fun."

Theo can't help but laugh, glad to feel that hearing Max say that doesn't actually make him jealous, anymore. Sure, it's not that he really *wants* to hear it, but it doesn't bother him like it used to. He's not sure why. Maybe it's simply because he has just completely accepted Max for who and what he is, promiscuous past and all. And Max's assurance that Theo is the only one he's been with that actually matters, probably helps a lot, too.

The pounding in the wall continues, along with the girl's moans, which Theo can now hear sound pretty exaggerated and monotone, like they're mostly there to egg the guy on, and the guy's grunts and moans sound more like he's lifting weights, than having sex.

Max groans loudly in frustration, rolling his eyes.

"Oh, for the love of—" he mutters, before actually turning to the wall and banging on it with his fist.

"Come on, guys!" he yells. "Give it up, you're trying too hard!"

Theo's eyes widen in surprise, but the couple in the other room definitely heard Max's reprimand, because they've suddenly stopped moving, and Theo swears he can hear the girl make what sounds like a noise of agreement. The guy replies something, which the girl apparently refutes, because then the guy groans in frustrated disappointment, and judging from the distinct sound of the bed creaking, he rolls off of her. And Theo can't help but laugh out loud, turning to his boyfriend.

"Well, what do you know?" he says, and Max chuckles, leaning back against Theo's chest, humming in satisfaction.

"Yeah," he says, snaking his arm around Theo's torso to hold him closer, and for a few seconds, they both just enjoy the newfound silence.

Theo trails his fingers along Max's tattoos, looking down at him, as Max closes his eyes, and suddenly, he's just hit with a surprising pang of sadness.

"I'm really gonna miss you," he says, and Max hums in agreement, before he seems to think of something, and all of a sudden, he tenses up.

"Oh, shit," he says, sounding surprised, more than anything. "I totally forgot. Fuck, I'm such an idiot."

Theo frowns, mildly alarmed.

"What?" he says, and Max props himself up on his elbow, to look at Theo properly.

"There has been a slight change of plan," he says, and when Theo just stares at him, a bit apprehensively, he explains. "Turns out... I'm not actually leaving."

Theo just blinks, trying to process what Max just said.

"Wait, what?" he finally blurts, and Max nods, almost excitingly.

"Yeah," he says. "I'm staying. Awesome, right?"

Theo just blinks again, thoroughly confused, his mind kind of reeling.

"But what about your dad?" he asks, his tone conveying his confusion. "What about his job—?"

"Oh, he's still going," Max explains. "And my mom. But not me."

And Theo stares at him, completely dumbstruck, for what feels like several seconds.

"What?" he finally says, frowning, with a quick shake of his head. "Rewind, here. What the hell changed? Not that I mind, but you know... What happened?"

Max sighs, as though gearing up, like he momentarily forgot that this is all news to Theo.

"Well, I found a place to stay," he finally says. "With Gavin."

Theo's eyebrows go up.

"Really?" he says, and Max nods.

"Yeah," he says. "He heard about the move, and got all pissed about mom and dad not asking him about it. He came over and asked what the hell they were thinking, seeing as how I'm graduating soon, and that him standing for that was 'not bloody likely'. That's a direct quote, by the way."

Theo just stares, stunned joy blending in with the confusion.

"So, what, you're staying with him, then?" he asks, and Max hums in confirmation.

"Looks like it," he says. "Him and his wife. They've got a spare room, anyway, so he said I could move in, whenever. And he's practically family, so..."

He sighs, a bit tiredly.

"And honestly," he says, "the thought had occurred to me. I just didn't wanna ask him, felt like that would be asking a bit too much. Guess I'm lucky that he apparently didn't think so."

Theo remembers Max mentioning how he didn't want to impose on anyone, back when Theo suggested that he might come stay with Theo's family. He must have thought of Gavin, even then, but been too afraid to ask him.

Still though, it takes several seconds for this news to sink in, for Theo to actually allow himself to be happy about it. He has been accepting a much sadder version of the situation for the past few weeks, after all, so it's a bit difficult. But Max waits patiently, and when the news eventually does sink in, Theo smiles, and he pulls Max's face to his own to kiss him, eagerly.

"Wait," he says then, after a moment, pulling away. "Why didn't you tell me, sooner?"

Max looks a bit sheepish.

"Well," he explains. "I just found out, yesterday. And I kinda wanted it to be a surprise."

Theo frowns.

"Is that why you've been in such a good mood, all night?" he asks, thinking of how Max has been unusually smile-y and happy, despite the less than ideal conditions of a high school dance, and Max nods, with a slightly sly expression. He quirks a smile.

"And also, without the excuse of me moving away, I might have had to actually admit that I kinda wanted to go to the dance."

Theo raises his eyebrows, amused.

"Oh, you wanted to, did you?" he asks, and Max groans, kissing him.

"Maybe," he murmurs against his lips. "But only 'cause it's you."

Theo laughs.

"I can live with that."

The mood feels considerably lighter, after that. Not that it was anything else before, but now, Theo feels completely elated, and for the better part of half-an-hour, he and Max just lie there, curled up together, and Theo just feels so happy.

Max is staying. Theo doesn't even care about the fact that rationally speaking, they could still have reunited after graduation, even if Max did move away. Because he can't be rational, not when it comes to Max. He just can't, and he can't imagine being without him, whether it's for days or weeks or months. He's just so incredibly relieved that that won't be happening, because he honestly feels like he wouldn't have known what to do with himself.

And he suddenly feels an intense surge of gratitude toward Max's surrogate uncle, who swooped in to save the day. *Very deus ex machina,* Theo thinks to himself, and vaguely wonders what would have happened, if Gavin hadn't come along, seeing as how Max seemed to have decided against actually asking him for this huge, personal favor.

A few more minutes of silence pass, until it's suddenly once again broken by the couple in the other room. Theo can clearly hear the guy say something along the lines of *you wanna go again?* And Max groans, apparently not yet asleep, resting against Theo's chest.

"No, she doesn't!" he yells. "Go to sleep, it's embarrassing!"

The couple doesn't go again, as though actually heeding Max's obnoxious advice, and Theo laughs.

"God, you're an asshole," he says affectionately, and Max hums in approval, cuddling closer again and pressing a kiss against Theo's skin.

"I know," he says. "You still love me?"

"Of course, I do."

"Good," Max says. "Then that's all that matters."

CHAPTER 31
PHOTO

Theo wakes up to the light touch of fingertips again his back.

It tickles a little, but it still feels nice, and it still makes him sigh contentedly, as he lies on his stomach, hugging the pillow. He doesn't open his eyes. Instead, he keeps them closed, so as to fully appreciate the way that touch feels, and when he hums a little, he can practically sense Max reacting, noticing that he's awake.

Max's fingertips trail down along his back, before the warm palm of his hand starts smoothing over Theo's skin, and Theo sighs again, as he then feels the distinct touch of lips against the back of his neck. It's soft and warm, with only hint of that hard metal piercing, and Theo grips the pillow just a little bit tighter, as he feels those kisses move downward, slowly, trailing down along his spine.

"What are you doing?" he murmurs, his voice cracked and slightly slurred, with sleep, and Max doesn't seem surprised to hear it.

"Worshipping," Max says. The one word is tender and soft, completely sincere, and Theo smiles, keeping his eyes closed, as Max continues to move down along his back, pressing his lips against Theo's skin in one kiss after another, until he reaches the middle.

"I was kinda watching you sleep," he murmurs, slowly kissing even further down along Theo's spine. "Although, that probably just sounds creepy."

Theo smiles, opening his eyes and seeing the blurry outlines of white sheets, illuminated by sunlight.

"Not creepy," he says, and just as Max reaches the base of his spine, Theo makes a move to turn over, rolling over to lie on his back, and he looks up at his boyfriend. Max is lying on his side, propped up with his elbow against the pillows, his face leaning into the palm of his hand.

"Great," Max says. "Then I don't have to be ashamed of all those pictures I took from the tree, outside your window."

Theo frowns.

"I don't have a tree outside my window," he says, and Max frowns even deeper, in thought.

"Well, fuck," he says. "Then who was I taking pictures of?"

Theo narrows his eyes at him.

"If you don't remember," he says, "he can't have been that impressive."

Max cocks his head.

"True," he says, before falling silent and letting out a small breath. He just looks at Theo for a moment then, his eyes softening, like they tend to do, where Theo is concerned. And just like always, Theo can feel that familiar flutter in his stomach, the one that makes him want to pinch himself, like this entire feeling and situation is just too good to be real.

Max squints a little, like he just had a thought, and Theo frowns, as Max turns around and leans toward the small bedside table to get something.

"What are you doing?" Theo asks, but Max ignores him, falling back onto the bed, his phone now in his hands. He activates the screen and navigates through a couple of apps, before propping himself up on his elbow again, phone in his hand. And before Theo knows it, he has snapped a picture, by the sound of it, and Theo blinks.

"What?" he says dumbly, and Max looks at the phone, examining the picture he just took.

"You look kinda perfect, right now," he says. "I wanted to save it."

Theo frowns, but still feels his heart do a little backflip at those words.

"I just woke up," he says, and Max hums in agreement.

"Exactly," he says, and a second later, he has taken another picture, catching Theo unawares.

"Hey," Theo protests weakly, gesturing at the phone in Max's hand, as though it's a fly he's trying to swat away. "I just woke up."

"And that's the best part," Max says, taking another picture, before expertly yanking the phone out of Theo's reach. "You look all sleepy and adorable. I need these pictures."

"No, you don't," Theo says doubtfully, once again attempting to take the phone, but Max rolls over onto his back, keeping it in his hands and going through the photos.

"Yes, I do," he says, eyes on the screen. "I need them for science."

Theo narrows his eyes at him, before striking fast, and managing to snatch the phone from his hands. Max turns to him indignantly.

"Hey," he says, trying to get the phone back, but Theo uses one hand to push him away, while he gets up into sitting position.

"No," he says, accessing the phone's camera, while managing to swat away Max's hands. "It's for science."

Max reaches for it again, but Theo evades his attempts, and ends up sitting on top of him, straddling his hips.

"Give it back," Max says, but Theo ignores him, using his new vantage point to snap a picture of a rather sleepy and annoyed-looking Max, lying underneath him. And Max groans, reaching for the phone, but Theo holds up his hand, keeping it out of range.

"For science," he repeats, but Max tries again, and Theo looks at him pointedly. "*Science,* Max!"

Max seems to give up, then, and he lets his hands flop down onto the mattress, on either side of him. And Theo slowly lowers the phone, snapping another picture, one which makes Max look like he hates everything.

"Aw, look at that," Theo says affectionately, turning the screen toward Max, so that he can see the picture. "It's your murder-look."

Max narrows his eyes at him, the black eyeliner from last night still there, albeit just slightly smudged.

"You really shouldn't be so happy to be on the receiving end of that," he points out, but Theo ignores him, taking another picture. This time, Max looks more relaxed, and by the next picture, he looks downright content. It makes Theo smile a little.

"Alright," Max says, reaching for the phone again, which Theo once again holds out of reach, over his head. This time, though, Max actually sits up, wrapping one tattooed arm around Theo's waist, while using the other to reach for his phone. He groans pathetically.

"You're being mean," he says in mock hurt, and Theo smirks a little.

"And you're whining," he says, raising his eyebrows. "You know who whines? Babies."

Max frowns at him.

"Wow," he says dryly. "Great comeback."

"I have my moments," Theo says, looking back up at the phone he's holding above his head, scrolling through the pictures he just took. Then Max uses his free hand to cup his face, though, and he pulls it down toward his own, pressing their lips together in a kiss. And almost immediately, Theo closes his eyes and kisses him back, relaxing into it, melting against that warm body, while Max moves both hands down to his back. His touch is slow and urgent and tender at the same time, against Theo's skin, and Theo tilts his head to kiss him deeper, letting out a soft, contented moan.

Then he can't help himself; he lowers the phone, moves it to the side, and snaps a picture. And Max slowly pulls away, just enough to look up at him.

"Did you just selfie us?" he says dryly, but Theo is unfazed, smiling teasingly as he brings up the picture and looks at it.

"Couldn't resist," he says, and as he looks at the photo he just took, he feels a little warm inside. It was mostly meant to be sort of a joke, but... The photo is actually really good. Max's eyes are closed, and his entire expression just looks completely blissful and soft, mirroring Theo's, as they kiss, as though kissing each other is the best, most perfect thing in the world. It makes Theo smile a little.

They look happy. Completely and utterly happy.

"Can you send me this?" Theo says, his voice just above a murmur, and Max frowns a little.

"Sure," he says, before gently taking the phone from Theo's hands and looking at it. And Theo watches his expression soften, as those blue eyes watch the photo, taking it in.

"Oh yeah," Max says, falling down onto his back, phone in his hands. "That's my new background."

Theo frowns in disbelief.

"Really?" he asks, honestly a little surprised, since Max generally isn't the type to engage in such sappy, relationship-y activities.

"Yeah," Max says fiddling with the settings on his phone, apparently implementing his plan. "Curse you."

Theo smiles a little then, and leans down to rest his elbows on either side of Max's head, as his boyfriend tosses his phone aside. Theo absently lets his fingers run through Max's black, messy bedhead, while those dark blue eyes just look at him, Max's hands moving up to settle against the small of Theo's back. He sighs.

"You've ruined me," Max says, but Theo just kisses him, softly.

"You're fine," he murmurs against his mouth, Max's hands smoothing over the bare skin of his back. "And I'm really glad you're staying, by the way."

Max hums against his lips, clearly remembering the conversation they had last night, about Max not moving away, about him actually remaining here, with Theo.

"Me, too," he agrees. "Just having a little trouble relaxing about it, just yet."

Theo pulls back a little.

"Good stuff happens, you know," he says, tilting his head, and Max raises his eyebrows doubtfully.

"You're saying, have faith?" he asks, and Theo nods.

"Yeah," he confirms. "Faith. And if nothing else, if this does blow up in our faces, we can at least enjoy it, until it does."

Max seems to consider that, before he seems to accept it, and he nods, pulling Theo closer again, to kiss him on the mouth.

"I can roll with that."

Their stay at the motel isn't very long, this time around. After lazily lying around for a bit, and taking a long, hot shower together (hot due to other reasons, as well as the actual temperature), Max and Theo start making their way home. They luckily don't spot the couple from the other room, on their way out, and after handing in the keycard at the front desk, they leave the motel.

They part ways eventually, Max heading home to his house, while Theo goes in the other direction, although it takes quite a while before they actually manage to pull away from each other. As Theo reaches the front door of his house, he misses Max, already.

Neither Theo's mother, nor Riley, seem the least bit surprised at seeing him come home like this, in the middle of the day. He didn't even text them last night, to let them know he was staying out, but they seem to have counted on that he wasn't coming home, then, anyway. At least, judging from the way Riley looks at him pointedly, as Theo makes his way into the kitchen; he looks brotherly teasing, and a little grossed-out, all at once.

"Finally home, huh?" Amy asks, looking at her oldest son, as she sits at the kitchen table, a cup of tea in her hands. "Did you have fun?"

"Yeah," Theo says, sitting down at the end of the table, exhaling heavily, as he does. He didn't really notice it before, but as soon as he got outside and into the sunlight, a throbbing hangover started creeping up on him, leaving him heavy-headed and tired, and he rubs his eyes.

"I'll bet," Riley says, and Theo looks up at him. Riley is making a sandwich, and he eyes Theo up and down pointedly. Theo glances at his outfit. He's wearing the exact same clothes as last night, although without the tie, which he opted for bundling up in his pocket, rather than wearing, on the walk home. But he gets Riley's point; it's the fact that he is wearing the same clothes as last night, that's the point.

Theo glares at his brother, who simply smiles wickedly and looks away, resuming his sandwich-making.

"Well, I'm glad you had a good time," Amy says sympathetically, with a small smile, and Theo looks at her. "You deserve to have some fun."

Theo smiles tiredly, before remembering something.

"Hey, by the way," he says, straightening a little in his seat, instantly more alert. "I've got to tell you something."

He proceeds to tell his mother and Riley what Max told him, about Max finding a place to stay until graduation, meaning that he won't have to move, after all, even though his parents still will. Riley is happier about the news than Theo somehow expected, and Amy looks a little surprised, but pleased.

"Well, that's nice of him," she says, about Gavin offering to take Max in. "And he's right, too. I hate to say it, but moving, and changing schools, when your son is so close to graduating... It seems a little irresponsible, to me."

She gives Theo a pointed look, and Theo suspects that she has been dying to say that about Max's parents' decision, ever since she first heard about it, but has kept her mouth shut. And he can't blame her; she hasn't even met Max's parents, and judging other parents' actions concerning their kids is something that she generally tries to stay out of.

"Yeah," Theo agrees. "Good thing Gavin saw it that way too, or else, we would have been pretty screwed."

His mother gives him a sympathetic smile, no doubt noticing how her son uses the word *we*, as though Max moving would affect both of them profoundly. Which it would, of course. Theo is pretty sure she has come to realize that, now.

They all sit there for a while, talking and just generally having a lazy day off, when the front door suddenly opens and Theo's dad steps inside. He looks a little surprised to see them all sitting there, and he frowns a bit, absently wiping motor oil off his hands with a rag. No doubt, he has just come from the garage, after fiddling with his car.

"Eric," his wife says, looking at him a little pointedly, "Theo just told us that Max isn't moving, after all. He found a place to stay, 'til graduation. That's nice, isn't it?"

Eric doesn't reply right away, instead just stands there, rubbing his hands with that rag that looks almost too dirty to actually serve a purpose, by now.

"Uh, yeah," he finally says, sounding a bit distant. He looks down at his hands, nodding. "Yeah, that's good."

He leaves it at that, only glances up at his family, before making his way upstairs, no doubt to clean up. And Theo clenches his jaw a little, annoyed, despite himself.

"He knows he's gonna have to come around eventually, right?" he says, turning to his mother, while Riley just sits there, eating his sandwich, observing the exchange.

Amy sighs.

"I know," she agrees tiredly. "But you know how stubborn he can be. He tends to have a hard time dealing with being proven wrong."

She takes a sip of her tea, and Theo exhales heavily, knowing that she has a point, but still. He just wishes his dad would stop finding this whole thing so awkward, and just accept it.

♦

It's weird, Theo thinks, how with everything that's been going on in his personal life, these past few months, school is actually still a thing.

Despite all the stuff with Max, his parents, their families, not to mention the whole deal with Michael and Hannah, and even Luc, *school is still a thing.* Theo *still* has to sit around and study, as though he doesn't have enough on his mind to deal with, already, and while he sits in the library, spending his third consecutive afternoon there, he is moments away from just flipping the table over, in frustration.

He can't believe this. He can't believe it, and the only thing that's really keeping him sane, at the moment, is the thought of the news Max gave him, about a week ago. The fact that he's *not* going away. It's enough to make Theo smile just a little bit, in the midst of his studying for that stupid History test, a few days from now.

Theo likes the library. He has never been particularly bookish, like Riley, but he likes the stillness of it, the way all the bookshelves feel almost like protective walls, isolating the entire, large room in silence. It helps him focus, away from loud noises and distractions, since he tends to sit in a more secluded part of the library, away from where groups of students usually sit and talk a little too loudly for it to be manageable.

It's after almost two hours of studying, that Theo hears someone approach, and he's almost a little embarrassed about just how well he recognizes the sound of Dr. Martens against any surface, by now.

"There you are," Max says, as he makes his way over to the table where Theo is sitting. Theo looks up at him, smiling a little at how he knew it was Max, even before he spoke. "Ambitious, as usual."

Theo raises his eyebrows at him, doubtfully.

"I wouldn't exactly call it 'ambitious'," he says. "More like 'mediocre and overcompensating'."

Max pulls up a chair, reverses it, and sits down next to Theo, straddling the chair and folding his arms against the backrest in front of him. He leans his chin against his arms, those blue, black-lined eyes locked on his boyfriend.

"You're a lot smarter than you think, you know," he says, his tone dry, yet oddly soft, and Theo gives him a small smile.

"Says the genius," he teases, and Max groans.

"I'm good at math," he says. "That's pretty much it."

"And yet, you manage to keep up good grades, in all subjects, while spending half as much time studying, as me."

Max shrugs.

"I may also have a good memory," he says. "Which is basically all these tests measure, really. It's incredibly unfair."

He actually sounds sincere, at the end, which surprises Theo a little. But he knows he has a point; memorizing a bunch of facts hardly feels like actually *learning*, most of the time.

Theo turns back to his notes, which sum up most of what the upcoming test will be about, and Max watches him for a moment, before nudging him gently.

"Hey," Max says, and Theo turns to him. "I've got some news,"

"Really?" Theo asks, before seeing Max's now slightly excited expression, and he widens his eyes a little.

"Oh god, you're not pregnant, are you?" he says, in mock serious anxiety. "'Cause I don't know how I would explain that to my parents."

Max just shakes his head, though.

"No, it was a false alarm," he says in a casual tone, waving his hand dismissively. "Just a food baby."

461

Theo nods, letting out an exaggerated sigh of relief, before turning back to his notes. Max nudges him again, though, to retain his attention.

"However," he says, "I think my actual news is a bit more exciting than a hypothetical child."

Theo looks at him skeptically.

"I don't know, man," he says. "It would be pretty impressive if you could actually pull that off."

Max glares at him.

"I'll keep that in mind," he says acidly, narrowing his eyes. "Now, you wanna hear what I have to say, or not?"

Theo smiles a little, before pointedly putting down his pen and folding his arms against the table, turning to Max and meeting his dark blue gaze.

"You have my undivided attention," he says, and Max glares a little more, before taking a breath.

"I got a job," he says, but when Theo's eyebrows go up in surprise, he revises a little. "Well, sort of. It's at Gavin's studio, and it's more of an apprenticeship. He's been talking about it for a while, and I guess he finally decided, now that I'll be living with him, and all."

Theo frowns.

"Like... tattooing?" he asks, and Max cocks his head.

"Piercing," he says. "As far as I know, I don't really possess the artistic skills required to actually brand images into someone's skin."

He cocks his eyebrows.

"But shoving a needle through someone's tongue," he says, almost gleefully, pointing at Theo, "that, I can do."

Theo squints at the less than pleasant image, which Max notices.

"Well, not just tongues," he says casually, a little defensively. "Actually, tongues probably won't be the first thing I'm allowed to pierce."

Theo groans.

"Tongues are difficult," Max goes on, gesturing at his mouth. "Lot of nerve-endings."

Theo groans again, louder this time, and Max tilts his head, glancing away.

"Okay, fine," he says, sounding bored. "I might be exaggerating a bit. Piercing your tongue is pretty harmless, really."

"Just please stop saying *tongue*," Theo mutters, and Max smiles wickedly. He can tell so clearly when Theo is uncomfortable, and he loves teasing him about it, hence all the unnecessary repetition.

"Tongue," he says pointedly, and Theo glares at him, to which Max simply responds by sticking out his own tongue, piercing and all. And Theo groans tiredly and turns back to his notes. He hears Max chuckle affectionately, though, and then feels him press a kiss against his cheek, making Theo look up at him again. Max looks expectant, a little amused, and Theo can't help but smile.

"Congratulations," he says fondly, and Max smiles a bit wider.

"Thank you," he says, leaning his chin back against his folded arms. "It's more of a part-time thing, and while I'm learning, it's cleaning up the place that I actually get paid for, mostly. But it's something. At least, for now."

"I didn't even know you wanted to be a piercer," Theo says, frowning a little, and Max hums in thought, glancing absently at Theo's notes.

"Yeah," he says. "I think I mentioned it to my parents, once, and they went apeshit, saying how it's 'not a real job'."

He looks up at Theo.

"Not that my definition of a job is any less than simply doing something you get paid for," he says. "But I guess I got their logic, and I still kinda do. And it's not like my dream is sticking needles into people, but at least I'll have a job. I just have a hard time imagining myself doing something... *ordinary*. You know?"

Theo nods.

"Yeah," he says, because he does know, and he feels kind of the same. "I do."

"So it's not necessarily permanent," Max continues. "But it might be, who knows, if I like it. We'll see, after graduation."

Theo smiles a little.

"What do you wanna do?" Max asks him. "After."

Theo shrugs, letting out a sigh.

"I don't know," he says, picking up his pen and fiddling with it between his fingers, as he glances down at his notes, not really seeing them. "I kinda feel like I want to travel, or something. For a year, maybe. Then, college."

He lets out a small huff of laughter.

"Not that I have any idea what I'd want to study," he adds, and Max smiles. Theo can see it, out of the corner of his eye. "I just don't want to end up in an office somewhere, or doing something that just makes me want to stay in bed, every day. I want it to matter. You know?"

He looks back at Max, who's now tilting his head a little, leaning against his folded arms, with an expression as though Theo is simply the most beautiful, most interesting thing he has ever seen.

"I get that," he says, his voice low. "I think I want that, too."

And Theo nods, before getting an idea.

"We should do it," he hears himself say, without really meaning to, and Max blinks.

"What?" he says, and Theo suddenly feels a little apprehensive about saying that, but figures he might as well roll with it.

"You and me," he says. "We should do that."

Max raises his eyebrows a little.

"Like the circus-thing?" he asks, clearly joking, and Theo scoffs, a small, slightly insecure smile on his face.

"I'm serious," he says, and he can see Max finally grasp that. "We should. I mean, if you'd want to."

Max just stares at him for a few moments, making Theo feel increasingly anxious about suggesting something so bold. But then, Max smiles a little, with complete sincerity, as though himself surprised at how much he actually agrees with the suggestion.

"Yeah, we should," he says, and Theo feels his heart skip a beat.

"Really?" he says, and Max lifts his head up, straightens in his seat, his arms still folded against the backrest.

"Yeah," he says, sounding a bit more confident, now. "Just go off after graduation, screw around, travel the world, road trip across the country, or whatever. Just figure out what to do. Then, college. 'Cause believe it or not, I actually wanna go."

Theo quirks a small smile.

"I'm pretty sure you could get into whatever college you want," he says, and Max cocks his head.

"So, I'll get into the one you go to," he says, and he says it so easily, like he's completely certain that's what he'll be doing, a year from now. And Theo can't help but smile, despite the tiny possibility that maybe Max won't feel that way, when the time comes. Because right now, that's how he feels, and it's how Theo feels, and it doesn't look like that will be changing anytime soon, and that's all that matters.

Theo nods.

"Sounds like a plan," he says, and Max smiles.

"Yeah, it does," he says a little smugly, as though he was the one who came up with it. Then it seems to sink in, though, and he sighs. "Wonder what my parents will think of *that*."

Theo shrugs.

"Does it matter?" he asks, and Max just looks at him. "You're legal, it's your life."

Max doesn't immediately respond, instead narrows his eyes, a slow smile spreading across his face.

"Now, that rings a bell," he says, and it takes Theo a moment, before he remembers that that's almost exactly what Max said to him, back when Theo asked him about his tattoos, after seeing them for the first time. And he smiles self-consciously, looking down at his notes.

"Yeah, well," he says, actually blushing a little, for some reason. "What can I say? You've made an impression on me."

He hears Max exhale softly, as he leans in closer and plants a soft kiss against his throat.

"Good," he says. "And the same goes for you, by the way."

Theo glances at him, sees the utter sincerity in those eyes, and he can't resist kissing him on the mouth, gently. Then something occurs to him.

"Speaking of parents," he says. "Shouldn't I meet yours? I mean, since they're moving away. Seems like it's about time, doesn't it?"

Max actually sighs heavily, as though a little frustrated, and he pulls away.

"Right," he says tiredly, ruffling through his hair with his fingers. "That."

He glances to the side, sighing again, deliberating, as he rolls his tongue piercing between his teeth. He must know, as well as Theo, that that one brief encounter with his mother doesn't exactly qualify as having *met the parents*, and that Theo has a point. With all the time Max has spent at Theo's house now, hanging out with his family, and with everything the two of them have been through, it seems only right that Theo should meet his parents. And especially if they're leaving; god knows if Theo will ever really get the chance again.

It's not that he really *wants* to, per se; those short moments of interaction with Max's mother were enough, really, awkward and kind of rude, as they were. But still.

"Yeah, I guess you're right," Max finally says, turning back to his boyfriend, absently rubbing his hand against the back of his neck. "Maybe even do it right, this time."

Theo frowns.

"How do you mean?" he asks, and Max shrugs, a little uncomfortably.

"I don't know," he says. "Like, dinner, or something? That's how I met yours."

Theo thinks about that. *Yes*, that makes the most sense, he supposes. Even though just the thought of it makes him weirdly uncomfortable. Honestly, had it been any other parents, it probably would have been fine; even apart from the fact that they're his boyfriend's parents, Theo has more experience with situations like that, than Max, and therefore tends to find them easier to handle. But Max's parents just seem so... cold. He's not sure how to deal with that.

"Sure," Theo says, nodding. "Yeah, we should do that."

Max looks at him skeptically.

"Should we?" he says, his tone matching his expression. "Really? 'Cause, honestly, I don't think they'd care much, either way."

"I would," Theo says, surprised at how sure he sounds. "Like you said, we should do it right."

Max seems to deliberate for a moment, looking at him, before he finally sighs in something like defeat.

"Alright," he says, nodding. "I'll set it up."

Then he sighs again, heavily, as he leans back against his folded arms, an oddly tired, bitter look on his face.

"Dinner with the Collins family," he mutters, sounding anything but excited. "Awesome."

CHAPTER 32

SPRING

The night of the dinner arrives so much faster than Theo
expected.

A few days later, and just a few days before Max's parents are
moving, Theo comes over to their house. Max is still living there,
not really moving into Gavin and Amanda's place until after his
parents leave, so when Theo arrives, Max is the one who greets
him at the door.

"Hey," he says, as Theo steps inside and stomps some snow
off of his shoes. It hasn't snowed properly for a few weeks, not
since that snow day they spent at Theo's house, with only the
occasional falling of tiny, white flakes. But still, it snowed *a lot*,
that time, so it's taking ages for it to melt, especially seeing how
it's still pretty cold, outside. It's gradually getting better, though;
you can even see the ground, in some places.

"Hey," Theo replies, as Max gives him a kiss. "How's it going?"

He asks mostly out of nervousness. Because he realizes that he is surprisingly nervous, and he just needs to say something, instead of just standing there in tense silence.

Max groans a little, glancing toward the doorway Theo knows leads into the kitchen.

"Pretty good," he says, "so far. But if you wanna run, I don't blame you."

Theo chuckles, a bit more nervously than intended.

"I'm not running," he says, and Max raises a pierced eyebrow at him.

"You sure?" he asks. "I'll make up a cover story. Like, you slipped on some ice and hit your head, or you were kidnapped by ninjas. Maybe, you found Narnia."

He adds that last suggestion with a slightly hopeful look, and Theo smiles a bit wider.

"First off, I'm not going anywhere," he says, taking off his scarf and jacket. "And second—"

He cuts himself off, leaning in to place a kiss on Max's lips.

"You're adorable."

Max groans a little, before letting out a defeated sigh.

"And you're way too responsible and honest," he says, like it annoys him to no end, and Theo takes his hand, lacing their fingers together.

"I like to think that's why you love me," he says, kissing Max's temple, and his boyfriend groans softly.

"You would be right," he grumbles, and Theo smiles, as they make their way into the house.

For once, both Max's parents are home. Given how they have a lot of stuff to do, like packing and making preparations, with the move so close, they have both taken a little time off from work, these last few days. At least, according to Max, who himself has been spending an increasing amount of time getting all his stuff together, for his move to Gavin's house.

469

So when Theo steps into the kitchen, he's prepared to see Max's dad, but he's still a little surprised, and when the man turns around, Theo tries his best to seem unbothered.

"Oh," the man says, straightening a little as he makes his way over. "You must be..."

He trails off a little, and Theo can practically feel Max tensing up, next to him.

"Theo, dad," Max says, a little stiffly. "You know, my boyfriend, the guy we specifically invited over, so you could actually meet him?"

Max's father nods, as though forgetting Theo's name is a completely reasonable mistake, and Theo almost starts a little at Max's way of addressing him. His father doesn't seem to care, though.

"Right," he says, turning to Theo. "Of course. I'm William, but most people call me Bill. Pleased to meet you."

He extends his hand, and Theo shakes it, uncertain how to feel about this whole, slightly awkward situation, but he manages to stay polite.

"You too," he says, and Max's dad—Bill—gives him a small, tight smile. He doesn't really resemble Max, at least not from what Theo can tell, and neither does Jeanine, from what Theo remembers. Then again, that might have something to do with the fact that where Bill has brown, sleek hair and a clean-cut look of dress pants and a shirt (he looks like he's just come home from work at an office), Max is the complete opposite, with his black-dyed hair, makeup, piercings and completely different style. So yeah, it's hard to spot a resemblance. So far, Theo has only observed that Jeanine and Max seem to share the same eye color, and that his father might have a similar jawline. Or something.

"Theo," Max's mother says, making her way over to them. "So good to see you again."

Theo is ninety percent sure, at this point, that she only knows his name because Max just said it, but he doesn't mention that. Instead, he just gives her a small, polite nod and smile, keeping his hand locked together with Max's. And he swears he can see both Bill's and Jeanine's eyes flit down there, as if a little confused at seeing their son actually hold hands with someone, before they quickly look back up, rather casually.

"Right," Jeanine says, after a moment. "Dinner's just ready, so..."

They make their way into the dining room, where the table is already set, and Theo feels a little apprehensive as he sits down. Max sits down right beside him, though, and gives him a supporting glance. Supporting, in Max's case, meaning a look of bored, slightly sympathetic annoyance, as if to say *I know, it sucks, right?* But Theo knows that's simply Max's way of showing said support, so he appreciates it, all the more.

As they all start eating, the one word Theo can really think of to describe the general atmosphere, is *cold*. It's weird, but despite there being actual conversation and occasional attempts at asking polite questions, Theo can't help but feel like none of it is really genuine. It's like by some kind of script, and when he glances at Max, he can't decide if he looks more bothered and uncomfortable by the whole thing, than Theo.

No, wait, scratch that. Max doesn't look uncomfortable; he looks angry.

"So, Theo," Bill says, and Theo looks up. "What do your parents do?"

Theo blinks, at the slightly unexpected question. Sure, it's an ordinary enough inquiry, but he can't help but notice the contrast between that, and the way his own mother asked Max about what *he* liked to do, rather than what his parents did for a living, when she first met him.

"Uh," Theo starts. "My mom's a grade school teacher, and my dad's a mechanic."

Bill nods.

"Teaching," he says, taking a sip of water. "A noble profession, at least."

He says it in a way that makes Theo unsure if he's being jokingly dramatic, or not, and he ends up just nodding awkwardly, even though Jeanine smiles good-naturedly, like she's finding the whole thing rather pleasant.

Although then, Theo can't help but wonder what, exactly, Bill's response implies.

"How so?" he finds himself asking, knowing that he probably shouldn't. And Bill looks a little surprised, for a moment, the rather hard planes of his face a little tense.

"Well," he says, "taking care of the next generation. Sharpening young minds, and all that. It's an important job, a good one."

Theo frowns a little, knowing that he really should probably just keep his mouth shut, but he can't help but feel like this man is deliberately saying that the opposite of those things applies to his father's job.

"As opposed to fixing cars?" Theo asks, before adding: "I'm sorry, it's just... I'm pretty sure both jobs are important, in their own way."

And Bill just looks at him, as though honestly surprised at his words. He even looks a little confused, and Theo briefly glances around the table. Jeanine looks a little taken aback, which worries him, but then he notices Max, who's leaning with both elbows on the table, relaxed, and spinning his fork slowly with his fingers, its tip pressed against his plate. And Theo swears, he even looks a little amused, with a tiny, almost proud smile on his face.

"Of course," Bill says after a moment, and Theo turns back to him. "But some jobs are just more... valuable, than others."

Theo straightens a little.

"Do you fix your car, yourself?" he asks. "When it breaks down?"

"Well, no, but—"

"Do you take it to a mechanic?" Theo isn't lost on the sheer dryness of his tone, and out of the corner of his eye, he swears he can see Max actually *smiling*, now.

"Yes," Bill says, a little impatiently. "But what I'm saying is, that some people contribute more to the economy."

"Like who?"

"Well," Bill says, apparently attempting to salvage the situation. "Like teachers. Or doctors, or business-owners."

"I'm pretty sure all of those need vehicles for transportation," Theo retorts, shocked at what he's saying and vaguely wondering what the *hell* he's doing. "And I'm also pretty sure that my dad contributes to the economy, just fine."

"Well, does he have his own business?" Bill asks, as though trying to prove a point, and Theo shakes his head.

"No," he says, plainly. "But neither do you."

And *god*, Max actually chuckles then, and his father looks at him, along with Theo.

"Max," he says sternly, but Max just shrugs. He's still slowly spinning that fork against his plate, now resting with his chin against the palm of his other hand, both elbows on the table.

"What?" he says, grinning lazily, looking completely relaxed and oddly entertained. "It's funny."

His father doesn't seem to think so, though.

"Why can't you just behave?" he says, sounding a little annoyed, but Max is unfazed, raising his eyebrows a little.

"Well, we can't all be Stepford residents, now can we?" he says, simply. "And besides, I wouldn't exactly call your blatant bigotry *behaving*."

Theo looks back at Max's father, who straightens in his seat, clearly very annoyed by now, in his own uptight way, but before he can say anything, Jeanine interrupts.

"Okay," she says, getting up from the table, "I think it's time for dessert. Bill, do you mind?"

She looks at her husband pointedly, who grits his teeth, before exhaling heavily and getting up, as well. No one says a word, as he accompanies his wife into the kitchen, and as soon as they're gone, Theo lets out a deep, almost gasping breath, as the realization of what he just did suddenly hits him with full force.

"Oh my god," he says, looking down at his cleared plate. "Oh, shit."

Max doesn't say anything, only laughs a little, but Theo still buries his face in his hands.

473

"Shit, I'm so sorry," he says, shaking his head, his voice muffled against his hands. "Oh, god."

He feels absolutely *mortified*, but Max doesn't seem too bothered about it.

"No, don't be sorry," he says, probably still grinning, sounding positively gleeful. "Please, don't be sorry."

He nudges Theo gently, and Theo hesitantly looks up. Max seems way too relaxed and entertained by this, according to him.

"Are you kidding me?" Theo says, trying to keep his voice down, embarrassed enough about the whole thing to even think about Max's parents hearing him. "What the hell was that?"

He gestures a little frantically at the table, then at the kitchen, as though making his rhetorical question clearer, but Max just puts his hand on his waist, leaning in to kiss him on the cheek.

"That was *awesome*," he says, smiling like he means every word, like he's moments away from bursting into laughter again. "Really."

He keeps looking at Theo, who at first feels a little annoyed. But then he notices that slight pride in Max's expression again, and he softens a little.

"Yeah, well, I'm pretty sure your dad hates me now," he says lamely, vaguely thinking about how that mirrors what Max said, the first time he had dinner with Theo's family.

Max rolls his eyes, with a small groan.

"He's an elitist with a stick up his ass," he says. "I don't think he's even aware of just how many people he actually hates. It's just all about 'serving a purpose', and whether you're useful or not."

He looks at Theo pointedly, expression a bit more serious.

"And what he said about your dad was totally out of line."

Theo sighs quietly, again thinking back to that night and what he said to Max, after he had talked back at Eric. He's honestly vaguely amused at how similar the two situations actually are, really.

"Yeah," he says. "Thanks. But still, I can't believe I said that. I mean, that was—"

"Awesome," Max finishes for him. "You stood up to him, and not a lot of people would do that, especially not when it's your boyfriend's dad, who you're meeting for the first time. Not to mention, it was very entertaining."

He quirks a small smile, pulling Theo a little closer.

"I'm impressed," he says, and Theo raises his eyebrows at him.

"Impressed, because I called out your dad?" he asks doubtfully, and Max cocks his head.

"Well," he says. "I do that all the time, but to see him actually react for once was weirdly satisfying. And I love it when you get your sass on."

He smiles a little wider, cocking his eyebrows suggestively along with his blatantly teasing tone, and Theo sighs, unable to help smiling back. He shakes his head, scoffing as he looks back down at his plate.

"Well, this is going well," he says sarcastically, and Max kisses his temple.

"I'd say so, yes."

Dessert is a slightly tense affair, but with Max now considerably more relaxed, rather than angry, it's a bit easier. Jeanine makes a new effort at talking to Theo, as well, but Theo can tell that she still doesn't really take him too seriously. It's apparent with both of Max's parents that they don't really feel like what their son has with this boy is much to concern themselves with, that it will indeed pass, soon enough, and it's an attitude that obviously doesn't really help the situation. It's also one which makes Theo feel gradually more annoyed, and he vaguely thinks of how different Max's parents' response is to the relationship, compared to his own mother's, or even his father's. His dad may not approve, sure, but at least he takes it seriously.

Theo keeps these thoughts to himself, though, and as the night goes on, he can't help but notice how at least Max's mother actually, gradually, starts looking at him a little differently. It's like she's trying to figure him out, like she doesn't quite understand him, and Theo isn't sure if he should be comforted or unsettled by that. But it's at least a change-up from her blatant indifference toward him, which he supposes is a good thing.

When dinner is done, Theo has to leave early, because it's a school night, and although he really wouldn't mind spending more time with Max, he kind of feels the urge to leave. He doesn't really want to be around Max's parents longer than necessary, and he's completely sure than neither Max nor his parents mind.

So Theo gets ready to leave, after thanking Max's parents for dinner, and he's in the middle of putting his jacket on, when Max is called into kitchen by his father, to help out. Max groans and glances at his boyfriend.

"I'll be right back," he says, and Theo nods, as Max leaves.

He's barely left alone in the hall for more than a second, though, before he spots Jeanine, on her way back from the bathroom, and she stops dead, as she sees him. Theo tries to give her a polite smile, and feels pretty confident that he has managed, but it doesn't seem to be enough. Because, to his surprise, she makes her way over to him, and he doesn't move.

"Theo, is it?" Max's mother says when she approaches him, and Theo suppresses the urge to very clearly, and rather disrespectfully, articulate that that *is* in fact his name, as has been stated several times, already. Instead, he just nods.

"Yeah," he says, adjusting his scarf, before starting to zip up his jacket.

Jeanine nods, as though deliberating.

"Look," she says, "I don't know you. But you seem like a good kid. And I don't know what it is that you and Max have, what you're doing... But it seems to have a good effect on him. And I haven't seen him smile like that in a very long time."

She sighs quietly, glancing away for a moment.

"I know we don't talk much, him and I." She looks back up at Theo, looking more sincere than he somehow expected, albeit a little uncomfortable, like she's still having trouble talking about the relationship in any serious sense. "But I can tell. So, I'm glad he's found something like that, whatever it is."

Theo just stands there for a moment, a little stunned, half-expecting her to continue. She doesn't, though, and when he realizes that, he nods slowly.

"Uh, okay," he says, feeling rather awkward at her weird, compliment-like confession, vaguely wondering if she would be telling him this, if she and Max's father weren't moving away. "Thanks."

Jeanine seems to sense his awkwardness, and she smiles a little, the expression softening her features. Theo gets the feeling that he would probably find her really sweet, if only she knew how to communicate better, especially with her son, and it's a realization that honestly makes him a little sad.

He has only spent one evening with Max's parents—he can't imagine what it must be like to grow up with them, to be judged so harshly solely based on your accomplishments. He can't really imagine not having the emotional support of his own mother, or Riley, even his father, despite his distant way of expressing how he cares. Having this instead, this indifference, this lack of trust and lack of interest, from your own parents, about your life and relationships and opinions...

It just seems very lonely.

Max eventually comes back, just as Jeanine leaves, and he glances at his mother, before shooting Theo a slightly confused look. Theo only shrugs, though, and Max drops it, instead moving in closer.

"Well," he says, tugging a little on the front of Theo's jacket, like he tends to do. "Now, you've met them."

"I have," Theo confirms, and Max looks at him, a little apprehension hidden under that easy expression.

"And?" he asks.

"And," Theo replies, "I honestly don't think I'll be missing them, when they go."

He realizes how downright insensitive that sounds, but he knows that Max gets it, that he appreciates the honesty. And sure enough, Max nods, before scoffing lightly.

"But we did it right," he says, smiling humorlessly. "We tried."

Theo smiles genuinely then, and he pulls Max in closer.

"That, we did," he says, giving him a soft kiss. "And I'm proud of you. I know you weren't exactly up for this."

Max huffs a small laugh.

"Proud, huh?" he says. "That's a new one."

Theo hums in confirmation, kissing him again.

"It's true, though," he says. "And even though this kinda sucked, I would do it again."

He catches Max's little smile, as he covers his mouth with his own, in short, soft intervals.

"Really?" Max says, a little doubtfully, a little hopefully, and Theo just looks at him, pushes his hair back with his fingers, so that he can really see those dark blue eyes. And he nods.

"For you, I would."

♦

Things start happening pretty fast, after that. In a matter of days, Max's parents have emptied their house and moved out of it, and by the time they're off settling in at their new place, several hours away, Max has practically made himself at home at Gavin's. With a little help from Theo, it doesn't take him long to unpack and get his posters plastered on the walls, and although his new room is slightly smaller than his old one, and actually much brighter, he makes it his own pretty quickly. He and Theo spend most of his first weekend there unpacking and fixing it up, and Gavin treats them to pizza, while pointing out how Theo really should get a tattoo.

"I'd be happy to do it," Gavin says, in that British, burned-whiskey rasp of a voice, and with that wicked smile that Theo still hasn't gotten quite used to. And Theo says thanks, but no thanks, at least not yet. Although, he must admit that he's starting to feel like getting a tattoo actually might not be a half-bad idea, somewhere down the road.

Despite his new living situation, Max still spends a lot of time at Theo's house, even more than before. It's not that he doesn't like it at his new home, because he does, but as he puts it, it can get a bit much, and he doesn't want to impose more than necessary. Instead, he's trying to *ease them into it,* these people who have taken him in, while Theo points out that Gavin and his wife *did* invite Max to live with them, after all, of their own accord.

He gets Max's point, though; even though the whole solution to his problem has been resolved, Max is still a bit apprehensive about simply accepting it. He's still waiting for it to blow up in his face, as though his new surrogate family will suddenly change their minds, and throw him out. Theo doubts very much that that will happen, but he decides to simply let Max come to terms with that, himself. He needs to realize, after all, that he's not a burden, like he seems to think, and that he's actually worth the time and energy he feels is simply wasted on him.

Max is having dinner at Theo's place, tonight, which has become a very casual affair, compared to the first few times it happened. Both Riley and Theo's mother have accepted him wholeheartedly, and it makes Theo smile to see just how much Max appreciates that. He's still not quite used to this, after all, to actually be part of a warm and supportive family environment, and Theo can tell that it makes him happy to be, even if just for a night.

Eric generally isn't home, when they have dinner; he tends to work late at the garage, a few days a week, and Theo has honestly kind of gotten used to that. In other words, he and Max still don't interact much, so when it turns out that Eric will actually be home, this time around, Theo is a little surprised. And a little anxious, honestly, because as far as he knows, Eric still feels apprehensive about the whole relationship between this odd boy, and his son.

Theo, Max, and Riley are in the process of setting the dining room table (which they have to use, since they're more than four people, for once), when Eric shows up. He looks a little uncomfortable as he enters the room, but when he clears his throat a little, they all look up. And to Theo's utter surprise, he's actually turned toward Max, like he's the one he wants to talk to.

"So," Eric says gruffly, while Max just looks at him, as though unsure whether to prepare for a cold shoulder or a verbal beatdown. Not that Eric has ever said or done anything bad to him, at least not since that first dinner, ages ago, when he talked like that. But still. He seems to take a small breath, and Riley and Theo both watch, as casually as they can, while their father tries to speak.

"You're not moving, then," Eric says, and Max nods, before another few seconds follow, in oddly tense silence. Then Eric exhales.

"Listen," he says, a bit apprehensively, as though he would rather not be having this conversation. "I know we haven't gotten along. I haven't exactly been... welcoming."

Understatement, Theo thinks, but he says nothing.

"And you're a bit of a weirdo." He sounds strangely honest, but where most people would be uncomfortable or offended, Max just cocks his head, with an expression that says Eric has a point, and that he personally agrees. "But you seem to make my boy happy. I have no idea how, but you do. So..."

Eric glances away, looking downright miserable, like he just wants to end this whole conversation.

"So, I guess what I'm trying to say is," he continues, "I'm glad you're staying."

No one moves a muscle, and Theo only vaguely notices that Amy has made her way into the room, as well, and that she's just standing there, as stunned as everyone else. Eric looks up at Max, and for a little while, Max doesn't respond, just blinks, in a way that makes him look more baffled, and more human, than Eric has probably ever seen him. Then, finally, he nods.

"Thanks," he says, and Eric lets out a small breath, as though relieved. Then he nods as well, and says nothing more, while carrying on like the conversation didn't happen, making his way into the kitchen to help out.

It did happen, though. It did happen, and Theo meets Max's eye.

"Did he just—" Max says, gesturing vaguely, and Theo feels a little stunned, for a moment, before he nods. And Max looks at Riley, who just shrugs, and they all hear Amy let out a relieved sigh, as she turns around to head back into the kitchen.

"Finally," she murmurs, and Theo can't help but smile.

♦

The sun is shining. For once, in what feels like ages, the sun is actually shining, and the sky is actually a brilliant blue.

It has been a couple of weeks now, since Max's parents moved, and although Theo figured it wouldn't make much of a difference to Max, he can't help but notice that his boyfriend seems lighter than before, more relaxed. It's almost as though just being away from that house, and instead just being around people who genuinely care about the little things, like how his day has been, his opinions, how he feels, what he likes, is really making a difference. It's really making a difference, and Theo can see that the change he has slowly seen take place in Max, is reaching a new level, somehow.

His personality hasn't changed, but rather the way he sees himself. Where he used to see himself as a waste of space with no real worth, Max has finally realized just how untrue that is. At least, from what Theo can tell. Because he swears that that look in Max's blue eyes is completely different, than it was a few months ago. And it makes him so very happy to see.

It's in the middle of the day, at school, and Max, Theo and Cassie are making their way outside. There's no real reason for it, but the sun is *finally* shining, and that's enough to lure them out. So although it's still pretty cold, it's surprisingly warm in the sunlight, and Theo even notices a few small buds, on a bush they pass by.

"Look at that," Cassie says happily, as she notices them, as well. "Looks like spring's coming early."

"You realize that all of that is gonna die," Max points out, gesturing at the bush, "when it starts snowing again."

Cassie glares at him.

"Must you?" she says. "It's spring!"

"It's winter," Max retorts. "Winter, and an unusually warm and sunny week."

"Don't be such a buzz-kill," Cassie says, as the three of them walk along, and then actually grabs Max and puts her arm over his shoulders, tugging him to her. She gestures at the horizon dramatically. "It's a new day."

Max raises an eyebrow at her.

"What's wrong with this one?" he says, attempting to escape, but Cassie just pulls him closer.

"New day!" he repeats vehemently, and Max groans a little, his walking kind of awkward, from her clinging to him, like that.

"Alright, alright," he says. "I get it. New day. Why don't you ride off on your unicorn, and embrace it, or whatever."

Cassie raises her chin haughtily.

"Maybe, I will," she says with some smugness. "And you're not invited."

"I'm pretty sure I'll survive," Max replies dryly, and Cassie plants a kiss on his cheek, making him groan again, before she finally releases him and actually *skips* away, leaving Max and Theo walking at the same pace.

Theo chuckles fondly.

"Well, aren't you adorable," he says, watching Max throw Cassie's back a slightly murderous look.

"She's the one with rainbows coming out of her ass," Max retorts, but Theo only smiles wider.

"Nothing wrong with that," he says teasingly, taking Max's hand. "And she's right. It's a new day."

Max glances at him, and although his expression stays the same, his blue eyes are smiling.

They reach a small, grassy knoll, near the edge of the schoolyard, and find Cassie just standing there, face tilted upwards and eyes closed, as though simply soaking up the sunlight. She hums pleasantly.

"Finally," she murmurs against the brilliant blue sky, which hasn't got even the smallest cloud in sight. Theo glances upward.

"It's still cold, though," he points out, because it's true; they've been outside with open jackets for barely ten minutes, and he's already starting to feel chilly. Although, he must admit, it's much warmer than usual, and the sunlight definitely makes it ten times better.

"Don't care," Cassie says, before sniffling, sort of proving Theo's point. "Worth it."

Theo quirks a small, easy smile, and makes his way over to stand next to her. He barely gets there, though, before Cassie's phone beeps, and her attention is diverted. She takes her phone out of her pocket and looks at it.

"Oh," she says. "It's Emma, she's inside."

She looks up at Theo and Max.

"I'm just gonna go get her," she says. "I'll be right back."

She glances up at the sky and emits a tiny, pathetic whimper of longing, before hurrying off toward the school entrance.

Theo lets out a deep sigh, before standing so that he faces the sun, and he tilts his head back a little, closing his eyes. It really does feel nice, like he can practically feel his skin soaking up the light.

Then Max scoffs, and Theo turns to him, at his side, expecting some kind of teasing look. But that's not what he gets. Instead, Max is looking over at the other end of the schoolyard.

"I just realized something," he says, and Theo glances over there, before looking back.

"Yeah?" he says. "What's that?"

"Five months," Max replies, turning to him, and Theo frowns.

"What?" he says, and Max cocks his head slightly.

"Our first kiss," he explains. Then, he looks away again and points toward the school building over on the other side. "Over there. Five months ago, today."

Theo keeps his frown, looking over at where Max is pointing. It is indeed the building behind which Theo found Max, that day, forever ago. Where they ended up arguing about superheroes,

…then somehow wound up making out against the wall for half-an-hour. He smiles.

"Oh, yeah," he says lightly. Then he frowns again, turning to Max.

"Wait," he says, "you're keeping track?"

"Hey, don't get a big head, alright?" Max says it almost warningly, pointing at him, with a deliberate look on his face. "The only reason I remember the date is because I had a test the next day, and thinking about you fucked up my studying. It cost me a few points."

"Uh-huh," Theo says teasingly, giving him a pointed smile, and Max rolls his eyes, suddenly looking a little uncomfortable.

"Don't," he says, while Theo squeezes his hand, and Theo smiles wider.

"I keep telling you," Theo says, in a smug tone he knows Max hates. "You are a romantic, you just won't admit it."

Max tilts his head back and lets out a groan.

"Forget I said anything," he says, closing his eyes.

"Never," Theo says, and when Max glances at him and their eyes meet, Max even smiles a little. And the sun shines a little bit brighter.

They stand like that for a few seconds, in silence, before Max releases Theo's hand, and Theo looks down. He watches as Max takes out a pack of cigarettes, and he manages to suppress that feeling he's gotten more and more lately, that apprehensive one he gets, whenever Max smokes.

Max takes out a cigarette and secures it between his lips, before taking out a lighter from his pocket, flicking it to life and bringing it up to his mouth. Theo watches as he does it, but then, suddenly, Max pauses. He lowers the lighter and plucks the cigarette away with his hand, simply looks at it for a few seconds, turning it over between his fingers, like he's thinking. He presses his lips together.

Theo is a little stunned, when Max then simply throws the unlit cigarette away, landing it somewhere on the frost-covered ground, and Theo raises his eyebrows. Max then looks down at his pack of cigarettes, before doing the same thing with that, throwing it somewhere in the bushes, and he takes a deep breath, while he puts the lighter away. He turns to Theo.

"New day, right?" he says, and Theo just looks at him, stunned, for several moments. Then, he smiles, taking Max's hand again and lacing their fingers together.

"Yeah," he says. "Sounds about right."

30929399R00292

Made in the USA
Lexington, KY
24 March 2014